THE COBRAS OF CALCUTTA

Grant Sutherland was born in Sydney and grew up
in Western Australia. He now lives with his wife and
children in Herefordshire, England.

www.grantsutherland.net

THE
COBRAS
OF CALCUTTA

*The first volume
of the Decipherer's Chronicles*

GRANT SUTHERLAND

PAN BOOKS

First published 2010 by Macmillan

This edition published 2010 by Pan Books
an imprint of Pan Macmillan, a division of Macmillan Publishers Limited
Pan Macmillan, 20 New Wharf Road, London N1 9RR
Basingstoke and Oxford
Associated companies throughout the world
www.panmacmillan.com

ISBN 978-0-330-47104-6

1 3 5 7 9 8 6 4 2

A CIP catalogue record for this book is available from
the British Library.

Typeset by Ellipsis Books Limited, Glasgow
Printed in the UK by CPI Mackays, Chatham ME5 8TD

Visit www.panmacmillan.com to read more about all our books
and to buy them. You, will also find features, author interviews and
news of any author events, and you can, sign up for e-newsletters
so that you're always first to hear about our new releases.

THE
COBRAS
OF CALCUTTA

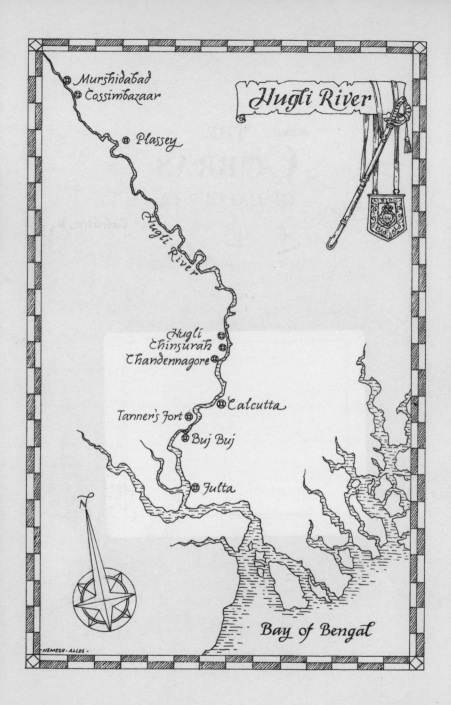

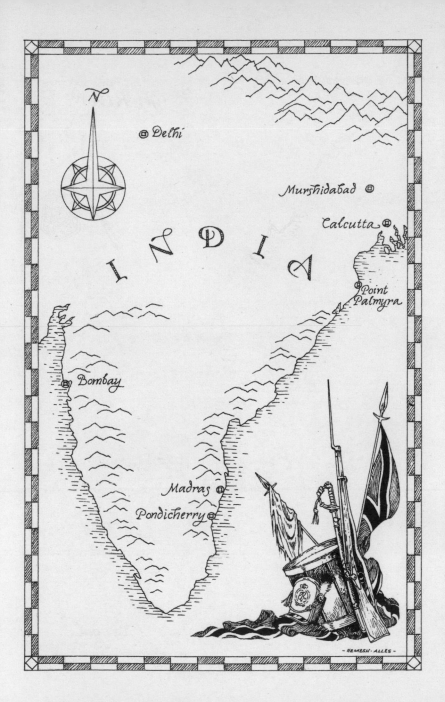

N

⊙ Delhi

Murshidabad ⊙

Calcutta ⊙

INDIA

Point
Palmyra

⊞ Bombay

Madras ⊞
Pondicherry ⊞

- HEMESH·ALLES -

A Note appended to the Chronicles of Alistair Douglas

I was born in Orkney, in the town of Stromness, in the Year of our Lord 1739, and now that my allotted three score and ten have come upon me I have returned here like a salmon to the spawning ground to make what peace a man may with himself before he goes down into the grave.

The uncontemplated life is not worth living. Sagacity? Or the threadbare wisdom of a man who has thought too much and lived too little? No matter. Each ends as he must, and now that the sap of life is going from me I oft-times catch a word or a thought that throws me very far from here. Contemplation comes, whether I will it or no.

In body, my daily round is settled. Returned to the house at midday, I sit down to a table prepared for me by Mrs Murdoe, who is the child of Molly Urquhart, who was twelve when I was nine and kissed me up by the kirk wall and laughed to see my colour rise. Mrs Murdoe is a dour but a good woman, and frets when I do not eat, and has finally agreed to sit with me for company, though she will take nothing herself but only afterwards when alone in the kitchen. She has a granddaughter, a lass who laughs as Molly laughed. It cheers my heart to hear her. Sometimes the years are as nothing.

Each day after Mrs Murdoe has left the house, I take a slow turn about the field by the kirk and then return home and go into the library and close the door. From the desk that was my father's I can see out of the high window and over the barn to the sea. The ships still come and go from the harbour, bearing men about their business, and cargo and the gilded dreams of London merchants whose guineas venture ever farther than their souls. It is said gold is the engine of empire. And they who say it are not entirely mistaken – even if the words be uttered by some as a curse and by others as a holy benediction. Where the empire is, there is trade, and in every corner of the world a British coin will have good value. Yet even a Lombard Street banker is more than only a machine for the manufacture of money; and were the empire not more than this also I am sure certain I would not have served her with my life.

It may be that I am too much within myself these days. I catch it at moments in the sideway glances of my neighbours. Still. Nothing to be feared, nothing to be done. I am beholden to no man. Grey hair has its privileges. And yet silence will be filled, even in solitude, where the clash of thought makes sound. Alone, I think; but in thinking, the threads of my life grow only more deeply entangled.

Peace and civility and good order. These necessary things do not come to us as manna from heaven. I knew as much as a lad. It was only as a man that I learned the harder lesson, how they must be won in never-ending battle, aye, and fought for, sometimes with guile and stealth, and sometimes most bloodily, with the accounting to be made to God. As my day draws in, the remembrance of the deeds of my life is a lengthening shadow. I have killed men – not all of them French – with never a thought for the holy commandments.

The Hindoos believe that every deed of a life stays with us, causing us to be born into another life with such a form as accords with our previous actions. Many a fine gentleman will laugh this belief to scorn, knowing himself to be self-raised by his own diligence and perspicacity – as if the lowliest maid who toils in faithful service is not more diligent and hard-working, and oft-times more perspicacious, than her master. For some the end comes too early, and for some too late, and few they are who get what they deserve in the end, neither the honours nor the whippings. The Hindoos do well not to look to this life for justice. For myself, when I think on my own actions, the nights can be both long and lonely.

But no night is for ever, unless it be the last, and each morning I am Alistair Douglas plain once more, or old Mr Douglas, who goes about the town like every other man with his soul undiscovered and the small-change of the day's doings on his tongue. Of late, the gentlemen of the old men's bench near the Black Bull have taken to offering me a seat with them. I smile and give them good morning and pass quickly on to the harbour.

The packet boat comes weekly and between-times all manner of vessels put into Stromness. I never thought, after my many travels and the bitch that the sea has been to me, that I would still be drawn by the siren call of the ships, but so it is, and here I may be found most every morning but Sunday. The correspondence that comes to me from London is now but a trickle, but that which comes I am glad of. Joseph and Nathan, my only regular correspondents, write to me even now as though my opinion might still weigh with them; to have had even one such friend, a man may count himself blessed. And there are other letters too, unexpected, and from far-off places where once I pursued my work under heaven. Upon receiving such a missive, it can feel as if the ripples of my own past have crossed the wide ocean of time to touch me at last, an old man in Orkney. I reply to those that need reply; some I keep. A rare few I forward to the department in London, and to these last I generally feel obliged to append a note or letter so that the decipherers or the minister or the king are none of them misled. No knowledge or understanding that comes of men comes at once, both full and entire.

This daily excursion to the harbour is but a prelude to the real business of my day. For with Mrs Murdoe returned to her own house, and I alone then in my library, all correspondence complete, I am at liberty to turn to the Chronicles which are the needful labour of my waning years and such a testament as I had never thought to leave. Here is, if you will, my life relived in quill and ink. Nor had I thought to make old bones, and therefore has this late scribbling come upon me like a ghost fiddler to the ended ceilidh. The guests have one and all departed, but when the spirit enters me I hear it rise again, the vanished music. Not every tune is joyful, nor yet every one a keening plaint of grief, but each one has its proper place and time.

From the shelves I take down the dusty papers, the letters that I sent my father when I was but young, the copies of department reports bound in red ribbon, and the notebooks and the papers. And from the cabinet I will often take some treasured thing – like this pebble from Cook's beach in Tahiti – and place it here before me on my desk, to be a talisman, while I take up my quill and remember.

For whom do I perform this final service? Not for Nathan, nor Joseph, nor yet for the decipherers nor any minister, nor even yet for the king, but only for myself, I think. And perhaps for others too, in aftertimes. But leave that aside.

Here in the writing of these Chronicles, I am determined to make report of my actions to my own soul as to the king of kings, following truthfulness as close as any man dare. Read it who may, this is the life I have lived, such as it was and is, written for all time on the face of the world.

I, Alistair Malcolm Douglas, have roamed the earth, a spy for the Crown. God's mercy on my soul.

CHAPTER ONE

*T*he sepoys were restless. I had noticed this on coming away from the factory, but I had been settled at Cossimbazaar two weeks only and it did not then signify with me. Men about to hunt are all of them restless, be they hard men to hounds in the green fields of Leicestershire or a platoon of sepoys gone pig-sticking on the hot plain of Bengal. I was new to them also, and young, being barely seventeen years of age, and there were among them men of fifty years and more.

'Mr Douglas, will you take the lead till we come to the river?'

It was Mrs Watts who spoke. I daresay she saw that I needed some guidance. Her husband William, the chief of the factory, had given me charge over the hunting party but I had received no particular instructions. In truth, provisioning society and amusement for wife and family is a great trial to any factory chief upcountry, and a newly arrived writer, such as I, must have seemed a godsend at that moment to William Watts. Though he did not say it, I was the most dispensable member of his staff, a fact I knew as well as he, and though my proper business in Bengal was to serve the East India Company and make my fortune, neither did I chafe at being so lightly turned from this labour.

So now I took my horse forward and Mrs Watts and Mrs Fortescue, the boy and the two girls, followed after me, and twenty *sowar* cavalrymen behind, and we trotted out of sight of Cossimbazaar toward the river. I am sure I thought myself the finest fellow in the world.

After a mile we passed over the dry riverbed and then Harran Khan, the *risaldar*, the leader of the *sowar* band, rode up to me and pointed to our destination in the Chantok foothills. When we set off again, I fell back to ride alongside Mrs Watts's buggy.

'Harry says we shall be there in an hour.'

'There is no hurry, Mr Douglas,' Mrs Watts replied, not unkindly. 'I hope you are not aggrieved that we have taken you from town.'

I assured her that I was not aggrieved, not in the slightest.

'I am pleased to hear it. It does a young man little good to be locked in the counting house with the whole world in flower outside his door.'

Mrs Watts, I may say here, had the reputation among the company officers of a most singular woman. Having arrived in India with her husband at the commencement of his appointment, she was said never to have uttered a word in public against his superiors, never to have complained of any lack of society or amenity in her situation, and never to have urged her husband to rapaciously mint coin from the advantages of his position the sooner to return her to her rightful place in English society. In short, she was as unlike the other company wives as it was possible to be.

Her father had once been the governor of Fort St David, south of Madras, and she had been twice widowed before she married Watts. She was not yet thirty, but a certain carelessness of the tropic sun had given her a darker complexion than most of the English ladies in Bengal. She was handsome rather than pretty, and with eyes slanted down at their corners, which gave her face a thoughtful cast.

'I'm told you were at Harrow,' she said, and when I acknowledged the fact she mentioned some nephews of hers that were there also. I knew one of these, and so we talked of him, and also of Harrow, and then of the qualities and shortcomings of a classical education, of the rise of religious enthusiasm she detected and deplored in the recently arrived alumni of both Harrow and Eton, and from there we moved on to Pitt and the Duke of Newcastle, and the battles against the French in America. It was a conversation that might have taken place in any fashionable London drawing room, a conversation the like of which I had not had since my recent arrival in India. She smiled often as we talked, and when she did there came quick creases to the corners of her eyes. Time passed quickly in her company, she was the pleasantest woman, and within the hour we came to the pig-sticking ground.

A tent had been pitched beneath the shade of some trees close by the ruins of a Hindoo temple. While the sepoys unharnessed the horses, Mrs Watts and her party repaired to the camp chairs by the tent to take some refreshment and I took myself off to consult with Harran Khan.

The hunt, such as Harry described it to me with sweeping gestures left and right, was to take place across the flat scrubby ground just below us. Harry warned that a startled pig was unpredictable, but he felt that with the sepoys at his disposal he could put on a good show. From the vantage of the tent, he said, there should be a decent view of the sport. Until this point there had been no mention as to whether I would remain a spectator up at the tent or ride down to take part in the hunt. Now I took the opportunity to tell Harry that I would stay by him till I had seen how the pig-sticking was done. 'Then you can give me a spear, I'll try my own hand,' I said with the calm and steady courage of total ignorance.

Harry said nothing to this, which I took for a sign of manly approval. I did not know Harry well at this time.

Returning to the tent, I found Mrs Watts and her party refreshed and revived. My description of the proposed hunt, however, was met with such general indifference that I forbore to elaborate the particulars of the plan as related to me by Harry. Indeed, only Mrs Watts seemed to pay my talk of the hunt the slightest heed. For the rest, the girls had taken out their sketchbooks and were busy drawing the temple ruins. The older woman, Mrs Fortescue, withdrew into the tent, reclined on the camp bed and closed her eyes, and the lad George, Mrs Watts's boy, walked around the tent slashing at the dead grass with a stick. It was only at the news that I, too, would take part in the hunt that a real interest was finally awoken in Mrs Watts. A quick line formed in her brow.

'Are you quite sure?'

I mentioned the packs I had hunted with in England.

'Yes,' she said doubtfully. 'Even so.'

'I'll stay close to Harry.'

'Please do. I should not like to have to explain to my husband how it was that I allowed one of his promising young men to break his own neck.'

'I've no intention of doing so.'

'What man does? But I will not oppose you, Mr Douglas.' She asked for my spyglass the better to view the sport, and I gave it her.

No Hindoo ever died from too great a hurry. The heat, no doubt, is partly responsible for the lethargy that will sometimes settle over whole cities, but their religion, too, gives them a sense of time unlike that of the modern European. In this I believe they are more akin to those ancient people who made Stonehenge and the Ring of Brodgar, people to whom eternity seems to have been ever near – which is to say that the organization of the hunt proceeded with a quite unexampled tardiness.

Harry rattled his orders at them with proper ferocity, pausing now and then to push a knuckle over his thick grey moustache. But this rattling seemed merely a matter of form and the men went about the business of preparation in the manner of those who practise some well-rehearsed ritual. I was as impatient about this as any young man might be, but I managed to hold my tongue until the horses and weapons and men were finally in readiness, and then I rode across to the tent where chai was now being taken. Mrs Watts was not there. Her lad, George, directed me to the ruined temple. After walking through its fallen doorway I discovered the unexpected sight of Mrs Watts, the spyglass resting on the shoulder of a broken stone idol, studying the plain to the north just like some general surveying a battlefield.

'We're ready for the off.'

'Very well, Mr Douglas.' She did not set aside the spyglass.

'Harry does not expect we will be hunting to the north.'

'You have said.'

She did not move, and it then entered my mind that there was some particular purpose to what she did here. But before I could ask what she saw there to the north, she put aside the glass and came away from the temple. As we walked to the tent, I told her that the hunt should be over in two or three hours and that, as I had promised her husband to have everyone safely returned to Cossimbazaar before nightfall, I would be much obliged if she could keep her party from straying too far from the camp. She assented and, with a final friendly warning about the great value of my neck, she wished me good hunting.

I joined Harry and, accompanied by the beaters with their drums and flutes, and the *sowars* with their spears, we rode down to the plain. And there, for two of the most exhilarating hours I have ever spent astride a horse, I forgot about Mrs Watts and the spyglass.

The first pig put up by the beaters charged straight out of the scrub directly in front of Harry and me. It saw us and veered away beneath a spray of stone and dirt, with the banshee cry of Harry Khan ringing in its ears. Harry set after the thing like a man demented, and no more thought for me than for the Emperor of China. His spurs raked the flanks of his horse and it flew after the pig, and then my horse caught the fury and bolted on after. Ahead, the swerving, racing pig; behind, a wild flurry of twisting and turning horseflesh; and somewhere off in the scrub, the raucous flutes and whistles and drums.

We chased hard till the horses were lathered, then Harry's mount picked up a stone and the pig got away from us. The language Harry spoke then was not such as I recognized, but neither could I mistake its meaning. As he swapped his horse for another brought forward by one of the *sowars*, Harry called to me, 'Again?' and I answered, 'By God, yes,' and his eyes gleamed then and he mounted up and we rode out ahead of the beaters.

We soon picked up another pig and chased and lost it, but the third was not so lucky. It took horsemanship of the very first order just to get alongside the thing with its tusks scything at the legs of our horses. But the way Harry rose out of the saddle to reach right over the swerving pig at full gallop and the force with which he struck the spear home between the pig's shoulder-blades – it was truly prodigious. When he dismounted to retrieve his weapon, I trotted back to him and told him as much.

There was no canting modesty about Harry; he lifted his head and laughed, for his blood was up. Then the beaters ran through the scrub to join us; they inspected the stuck pig and proceeded to cut out the tusks. Harry offered me one of his own spears, and I hesitated a moment in surprise before taking it. But it was as I took it that I became aware that the busy chattering of the beaters had suddenly died. They looked past me and Harry, who was silent also, and when I turned in the saddle I saw the cause.

Not thirty yards distant a *sadhu* was passing. Now a *sadhu*, a Hindoo holy man, was not in the normal course of things an unusual sight, for in the cities and towns one saw such men daily in the streets by the temples. But out on the plain, miles from any village and in the midst of our temporary pig-sticking ground, the fellow appeared among us like the very strangest apparition.

The *sadhu*'s hair and beard were long and black, streaked with lines of grey. He was naked but for the grubby loincloth. His forehead was decorated with priestly white and red markings, and he carried in one hand a short metal trident, such as with us might signify Neptune, but with the Hindoo denotes the destroyer god, Shiva.

I stood in my stirrups, about to hail the man, when I felt Harry's hand touch my leg. He shook his head, indicating I should allow the *sadhu* to pass undisturbed.

The man came on till really quite near to us. For all the mind he paid to us we might have been creatures of no substance. His path took him through the line of beaters and, deviating not a foot from his chosen way, he walked on by them without a glance. His dark eyes seemed fixed on some inward point, not of this world.

The beaters, once the *sadhu* had passed, immediately became voluble again and gathered about the stuck pig. Harry began to advise me on the proper use of the spear, of what I should do on closing with the quarry, and what I should watch for in its devilish actions. By the time the beaters went into the scrub again the *sadhu* was far from my mind.

We hunted for one hour more, during which time I missed two pigs while Harry stuck two. Then, on a wild chase for a boar, my horse stumbled and I very nearly succeeded in breaking my neck just as Mrs Watts had feared. As I picked myself from the ground, Harry caught the reins of my loose horse and led it back to me, and after briefly looking me over and satisfying himself that I had suffered no serious injury, he pointed to my spear which lay on the ground behind me. It had been broken in two by my fall.

'You must release it. Throw it from you.'

'Next time I shall.'

'If you hold it when you fall – better not fall.'

I remounted, thoroughly chastened. Though bruised and rather shaken by the thought that I had nearly impaled myself, I still meant to go on. But then after taking some water I looked about me and was more than a little surprised to see how far we had come from our camp. Harry gave me his spyglass and I peered over the low ripples of heat back toward the hill. I made out the ruins of the temple, and then, further along the ridge, the white tent. Faint figures were discernible up by the tent. And on the slope below the temple ruins I saw a slow-moving figure, climbing alone. Upon bringing the figure into focus, I recognized it to be the *sadhu*, walking now with his trident as a cane.

Behind us in the scrub the beaters began drumming. Harry was keen to return to the hunt. The other *sowar*s now rode up to discover what had happened to us, for they were as eager as Harry to be after the quarry. I shaded my eyes and took a quick reckoning on the sun. Then I said to Harry, 'Hunt your way back to the river. I shall bring Mrs Watts and the others and meet you at the crossing in two hours.'

This decision being completely in accord with Harry's wishes and those of his men, in very short order they left me. Turning my horse from the sound of the beaters, I set out for the camp at a trot.

I was perhaps a mile from the camp when I stopped to take water again and again raised Harry's spyglass. The *sadhu* was by now just below the ruined temple. Moving the glass first to the tent and then back to the temple, I saw to my consternation that Mrs Watts had returned to her earlier viewing place by the idol in the ruins and that she was alone there and appeared to have no inkling of the approaching half-naked holy man.

I will not say that I feared for her, but rather that I had a sudden uneasiness at the thought of the startlement it would cause when the *sadhu* appeared unannounced at her side, for the temple ruin was now the man's clear destination. Putting away the spyglass I trotted on and then, after further thought, rose to a canter.

I arrived at the temple directly and, dismounting, looked down the slope. There was no sign of the holy man. I hurried to the temple doorway and was about to call out to Mrs Watts when, through the opening, I saw her. She stood by a large stone block upon which lay the *sadhu*, on his back, perfectly still. She leaned over him, further-more, in such a manner that their faces were almost touching. She was listening to something he said. The sight was so peculiar that I hesi-tated and then I said, 'Mrs Watts?' and stepped in. Without turning her head she replied, 'Bring me your flask.'

I brought it to her. She put a hand beneath the *sadhu*'s head and tried to raise him. She put the flask to his lips but he would not take the water; it ran down his cheek and she let his head rest again.

'What is wrong with him?'

'He has been poisoned.'

I looked at her in surprise, but she offered no further explanation. She continued to regard the *sadhu*. After a time he whispered some words in his own tongue. She took one of his hands and placed it on his chest, and then she went around the stone block and did the same with the other hand.

'Can he not be purged?'

'He does not choose to live.'

'You know this man,' I said, for I had not yet learned to hold my thoughts close. I cannot say how I knew it, but only that it was implicit in her manner toward him and in her stillness when I had first discov-ered them. She made no reply to this remark and when the *sadhu*

12

whispered again she put an ear close to his lips. When she next lifted her head, I said boldly, 'We must take him with us.'

'We shall do no such thing. I have told you, he has chosen to die.'

'But with proper care—'

'If you would be so kind as to keep my children and the others away from this place, Mr Douglas. I will stay here while you strike the camp. When you are prepared to depart, please come yourself to fetch me. And I would be obliged to you until then for your silence.'

It was fully an hour before the camp was struck and Mrs Watts's party had readied themselves for the return to Cossimbazaar, and all through that hour I was in a state of constant distraction. I looked in the direction of the temple frequently, but there was no sign of either Mrs Watts or the *sadhu*. I could not fathom any plausible connection between such a pair, but in reflecting upon Mrs Watts's earlier actions, first her going to the temple ruins and then how she scanned the plain with my spyglass, I could not help but wonder at the coincidence that had brought the *sadhu* to this uninhabited place on precisely the day of our hunt. And as to her parting injunction for silence, frankly it troubled me, and amidst the bustle of striking camp my thoughts on the matter became no clearer.

As the *sepoys* carried out the final loading, I went back to the temple. It was silent within the fallen walls but for the scraping and trilling of insects in the heat. The *sadhu* lay motionless on the stone, his trident now lying beside him. Mrs Watts sat on another stone nearby, looking out through the ruins across the plain.

I said, 'We are ready.'

After a time she roused herself and went to the broken idol and retrieved my spyglass from by its feet. She gave me the spyglass and stepped past me while I continued to stare at the motionless figure of the *sadhu*. She stopped and said, 'He is dead,' and looking at her now I saw that she was grieved, and so, not knowing what else might be said, I told her I was sorry for it.

'Do not be, Mr Douglas. The world can hurt him no more.'

She did not seem unsteady but there was something made me offer her my arm, and she took it, and so we came away from the temple. Nothing further was spoken between us of the *sadhu*, and nothing more done for the body, but we left it there and by nightfall I had returned Mrs Watts and her party to Cossimbazaar.

CHAPTER TWO

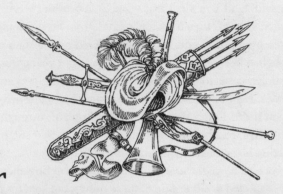

'You are a friend to the boar, I hear,' said Edward Fairborough, clapping me on the back when he came to fetch me the next morning. 'A friend to the boar and a danger to yourself, God help us.' I had been under Edward's watchful eye since my arrival in Cossimbazaar and fully expected to remain under his tutelage for some weeks to come while he broke me to the East India Company harness. 'Are those figs, dear boy? Don't mind if I do.' He gathered several into his pocket while I finished pulling on my boots and then we left my quarters and went into the factory yard.

There were not two score of us British servants of the company in Cossimbazaar, and though the native population was fully several thousand, the life of the place centred upon our trade and the trade of the French, and that trade centred upon our factories. Our own factory yard was a compound surrounded by a low wall, the compound comprising the warehouses and storerooms through which the trade-goods passed, the rooms where the business of negotiation and book-keeping was done, and the quarters where the company men lived. As we crossed the yard now, Edward recounted the story of my hunting exploits, such as he had heard them. It was a tale I barely recognized, and I said as much.

'Never fret yourself,' he told me. 'In two days you'll recognize none of it. Don't let it trouble you. Harry thinks you'll do, that's what matters.'

It pleased me to hear this. I admitted that although considerably less than half his age, I had struggled to keep up with Harry.

'Yes,' he said, 'and you shall not want to get on the wrong side of the man either.' Edward then took a notebook from his pocket in preparation for the brief prospectus he always offered me on the morning's business. He had been in India some seven or eight years, the last two in the Cossimbazaar factory, and there was little he did not know about the company's way of business and its trading rights and privileges in Bengal. I had heard from other writers that Edward, through trading on his own behalf, had become wealthy. There was also some rumour of a connection he had made with a young lady in Calcutta, and it was generally expected he might soon, therefore, return to England. Edward himself never alluded to either one of these things, but kept his personal affairs close. Indeed, he seemed so to thrive on his work (and on the climatic conditions that had done for so many) that he was, as you might say, 'in the pink'. A little too much weight about the girth perhaps, and the fullness of his cheeks made his face round like a melon, but otherwise he was the very picture of robust good health. Like most of us he dressed in shirt and breeches whilst about the factory, and donned a jacket to ride out or to meet the native traders who came in to meet with us. His wig I saw upon a peg in his bungalow but hardly ever upon his head. He was a man too busy with the interests of the company and himself to have much time for his own appearance, and so his dark hair was often awry. Now he brushed his wayward fringe from his eyes and consulted his notebook and frowned. 'Rahindrah Roy to start the day. A liar and a cheat. His father controls most of the boats on the river, so kid gloves there. Best you say nothing, and leave Mr Roy to Uncle Edward.' Edward, I might add, was thirty years of age and no relation to me whatever. 'After that, old Lahal may drop by. Not a bad old bird, Lahal. Good cloth, too, if you can get your hands on it. Sends most of it to the French down in Chandernagore, the old sod.'

He continued in this vein till we came to the cloth warehouse where a bullock cart was being loaded with large bolts of fabric. Edward stopped when he saw this and called to the turbaned supervisor. Receiving the brief answer, 'Watts Sahib,' Edward then went himself to look inside. Evidently he did not like what he saw, for his bonhomie vanished on the instant. After exchanging a few words more with the supervisor, Edward moved swiftly across the yard toward the Wattses' residence with me, in some perplexity, trailing after him.

Up on their verandah, Mr and Mrs Watts were taking their breakfast. They made a handsome couple – he must then have been thirty-four years of age. Watts was not at all a physically imposing man, but unlike Edward he took some care of his appearance. Even now at table on his private verandah he wore his jacket, and when his breakfast was done he would most certainly put on his wig before making his morning round of the factory. On seeing us approach, they both bade us good morning and then, as Edward went up the steps at a bound, Watts thanked me for the good care I had taken of his wife and her party the previous day. He made no mention of the *sadhu*. Mrs Watts smiled pleasantly and said not a word.

'You save me a journey, Mr Fairborough,' said Watts, turning to Edward. He could not fail to see Edward's agitation. 'I was to come to you presently about our need for more space in the cloth house.'

'I have just looked in.'

'I thought it best they begin early. You will forgive me that I did not inform you earlier.'

'I was not told of any large shipment due.'

'The space is required.'

'Where has the cloth been taken? What has been removed – I looked but briefly – what is gone is not all company goods.'

'Just so. In point of fact, very little that has been removed is company property. It is the private stock, for the most part, that has been shifted. Mine as well as yours and that of the others. But it is safe enough in temporary storage about the town.' Watts then named some Hindoo traders with whom the goods had been stored. At these names, the first heat of Edward's agitation abated a little. 'The transfer has been effected without undue comment,' Watts concluded. 'It would be pleasing to me should that happy situation continue.'

Presented with this fait accompli, there was nothing left for Edward to say that would not put him in direct and unseemly conflict with his superior. He therefore contained himself, but there was no mistaking his belief that an unwarranted liberty had been taken. He had been touched at the point an East India Company man feels keenest, his own private interest, and even now he could not fully conceal his displeasure.

Watts then invited us to join him for breakfast. We declined and were about to depart, when he said to me, 'It was you, I believe, wrote that letter to Monsieur Marais in Chandernagore.' Marais was a Frenchman, an employee of La Compagnie Française des Indes Orientales – the French East India Company – who had caused Edward some trouble with one of the Bengali merchants. Upon discovering my facility with the French language, Edward had me draft a letter to Marais complaining of the fellow's ungentlemanly conduct. I was surprised now to discover that this letter had passed through Watts's hands. I confessed to the authorship and Watts said, 'I would prefer you not enter into any further correspondence with Marais. Or with any other Frenchman in Bengal.'

'I have no reason to.'

'I am glad to hear it.'

Watts then turned to Edward again and engaged him in talk of various company matters unrelated to the movement of the cloth. It was a palpable olive branch, and after some minutes more we retreated down the steps. But as we re-crossed the yard the fully laden bullock cart was departing the cloth house, and at this sight Edward's face darkened again. When I asked him how that letter had come into Watts's hands, he gave me no answer, so I was left in some wonder as to the matter and as to the meaning of the words Watts had spoken to me.

Rahindrah Roy sent a boy to inform us that he was currently indisposed and would not be coming to the factory. Edward sent the boy off with a sharp burst of Hindoostani of which I understood little, but I could see that Edward thought himself slighted by Roy's non-appearance.

He brooded on it and after a short time went into the factory yard and enquired after the boy, meaning I suppose to give him a further message for his master, but the lad was not to be found. Returning indoors, Edward called for his man to bring a pitcher of water, and then, as if to put the generally disagreeable start to the day from his mind, he brought out the contracts and ledgers relating to the merchant Lahal's trade with us and showed me how it was recorded and what I must write and what should be left to the native clerk. Much of this I had some notion of from my few weeks in the Calcutta factory, but Edward was rather more particular than most about these records and he made sure that I should strive to understand them as he did.

Through the open door of our room we saw the oxen carts come and go from the yard, and Edward went out once or twice to deal with some problem while I stayed at the desk we both used and looked around me at the ledgers and books, the broken tally-board on the wall and the dust drifting in from the yard and wondered if I should ever now escape from it. And if I did not escape from it, I wondered what I must then look forward to and what my life should be – a careful maintaining of my health, a careful marshalling of money, and then, and at best, an emergence after several years as a second Edward Fairborough.

Later, while we bent over some ledger together, I said to him, 'Yesterday, when we hunted, a *sadhu* surprised us.'

'Eh?'

'He just seemed to appear. There was no village nearby.' I enquired of Edward what he knew of these men.

He could tell me but little. He said they had the reputation among their own people for an astounding self-control and he told me of a *sadhu* he had himself seen who stood in the river by Cossimbazaar and drew his own innards out through his anus and washed them and then, apparently satisfied with his efforts, put them back and went on his way. 'Never saw the like in Hampshire, I assure you.'

'Their purpose then is wholly religious?'

'No damned purpose at all from what I can see. Beggars, most of them. I never saw one with anything to trade, so I never went near the fellows. If you've got your wits about you, you'll do the same. They won't thank you for too close an enquiry into their affairs. If it doesn't touch on company business or your own purse, stay well clear of it. A lesson I could wish better learned by one or two others besides yourself.' He bowed his head in the direction of the Watts residence, but did not expand on the remark. Then he tapped his finger on the open ledger and continued with my induction into the mysteries of the well-kept book.

We were interrupted in the mid-morning by some traders and agents who came in to take chai with us. Edward put aside his papers and called for his man to bring cakes, and the traders and agents then settled by the low table near the window – some on rickety chairs and some on dusty cushions – and there was gossip about their tight-fisted bankers in Murshidabad and the character of the new nawab of Bengal. It was late morning before the merchant Lahal arrived. He came in quietly and sat with the others and took chai, but after a time, and at some private signal from Edward that escaped me, the lesser traders and agents melted away to leave Lahal alone with us.

Lahal was a portly man, dressed in white *shalwar-khemis*. His beard was white also, but his upper lip was shaven. A company man might conduct all of his business affairs through agents, but the shrewder among them, like Edward, used the agents, paid the necessary commissions, but always maintained a personal contact with the important merchants like Lahal. A superior tray of cakes and sweetmeats was now produced by Edward's man. Though Lahal broke some of these for politeness's sake, I noticed that he ate not a crumb. He laughed often, his eyes wrinkling to merry slits, but there was about him that which I did not altogether like nor trust.

He talked with Edward about the cloth trade and they moved between English and Hindoostani in a manner that made it hard for me to entirely follow. The gist of it, though, was clear – Lahal was bringing a shipment from the north and he was holding out to Edward the prospect that the shipment might bypass the French and come to us. Edward behaved as though such opportunities were quite commonplace, but Lahal was neither deceived nor offended by such pretended nonchalance and he smiled and looked from Edward to me and back, nodding merrily. When Lahal was gone, Edward made a short drum roll with his fingers on the desk.

I said, 'He promised us nothing.'

'One step at a time, dear boy.'

'Do you trust him?'

'I trust him to look to his own interests. Our business is to make him see that he can best do that by trusting to us.'

'He seemed guarded.'

Edward laughed. 'An open heart and an open hand might do very well for the gallants of Mayfair, Alistair. Lahal resides in Bengal.'

Raised voices sounded suddenly in the yard, and, looking out, we saw three carts that Edward had earlier sent down to the river. They should have been unloaded down at the river-dock, but now, to all appearance, they had returned fully laden. Edward went out to discover the cause of the problem. He spoke with one of the drivers and returned a minute later with a face like thunder.

'*Syce! Doh horse, shighra!*'

We rode out from the factory down to the Begrathi, a Ganges tributary (and upper arm of the Hugli) that ran hard by Cossimbazaar, and there we dismounted by the dock. On my earlier visits, the river had been crowded with boats and life. Today the scene was altogether different. There were only three vessels tied up to the dock, and each one of them was under repair. On the first boat a group of naked boys was playing, jostling and pushing each other into the muddy water. Apart from these boys, nothing moved on the river. Edward called to them, asking for the whereabouts of Roy, but then a man came out from the second cabin, buttoning his shirt, and from Edward's muttered remark I knew the man for Roy.

He was a small fellow, and darker than most in Cossimbazaar. There were deep wrinkles near his eyes as sailors get from the constant glare of water. Edward brushed aside Roy's apology for his failure to keep the morning's appointment. Instead he asked after the boats, where they had gone, and where Roy's father might be. Roy finished buttoning his shirt and then made a lazy motion with his hand downriver.

'And these are all that remain?' said Edward, barely able to restrain his anger.

Roy cast a casual eye over the decrepit hulls, and then said, 'Also that,' and pointed across the river to where a child's boat was beached in the mud, tied with a rag to a tree. At this calculated insolence, Edward planted one foot forward.

'May I ask why your father discovered the urgent need to remove his boats while they are under contract to us? And with never a word to us?'

Roy gave no answer.

'The boats must be returned here. We have need of them.'

'I will speak of your request with my father.'

'Do not mistake me, Mr Roy. It is not a request I make but a demand that your father's contract be properly fulfilled.'

'Is there a letter from Mr Watts?'

'I need no letter from either Mr Watts or anyone beside. I have your father's signature, and his seal, on a solemn contract. And so I would be obliged if you would immediately convey to him my instruction that the boats be returned at once to where they are required. To this place, where he has contracted to supply them.'

'If he is willing—'

'Should he prove unwilling, I will then report to Mr Watts that your father has broken his contract with the company. The consequences of such a report, I think you know.' At this threat, Roy, who had till then been enjoying the sight of Edward struggling to govern his fury, gave us the look of the very Devil. I feared some incident might occur between him and Edward and wondered what I might do to prevent it. But then the naked boys cried out and pointed upriver and a number of heads came bobbing from the cabins. Some distance away, up on the riverbank, a large number of horsemen were riding toward us. I fetched my spyglass from my saddle, observed for a moment the approaching riders, and then passed the spyglass to Edward.

'They are armed.'

He seemed not to credit my opinion. But then he looked himself and said, 'They are soldiers.'

'Company soldiers?' I squinted into the distance but they were too far.

Edward lowered the glass. 'What think you, Mr Roy? Are they company?'

Roy's discomfort was answer enough. They were not company. It was now only too clear that Roy's father had been forewarned in some manner of the arrival of these Moorish troops and had consequently withdrawn his boats to safety. But neither father nor son had chosen to forewarn us at the factory. I thought for a moment that Edward might knock Roy into the river. But with a supreme effort he finally turned his back on the man and we went to our horses and rode to the factory.

Once inside the yard, Edward ordered the tallyman to close the gates and he called for Harry to bring some sepoys to stand guard there. Watts came onto his verandah to discover the cause of the disturbance. Edward waved riverward with his riding crop. 'Troops. The nawab's men.'

'How many, Mr Fairborough? And how far?'

A sharp cry from by the gates then drew everyone's eyes. A column of foot-soldiers was in the town, moving along the main street and advancing toward the factory.

'Harry!' called Watts. 'You are not to fire on them. Mr Fairborough, you will have the warehouses closed and secured. Any man who has no proper weapon ready, come here to me.'

I assisted Watts in bringing a number of pistols from the gun locker inside his house. Mrs Watts seemed to understand the situation on the instant. She reported to her husband that their children were safe inside and then she withdrew herself to tend to them. As Watts issued the pistols from the steps of his verandah, he warned that they were to be used only in self-defence and that any man who disobeyed would be dismissed from the company's service.

The weapons all being taken, I went to fetch my own pistol from my quarters. Loading it, I felt a full measure of excitement, albeit touched with a quite reasonable apprehension. And I prayed a silent prayer, also, that if the worst should happen and the soldiers break through, I might show the courage I believed was in me and at the very least acquit myself like a man. Returning to the yard, I looked to the gates in full expectation that the massed ranks of the nawab's soldiery would by now be gathered there. My expectation was wholly confounded. The column of soldiers had stopped in the town and now appeared to be dispersing to the shade of the roadside stalls. I crossed to where Harry stood.

'Will they attack us?'

'Am I the nawab?' he growled and would have cuffed me, I think, had I been any younger.

There was no great alarm or noise in the town. In fact the soldiers seemed to be moving among the people quite peaceably now, some of them even buying refreshments from the stallholders. After a time, one of their officers came alone to the gates. (I recognized him for an officer – by the fine helmet that he wore and by the chain mail and breast-plate – before Harry confirmed it.) This fellow conversed with Harry through the gates, dropped his sword on the ground and put his pistol down beside it. Harry then opened the gates to him and led him to where Watts stood observing all from his place on the verandah.

When I saw that Edward and several others did not scruple to hurry across, I went also and arrived to see the nawab's officer hand Watts a scroll, which Watts opened and read in silence. He then turned to his second, Mr Cole, saying, 'The nawab invites us upon a safe-conduct to attend him, that we may present our felicitations on his ascent to the throne.' He regarded the officer a moment, and then glanced beyond him to the soldiery within the town. Had they so wished, they might have driven us from the factory and directly into our graves. 'Having given the matter due consideration,' said Watts, 'I believe it would be churlish of us to refuse so thoughtful an invitation.'

CHAPTER THREE

M r Watts, Mr Cole and I made up the small party that rode from Cossimbazaar with the nawab's escort that same day, the twenty-fourth of May. Watts had not ordered me to accompany him, but he required someone to serve as a messenger should such a need arise and, when Harry recommended me, Watts enquired of me whether I might be willing and I assented.

Edward, in the hour before my departure, did me the doubtful service of recounting certain rumours, some of which I had myself already heard. Rumours which, if true, went some way toward explaining the sudden irruption of the nawab's troops into Cossimbazaar. It was said that Siraj ud-Daulah, the new nawab, had come to power one month earlier only after beating out a contender for the throne whose cause the company had secretly supported. To make matters worse for us, the British governor in Calcutta, Drake, had refused to give up to the new nawab a fugitive Bengali tax collector, a rogue who had taken sanctuary under company protection in Calcutta after defrauding the nawab's treasury to the extent of some several million rupees. Governor Drake, who Edward assured me was a fool, had made an unnecessary show of his defiance of the nawab.

As Cossimbazaar lay not far distant from the royal city of Murshidabad, we were the first to feel the full extent of the young nawab's displeasure – so Edward concluded. What conclusion Watts had reached, none knew, for he kept himself close-quartered in the time before our departure, speaking only with his wife and family.

After our small party and escort had ridden some way along the bank of the Begrathi, we turned away from it inland, and then Watts fell back and rode beside me. Our horses put up a small cloud of dust, and upon seeing me crane my head to watch the vultures wheeling high above us, Mr Watts remarked to me, 'It is a long way from Orkney, is it not?'

'Aye.'

'Aye.' He smiled, a rare sight that day.

We rode in silence for some considerable time, till the heat at last began to ease. A flock of birds like sparrows passed over, sailing to their nightly nesting. The native soldiers of our escort talked among themselves, and though Watts seemed withdrawn now into his own thoughts I was sure that he listened, for by Edward I knew that the Persian of the nawab's court was familiar to him. It was coming on to dark when we veered from our course again. I made sure to take a quick reading from my compass, and then looked up to find Watts regarding me.

'I trust that you did not think me uncivil that I perused your letter to Chandernagore. I saw by your look that Mr Fairborough had neglected to inform you of it.' I made no reply. The reading of a private letter seemed to me a low, not to say ungentlemanly, act, which did not accord with the good reputation Watts had in the company. But I had quite forgotten it in the midst of the larger events of the day. He added, 'It was no Harrow-schoolboy French that you wrote.'

'There is a Frenchman attached to my family. I have babbled with him in the tongue since my cradle.' Watts waited for some further elucidation of the strange circumstance of a French gentleman attached to a Scots family in far-off Orkney, but I gave him none. This was a hare I would not start. Enough to say that the man closest to me in all the world since my own father's death was a retired French officer, maimed at Culloden, and that I had long since learned to avoid speaking of it. 'Had I known of the prohibition, sir—'

Watts lifted a hand, signifying that we should not dwell on the unfortunate misunderstanding with respect to the letter. 'It will surprise you, I think, if I tell you that I once dined in your father's company.' It did indeed surprise me. It surprised me exceedingly. 'It was in Edinburgh,' he said. 'He gave a number of public demonstrations at the university. I was fortunate enough to attend one of these.'

'That would be a dissection.'

'A dog, if I recall. Afterward we dined with the Poker Club. Perhaps I should have mentioned it before. But I fear that in the present times it will not do for a Scotsman to be ever playing on the Caledonian pipes. And you will now be wondering if your father did not write to me of you. Be assured, he did not. Our acquaintance was of the slightest. I daresay he scarcely noticed me. Certainly he little thought then that his dining companion would these many years later be riding with his son under armed escort through Bengal. Does he continue with his experiments?'

'My father died last year.'

He pressed his lips tight together, then said, 'Forgive me that I prattled so.' I told him it was no matter, that I should have told him of it had I known of their previous acquaintance. 'But such scientific enquiry holds no appeal for you,' said he.

'It appeals to me greatly.'

'And yet with the shining example of your father before you, you have chosen the life commercial.'

'I had hoped for an army commission. It was not to be.' The bitterness and regret, alas, were with me still. And though I had thought to conceal it, there was in my voice that which caused Watts to turn a penetrating eye on me, but how to tell him it was my father's disastrous last year of life that had brought me to this pass, with no estate in the world left to me, and no money to buy a commission, and only my junior place in the company now to rely upon?

I was spared further examination and scrutiny when ahead in the gathering darkness we saw the first fires of the nawab's camp. Our horses pricked their ears and our pace suddenly quickened.

'Great God,' said Cole when we came closer and the full extent of the camp opened before us.

Watts paused and looked gravely over it all. Then he rode on with no more outward show of concern than an English gentleman might reveal on being escorted through the Royal Park at Windsor. And so we entered the camp, that gathering of multitudes, a mass of men and horse and weapons the like of which had not been seen in that country for many years – the great army of Siraj ud-Daulah, the mighty nawab of Bengal.

The nawab did not receive Watts that evening, nor yet the following morning. Three of our escort had been stationed outside our tent, and whensoever any of us wandered we found ourselves shadowed by one of these martial fellows who kept their scimitars always strapped to their belts, and their watchful eyes upon us. It surprised me that we were allowed to wander so freely about the camp, but when I said as much to Watts he remarked that this freedom was intentional and that we were meant to understand from what we saw that the nawab was no paper tiger.

For myself, I used that freedom to the utmost. I went about the camp with my shadow and looked at each part of it unmolested. It was something like a travelling city, every division of it having its own tradesmen and camp-followers – blacksmiths worked their makeshift forges, baggage-men tended the supply carts and there were so many women and children in some places that it appeared whole villages must have decamped here. In the meadows around the perimeter, strings of hobbled horses were tied, and set apart from these were the elephants and their mahouts. I could compare it with nothing in my experience. It was like the pages of Livy come alive, the Punic army of Hannibal re-arisen.

All through that first day more soldiers arrived at the camp, columns of mounted troops and foot-soldiers, each column received with wild ululations and the beating of drums. Watts's habit was to keep in his saddlebag a book with which to pass the idle hours of his travels, and for most of that day he sat outside the tent and perused the pages of Marcus Aurelius, looking up sometimes to observe dispassionately the steady increase of the nawab's great army. In the late afternoon Cole scanned the horizon with his spyglass and announced unhappily that yet more soldiers would arrive in the camp before nightfall.

Though I blush in shame now to confess it, there was in me some goodly measure of youthful anticipation. In my defence I will say that the sight of an army was new to me, and that my schooling in Bengali politics being all from Edward Fairborough, I did not then truly understand what this great gathering of men and arms might eventually portend. (A defence, I know, that is weak enough.)

In the early evening we were summoned to attend the nawab. Or, truer to say, Watts and Cole were summoned, for immediately we entered the *durbar* tent I was ushered to one side and could only watch as the others made the long walk up through the two lines of tent-poles into the presence of the nawab, Siraj ud-Daulah. The cavernous interior was lit with flaming torches mounted on spikes thrust into the ground. There were scores of courtiers and soldiers in there, some standing in small groups, some lounging on cushions, most of them talking quietly among themselves and behaving as if they had not noticed the arrival of Watts.

My escort evidently saw no need to stay close by me in the tent, and I moved forward alone through the throng to gain a better vantage of the dais. There was empty ground between the dais and the courtiers, but I saw that none might cross uninvited and so I stopped there. The nawab wore a white turban, heavily threaded with gold. A coat of the same cloth was tight about his narrow shoulders. Though the nawab and Watts talked together, not a word of it reached me, and I therefore studied the nawab's face, trying to read in it the lineaments of his character. The company gossip painted him as capricious, and somewhat cruel, but he had held the throne barely a month and so I discounted this talk, for none but the intimates of his court could have yet known his character. The strongest impression I had at that first sighting was of his extreme youth, for he looked to me even younger than his reputed twenty-three years. Indeed, he had the unblemished face of a boy. He toyed with the gold bangle at his wrist while Watts spoke to him, and occasionally lifted his eyes and peered at Watts in a manner of studied disagreeableness. His dark eyes were feminine, and made more so by the kohl (which is a native cosmetic) that had been applied to them. All this, and the few thin wisps of hair on his upper lip, gave him a look not of manliness but rather of languid petulance.

'*Asalaam alaikum*, Mr Douglas.' I turned in surprise. It was a plump Hindoo at my shoulder who had addressed me so softly, though in the Moorish fashion. Like me, he had been watching the scene at the dais and he continued to watch it while he spoke. 'Mr Watts has not become impatient? But you have had a day to recover from your ride. You have slept well?'

'We slept,' said I, for the fellow seemed to expect some answer of me.

'And you have clean water? The southern well has the cleanest water. I find that it draws best in the hour before sunrise.' He paused and then looking to the dais remarked, 'Mr Watts is a gentleman.' I had been warned by both Watts and Cole not to speak loosely with any of the nawab's men, so I made to move away from this garrulous and rather too friendly stranger. As I did so, he touched my arm. 'Perhaps you will tell Mr Watts that Sri Babu sends him salaam.' He turned from me and at once fell into conversation with his neighbour while I immediately withdrew myself from there lest he again accost me. I was unsettled too, and cursed the fellow to myself, and yet from my new place at the rear of the tent I found myself looking out for him. But I could not see him now, for he was lost among all the others in the dancing shadows of the torchlight.

'You will regret your lack of reading matter, Mr Douglas,' Watts said, letting fall the flap of our tent as he followed Cole and me inside. These were the first words he had spoken to me since our coming away from the *durbar* tent. 'The nawab has invited us to remain here as his honoured guests.' Watts had till now given no sign that his audience with the nawab had been other than acceptable and within the bounds of common diplomacy. But now here in the privacy of our own tent his displeasure was writ bold upon his face. He waved me to a place by the tent-opening where I might keep watch on our escort who sat by the fire outside. Watts then launched into a quiet but earnest discussion with Cole on the whole proceedings that they had just been through. I overheard enough of this rehashing to understand that Edward's surmise was at least partly right: the nawab had indeed complained to Watts, but not only of that fugitive Bengali tax collector. He had also protested against the company's building of fortifications around the Calcutta factory and had accused the company of abusing the royal *dustucks*, our duty-free trading privileges.

Cole seemed willing to give the nawab's complaints against the company some credence. But Watts, after several minutes' discussion, and after thoughtfully weighing each argument, finally dismissed the nawab's complaints with a decisive sweep of the hand. 'These are but pretexts. He is the creature of the French and they will now follow the Golden Rule and do unto us as we should most surely have done unto them. He will move against Calcutta, and little enough we can do to stop an army such as this.' In his agitation, Watts paced the tent and then came to the opening just by me and looked out across the camp.

I said, 'Sri Babu sends you his salaam,' and Watts turned to me sharply. His eyelids drooped and the sudden intensity of his gaze made me wish I had not spoken. 'He addressed me by name,' said I. 'I did not parley with him.'

'Salaam?'

'Yes.'

'And nothing beside?'

'He said he thought you a gentleman.'

Watts continued to peer at me. He asked me what more was said.

'He asked if we had slept. He asked if we had clean water. I told him that we had slept.'

'Clean water?'

'He said that should we require clean water, the southern well drew best in the hour before sunrise. Then he sent his salaam. That was all.'

I began to explain that I had not invited this Sri Babu's confidence, but that he had thrust himself upon me.

Ignoring my hurried explanation, Watts cast his gaze upon the ground and reflected for some considerable while. 'Do not trouble yourself, lad,' he said at last. 'It was not badly done.' He glanced up. 'You understand that we are the nawab's prisoners.'

I nodded. I had not known it till now.

He said nothing more, but went and lay on the cushions of his charpoy, draped an arm over his forehead like a man exhausted, and stared up at the roof of the tent. He did not close his eyes, nor, it seemed to me, cease in his thinking.

In the hour before sunrise the crescent moon was low in the western sky and the tents of the camp threw a wide forest of shadows. Some few soldiers had risen early to stir the embers of the campfires, but most remained asleep, and no one challenged me as I went to the well. I made sure to stay clear of the horses, just as Watts had instructed, lest any man mistake my actions for a foolhardy preparation to escape.

I had brought a pail from our tent, and coming upon the well I set this down and lowered another pail which was attached to the rope on the windlass. Far below me I heard the soft splash as it touched water. Then I jerked the rope.

'You are alone, Mr Douglas.'

I own that the hairs stood on my neck. There was no reason for it, but only the warnings Watts had given me. I said, 'I am.'

'Please to keep drawing your water.' There was a movement on the far side of the well and I saw the figure of Sri Babu emerge from the shadows. He wore just a dhoti. He was bare-chested and looked like a man going about his morning ablutions. 'It is clean, as I told you.'

'Mr Watts has asked that you speak to me as to him.'

'He thought, no doubt, to provide us with some matter?'

'I must ask you what is intended with this army. And if you know of any French commitment to the nawab.'

'May Mr Watts not come himself tomorrow?'

'He said I was to tell you that he thinks it imprudent.' I could see enough of Sri Babu's face to read his hesitation. I could see he considered that passing information through me might be not only imprudent, but also unwise.

But at last he said, 'The nawab's generals encourage him in his new-won power. This army is the consequence of their encouragement.'

'Will they march on Calcutta?'

'It seems possible, does it not? The nawab has sent envoys to the French in Chandernagore and to the Dutch. He now waits for their return.'

'Then the French have yet to commit themselves.'

'As to a formal commitment, I have no knowledge. As to their inclination, it is not to be doubted. I have heard there was no bloodshed in Cossimbazaar.'

I told him that the soldiers did not enter the factory, and then I immediately checked myself. This was such an exchange as Watts had warned me against. I saw then that Sri Babu had with him that small tin pail the Hindoo will frequently have about him at his prayers, and now he placed this on the wall of the well. But when I offered to fill it for him, he quickly declined the offer, and only later did I think that he must have considered my touch on his prayer-water unclean

He said, 'There is a great difficulty with Governor Drake.' I made no response. Mr Watts had instructed me with particular fervency that I not be drawn to offer an opinion on the character of any man connected with the company. I lowered the roped pail into the well again while he went on, 'If Drake could be persuaded to release the tax collector Das, the nawab might yet be swayed.'

I remarked that Mr Watts had little opportunity to persuade any man of anything while he was held the nawab's prisoner.

'He believes himself a prisoner?'

'The thought was mine,' I said, for I heard in his tone a quickened interest that I did not understand. I was disconcerted to find myself so little the master of my own tongue.

'Indeed.' He took thought a moment. And then he enquired if Mr Watts had either quill or paper.

'Quill and paper, he has. A method of delivery, he has not.'

33

'Then you will please to tell him that I will depart for Calcutta in one week.'

I filled my pail and took it up, ready to leave. I had no wish to speak more.

He said, 'You are in some hurry to be gone.'

'Is there more you would tell Mr Watts?'

He considered that awhile, and then said, 'You may tell him, Salaam.'

'The good sense of Governor Drake is a rather slender reed for us to lean upon,' murmured Watts when I had made my report to him. He drew his blanket closer about him and shut his eyes. 'Your diligence is appreciated, Mr Douglas. As is your discretion.' After that he rolled over and within minutes was asleep.

It was not many days before the novelty of our situation began to pall. We had each had our turn with Marcus Aurelius, and even I, by the sixth day, had had my fill of watching the elephants bathe in the river. Each day Watts petitioned through our escort for a further audience with the nawab and each day the petition went pointedly unanswered. These deliberate discourtesies were met by Watts with an outward stoicism, but I could see that he did not forget the slights – each one went into the balance against our host, a balance that had weighed heavily against him since the uninvited arrival of his troops in Cossimbazaar. By the time the nawab condescended to grant a second audience, on our seventh day of captivity, both Watts and Cole had long since formed their own decided opinions on the man.

Watts was firm that I should not go with them this time. 'The swallow has a freedom the peacock cannot dream of,' he said by way of consolation. (A translation from the Persian, I believe. He was fond of such things. And to my young ears, no consolation whatever.) When they went, I was left by our tent with only three of our original escort for company. None of them spoke English, and my Hindoostani was of the most rudimentary kind, in consequence of which the passing time weighed heavy on me, and so after an hour I took myself down to the bare patch of earth where the soldiers practised with their swords, and sat there and watched them. They did not use their swords after the British or French manner. The first time I had seen their strokes I thought them ill-judged, but in the past few days I had studied their practice enough to know that it was not ill-judgement, but the shape and heft of their weapons that made them move as they did.

There was little talk among them as they carved at the air. They were drilled by an officer who knew both his men and his business, and I could not help but think of the empty barn at home, and of Jean-Paul flourishing his walking cane about my head as I attempted to master what he had taught me and calling in his friendly fashion, 'Encore, Alistair. Encore, Monsieur Lazybones,' which he thought the very height of British wit. I hoped if I waited there long enough they might offer me a sword, but, just as on the previous days when I had sat there, no offer was forthcoming, and when the practice finished I returned to the tent and lay down beside it in the shade.

It was evening before Watts and Cole returned from their audience with the nawab. Neither man was in the temper for polite conversation, and when I remarked on the lateness of the hour Cole turned on me with some asperity. 'You will pardon us, Mr Douglas, but our kind host did not deign to admit us into his august presence till we had sat for some hours, sweltering. We have been pickled in our own perspiration. By His Highness's royal decree.'

Watts loosed his collar while I went to dip two kerchiefs in water for them. When I returned, each was sat on his own charpoy with shirt unbuttoned. I gave them their kerchiefs and asked if, having now seen the nawab, we would be permitted to leave in the morning.

Watts dabbed at his neck with the wetted kerchief and indicated that Cole should take up position by the tent entrance. Once Cole was there, Watts set his elbows on his knees and leaned forward to me.

'You have heard of the Armenian, Coja Wajid.'

'The merchant in Hugli.'

'He has the most extensive trade with us and the other Europeans. He has as much to fear from an upset to the company as any. Sri Babu is Wajid's man. Wajid has sent him to attempt diplomacy with ud-Daulah. Though I am near certain that Sri Babu will fail, while he makes the attempt we must assist him.' Until this time I had been allowed to form my own notions as to the nature of Sri Babu's position. The notion I had formed was that he was in the pay of the company. Though the truth was not too far from this, yet the reason for my now being taken into Watts's confidence eluded me. Then Watts said, 'I must ask you now that which I have some doubt I have any right to ask you. I must ask if you will carry from me a letter to Governor Drake.'

'I will.'

Watts put up his hand. 'Not only to Drake. I would give you private messages also to some others in Calcutta. You would carry them where they cannot be discovered.' He touched his temple. 'I would arrange it that Sri Babu travelled with you. If I write a letter of advice to Drake such as is agreeable to the nawab, then you may be sure you will be given your liberty to deliver it.'

Would Governor Drake not be more inclined to take advice if it were delivered directly by Watts, I wondered.

Watts said, 'I am certain that neither I nor Mr Cole will be permitted to pass from the reach of the nawab for some time yet. While the game is playing, he thinks to keep us from the board.' At these last words there came such a glint in Watts's eye that I knew he meant to do all in his power to thwart the nawab's intention, though how he might manage this from his captivity I could not then imagine. 'Also,' he said, his tone softening, 'it may be you will go by way of Cossimbazaar. My wife will by now look for some news of me. And there may be that which you can do for my family. At the very least you will carry them my prayers.'

This personal concern rising so tenderly amidst his sea of wider troubles was deeply touching. Safe in my own bachelorhood, I had not given proper consideration to how this separation from his family, and the manner of it, must be affecting him. Though it was the first time, indeed, that he had alluded to his family since our leaving of Cossim-bazaar, I saw now that he had thought on them constantly.

I said, 'I would be honoured,' and so saying I gave Watts my hand, and in this manner, and in this moment, did I first bind myself in all innocence to the secret service of the king.

CHAPTER FOUR

*I*t was but a few days later that I left the nawab's encampment in the company of Sri Babu and his manservant. We rode toward Cossimbazaar with Sri Babu sometimes riding in front and sometimes behind and, though he was much too subtle a fellow to question me directly on the contents of the letters in my saddlebags, his conversation drifted over matters on which Watts had warned me to maintain a firm silence – company business, the intentions of the nawab and the characters of men such as Watts and Governor Drake. Forewarned, I was able to turn aside his casual-seeming enquiries and after a time Sri Babu ceased to probe and became then a quite agreeable companion. His knowledge of Bengal was such as was rare to find in any man, native or company, for through his service under the merchant Coja Wajid he had travelled extensively, and for many years, all about the province. He answered my questions freely. It was clear that he thought me worth little.

The first part of our journey passed without incident and we arrived at the Begrathi River near midday. There were several boats moored on the riverbank and Sri Babu went down to the *syrangs*, the boatmen, who were making offerings at a Hindoo shrine there. He squatted among them – he appeared to be known to them – and after some while conversing he made his own offering at the shrine and came away.

'We will not go to Cossimbazaar,' said he, climbing the bank to rejoin me.

Somewhat taken aback by this presumptuous declaration, I reminded him of the letters that I carried to Mrs Watts and others in the factory.

'The factory is taken,' he said. 'The nawab's men have taken it.'

'And Mrs Watts? And her children?'

'No one is hurt. We cannot go there. That is all.'

I protested that as the nawab had given us a safe conduct we had no reason to fear for ourselves. Sri Babu remounted and looked down at me with something like contempt for my naivety. His manservant then brought forward my horse and they waited for me to remount. I said, 'You are certain that Mrs Watts and her children are safe.'

'They are prisoners. If we go there, we will be held.' He turned his horse from the river, and when he had gone a short way I climbed with reluctance into the saddle and rode after him, though I did not know if what we did was right.

At dusk, having skirted wide around Cossimbazaar, and ridden for some several miles more, we sighted a village. The manservant was sent ahead to discover whether it was safe for us to proceed or no, and he soon returned to report that several of the nawab's *sowar*s had stabled their horses in that place for the night. They had, he was told, ridden from Cossimbazaar in pursuit of some company men believed to have escaped from the factory. The news gladdened me, but Sri Babu fell to questioning the man further, refusing now to translate any word more for my understanding. From the glances the manservant cast toward me, I began to have a certain apprehension.

I said, 'If you fear to be discovered with me, I will make my way alone toward Calcutta.'

'We will go together,' said Sri Babu. 'Already the *sowar*s in the village will be hearing of my man's questions. We cannot rest here.' He turned away from the village, urged his horse to a canter and I went after him.

The night in those parts falls quickly and it was not long before we were under the cover of darkness and could allow our horses to walk again, sure now of not being followed.

In an hour the moon rose. The track lay clear before us in the moonlight and we made good progress despite the fatigue of our horses. But near to the river there were many trees and bushes all about, and many shadows, and I believe this is the reason we none of us saw the dark figure till he stepped boldly and directly into our path with pistol raised, and cried, '*Dhat!*' which is to say, 'Halt!'

He barked further commands in Hindoostani and Sri Babu and the other cautiously showed their open hands and dismounted. The fellow's pistol swung threateningly in my direction. He shouted now, and in some trepidation lest he, in his rage, inadvertently touch the trigger and dispatch me to Kingdom Come, I hastened to dismount. But I caught my foot in the stirrup and as I struggled to free myself and get down I distinctly heard him say, 'Come on you dozy blackguard.'

The voice, to my astonishment, was known to me.

'Fairborough?' He was already launched upon Hindoostani again, but stopped abruptly at hearing me. 'Edward,' said I. 'It is Douglas. We are come from the nawab's camp.'

'By God. Are you prisoner?' His pistol swung with menace toward the others. I swiftly assured him I was no prisoner, and that these two were my companions.

'Mr Fairborough I am known to you also. Sri Babu. This other is my man.'

Fairborough stepped closer, the better to examine Sri Babu's face and then the servant's. Finally satisfied that he was not the victim of some elaborate ruse, Edward let out an oath and lowered his pistol. The threat of an untimely death now being removed from all parties, Edward and I fell at once to interrogating each other, but we were quickly cut short by Sri Babu's warning that that we should continue our conversation as we rode. When Edward confessed himself horseless Sri Babu gave him that of his manservant and we left the servant there and proceeded at once on our way southward.

Edward now told me that he had indeed escaped the factory, but, contrary to the belief of the soldiers who searched for him, he had done so alone.

'I got out in a bullock cart. Harry dropped some sacks on me. I got myself down to the river and paid a *syrang* to ferry me down to Calcutta. Fellow brought me this far then he took fright and set me down.'

I asked him about the factory and the welfare of Mrs Watts and the other women. He said that Cole had come to the factory that same morning with an order to hand over all cannon and ammunition to the nawab's troops. 'No one liked to do it. But it was an order from Watts. And Mr Cole was insistent. Of course, the moment the Moors had our cannon, they marched in. Nobody hurt though. Mrs Watts, the children, all under the protection of the Moors' senior officer.' The nawab's seal, he said, had been placed on all the warehouses to prevent looting.

Edward asked me then how it was that I came to be passing at that place where he had accosted us and I told him as much of the circumstances of my coming there as I felt I might with Sri Babu listening in to our conversation. Several times during my narration Edward broke into intemperate exclamations against the nawab and when I was finished he remarked that Governor Drake, at least, would know how to deal with the man. I suggested that Drake might wish to reach a compromise with the nawab (I understood from Watts that this was the probable mission of Sri Babu).

'You do not know him,' said Edward, speaking of Drake.

And indeed I did not, but I knew the slight regard in which Watts held the governor. Yet there was something in Edward's firm tone, and Sri Babu's presence, made me forbear.

After some few more hours' riding we left the track and hobbled the horses near a water trough in a grove that was known to Sri Babu. We set no fire, but ate the flat bread from our saddlebags, then each spread a blanket by his saddle and we lay down to rest. We were far now from the nawab's troops and Cossimbazaar. Edward was soon asleep, and Sri Babu urged me to do the same, saying that he would keep watch. But I did not sleep, and with occasional words and movements I made certain that Sri Babu could not mistake my wakefulness, till he said at last, 'You do not sleep, Mr Douglas.'

'No. Nor will I.'

'We should leave here before sunrise.'

'I shall wake you.'

Within minutes his breathing was steady, he seemed to sleep, and I lay with my eyes open through the night and watched the stars move slowly across the heavens.

The next day, which was the fifth of June, we travelled without incident, and on the sixth we came to the town of Hugli where lived the *faujdar*, the nawab's chief officer in the region. Here also, and not by coincidence, was the residence of Sri Babu's master, Coja Wajid, the greatest merchant of Bengal. The *chowkays*, that is to say the toll-keepers, at the edge of town gave Sri Babu the most pronounced and obsequious salaams as he rode by them. But as Edward and I passed, these same fellows looked at us with a coolness that was equally remarkable, for we were accustomed to being viewed by such officials with some high regard, as being ourselves honourable servants of the Honourable Company. I glanced at Edward, and he at me, and we rode on in watchful silence.

The common Bengali merchant is not given to outward shows of wealth lest he thereby make himself a prey to the avarice of the nawab and the nawab's court; and only the most powerful of them ever dare to live in a manner proportionate to their fortunes. And yet the house of Sri Babu's master, Coja Wajid, was almost a palace. It was located just outside the fort where the *faujdar* resided, but near to the fort-gate, and encircled by its own low wall. As we came to this wall a syce (which is a native groom) appeared and Sri Babu dismounted and gave the man his horse.

'We cannot stay here,' said Edward quickly.

Sri Babu protested that he would be but a short while, that we must ride on together. Edward remained firm. Finally Sri Babu bowed his head in acceptance, then he said, 'But as Coja Wajid's guests you will not refuse to take fresh horses,' and he beckoned another syce forward and commanded new horses for us. We allowed ourselves to be led to the stables while Sri Babu went in search of his master.

While our mounts were prepared, sweet syrup was brought to us, and also plantains from Coja Wajid's garden. We did not tarry there, but, when the horses were ready and ourselves refreshed, we straightaway remounted and rode from the yard onto the main road south. We had not stopped in the place above fifteen minutes.

But fifteen minutes was all it took for messengers to be sent on ahead of us. We knew our mistake the moment we were ordered to dismount by the *chowkays* at the southern edge of the town. They requested us to present our *dustucks*, which is like a trader's travelling-pass, and we did so, having no right to refuse them. After several minutes inspecting the *dustucks* to no real purpose, they then took note of our horses. They asked us where we had got them.

Edward, in a cold fury, replied, 'You may ask Sri Babu. I expect he will be along in an hour,' and so saying he tethered his horse and then went and flung himself down in the shade of the nearby trees. I soon joined him there, but it was some while before Edward could calm himself sufficient to speak with me. And when he did there seemed an unwarranted heat in his remarks upon the trick Sri Babu had played us.

'We shall be in Calcutta tomorrow,' said I. 'It is but a delay.'

'It is a delay that keeps me from the most important business of my life.'

'Mr Watts would be very grateful for your concern.'

'Watts? He has no need of my concern.'

'The others in the Cossimbazaar—'

'Pray, no more of the others in Cossimbazaar. My every thought now is on Calcutta.' He looked at the *chowkays* who watched us from their kiosk. He said to me, 'I have never asked you: did you make the acquaintance of the governor's sister, Elizabeth, while you were in Calcutta?'

'No.'

'You must surely have seen her.'

'Yes.' I turned an eye upon him now.

'Well?' said he.

'She is very fair.'

'That is all?'

'She is the fairest of all the young ladies in the settlement.' At this Edward seemed so pleased that I could no longer doubt his meaning. I said, 'Am I to take it that this "most important business" of yours concerns the governor's sister?'

Abashed now, he stretched back on the ground and told me to keep a watch out for Sri Babu.

In the event, it was near four hours before Sri Babu came, and then our *dustucks* were returned to us and we were able to proceed, all three of us together, to Calcutta.

The town of Calcutta was no small affair even then, but a place of perhaps a hundred thousand souls. Sited on the eastern bank of the Hugli River, its natural boundaries were the river itself on its western side, Surnam's Garden to the south and Perrin to the north. From Perrin stretched a ditch (called the Maratha Ditch in honour of those warlike Hindoos against whom the defence was first made) and this ditch wrapped around the back of Calcutta to the east, and then down toward Surnam's Garden by the river, petering out before it arrived there.

We crossed the ditch over the Chitpur Bridge, just by Perrin's Battery, and I noticed Sri Babu cast a studious eye over this battery and also over Kelsall's Octagon, the folly (upon which a fair-sized gun might easily be mounted) that had been recently repaired on the other side.

From this point we rode first through the black town of Calcutta, where the Hindoos and other people of the country resided and where the bazaars were, and which, in extent, was the largest part of Calcutta. After two miles of crowded houses and bullock carts, devotees making offerings at any number of roadside shrines, camels carrying bright-coloured blankets and coolies throwing water upon the dusty streets, we entered the settlement. Here, nearer to the fort, lived the Armenians and mixed-race Portuguese (called topasses) and the servants of the company. Sri Babu peeled away from us in the direction of Omichand the merchant's house, while Edward and I went by St Anne's, coming last of all to the centre of all, which was Fort William itself, wherein was the factory house. We rode directly in through the fort's open gates and were taken by the officer of the watch to the secretary to the council and governor, Mr Cooke.

Mr Cooke desired that we return at a later hour when Governor Drake might be disposed to receive us.

'The Cossimbazaar factory has been taken,' said Fairborough again, in exasperation at the deliberate obtuseness of the fellow. 'It is even now in the hands of the nawab's soldiers. Our people are prisoners.'

'And this is your business with the governor?'

'I have come from there directly. Mr Douglas has been in the nawab's camp. He has letters for the governor from the hand of Mr Watts.'

'Mr Watts has already sent report that the nawab's troops are in the neighbourhood of Cossimbazaar.' Cooke extended his hand. 'I will take the letters.'

'I am instructed by Mr Watts that I pass the letters into the hand of the governor and no other.'

'Come, come.' Impatiently he reached toward the parcel in my hand.

Edward stepped between us. 'You will please to inform Governor Drake that we shall call on him once we have refreshed ourselves. We are invited to breakfast with the officers.'

'As you will, Mr Fairborough.' Cooke seemed undisturbed that the officers were to hear the news in advance of the governor. He inclined his head to Edward in a smiling but distinctly uncivil manner.

The officers had their mess in a room adjoining the garrison barracks which was near to the forge, and we breakfasted to the sound of the blacksmith's hammer ringing out across the yard. Unlike Cooke, the officers were only too eager to hear Edward's report on the state of affairs in Cossimbazaar. That the nawab's soldiery had laid siege to the factory they already knew, for word had come downriver ahead of us; but the manner of it, and Edward's confirmation of the final fall, these were novelties and they interrogated Edward keenly all the while that he ate. In the course of this interrogation my own insignificant role was discovered and the stream of their questions was at once diverted

to me – how many were the nawab's soldiers? In what state of preparedness? On what matter was Mr Watts conducting his talks with the
nawab? To each of which I pled ignorance and the inexperience of
youth and, though some few became vexed with me, the stream was
soon re-diverted to Edward, and I was able to bolt the last of my mutton
before slipping away to the pump behind the mess where I washed.
The saddlebags, with the letters, I kept very near.

Within the hour we stood again before the governor's secretary.

'Governor Drake has put by a quarter-hour to hear you. Do not
exceed the allotment or I shall have to call you from there.' Cooke
rapped on the governor's door, opened it and waved us in.

'Mr Fairborough,' said Governor Drake, nodding, but he did not rise
from his chair. He was barely older than Edward, perhaps thirty-five
years of age. He was president of the Fort William Council by right of
seniority and his uncle a director of the company in London, a circumstance which did his standing among the British in Calcutta no great
harm. 'Cooke informs me that you offered the nawab no resistance.'

'Mr Cooke knows nothing of the matter.'

'Well then. Who now controls the Cossimbazaar factory?'

'It was in no manner possible to defend the factory against such an
army.'

'I have it by report that Mr Watts surrendered with no shot being
fired. May I have your confirmation of it?'

'Mr Watts is held at the nawab's pleasure. But Mr Douglas knows
more than I. He has been with Mr Watts in the nawab's camp. I believe
he has brought you letters.'

The parcel was in my hand and I passed it now to Drake. He asked
me when I had left Watts and I told him the number of days. He broke
open the parcel and then the wax on the letters. He commenced reading
while he spoke to Edward.

'What damage has there been to the company's goods?'

'The warehouses were sealed up by the nawab's order. There was
no looting.'

'The buildings?'

'Untouched.'

'There is some benefit, then, in an abject surrender.'

'No injury has been done to any in the fort. I have not always agreed with Mr Watts, but in this matter he is not blameable. Our garrison was paltry. In no way sufficient to admit of a real defence.'

'I am sure Mr Watts will be given the opportunity to make his own case before the director in good time, Mr Fairborough.'

'Sir,' said I. 'I have also a private verbal communication from Mr Watts.'

'Indeed.' Drake lifted his eyes from the letter and regarded me in a manner meant to be intimidatory. It might have succeeded had I not so often withstood a much heavier scrutiny within my own father's study. 'Was there shortage of ink to Mr Watts?' said he.

'Mr Watts feared lest his private thoughts be discovered by an inter-ception of the letters. He believes—'

'Pray, hold a while, Mr Douglas.' He returned to reading Watts's letters. I felt Edward's gaze upon me now, for I had told him nothing of any private communication from Watts. Finally Drake looked up. 'And you have some addendum to this?' When I hesitated, Drake said, 'Had Mr Fairborough been available to Mr Watts, I am certain he had carried the message. Speak.'

'Mr Watts bade me commit his words to memory. They are these, sir – "*The nawab of Bengal has assembled an army of fifty thousand and more, under pretence of his dispute with us on the question of the* dustucks, *and of your military building-works, and of your supposed harbouring of Krishnan Das. I am satisfied that he means to march on Calcutta before month's end. Cossimbazaar lying nearer to his hand, he has fallen upon us first as an earnest.*

"*I am certain that a large gift in the Bengali manner may yet answer. Send Krishnan Das from Calcutta, then let Coja Wajid's man, Sri Babu, or Omichand open negotiations with the nawab on the council's behalf.*" That is all, sir.'

'The man now instructs me.' Drake seemed angered and appeared to have paid no mind to the message. 'And through the mouth of a junior.'

'There was a fear the letters—'

46

'The letters bear his signature, Mr Douglas. Unlike your, no doubt, impeccable recitation.'

'I will vouch for Mr Douglas's memory,' Edward broke in. 'His veracity, of course, is unquestioned.'

'This strays from the point. Have you any further such messages, Mr Douglas? No? Then I must thank you for the pains you have taken. But before you leave, perhaps you might acquaint me with Mr Watts's state of mind when you left him.'

'I do not take your meaning, sir.'

'Did he show himself, perhaps, fearful?'

'He is not fearful – somewhat anxious, possibly, in his dealings with the nawab.'

'Indeed.'

'The nawab shows no proper courtesy to either Mr Watts or Mr Cole. To any real understanding they are now his prisoners.'

'This so-called army. Saw you any particular sign of it?'

'Sir, we were encamped in the very midst of it. I have walked among the tents. It is a real army, and it grows daily.'

'But the army was itself unmoving.'

'Making ready to move I should say. And, though it is my opinion only, in full readiness to fight.'

Drake did not like to hear any of this, though it can have been little more than irrefutable confirmation of what he had already heard from the company's native spies. He turned to Fairborough. 'There is neither treaty nor law would support such an action. The nawab is in the wrong entirely. I have writ to him many times to tell him so. If he thinks now to intimidate us – if he thinks to extort by force what he cannot have by law – he shall learn his error. Thank you, gentlemen – Mr Cooke!'

'May I call on you?' said Fairborough, suddenly aware that our interview was ended. 'On that other matter I wrote you of.'

Drake rose from his desk, as though he had not heard. But Fairborough, though clearly discomfited by Drake's abrupt manner (and, no doubt, my presence), was too full of his matter to now restrain himself. 'My capital, I believe, is now sufficient, indeed it is ample—'

'Mr Fairborough, I congratulate you that your trade has prospered.

I am sure that my sister and her fiancé, Lieutenant Harding, congratulate you also.'

Edward stood motionless. He did not speak but only stared, appearing for all the world as if he had taken the thrust of a rapier. Drake, who was no stone, must surely have felt the awful weight of what his sister had done. Indeed, as in loco parentis he might well be judged equally culpable, and there was certainly something very strained in his ensuing brief relation of the recent departure of his sister and Lieutenant Harding to London by way of Madras. I doubt that Edward heard much of it. His face was ashen.

'Cooke!' Drake called again when he was done, and I own I was glad when that damned fellow came.

CHAPTER FIVE

*S*t Anne's Church, just outside the walls of Fort William, had the appearance of one of the lesser City churches of Wren, with the singular difference that its roof tiles were made of brown clay dug from the banks of the Hugli. Inside, the illusion of English sanctity was more complete – the stone walls were whitewashed, the lead-lined windows clear and the altar was covered by a cloth – embroidered with a lamb and a cross – brought from England by St Anne's first rector. It was the current rector, the Reverend Bellamy, that I came to call upon now that I had left Edward in that solitude he had asked of me and which he, very understandably, required.

The rector was engaged in conversation with two women up by the altar when I entered and so I wandered about the rear of the church perusing the carved memorials of stone and wood set upon the walls there.

I did not, in truth, have any real notion of the import of my business with the rector, though Mr Watts had impressed upon me in the strongest terms that the messages I carried were for the governor and the Reverend Bellamy alone. In the nawab's camp, I had thought this

49

strange, but arrived now in Calcutta, it seemed almost an absurdity. For here were company men and company officers at every turn, men of action and enterprise, and yet my message was to be delivered to the one man among them who by faith and promise could not lift his hand against another – a man of the cloth and a person of some years.

'You knew the major?' The rector it was who had spoken. He had come to my side without my perceiving it and at his question I turned from the wall plaque that commemorated some recently deceased major of the company's regiment.

'I had not the pleasure.'

'A very doubtful pleasure, I do assure you,' said he. 'You are the young writer who went to Cossimbazaar.' I confirmed it, both surprised and gratified that any had noticed my departure after my brief stay in Calcutta. 'There is no service now till Evensong. I would recommend it over the morning service. I cannot recall when last I had a writer at the morning service.'

'You have heard that Cossimbazaar is taken.'

'I keep all her people in my prayers.'

'I am bid say to you – "The first shall be last and the last shall be first."'

'Are you indeed?'

'I have come directly from Mr—'

'Mrs Coates!' He called up to one of the women at the altar and put a hand on my arm to silence me. 'Do not wait upon my return. You may expect me at the evening service.'

On the steps of the church sat a Hindoo boy who jumped to his feet at the sight of the rector. There were lads like this attached to every soldier and servant of the company, but now the rector told the lad he was not needed and the boy went unhappily back to his seat on the church steps.

'A man may have any pleasure he pleases in this town, excepting privacy,' remarked the rector to me. We went south through the settlement and while we walked he would hear no word more of Cossimbazaar from me, but pointed out the various shops and houses and told me the stories of their occupants. The Europeans tipped their hats to him as we passed, but more striking to me were the Hindoos who, on seeing him, clasped their palms together in salutation just as they did with their own holy men, and like the Hindoo holy men, the rector paid them no mind at all.

'You will know Omichand's house,' he remarked, with a cursory wave to the only house in the settlement occupied by a native. When I said that the man I had ridden with, Sri Babu, had gone there immediately upon our arrival in Calcutta, the rector lifted a finger to silence me. 'Say nothing for the present.' A few minutes later we came to the burial ground. He talked with the gatekeeper awhile and then came to join me among the gravestones. He led me along a dirt path there. 'Here you may speak freely. It will not trouble you if we amble rather than sit? I am too often idle.'

I commenced by saying to him that I was just a messenger.

'I know who you are, Mr Douglas. Now, Mr Watts's message, if you will.'

It was unsettling to discover my name already known to him, for I had not given it – he had left me no chance to properly introduce myself since our first meeting in the church.

'Mr Watts and Mr Cole are held by the nawab. The nawab has gathered an army of fifty thousand or more.' I went on with my tale, reciting again the words I had carried to Governor Drake. While I did so, this man of the cloth, this man of some five and sixty years, fixed me with a look of quite singular and unnerving penetration. His face was thin, his body slight, but his eyes held me in a grip of iron.

This first part over, I then hastened to relay the next part of Watts's message – it was a numerical list of verses from the Bible. The rector asked me to repeat the list, which I did, and he then astonished me by at once reciting the list back to me with every number correct and in its proper place.

'And that is all?'

'That is all. Upon my word.'

'Mr Douglas. While you converse with me, I would that your yea be yea and your nay be nay. You need not swear by your word. Do we understand one another?'

The rebuke was not unkindly given and I nodded like the merest child.

'This army. Did it appear to you ready for war?'

'It seemed so to Mr Watts. The soldiers exercised daily. Both cavalry and infantry practised manoeuvres beyond the camp.'

He asked me when I had left Mr Watts and questioned me as to the reason I had ridden with Sri Babu. Upon learning of Fairborough's joining us, he would know of all the circumstances surrounding it and, in short, he made enquiry into every corner of my experience since my departure from Cossimbazaar. In consequence, the rector's understanding of the whole state of affairs was in the end as near complete as a man could hope for – certainly more complete than that of Governor Drake, who had asked me nothing. When I mentioned that Mrs Watts and her family had been placed under the protection of a senior Moorish officer, the Reverend Bellamy would hear more of that too, but there was no more I could tell him. I suggested he might speak to Fairborough.

'I will ask him to come to you.'

'You will say nothing to Mr Fairborough on my behalf,' he said with sudden firmness. 'And as to this conversation, or any other between us, I trust you understand what privacy is, or Mr Watts would not have sent you to me? I believe, Mr Douglas, that we understand one another.'

From the officers' mess by the stables I was directed to the upper floor of the southern wing of the factory, where I received further directions and eventually found the small cell-like room that Mr Cooke had seen fit to allocate Fairborough and me as temporary quarters. The two single bunks were separated by a writing desk that sat beneath a shuttered window.

'Edward?'

The figure on the left bunk rolled onto his back, his arm was draped over his eyes. 'No need to creep, my boy. I am not yet on my deathbed.'

'Shall I open the shutters?'

He raised his hand in a vague gesture of assent. I pushed back the shutters and the hot glare of tropical sunlight poured in. He was fully dressed. There was a pitcher of water on the writing desk. I closed the door and sat down on my bunk. His arm remained over his eyes. He said, 'You are wondering what you might say to me.'

'My presence there at such a time was unintended. I am sorry for it.'

'It was none of your doing.' I then, rather foolishly, commenced to offer him my commiserations. 'You may take your commiserations,' he interrupted me very calmly, 'and sink them into the deepest pit of hell. I have been slighted. But I will not be pitied.'

'I will leave you in peace.'

'Stay.' His arm came from his eyes. There was a great weariness in them, but they were not, as I had feared, the eyes of a man broken. 'In truth, I have pitied myself sufficient for the both of us. Is there water?' He sat up and in a draught drank the mug I poured for him. He asked me where I had been, for I had by this time been parted from him for several hours. Seeing the opportunity to move his mind on from the terrible blow he had suffered, I told him how I had been walking in the settlement, and up the Lal Bazaar as far as the Bread & Cheese Bungalow, and of how I had there remade the acquaintance of several writers with whom I had served briefly upon my first arrival in Calcutta.

'They say there is a muster of soldiers called for the morning. There is a fear that many are sick in the hospital.'

'Did you pass by any bazaar in the black town?'

'The stalls in the grain market were empty.'

'We will not be the only ones bringing report of the nawab's army. The Hindoos here have no stomach for a fight.'

The boom of a cannon sounded suddenly outside and we looked each at the other and were then both of us on our feet and through the door in an instant. A group of company officers were gathered already at the verandah's end. One of them was standing on the railing, holding tight to the upright with one hand and with his other hand waving his hat toward the river. We saw then, over the walls of the fort westward, the ship which had just saluted the fort. It was now moving away down-river. As we joined the officers, the company artillerymen on the fort's south-western bastion returned the ship's salute, a single cannon shot.

Around us the officers seemed in rare high spirits. One of those with whom we had breakfasted now noticed our presence among them. 'Gentlemen, if you will come with us, we will drink your good health.'

Fairborough asked after the business of the departing ship.

'She is to Fort St George. Inside two weeks if she gets the wind. Are you a betting man, Mr Fairborough?'

'But surely ships will be needed here.'

'Soldiers are needed here and she goes now to fetch them for us. You have put the spur to the governor and, if you join us downstairs, you shall have our gratitude in a glass.'

Edward demurred. They insisted. I found myself offered up by Edward to receive the brunt of their good will. As I was bundled along the verandah I looked back to see Edward retreating to our quarters. There was none of his customary bounce and vigour. Behind his back, his left hand held his right wrist and his shoulders were bowed. He turned in to the room, shut the door and I do not doubt that he at once closed the shutters.

CHAPTER SIX

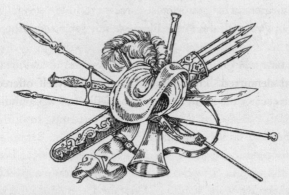

*T*he muster of company soldiers took place at mid-morning in
the fort and by midday the results were known throughout the settlement – seventy soldiers were in hospital, twenty-five were on various
company duties away from Calcutta and of the remaining one hundred
and eighty, only forty-five were European (the rest being topasses). The
talk was immediately of the need to form a militia from among the able-
bodied civilians and the primary concern of the council now became
the appointment of officers for this putative brigade. There was a good
deal of disgruntlement and jealousy among the company officers when
none of them was selected, but two council members, Manningham
and Frankland, were instead given rank over all of them. (It is indica-
tive of the prevailing feeling in Fort William that each side thought such
appointments a prize worth squabbling over, for it was still the general
opinion among them that success and glory would inevitably accrue to
the ranking defenders of the fort.)

All this went on while the necessary repairs to the fabric of the walls
were manifestly neglected, though I cannot say in good conscience that
the fault here was entirely Drake's. The military commander of the fort

was Captain Minchin, and he it was had set all the carpenters to work building and renewing the gun carriages needed for the guns on the ramparts, though it was the general talk of the soldiers that in most places the walls would not support the guns and only the bastions at each corner of the fort could be relied upon. Yet nothing was done to employ carpenters or masons for the necessary repair to the structure, and further – what now seems scarcely credible – several windows and high openings in the fort walls were not sealed up, but were left gaping.

It was some relief to me when the order came for the militia to report to the burying ground and I could for a time leave off my concern at the complacency of those preparations I was witness to within the fort.

'Do you prefer a shovel, monsieur?'

In the boredom of waiting my turn at the matchlock, I had been watching the coolies at work constructing a palisade across the road behind where we were standing. Captain Le Baume, the company officer who had spoken to me – somewhat to my surprise a Frenchman – had been calling the militia volunteers forward individually to assess the ability of each one of us to handle a gun. It had been a very dispiriting hour for him. I was the last in line. Now I stepped forward and took up the gun from the ground and loaded it at his order.

'Take your aim at the target.'

I set my left foot forward, shouldered the gun butt and braced myself.

'Fire!'

I fired.

He viewed the target at the far end of the burying ground through a spyglass then said to me, 'You have shot before.' I acknowledged it and he gestured to the powder. 'Reload.' I did so and, at his instruction, took aim and fired again. After viewing the target, he called me away from the others. He turned his back on them and lowered his voice.

'You will take ten of the Armenians. I will show you the ones. You will make them understand how to load the gun. Only load. No firing. When they understand, you will return them here.'

I took my ten useless charges to a place by the neighbouring ditch and attempted to impart to them the rudiments of loading a weapon. It was, to me at least, a very salutary lesson. They ranged in age from sixteen to forty-five, and there was not one among them able to attempt the simple feat of loading unaided. After an hour I had done all I could with them, which was little enough, and we returned to Le Baume to hear how the militia was to be divided into three parts, European, topass and Armenian, for the better direction of our abilities. After this he took aside three Dutchmen, one of the junior traders, a factor and myself and told us that the company officers would welcome any of our number who wished to volunteer for service in the company regiment. We each of us volunteered immediately and so came to an end my short service in the Fort William militia.

I went at once to find Edward to advise him of this chance of volunteering for the company regiment, fully expecting to find him in that same debilitated state he had sunk to since first taking the knock. I found him, instead, in a queer state of excitement whose cause he was only too happy to divulge.

'I am going upriver. I have volunteered.'

'Upriver?' said I in some surprise, for this was toward the nawab's army.

'There is a lieutenant leading the party. May I take your canteen?' He strapped my canteen to his belt while I asked what manner of party this was that he had joined. 'You will not dissuade me,' said he. 'There are a dozen of us riding up as far as Sukhsagar. We are to beat drums and make some commotion. All under cover of darkness.'

'To what purpose?'

'Ah, there is the genius of it. There is no purpose in it that any sensible man can see. Governor Drake is convinced it will frighten the Hindoos along the river. Captain Minchin calls it a diversion, though a diversion from what, there is no means of telling. Let us call it an escapade, shall we? Yes. That is it. An escapade.'

'Edward—'

'I will not be turned from this,' he said with a grim finality that silenced me.

I accompanied him down to the fort's river-gate, and out onto the Crane Ghat, which was like a small dock, where two boats were tied and where several company officers stood talking among themselves and laughing. It appeared that Edward was not alone in regarding this expedition as an escapade. Weapons were brought and drums, which the officers beat in high good humour, before the *syr syrang*, the head boatman, had the oarsmen take everything on board the vessels.

I did not think the nawab's army could be so near to us as Sukhsagar, and yet that was no reassurance to me as Edward and the other volunteers went aboard and the boats went out into the river. I stood on the ghat and listened to their laughter and the occasional beat of a drum and saw with some foreboding a flagon passing among them.

In the evening I walked about the settlement and made a circuit of the batteries and palisades that had been commenced on the main thoroughfares to the north, east and south of the fort (the river being a natural defence on the westward side). A ditch had now been cut across each thoroughfare, and, behind each ditch, a temporary wall or palisade was in the process of construction. It was at the eastern battery, on Lal Bazaar by the Great Tank, where the *dhobi* women had spread the washed clothes on the steps to dry, that I met the Reverend Bellamy again. He was standing with a small party of sightseers, people like myself out to see what was doing on our lines – a few ladies and some senior traders, who had just climbed out from their palanquins and were now listening to the junior officer at the battery explaining the council's plan of defence.

'Artillerymen will be sent to man the redoubt at Perrin's. A ship or two will support them from the river. If the nawab breaks through there, the natives in the black town must look to themselves.' The dashing young man then gestured to the battery before us, saying, 'Here is our next defence.'

One lady expressed a doubt whether such makeshift batteries as this could hope to hold back an army.

'Should the batteries be overrun, we will fall back to the larger buildings nearer the fort.' The fellow turned and pointed confidently. 'St

Anne's here on the east. Mr Cruttenden's house on the north side. The company's house on the south.'

'And should they be overrun?' she persisted.

'It will not happen,' he said, with a smile at her womanly fears. 'But allow the possibility – we will then withdraw to the fort. There we will withstand the siege while awaiting reinforcement.'

There seemed a general satisfaction with this. It was a satisfaction I did not share. The rector then bade his companions good evening and took my arm and we walked back down the avenue.

'Such at least is the plan,' he said once out of earshot.

'You have a doubt.'

'I have many doubts, Mr Douglas. But it is ever easier to have a doubt than to take an action. We must support those who have the responsibility for our common defence thrust upon them.'

When I told him of the quixotic expedition which Edward was even now embarked upon upriver, the rector remarked that most soldiers were but boys uniformed and that good sense and quietude were qualities not to be expected of them. We turned off the avenue and went to the palisade under construction between the houses of Omichand and Mr Coales (who was Governor Drake's father-in-law). Behind these houses began the houses of the Armenians and Portuguese.

'Do not turn your head, but mark the fellow who watches us from Omichand's verandah.'

'I have him,' said I.

'He is Omichand's *jamindar*. He works for Omichand as Sri Babu works for Coja Wajid. I will greet him as we walk by there. I would that you look closely at him.'

We passed in front of the house and the rector did as he had said; the two of them spoke together briefly while I pressed into memory the sharp lines of the fellow's aquiline face. As we came away, I said, 'I will not forget him.'

'But you are sure you have not seen him before now?'

'I have rarely walked by here.'

'I was not thinking of Calcutta. I wondered if the face might be familiar to you from your time in the nawab's camp.'

I considered this a moment, then shook my head; it was a face I would have remembered. As we went on to the church I asked him no more, for he was sunk in a studied silence that invited neither conversation nor question. Instead I thought on Sri Babu and of how he had turned in to Omichand's house immediately upon our arrival in Calcutta. I reflected also upon the reputation Omichand had among the Calcutta traders as a man with easy access to the nawab's court. The Reverend Bellamy's expression was grave and thoughtful. At the centre of those thoughts, I knew, was that fellow Omichand, but the matter of the thoughts was obscure to me and beyond any hope of my discovering.

CHAPTER SEVEN

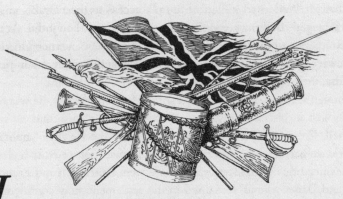

*I*n the morning I was roused from my bed by the sound of some
commotion in the square below. Dressing quickly, I went out onto the
verandah, where I found a company lieutenant leaning upon the balustrade with a nonchalant soldierly air. He watched a dozen company
soldiers and a few score sepoys in the square being formed into platoons
by the officers. I asked him what was afoot.

'Some of them will go to reinforce the redoubt at Perrin's.'

'Has the nawab's army been seen?'

'Neither seen nor even heard of by any reliable report – excepting
your own.' This with an amused, and quite galling, scepticism. 'But it
is as well we are prepared.'

The men below were armed with fine matchlocks and the officers
with pistols, but when I thought on the might of the nawab's army I
could not conceive what I saw below me to be worthy the name of
preparation. When I expressed my misgivings to the lieutenant he
dismissed this with a condescending jocularity.

'Soldiers are not like bullion, Mr Douglas. Their value is not to be
measured by quantity alone. Do not trouble yourself.'

I will not compare myself to Cassandra. I had no foreknowledge. I did not cry any warning in the streets. The most I can say is that I thought something very lacking in our state of preparedness and the measures being taken by the council to defend both Fort William and Calcutta. There was an arrogant complacency to it, bred no doubt by the long years of peace and high prosperity, and I could not help but feel that Mr Watts, had he led in the place of Governor Drake, might have arranged matters very differently. But who was I to judge them? The soldiers and the officers, the councillors and Governor Drake – these were men who had been years in Bengal and many other parts of India, their experience infinite by comparison with mine.

Though Edward, I knew, shared some of my misgivings, he was too deeply lost in his own private grief to sound any alarm and he was inclined, like most of the civilians, to defer to the weight of military experience barracked within the fort. And it was not we British alone who evinced this complacency, for there were Dutchmen and Frenchmen and Danes who all remained in the settlement, fully confident of their security within this, the greatest of the European factories in Bengal.

Down in the square the officers gave their orders now, the drummer started, and, as the men marched from the fort, I heard some of them laughing.

Edward returned from his escapade in the late morning with nothing to show for his night's work but a sore head and a confused tale of having lost a man overboard and then of saving him, though with some possibility that a *syrang* had in the process been drowned. As to the fright they had given to the natives along the river, he said there had been some shouting and a few stray shots fired in the wake of the din they had made with the drums, but that he was himself certain that as an aid to the defence of Calcutta it was precisely the useless folly he had expected.

'Drake is a damned fool. And they who put their trust in him are twice damned fools. I am the biggest damned fool of all.'

I remarked that I was glad to see he had recovered his good humour, at which he scowled at me and dropped onto his bed and told me not to wake him till the morning. But he woke himself after just a few hours' heavy sleep and came and found me at the ghat, where I passed the time playing at quoits beneath an awning with a few junior officers from the ships. Edward joined us in the game; it was the first I had heard him laugh for some days. Our game ended, he invited me to accompany him to the goldsmith's street in the black town. It was just such excursions we had taken together in Cossimbazaar, and it pleased me to find him in this way returning to himself.

We were carried there in palanquins, for Edward was no great walker, and kept the sides open, conversing as we went. And as we talked we could not fail to see around us in the black town that many doorways were boarded up and many small shops had their shutters closed and battened. We remarked it but did not take it for a portent, rather as a confirmation of the renowned Hindoo timidity. In the goldsmiths' street we got down and were immediately surrounded by a clutch of bare-footed boys with trays of sweetmeats who vied to entice us into the shops of their masters. Edward made his way directly into the first place decorated with a goldsmith's sign and the chattering boys parted before him as before a fifty-gun frigate.

The price of gold, the cost of carriage, the quality of workmanship – here was meat and drink for Edward and he soon had his magnifying glass from his pocket and was deep in debate with the goldsmith over the merits of the piece on the bench between them. From the first gold-smith to the second, from the second to the third, and Edward ever more like himself. And it was not only the gold he inspected, but diamonds too, which I might have wondered at had I had my wits more readily about me. Instead I merely laughed when he said that he meant to show me which of the merchants might be trusted, that is to say, which might cheat me the least.

'Good, but not the finest,' said Edward, running an expert eye over the wares placed on the scarlet silk before us. 'If you hope to do any business today, my friend – a necklace? Let me hold it.' He draped it over his palm while the goldsmith spoke to him in the local tongue. 'What do you say, Alistair? He claims it is a gaming forfeit from an errant rajah. We will give such an unlikely tale no credence. Still, it is a handsome thing.'

A boy ran into the shop and spoke to the goldsmith, who sent him immediately away. I bent closer to inspect the necklace on Edward's hand. The workmanship was exquisite – each link was a slender leaf of gold and the single diamond would have been no disgrace to a duchess. But Edward placed it on the silk, saying, 'We are done here. Come away.' The change in him was so marked that once in the street I enquired what terrible blunder I had made. I apologized if I had, perhaps, ruined his trade by showing too great an interest on my face. 'You were a child before a bright bauble. But at the present time, that does not signify.'

'Was the diamond glass?'

'It was as fine a piece as I have seen in some years. You saw the boy who came in? He brought news from the fort. Our good Governor Drake has declared an opening of hostilities against the nawab of Bengal.'

What effect Governor Drake intended by his surprising declaration I cannot say. What he achieved was a marked rise in apprehension and no change whatever in the general state of readiness to fight. The company soldiers drilled after their usual fashion within both the fort and the confines of the settlement, for without an enemy present, what could they do more? That the nawab had gathered an army about him, they knew. That the governor had requested reinforcements from Madras, this they knew also. And it was plain to even the lowliest sepoy that should all efforts at diplomacy with the nawab fail, there might come a time in the weeks ahead when they would have to fight. But that the governor should unprompted declare an opening of hostilities against the nawab, with the disposition of the nawab's force a mystery hid beyond the horizon, it was – as I heard a company sergeant remark – a bloody rum business. I can only surmise that Drake meant it for a show of his own boldness and resolution. If so, it failed utterly in its purpose.

And I can only think that the invitation that went out from Mrs Drake to most of the officers and senior traders that same day was a further part of her husband's attempt to demonstrate his calmness and resolution, for why else would it have entered her head to hold a soirée at such a time? I too was invited, being a guest in Fort William and Edward's friend, and on the following evening we arrived at Government House for the occasion, dressed in our new-borrowed clothes, with some wonder that such an event should be happening at such a time.

We were shown inside by a pink-turbaned Hindoo and another of these fellows offered us drinks from a tray. All the prominent European ladies and young women of the settlement had answered Mrs Drake's summons and these now made a focus for the clusters of officers and traders circulating about the stately room. There was an opulence to the governor's apartments that might have surprised even the company's director in London. It was decorated to that same excess that I had marked upon my sole visit to the governor's ballroom some two months earlier. No feature that might be gilded had been spared. And from the tapestries on the walls to the floor coverings and furnishings, every part of it was purely European, with no sign, except the dress of the servants, that the room was located in Bengal rather than halfway around the world in Mayfair.

'Brace up, Alistair,' said Edward and drained his glass. 'We shall not see another night such as this for some while.' And with that he left me and I wandered a short while about the room and made conversation with a few of the officers who seemed to have as little heart for the absurd occasion as I. It was a relief when we were at last called to our chairs and the musical part of the evening commenced. There were violins to begin with; two of the professional musicians from the settlement playhouse, and these had a real gaiety and liveliness to their performance. They were followed by a young woman on the pianoforte who had a fine ear and another who had not. Then a pair of sisters sang and then the violinists returned, after which Mrs Drake stood to invite us all to refresh ourselves for a short time before the next part of the evening.

I took a glass of water and went to stand on the balcony, for the evening was very still and the heat inside the room oppressive. It was June and the season for heat, which only breaks with the coming of the rains. We expected the rains daily. There were dark and heavy clouds beneath the moon now, but not a breath of wind to bring them over Calcutta.

'No need to hide yourself away, dear boy. Or are you come out here to recover from an excess of musically derived emotion?'

'I am come to recover from the heat,' I told the Reverend Bellamy, 'which I am sure I should not complain of.'

'To me, you may complain all you wish. But I would not complain to Mrs Drake. I see Mr Fairborough has returned unharmed from his expedition.'

'It achieved nothing.'

'I did not see your name on the list of militia.'

'I have volunteered to join with the company soldiers.'

'Have you indeed?'

'I had not thought to await my first battle in such a style.'

He smiled. 'I must tell you that Mrs Watts and her children are all well. They are unable to leave the French compound, but Monsieur Law has been a most gracious host to her. So she writes. Her friends – and you are mentioned in her letter – are to take assurance that all is well with her.' Upon my remarking that she might have hidden the true state of affairs for fear of her letter being intercepted, he said, 'By Monsieur Law? Though he is a gentleman, I think we may take it that he has a thorough acquaintance with all post that leaves his factory. Mrs Watts knows it too. But you may take it as my confirmed opinion that she and her children are safer with the French in Chandernagore than they would be with us here at this moment in Calcutta. But come. I have delivered my cheering news,' he said, taking my arm in his and turning me back to the room. 'The women here are most of them not as fierce as they appear – though you would do well to avoid those two.' He nodded to a whispering pair. 'The others are agreeable enough. Your friend Mr Fairborough, at least, appears to find them so.' And now at the far side of the room I saw Edward standing with his back to the wall, two young women facing him and they laughing as though they found him the very soul of wit. I had never seen him look quite so uncomfortable.

Bellamy then introduced me to Mrs Lethbury and her unmarried niece. The conversation ran lightly over the music we had heard, but then Mrs Lethbury began to lament the cancellation of the June Ball, for her niece must now be denied the opportunity to show her fine dancing step. 'One rather blames this new nawab. He does not show himself the most considerate type of blackamoor.' There followed more in this vein, all of which came, I saw, from the deep fears she harboured for her own safety. Then she turned to me. 'Now, Mr Douglas. I am told your friend Mr Fairborough is seeking a passage to England.'

'I do not believe so.'

'But it is certain.'

'I have not heard of it.'

'You have heard of it now,' said she, taking my denial for a disingenuous but forgivable dissimulation. 'And you may see with your own eyes that others have heard of it too,' this with a significant nod toward the two young women who held Edward trapped by polite conversation and laughter against the wall. I saw one of them touch his arm now, playfully, as she made her point. His alarm now was visible at twenty paces.

I remarked that we were none of us likely to stay in Bengal for ever.

'Just so,' said Mrs Lethbury. 'And that is just what a young man should consider. What gives the appearance of a fine bloom in Bengal is like to make a poor show in the cooler clime of England. The forward flower, I find, is never the finest.'

'I am sure you are right,' said I, anxious now to turn aside this blatant advertisement of her niece, a plain girl who looked quite mortified at hearing her aunt's words. The Reverend Bellamy, perceiving this, now drew the niece after him on a tour of the paintings hung about the walls.

'If anyone can appreciate the pictorial art, it is my niece. She has a quite lively talent herself.'

'Indeed.'

'I see you doubt me, Mr Douglas. But King George himself has

remarked upon her Hyde Park watercolours. And you will not doubt
him. Besides, you may see her work yourself when you call on us
Thursday next. You and Mr Fairborough both.'

'I cannot answer for Mr Fairborough.'

'It is decided. My niece will play for us. She has an ear as fine as
her eye, though you will never hear the girl herself say so.'

'You might have had some mercy on a fellow,' said Edward as we came
from Government House and crossed the square of the fort. 'You saw
I was under siege.'

'You put up no flag.'

'Your time will come, Alistair. And I will remember this.'

'We are invited to dine with Mrs Lethbury on Thursday next.'

'These people are mad.'

'She has a niece.'

'Dear God.'

'She is determined you must make the acquaintance of the niece
before your departure for England.' His face changed now and he
studied the ground as we walked. 'That is why you asked after diamonds in the goldsmiths' street.'

'I had intended to tell you once the matter was more settled. There
is the nawab to be dealt with first.'

'I am not put out, Edward. I am only surprised that you should
choose to go.'

'You think my mind has been loosed from its mooring?'

'I merely wonder what harm there could be in waiting a few months
before reaching such a decision.'

'You believe I should not go.'

'Edward, this past several days you have been a prisoner, an escapee,
and – if I may speak plain and if too plain it is but from regard for you
– a jilted lover. Think what harm you may do yourself by too rash a
decision.'

'And I suppose that I must now thank you for your plain speaking.
And for your regard for me. You are a boy.'

'Edward—' I said, for I saw at once how very ill-taken were my words.

'I pray you trouble your thoughts no further on my behalf. You may convey my regrets to Mrs Lethbury and her niece.' He turned from me and retraced his steps across the square and out of the gates into the darkness where a pair of nightwatchmen walked and where he might seek his own peace in solitude.

CHAPTER EIGHT

*E*arly the next morning I heard from an officer that three ships were to be sent down to take Tanner's Fort, a few miles to the south of Calcutta. It was almost the first sensible action I had heard of by the council, for possession of Tanner's Fort would give us the freedom of the river in that direction and on out to the coast. Edward being not yet returned from his nocturnal wandering, I went alone to the ghat to watch the departure of the ships. Once they were gone I went to the eastern battery which was to be my post should the nawab's army come, but the soldiers were only supervising the coolies there and had no need of me. Thence I walked down Lal Bazaar almost as far as the Maratha Ditch, when I suddenly heard some distant cannon fire from the direction of Tanner's Fort and turned and came back to the fort. A servant confirmed that Edward had in the meantime returned to our quarters and then left again, and so I went up onto the western battlements overlooking the river and turned my gaze southward. A small boat was sailing up the river.

For a quarter-hour I stood speculating on the fate of Tanner's Fort with the idle soldiers on the south-west bastion, and then the boat drew into the Crane Ghat and the news was shouted up to us that Tanner's had been taken without a single loss on our side. At this news the soldiers gave a half-hearted cheer and immediately went back to their dice. I left them and walked along the wall, thinking how different was the business of war from my imaginings, and I was about to descend when I saw some disturbance at the Governor's Ghat further along.

There was an upriver boat moored at the ghat and the company's *syr syrang*, the head boatmen, was watching two of his men searching the boat, while two others held the arms of the protesting tillerman. While I watched, they appeared to find what they looked for; it seemed to be some papers. The *syr syrang* at once leapt into the boat and slapped the tillerman hard about the head. He took the papers into his care while the tillerman was dragged after him toward Government House and I lost sight of them. There was something very strange in it. I came down from the bastion and out of the fort and my footsteps took me to a place near to the Government House entrance.

Had I had some more useful role to play or had Edward been with me, I had not then lingered there as I did. But I was still in that place a quarter hour later when the *syr syrang* and a lieutenant emerged from Government House. The lieutenant gathered up a number of soldiers standing nearby and gave them orders to load their guns and follow him to Omichand's house. I hurried to St Anne's to find the Reverend Bellamy.

'And you did not hear what they had found?' said he, when I had told him all I had seen.

'I am sure they were papers. A message of some kind.'

'And where is the lieutenant now?'

A single shot at that moment sounded from somewhere outside the church. He quickly closed the trunk he had been packing, got up from his knees and followed me out of the vestry. His boy on the church steps came after us and we hurried to join the people who were now converging on Omichand's house, for that was the direction of the shot.

As we drew near, we heard from the house the wild ululation and wailing of a woman somewhere in the upper storey, then we saw Omichand himself being led from the house by soldiers. Though they jostled him he made no protest, but walked on a little faster to be clear of them. He tried to walk alongside the lieutenant, but the lieutenant gave loud orders that he be taken to the Black Hole prison in the fort. Omichand now looked shaken, but he would not let the soldiers hold his arms. As they led him away, I saw him adjust his coat and his turban, which had been knocked awry by the jostling. The lieutenant stood for a moment with the rest of us and looked to the upper storey, where the ululation had suddenly died. Then a soldier appeared at a lower window.

'Sir, there is a room full of guns,' he said, and the lieutenant returned inside at once to see.

I too stepped forward, but Bellamy took my arm and said, 'Wait,' and when I raised my eyes to follow his gaze I saw what he had seen – smoke now came from the nearest window on the upper storey.

There was confusion among the soldiers and other people by us, but in the next moment another man rushed from the house. I recognized him immediately as Omichand's *jamindar*. The rector quickly turned to the soldier standing with us and said, 'You must not let this man escape.' The man at once called to the other soldiers and they rushed the *jamindar* all together. He pulled a dagger from the sheath at his waist. They paused on seeing this, but rushed him again and the fellow then did what no one expected – he turned the dagger upon himself and slashed at his own throat. But the soldiers had hold of him now and got the dagger from him before he cut himself free from life. His wound though was dreadful. There was a great quantity of blood, and the rector called for the surgeon to be fetched.

At this point I found Edward by me. 'Are there people inside?' he said. I told him there were soldiers and that we had heard a woman on the upper floor. 'They must be got out,' he declared and rushed through the door and I went after him in spite of the rector's protest.

We went straight up the stairs, Edward calling to the soldiers in the lower rooms that there was a fire above and that they should seek safety outside. Upstairs, Edward hurried down the central hallway, shouting in bastard Portuguese (the only tongue sure of being understood) that everyone must flee the house. Smoke came from beneath one door and he called over his shoulder to me, 'Do not open it!' Then he ran on to the last room and went in.

When I joined him he was in the middle of the room turning about in a slow circle, looking with horror at the several native women and children who lay slumped on the floor against the walls. 'Dear God, what has been done here,' he said hoarsely and crouched by one woman and drew the tight scarf from about her throat. He made the same inspection of the neighbouring child. 'They have been strangled.'

There was a rush of steps in the hall. We heard the soldiers break down the door and then a clanking of buckets and pails as water was brought to douse the fire. At last a soldier put his head into our room and ordered us to leave, but seeing the dead women and children, he fell suddenly silent.

Edward said, 'Is the fire contained?'

'It did not take hold. It is out.'

'You will please to call your lieutenant here.' The soldier nodded dumbly and withdrew, and I followed him into the hall and told him he must also fetch the Reverend Bellamy. Then I went into the room where the fire had been set. There was a pool of water across the floor, several buckets abandoned and, beneath the window, a pile of wet ash. I crouched and pushed a finger through layer upon layer of it. Papers and letters. Every layer blackened, incinerated beyond recovery.

'Whatever frauds he has committed,' said Edward, watching me now from the doorway, 'no judiciary may now uncover them.'

'You cannot believe this was done to protect a common thievery.'

'Common thievery never built a palace. And as you may see, there was none of his treasure lost in the flames. Nothing lost, but only the lives of the helpless. Oh, what a piece of work is a Hindoo. Omichand is a devil. I believe I could hate these people. Do not waste your life here, Alistair. I could hate them to the grave.'

Within hours it was a commonplace in the settlement that Omichand had been dealing privately and by secret means with the nawab and that he had kept a store of guns in his house in direct contravention of the governor's earlier order to deposit all arms at the fort. The strangling of the women and children was spoken of by some with horror and by others with a flippancy I could scarce believe till I perceived the secret terror beneath these unrepeatable remarks.

None slept easy that night in the fort or the settlement, nor yet in the black town.

The next morning we heard cannon fire from the direction of Tanner's Fort downriver, which was a thing no one had expected. Two hours later a boat put in at the ghat, where many of us had gathered. She brought news that the Moors had attacked and retaken Tanner's Fort.

'Drake has sent another ship down,' I told Edward when I found him, some hours later, in the smithy. 'Captain Minchin believes the Moors may be pushed out again.'

'Captain Minchin had better give his concern to Fort William.' He stepped toward the forge and gave the smith some direction as to the necessary breadth of the metal then being worked by another man at the anvil. A heavier hammer came out, the noise and the heat increased, and when Edward and I came away from there, I asked him what he did.

'The gate of the fort is unprotected. I have spoken with the mason. We will finish the ravelin and also a pit, if we have sufficient time.' He took me to the main gate and we went out to where a team of coolies was at work at the old ravelin, the half-finished defensive wall which had stood there unregarded all the while. The coolies were now finishing the wall and digging a deep pit to the front of it. Edward had by some means got a decision from Captain Minchin (which was the only instance I heard of our military commander's foresight in these final days) and now the work was progressing under Edward's own supervision. The rage that was in him when he had found those women and children was in him still, but colder now, and directed to some purpose. I could see he wanted no assistance from me and so I left him there, with the coolies who asked him no questions and offered him no sympathy but only worked at his quick command.

In the afternoon, the rumours of the approach of the nawab's army growing every hour, that fellow Krisnan Das (whom the nawab had wanted Drake to surrender) was caught by the company soldiers out near the Maratha Ditch attempting to escape the city. Drake immediately had Das thrown into the Black Hole with Omichand and the news of it caused a sudden desertion of the fort by many of the Hindoo servants. It was not a general panic, but the silent, unheralded withdrawal of these people was unnerving – as coming from some reason native to the country – besides being a great inconvenience to the general running of the fort.

On the day following, Drake gave orders for the burning of the houses in the black town near to the settlement.

CHAPTER NINE

'*A*listair!' I looked about me but could see no one. 'Lend a hand here!' he called, and then I knew it for Edward and broke off from the Reverend Bellamy and went across to the ravelin. Edward had some levering device assembled in the pit, and was hauling with all his strength on the bar, forcing a block into place in the foundation of the wall above.

'Are there no coolies?'

'Vanished into the smoke. For which we may thank Mr Drake.'

I shed my jacket and climbed into the pit to help him. We both of us now put our shoulders to the bar, but it moved not an inch. After a minute he said, 'Leave off. We cannot do it,' and he sat on the floor of the pit, his face very red and the perspiration running down his neck. 'What do they say now?'

'They say the nawab's army is near forty thousand strong. And that there are fifty elephants and more.'

'This pit will be the saving of the gates.'

'I have been assigned to the eastern battery. Monsieur Le Baume is my commander.'

'I am sure you will acquit yourself as well as any company officer.'

'Le Baume is a very experienced soldier.'

'I will allow Monsieur Le Baume to be the finest type of French officer. The enemy of my enemy is my friend. And if he does for the nawab, he is a gentleman. You have heard there are Frenchmen with the nawab.'

'They are artillerymen. And there are Dutchmen also. Monsieur Le Baume says they are the worthless outcasts of Chandernagore and Chinsurah.'

'Outcasts or what you will, they may do us much harm. Though I am certain your monsieur will not like to hear it said.'

We saw soldiers moving about on the north-eastern bastion now. They were loading the guns, and while we watched they fired once, made a long pause, and then there was a second shot, another long pause, then a third. It was the signal.

'When I am done here,' said Edward, putting his shoulder with renewed vigour to the lever-bar, 'I will join you at the battery.'

I climbed up from the pit. Our women and children were coming from all parts of the settlement in answer to the signal from the gun, not running or in panic, but everyone on foot as they retired to the fort, for the palanquin-bearers were among those who had deserted us. I then heard the sound of cannon to the north, near Perrin's. I knew it must be the first of the nawab's army engaging with our men on the outskirts of the city and I felt – God forgive me – a sudden thrill at the coming battle.

Monsieur Le Baume then hailed me from the fort ramparts. He bade me go down to the river to discover what kept the topasses who had been sent to fetch rope from the ships.

The Hugli at Calcutta is greater in size than the Thames at London and the several company ships moored there had ample clear water flowing between them, so that I was easily able to distinguish the topass boat as it finally cast off from the *Dodaly* and came in toward me at the ghat. Aboard the ship the sailors appeared in no hurry, but they went about their business on the decks and up the masts as if they had not noticed the cannon-fire so near to the city, which was a thing impossible as the firing was now very frequent. The topasses seemed touched by the sailors' lack of urgency and were some while getting the boat to the pier. The cart once loaded, I went ahead of the bullock driver and so we came again around the southern side of the fort.

From my setting out from the ravelin till my return there was a period of less than thirty minutes. And in that time, and to my disbelief when I first saw it, the ravelin wall had collapsed. Many soldiers were gathered there now and scrabbling with their bare hands at the rubble that was fallen into the pit.

'Where is Edward?' I called, but no one answered me. Chilled to the very marrow by their silence, I hurried to them and got down on my knees and dug. There was no talk, but each man now lifted free the stones and with some desperation.

How long we were about it I cannot say, but at last it was the mason who said, 'I have his hand here,' and I felt the blood drain from my face. But then he said in some surprise, 'It is warm. By Christ, he is alive,' and we all, with new vigour, dug out the stones from around the place.

Now Edward's shoulder came clear, and now his head. But as the weight came from his chest red spittle dribbled from his lips and the mason said to me, 'Get him free now, before he chokes. We must not kill him now.'

The lower part of his body had taken the heaviest of the fall and it was no easy business to get the weight from him. Once his upper body was free I put a hand beneath Edward's head and the mason took his shoulders. We turned him sufficiently to let the blood spill from his mouth. The blood ran for a moment and then stopped. The mason looked with fear in his eyes at what we had done.

I said, 'It is a good sign. He is not dead,' for I remembered something very like it from my father's experiments with the Kirkwall street dogs. At the least, I wanted, with all my heart, to believe that it was so.

A palanquin was swiftly brought by some soldiers, and many careful hands then lifted Edward's broken body into it, and I walked alongside as it was carried into the fort. The palanquin curtain stayed open and he lay so still that I several times put my hand on his arm to reassure myself he yet lived.

There were some rooms of the barracks set aside for an infirmary, and the soldiers put down the palanquin on the verandah of the barracks and then withdrew to their several posts about the fort. A Hindoo was folding linen on the verandah and I made him understand that he should sit by Edward while I went to fetch the surgeon. I turned in at the first door and stopped there, mute.

There was a soldier lying upon the table. The fort blacksmith held the soldier's right leg and the surgeon's mate the left. Two other fellows held the man's shoulders pinned to the table. The man's teeth were bared and he bit like fury into a strip of leather while the surgeon cauterized the gaping wound in the thigh. It made the hissing sound of frying meat.

'You have some business here?' said the surgeon without lifting his eyes.

I stammered out the story of what had happened to Edward. I said that I feared he might be dying outside in the palanquin even while we spoke. The surgeon made me no answer, but worked on. By several remarks that passed between him and the blacksmith, I understood that the fellow on the table was the first casualty from the nawab's assault and that others had been killed. At last the surgeon finished his work and tossed his knife into a bucket and came outside.

'Has he spoken?'

'No.'

'Has he been conscious?'

'I have seen no sign of it.'

'Well, he is alive at least.' He peered into Edward's ears and nostrils. 'I will set his legs before he rejoins us. I can do little for his ribs, but only bandage them. His skull is remarkably undamaged. Contusions, yes. He will need some strong opiate by him when he wakes.'

'Then he will live.'

'I pray that every one of my patients will survive my care, Mr Douglas. Regrettably, they are not all of them so considerate of my hopes. I will do what I can.' He called the men from inside and they came and moved the palanquin to a place beneath the window of the operating room. Soon splints and bandages were being passed out through the window.

Edward was stripped and washed, then his legs were straightened and bound and his torso swathed in bandages. The fall of stone had left a thousand cuts and grazes on him, but there was little bleeding. When I remarked upon this strange circumstance, the surgeon said, 'It is the inside of him took the weight. Till he wakes we cannot know the worst. You need not stay. There is nothing you may do for him.'

Another casualty from the nawab's first assault then arriving, the surgeon went to tend to him. I gave a few annas to the Hindoo servant (almost the only servant who had not deserted the fort by now), telling him that he should come and find me out at the eastern battery if there was any change in Edward's condition.

Captain Clayton had charge of the eastern battery and Captain Le Baume was under his command. When I arrived there, I found Le Baume and his small troop of soldiers and militiamen busy hitching bullocks to two carriage-mounted cannon.

'We will be an advance post at the jailhouse,' Le Baume told me when I reported to him. He pointed to an iron bar that I should take with me, and only when we reached the jailhouse, two hundred yards to the east of the battery, did the purpose of the iron bar become clear. Le Baume immediately set several men to breaking two embrasures through the jailhouse wall on the lower floor for the two cannon, and the rest of us he set to making loopholes in the walls upstairs, through which we might fire upon the Moors when they attacked us.

While we worked at loosening the stones we heard musketfire from the black town where the Moorish camp-followers now advanced in a wild carnival of pillaging and despoliation. From the upstairs windows we marked their slow advance toward the settlement by the black pillars of smoke that rose from the houses they torched on their way.

The two cannon at last arriving at the jailhouse, Le Baume called us all down to lend a hand with manoeuvring them, which was no easy matter, for the carriages were too wide for the door and had to be taken apart by the carpenters, reassembled inside and finally lifted back into their cradling. It was hot work and we had soon drunk the supply of water brought forward with us. After this, we returned upstairs to complete our work on the loopholes (of which we made about twenty), and it was there that Reverend Bellamy found me.

'Where is your captain?' he asked when he saw me, and he came over and looked with some anxiety out the window and up the avenue toward the Bread & Cheese Bungalow out by the Ditch.

Before I could answer, Le Baume came bounding up from below. Bellamy turned from the window.

'Monsieur, I have taken the liberty to come out and warn you. There has been a fellow escaped from us. He has ridden out to the Moors. It is Omichand's *jamindar*. I fear he has gone to direct the nawab's army to the eastern entry over the Ditch.'

Le Baume raised a brow, clearly surprised that such information should come from a man of the cloth. He assured Reverend Bellamy that every care was being taken with our preparations.

'I have no doubt of it, monsieur. My concern is that the nawab's men should fall upon you unexpectedly and in numbers overwhelming. You and your men are very exposed this far forward of the battery. I have said as much to Captain Clayton. But as he would not call you back, I have come out to warn you.' Le Baume asked when the *jamindar* had escaped. 'I only heard of it this hour, Captain. But I am quite certain of his intention to guide the nawab's army in from the east.'

All of us who worked on the loopholes had by this time set aside our tools, and now we watched Le Baume and awaited his response.

'Monsieur Douglas,' said he in French, 'you will take one man out to the Ditch. If the nawab's army approaches, return here at once to report it. Keep a watch till nightfall, then come in.'

My throat went dry. And there was in Bellamy's eyes a sudden look of concern at what he had wrought.

'Would it not be more wise to withdraw at once?' he asked Le Baume.

'I thank you for your warning, monsieur. But we were not sent here to withdraw. Monsieur Douglas?'

Le Baume gave me his spyglass and I selected a soldier. This soldier and I then took up our muskets and, with further instructions from Le Baume, we went out from the jailhouse and eastward up the avenue toward the Ditch.

As we walked, a heavy smoke drifted over us from the black town. By the sound of the sporadic musketshot, we knew that the Moorish pillagers drew steadily closer. It was almost a mile we walked till we came to the bungalow and the Ditch. Climbing up on the bank there, I raised the spyglass and looked northward. There was no sign of the nawab's army and so we settled ourselves to wait.

It was some hours we waited, talking little and keeping a keen watch to the north and an apprehensive eye always on the black town. I did not know then how much of a soldier's life is spent in waiting, and the time lay very heavy on me. But when the sun at last went down behind St Anne's and the fort at the western end of the avenue, I turned my spyglass northward a final time. There I saw the van of the Moorish army.

I called for my companion to wait, for he had started down the bank very eager now to return to the jailhouse before dark. There were Moorish cavalry in the van and behind these the Moorish infantry. There was no hurry in them. They advanced steadily toward us, though they were still perhaps a mile and a half distant.

'Is it the army?'

'It is,' said I and he came up again and I gave him the spyglass.

'Holy Jesus,' said he.

We could not see to the rear of the Moorish column, so great was the size of it. We hurried down the bank, and westward along the avenue.

It was nearly dark by the time we reached the jailhouse (in that latitude, there is no evening twilight), and when I made my report to Le Baume he went at once to the upstairs window. He raised his spyglass and looked toward the Ditch. Even with the naked eye, the Moorish torches were now visible. They were not moving, but had stopped out at the Ditch, just beyond the Bread & Cheese Bungalow.

'The main force will make their camp there,' said Le Baume.

'Will they attack us?'

'Not tonight.' We stood a while and watched the Moorish torches, ever increasing in number and shining brightly now as the darkness descended. 'Sleep now,' said Le Baume. 'You will go to the fort to receive our orders before sunrise.'

In truth, he must have known what small chance there was of me or any other in the jailhouse sleeping that night.

CHAPTER TEN

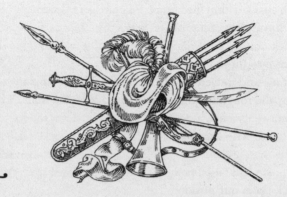

'The order is to give the Moors no quarter,' said Drake's secretary, Cooke, as he came out from the council chamber. There were three of us had been called there at first light, one from each of the batteries beyond the fort walls. 'The Black Hole is already full, we can accommodate no more. You must press it upon your captains that they shall not bring any prisoners within the fort.' He handed each of us the written order of the council.

'And if any Moor should surrender himself?' said I.

'No quarter is the order, Mr Douglas. If you do not understand the meaning of it, you must have the captain of your battery explain it to you.'

We three came out from the main gates. The others went north and south and I straight on past St Anne's to the eastern battery near to the playhouse. As Captain Clayton took the written order from me, musketshot sounded from the direction of the northern battery.

'Report to Captain Le Baume, Mr Douglas. Take him the council's order. And you may tell him from me that he should look to expect the Moors' attack within the hour.'

I went down from the eastern battery then, and up past the play-house to the jailhouse where Le Baume, eagerly took the council's order from my hand.

I said, 'They want no prisoners taken.'

'Bon,' said he.

When I told him of Captain Clayton's belief that we should expect a Moorish attack within the hour, Le Baume beckoned me to a window. 'You see those three houses? We have seen Moors there. When the main attack comes, those men will cover their infantry. If you see no enemy, fire into those houses.'

He left me and moved among the soldiers and company volunteers who sat by the rough loopholes we had made in the walls. There were fewer than twenty men, a dozen on this upper floor, the remainder on the floor below with the two cannon. Le Baume checked their muskets and powder and kept one eye on the streets below, for the musketshots from the north had faded now. Every one of us now expected an imminent attack upon our position.

As I knelt to load my pistol, the soldier at the window near me said, 'You would be better to use your musket.'

'I will keep the pistol ready.'

'Use the musket well and you will not need the other,' said he, and smiled in encouragement, for he saw the unwonted clumsiness in my loading. When he turned from me to peer out the window, the first Moorish musketshot sounded from the street and his legs buckled and he collapsed onto me. Cries and shouts broke out from all sides as Moorish lead suddenly poured in upon us through the windows. I lowered the shot soldier onto the floor and saw there was nothing to be done for him. The ball had gone in at his throat and out through his spine and, though the blood was still seeping out of him, he was dead.

'Move him!' I looked up, dazed, and found Le Baume shouting at me in French. 'Move him clear of the loophole. He is blocking the position.' He strode across the room and took hold of one the dead soldier's arms and I the other and we dragged the body from the window and left it by the rear wall.

'To your post, monsieur.'

'Shall I fire at those three houses?'

'Fire at anything that moves.'

I fetched my musket from the floor as another ferocious volley broke upon us. My back pressed against the wall by the loophole, I stared across the room at the dead soldier. The plaster on the rear wall had shattered and rained down upon him. He looked like a man no more but only a thing. There was a lull now in the Moorish fusillade and our soldiers thrust their muskets out through the loopholes and fired. The noise was deafening and the powder smoke bloomed into the jail-house air like a pestilential vapour.

I knelt and pushed my musket through the loophole. The Moors were not massed, but hurried about singly and in small platoons between the nearby houses. Seeing one such platoon momentarily stationary, I fired into them and then made the almost fatal error of raising my head to the window (I suppose from some instinctive, but absolutely foolish desire to see if my shot had gone home). I heard the ball that almost killed me very clearly, for it fizzed past my ear and smacked into the rear wall, sending down another shower of plaster. I ducked, withdrew my musket from the loophole and crawled aside to gather my wits and, with trembling hands, reload.

Le Baume called to me, 'You will not do that again, Monsieur Douglas.'

I shook my head, too shocked by the near-miss to even answer him. When he finished his own reloading he hurried to the stairs and des-cended and a moment later his voice could be heard urging the men at the cannons below to fire into the Moorish positions. The cannon fired like double thunder and the floor and walls shook. Le Baume could straightway be heard once more commanding them to reload and continue firing.

I now paid a more careful attention to the method of the soldiers about me. I saw that they spent barely a second exposed as they took aim and fired. Their intent was to throw as much lead as they might upon the Moors without themselves becoming targets – a very sensible method, and I adopted it with alacrity.

Yet so intense was the Moorish fire that after ten minutes, in spite of our caution, we had another man shot. He fell back from the loophole next to mine, clutching his shoulder and screaming. Le Baume was up the stairs in an instant. He called my name over the musketfire and beckoned me to him and I went and helped him prop the wounded soldier against the wall. Le Baume used the fellow's bayonet to cut away the jacket, the man crying out only now when Le Baume had to move him. With the sleeve off, and the wound finally exposed, Le Baume told the fellow to raise his arm. The man tried and failed and cried out in agony. Le Baume said to me, 'Use his powder and shot if you need it.'

'He should be taken back to the fort.'

Le Baume pointed to the window. 'There is our business.' Le Baume then instructed the wounded soldier to take sightings at the window for me and the fellow, very much to my astonishment, got to his knees and shuffled across to a place just by my window, all the while holding the loose sleeve against his bleeding shoulder. Le Baume hurried back down the stairs to the cannon.

I reloaded, and as I did so the wounded man essayed a few tentative glances out of the window.

'The house on the left,' said he. 'There are Moors at the bottom right window.'

I made my own quick glance to confirm it. Then I put out my musket through the loophole, sighted quickly, fired, and withdrew.

And so it went on for an hour and more, with the fellow sometimes sighting for me, and sometimes being in such an affliction of pain that he could only press his head against the wall and sob. The Moorish fire never relented and we lost another of our men, killed by a headshot (a fact only too visible to us till Le Baume pulled off the man's jacket and covered him), and two more men near me were wounded. Le Baume was up and down between the floors continually, firing out the windows and loopholes and peering out also, at the risk of his life, to discover the Moorish positions.

But, though our cannon continued to hold off the Moors, it was clear that our losses had caused a noticeable diminution in our rate of fire.

Each time I looked out, the number of Moors I now glimpsed increased, as did the weight of their fire upon us. At last Le Baume came up the stairs and crossed to me.

'Go back to Captain Clayton. Tell him I need two field guns sent forward here. Take these three—' he pointed to our wounded. 'And also the two others you will find downstairs.'

Le Baume immediately took my place at the loophole and I heard him calling the Moorish positions to the others, even as I helped the wounded down the stairs. There was one man lying dead below. The two wounded there had already withdrawn themselves to the rear exit, but there one had collapsed and could not walk, and neither could I carry him while I yet supported my fellow with the shoulder wound.

'Stay with him,' called I to the other wounded man who knelt by him. 'I shall have someone fetch you.'

The kneeling fellow seemed almost to welcome my words, for he slumped down at once by the wall, barely conscious.

Leaving the jailhouse with my party of walking wounded, I now discovered a surprising protection afforded us by the walled yard at our backs and by the empty houses nearby, and after a few minutes shuffling along under the protection of the walls, we arrived at the playhouse in safety. From there I ran the last twenty yards to the battery, where I found Captain Clayton coming down to meet me.

'We have had three men killed, sir, and five wounded. Monsieur Le Baume requests two field guns be sent forward to his aid.'

'Two?' said he, as though the request were excessive.

'Yes, sir.'

'Is there some problem with his cannon?'

'It is the great number of Moors, sir.'

He called an ensign to him, saying, 'I see we must get the Frenchman out of his difficulties.' He gave the order for two field guns to be taken forward, but with remarks about Le Baume both unworthy and disagreeable. 'And you, Mr Douglas, you are not needed here. You may return there and tell Monsieur Le Baume the guns are sent to relieve him.'

I own, when I had left the jailhouse, I had been glad to put it behind me, but on hearing Clayton speak so, I was almost equally glad to be returning there; for Le Baume's efforts were deserving of something more than these churlish rejoinders.

On my way back to the jailhouse, I passed those two wounded men I had left there being now carried back to safety at the battery. I told Le Baume of this and of the promised field guns and he clapped me on the shoulder and pointed me to the window. 'If you see a Moor, shoot him.'

The Moors' fusillade had grown heavier in my absence and, of the seventeen men who had started the morning under Le Baume's command, only seven now remained to him. The sight of the fallen redcoats, on our side, had made the remaining men attentive of their own safety and I believe it was only Le Baume's cajoling and the bold example he set that kept them firing now with any proper effect.

No finer sound came to my ears all that day than the first field gun when it, at last, fired from some place outside; and in the next minute Clayton's ensign came running up the stairs with re-inforcements. There was only a half-dozen of these fellows, but they were very welcome to us. When the second field gun fired, there was a lull in the Moorish musketshot and Le Baume and the ensign conferred, while we others called forward the newcomers to our aid by the loopholes.

'By Jesus,' said the gnarled soldier who positioned himself in safety nearby me. He looked about the large room, at the pummelled rear wall and the splintered ceiling and the blood upon the floor. 'By Christ, you've been in a fight here, boy.'

The Moorish muskets then reopened on us and we were in a fight once more.

With our field pieces now playing briskly over those houses the Moors had occupied, we had some respite from the full force of their musketry. I ventured now to imitate Le Baume and looked, for a few seconds, from a window.

There were dead Moors lying in the street near to the houses we had fired upon, but in no great number. And in spite of the fire from

89

our field guns, the Moors had not withdrawn, but rather many of them were now moving in the lanes and streets opposite, as though coming up to reinforce the others. With no hopeful feeling, I went back to my work at the loophole. After fifteen minutes these Moorish reinforcements began to have some effect, for their musketshot increased, so that very soon they were galling us very fiercely again. After an hour, and with yet more of our men shot, I saw the ensign and Le Baume in urgent conference at the head of the stairs, though I could not hear them above the musket and cannon and guns. Le Baume went downstairs and several minutes later there came a metallic knocking sound from down below.

'It is the cannon,' the soldier by me called when I asked him the meaning of the sound. 'The Captain is spiking the cannon.'

'Will we withdraw then?'

'If we live,' said he and did not smile but shot, without aiming, through the window.

For another hour or more we fought on, and when Le Baume came up to fetch us we had been winnowed to only six able-bodied men. Upon the floor were three dead and four wounded, only two of whom could walk. As Le Baume came toward me I saw that he too was wounded. His right hand was thrust into his buttoned jacket to support his arm and the cloth at his right shoulder was torn and stained dark with his blood. He was very pale and, when he came across to me, he leaned his back against the wall and said to me in French, 'We are called back to the eastern battery. Tell the men here they must bring the wounded. Any who are not needed for that must stay close to the field guns to cover the withdrawal.'

I shouted his order across the room. The men at once left off their firing and hurried to help the wounded. Le Baume shoved away from the wall and shook his head when I offered to assist him.

Downstairs, the two cannon had been dismantled and their carriages broken into pieces. A soldier was making a few final blows on the iron spike driven into the firing-hole. Le Baume inspected his work, but the job was well done and Le Baume had no further instruction to give the fellow, only to tell him now to withdraw with the others to the eastern battery.

At last Le Baume made his exit and I with him, past the place where our dead had been dragged into a heap together. It was a dreadful sight, though I but glanced at it in my hurry to be away from there. We joined the soldiers near the two field guns and the withdrawal was effected in stages, with one gun pulled back fifty yards, and set up to fire, and then the other gun falling back fifty yards behind it; and the whole exercise repeated, and we firing our muskets all the while at the Moors.

When we reached the safety of the eastern battery I overheard Le Baume tell Captain Clayton that he wished to withdraw his men to the fort to recover awhile. Clayton seemed disinclined to allow it.

'But my men must eat, sir,' Le Baume told him.

'There is no food brought forward for us either, monsieur. And your men cannot yet return to the fort as they are needed here.' Captain Clayton looked through his spyglass up the avenue. 'And it is my advice that you would do better to think of their powder and shot than of their stomachs.'

How Le Baume contained himself, I know not. As he came down from the battery the cannons mounted there fired upon the Moors now occupying the jailhouse.

'Go to the fort,' Le Baume told me quietly. 'Bring us what food you can find. And water.' He called his weary half-dozen men after him and they withdrew from the battery and went to rest in the shade of a house beyond the eye of Captain Clayton.

Within the walls of the fort there was no panic yet, but certainly fear was spreading, for all the people there had witnessed the injured brought back from the jailhouse (and from the northern and southern batteries, where the Moors had also attacked) and, at my hurrying across the square now, many called anxiously to me asking for some report of the fighting out on our lines. I made no reply to them, but went directly to the officers' mess, where I found the one native cook who had not fled. I ordered him to give me food sufficient for half a dozen men. He took me into the larder where there was food in plenty, but all unprepared. I took what was immediately edible – bread, fruit, salted beef and suchlike – and shoved it into a sack and then I filled an empty flagon at the fort's well.

While I did this, Governor Drake, his sword at his side, stood on the north-east bastion and looked out through his spyglass at the fighting. His secretary, Cooke, shouldered his way to me through the milling crowd in the square and demanded to know the situation at the jailhouse.

'We have abandoned it,' said I bluntly.

'How soon will Captain Clayton retake it?'

'The Moors are too many. I believe we will now try to hold the battery.'

'What?' said he, as though the thought of losing the battery had not occurred to him till now.

'Sir, I must go.'

'The governor's order is to hold the battery and the jailhouse and give no quarter to the Moors.'

I picked up the sack and the flagon and hurried away from the blasted fellow. The gate-door of the fort was opened for me, and I ran out, and up by St Anne's. Le Baume and the exhausted remnant of his troop had not moved from the place where I had left them. They fell with a great hunger upon the food I brought, and the flagon of water passed quickly among them and was soon empty.

In the time of my going to the fort and returning, the Moors had advanced into many of the settlement houses which had been earlier protected by our position at the jailhouse. They had got onto the roofs of these places and now fired their muskets with some good effect upon our eastern battery.

Le Baume spoke French to me, that the men might not understand him.

'If the Moors come through the park they will outflank both the east battery and the south. Captain Clayton and Monsieur Holwell do not need us here. We will—' he fell silent suddenly and looked past me, southward, where was an intensification of musketshot and much shouting. I followed his gaze and saw the red coats of our soldiers

92

standing upon the roof of Captain Minchin's house. The Moors were firing heavily upon them and they, in some desperation, returned their fire. What Le Baume feared had already happened: the Moors had broken through our line. 'Allez!' cried Le Baume, and I called to the others, 'Come!'

Stuffing food into our mouths, we snatched up our muskets and followed Le Baume across the park. We ran between the few trees there till we came to the protection of a low wall on the far side. But by then, the situation at Captain Minchin's house had changed. We saw now that there were Moors rushing in through the front door, though our own men were still upon the roof. The senior soldier among them was Ensign Blagg and, having seen our approach, he hollered down to us, 'We have no ammunition!'

Le Baume was very weak now and he said to me, 'Tell him he must order his men to fix their bayonets. He must tell us when he is ready. Our men will fire a volley through the lower windows. He must not hesitate then, but come immediately down the stairs and fall upon the Moors.'

I shouted Le Baume's instruction up to the ensign, who made no objection. I then told our own men to load and stand ready to fire in through the lower windows. Le Baume handed me his pistol and I loaded it for him, and a minute later the ensign called to us, 'We are ready!'

Le Baume was visibly weakening now from the loss of blood, but we watched him, awaiting his signal, and at last he said to us, 'Through the windows. Aim and fire!' and he rose himself and took aim over the wall. Then we all rose and aimed and there was a crackling volley of our muskets as we fired. When we crouched to reload and to fix our bayonets, as Le Baume ordered, there came a wild banshee cry from the house. I ventured a glance around the wall and was amazed to see the Moors fleeing the house in disarray. Once I had reloaded, I looked again and the ensign and several men under his command came rushing out with bloodied bayonets. They ran over to us by the wall, still shouting wildly, and Le Baume cried, 'To the fort!' for the Moors had got over their first surprise and were returning now to attempt to trap us behind the wall.

The musketshot flew on all sides and the confusion and shouting was very great. Le Baume was not too proud now to clasp a hand upon my shoulder as we retreated, for there was little strength remaining in him. Once we had retreated fifty yards, we came under the protection of our soldiers' muskets at the southern battery near the fort. When we finally reached it, I paused to let Le Baume recover himself and was myself astonished to see now the line of Moorish dead our small party had left in its wake.

'Bon,' said Le Baume, who saw them too. He rested his arm fully about my shoulders now and I took him back into the fort and the surgeon.

Nor was Le Baume the only one of us to need the surgeon. Ensign Blagg and most of his men were wounded and, from the batteries, others were now being carried into the fort. The sight of all these wounded suddenly arriving together caused a considerable agitation among the two thousand or more dismayed souls confined within the fort walls. For unlike the soldiers up on the parapet, these in the yard below could see nothing of what was happening outside, but only heard the guns and muskets. The arrival in their midst of the torn and broken bodies was a great shock to them, and there was a growing terror in the eyes of these civilians.

Having left Le Baume with the surgeon, I went out to Edward's palanquin and looked in. His eyes were closed and there was a good deal of perspiration on his brow. 'There is nothing may now be done for him, but only to wait and to pray,' said the Reverend Bellamy, coming from another wounded man nearby. He asked me what was happening beyond the walls, and when I told him he said, 'Come with me now. We must see the women to the boats.'

We went to the building where Mrs Drake and the other wives of the company men had been temporarily quartered with their children and, finding them in readiness to leave, we escorted them through the crowded yard and out through the river-gate onto the ghat. There were no servants with them, for the ships could not accommodate so many. In spite of this, we quickly discovered there were too few boats to take them all out to the ships and so we got but half of them into the boats, and the others must needs return with us to the fort and take refuge again in their temporary quarters.

Le Baume had by this time been dealt with by the surgeon. The lead was removed from his shoulder, which was heavily bandaged. But he had lost more blood whilst under the knife and was now white as he lay on the charpoy (which is like a bed with no mattress), too weakened to speak with me.

'The surgeon has asked for you to be taken out to the ships,' said I, at which his head went weakly from side to side as if he would protest the surgeon's instruction. I left him and hurried to the main gate, intending to go out and put myself beneath Captain Clayton's command at the eastern battery. But before I reached the gate, Captain Clayton himself came in there with a score of his men, and they all looking very relieved to have got themselves back inside the walls.

The confusion and lack of any proper command at this moment was very evident. For Governor Drake, in anger, came down from the parapet, shouting at Clayton that reinforcement was being mustered to be sent out to him and that he should not have retreated and Clayton answered that to hold the battery against the Moors was impossible and he had consequently spiked the cannon there and withdrawn. Mr Holwell, who had been Clayton's second at the battery, offered his own opinion on the matter and the whole disagreement among them was carried on in full view and earshot of the soldiers and civilians in the fort whose very lives were in the charge of these bickering gentlemen.

'If you cannot retake the battery, you must hold them at the church,' ordered Drake at last. 'The Moors must not get under our walls in the night.'

'My men must rest.'

'They may rest when they have stopped the Moors.' Drake turned and gave instruction to some other officers there that the large buildings just outside the walls – St Anne's and the company House and Mr Cruttenden's house – must now be occupied by our soldiers, so that the Moors might be kept back from the fort's walls. He told them that the council would meet after nightfall and that they should then receive further orders.

Captain Clayton reluctantly led his soldiers back out through the gates and several more officers, and perhaps two score men, went also to occupy the buildings in accord with Drake's orders. They were unhappy men all.

The Moorish musketfire was now much diminished, for it was coming on to dark and the Moors by custom do no proper fighting in the night. And having no great wish to serve now under Captain Clayton, nor seeing any usefulness in my being without the walls, I returned to that place by the surgeon's room where Edward was and slumped down exhausted by his palanquin.

The Moors had won the day, won it decisively, and there was no man in the fort could pretend otherwise. There was to me a real bitterness in this, for I was certain that had Drake condescended to heed the warning I had brought from Mr Watts, there might not have been this sudden and near-instant collapse in our defences. Indeed, the only one of our senior men to emerge from the day with honour in my estimation was Captain Le Baume, and he a Frenchman. Now that I could reflect in quietness awhile, I thought upon the fighting at the jailhouse and our rescue of Ensign Blagg and his men. I found that there was scarcely a moment of it that accorded with the soldiering of my imaginings, for fear and confusion had been my constant companions, with only the steadiness of Le Baume to keep me to my duty. I had killed Moors, of that I was certain, for I had several times seen the fellows go down at my shot through the loophole, but I did not think much on them now. I thought, rather, on our own dead and wounded and on the merest chance that had preserved my own life. This great part of chance in the whole proceedings of the battle was another thing new to my imaginings and it unnerved me to think on it.

After an hour the Reverend Bellamy came to me with word that some boats had returned to the ghat. I went inside and spoke to the surgeon and together we convinced Le Baume that he must be the women's escort out to the ships. He at last relented and then amazed both the surgeon and me by getting himself up from the charpoy. Yet he was terribly weak still and he put an arm over my shoulder. I supported him through the yard and down to the ghat. Again the boats were too few to take all the women, but I made sure of Le Baume's place and he was too weak to force an objection. Then Bellamy and I led the other women back into the fort and their quarters.

'If you can sleep, sleep now,' Bellamy told me, as we crossed the fort's crowded yard. 'Our line outside the walls will not hold long tomorrow.'

'Does the governor understand it?'

'He understands it very well. But our situation is now beyond his saving.'

'It was said we should be able to hold the fort for a month.'

'It was wrongly said. When the council meets tonight, they will discover no Davids among them to defeat the Moorish Goliath.'

He left me with Edward and went into the surgeon's makeshift hospital to pray for the dead and to minister to the dying.

CHAPTER ELEVEN

*T*hat night torches were lit all along the Great Ghat below the fort, and soldiers worked there, bringing chests and boxes and sacks down from the river-gate, loading them into boats to be rowed out to the ships. And out at the ships, the lanterns were lit and everything was very tranquil there.

'Mr Frankland,' said I, at last identifying his face in the flickering light along the ghat. He was with the last of our women and children there, who were being helped down into the boats. 'Captain Minchin sends his compliments, sir, and asks if you may take this letter.'

Frankland looked down at the note in my hand with some degree of suspicion. 'There is no room on the *Dodaly* for more freight, Mr Douglas.'

'The captain is not seeking passage for any goods.'

'If it is for himself, we cannot wait for him here.'

'Sir, I believe the captain hopes that you might represent to the *Dodaly*'s captain how severe is the want of munitions in the fort.'

'You must tell the governor.'

'The governor is in deliberation with the council.'

'I must see to the safety of these women. The captain is not alone in his troubles. We are all of us in extremities.' He snatched the letter and thrust it into his coat pocket without breaking the seal. The women and the others of his party were, by this time, embarked and he now climbed into the boat after them, the boatmen bent to their oars and Frankland went out to join his friend Mr Manningham, with the women, in safety.

I reported this all to Minchin, and also my fear that we would see no more of Frankland, nor yet any munitions from the *Dodaly*.

'Have you told any others of your fear?'

'No, sir.'

'Say nothing. They will sleep better if they may hope.'

From there I went down to see Edward. His eyes were closed and, when I put a hand to his brow, the fringe of his hair was damp, and damp too the kerchief that lay beside him on the pillow. I settled the blanket over him and sat with my back propped against his palanquin and looked across the square. There were many lanterns and small fires burning within the yard of the fort and a multitude of people clustering like moths around the campfires. It appeared that almost every person in Calcutta with some close connection to the company had fled here to take refuge – Hindoo servants from the settlement with their families; the Armenian merchants with their families; all the topasses; even some Dutchmen and Danes. And now they were all encamped in the midst of us, perhaps two thousand or more; were the siege to continue more than a few days they would finish up all the provisions that we had. And, with so many crowded together, sickness must surely come upon us.

'Who is it?'

Turning, I saw that Edward's eyes were open and he looked in some bewilderment at all the people in the fort. 'We have abandoned the town to the Moors. These have taken refuge with us.'

'How long?'

'You have been here one day. Do not tire yourself with speaking.'

'I am going home to England.'

'Yes, but you must rest now.'

'I will find me a good wife there.'

'I am sure of it.'

'She will have my children.'

'You must sleep.'

'Listen.' With an effort, he lifted his head to see me the better. He spoke between breaths, haltingly. 'The children. The first child. I have been thinking on it. If you would – do me the honour – if I may ask on the behalf of the wife I do not have – if you would consent, that is – to be godfather to the child.'

This took me unexpectedly. 'When you are well, we will speak of it.'

His fingers found my arm on the palanquin's sideboard. 'I am well enough to know my mind. In mind, Alistair, I am better than I have been for some months.'

There was no strength in the grip of his fingers, though his eyes held me.

'Then the honour would be mine,' said I.

He pressed my arm, but the effort made in speaking had drained him. Spent now, he dropped his head to the pillow and closed his eyes again. When I touched his brow there was now a river of perspiration. I dabbed at his brow with his kerchief and his body went suddenly rigid with pain. I feared he was dying.

I fetched the surgeon and the man prepared a strong opiate for Edward. When Edward had drunk it the pain soon seemed to release him, and he lay quiet then and unmoving.

Through the night his fever rose and fell and rose again, and though several times in the night I slept, it was but poorly, for I was almost ill myself with fatigue. I own I had a great apprehension of the morning and the inevitable renewal of the Moorish attack. Each time that I woke, I lifted myself from the boards by the palanquin and looked in on Edward, but he never tried to speak to me again, nor did his eyes open, but he murmured continually and sometimes cried out. There was no meaning in his words now, only confusion. The last time that I slept I dreamt of a fierce wind blowing across the drifted snow in Orkney, and when I woke the fort was stirring and the darkness was going from the sky along the eastern parapet.

I went and splashed my face at a bucket by the well, and brought Edward a flask of fresh water. The Reverend Bellamy was with him now.

'But you are here, Mr Douglas,' said he in surprise when he saw me. 'I was told you had gone out to the ships with the women.'

'It was Mr Frankland took the ladies on board.'

'Indeed. Mr Frankland and Mr Manningham would both appear to have an uncommon concern for the women's welfare.'

'They may be as safe as they please, if only they send us more powder and shot from the ships.'

'I would not trust in the ships. The most of them have fallen down-river in the night.' I was too shocked by this news to speak a word. It seemed almost inconceivable to me that the ships should so callously and needlessly abandon us. 'Only the *Prince George* remains to hope on,' said he. 'But I fear we must now look to ourselves for our own salvation.' The Moorish musketfire suddenly started, and with it, a scrambling confusion of all those in the yard to seek the cover of the walls. The crying of the children was most pitiful. 'The siege may end badly,' Bellamy said to me quietly. 'If it does – I will speak plain to you now, Mr Douglas – if the fall of the fort seems to you imminent, I must ask that you come to me here. There is some important service that you may do for me. Do you understand me?'

I nodded, though in truth it was only the earnestness of his intent that I understood. His gaunt face was very stern, and his gaze went right into me. I gestured toward Edward. 'Have a care for him,' said I, and then I went to the parapet, and was amazed to find there Le Baume.

'But how could I stay with the women?' he said in answer to me.

'You are bleeding.'

'It is nothing,' said he, but I think he knew already he would not be fighting that day as he had hoped.

The departure of the ships was all the soldiers spoke of at first, and that most bitterly, but then the sun came fully up and the enemy opened their cannon upon us. There was no more talk of the ships, but only a sharp firing and reloading and a steady cursing of the Moors. Le Baume used his pistol for a while, but his loss of blood quickly weakened him. Then he reloaded for the others and called his encouragement to them.

Under the cover of night, the Moors had occupied every building close to the fort, and though we directed cannon and musket at them now, yet we could not dislodge them. The pair of cannon by the courthouse kept up a steady rain of double blows upon our walls.

Had there been some proper discipline among the nawab's troops it is certain we would not then have killed them in such numbers. But once the sun had risen (and the news no doubt spread among the Moors of our abandonment by the ships) they grew ever more bold and reckless. Several times they rose up from the batteries and swept out from the cover of the buildings in a great wave across the open ground toward us.

We cut them down like the grass.

In the late morning I turned to speak with Le Baume after one such attack and found him slumped against the parapet. His face was white. I opened his jacket and found his shirt soaked in blood.

'You are going back to the ships.'

'No.'

I called another soldier to me and together we took Le Baume down into the yard and across to the river-gate. The gate was opened for us and out on the ghat there were perhaps a dozen small boats, the boatmen in some quandary whether they should stay now or get their boats to safety. We put Le Baume into one of these boats and there were some topass women there, crying and in terror of the Moors. I told them to get into the boat also, and take care of Le Baume, for he was unconscious now.

'Take them down to the *Dodaly*,' said I to the boatman, and I waited only long enough to see the boat move out into the current and turn downriver.

Inside the fort, I took up my musket again, but there was a want of powder among the soldiers. I knew we could not hold the Moors off for very much longer.

Then it happened that as I was taking some powder to the guns at the south bastion, a cry went up from the soldiers overlooking the river. I ran across to them, crouching and keeping my head down.

When I looked myself over the parapet, I saw on the Great Ghat and on the river just below the fort a scene of chaos and panic. The river-gate had been opened, and a great many people had rushed from the fort. There were now two hundred and more down there, shoving each other, some of them fighting and falling into the water. The last boats that had been tied there were now leaving the ghat, and as more people came out from the river-gate I heard the officers inside shouting for the gate to be closed. And then I saw what the soldiers beside me had already seen. In one of the fleeing boats sat the supposed leader of our defence, that brave gentleman Governor Drake.

One of the soldiers near to me raised his musket, and there could be no doubt of his aiming direct at the governor.

'Hold!' cried I. But I was met by such fierce and threatening looks from the soldiers there that I saw I could not pass through them to prevent the villainy. There was a crack, and a puff of smoke.

'The devil!' cried the marksman and spat, for he had missed his mark. Drake drifted fast on the tide, downriver toward the safety of the ships.

'Gentlemen, hear me! You will know by now that Mr Drake has left us. I will not hide it from you, but say it openly – he has deserted his post, and by this action caused many others to likewise abandon the fort. Be assured it was his decision alone and done by no order of the council. Since his going, the council has met and decided that Mr Drake has forfeited the governorship. In his stead – and that you may not be leader-less in our extremity – the council has elected me governor. It is a position I intend to hold with honour, and as a surety to which, I make this promise to you now – whatever fate deals to us, I will be the last man to leave the fort.

'We have signalled the southern ships to return upriver here to their proper stations. A messenger has been sent to the *Prince George*, ordering her to fall down and anchor by the fort. In short, preparations for an orderly retreat from the fort are in hand – should such a retreat prove necessary. But for the present we must not neglect to do all that we are able to do for ourselves.

'I believe the fort may yet be held. And should you, by a stout defence, hold her on behalf of the company, the company has means to be grateful. As an earnest of the company's gratitude, I pledge a reward of three chests of rupees to be divided among you promptly upon the enemy's withdrawal.

'Every man to his post now, and God be with us.'

All the time that Mr Holwell spoke, shots were fired, both by the Moors and by us. Being close by, I heard him, as did perhaps thirty others near at hand on the wall, but most were too distant or too fully engaged with the enemy to very much care about our new governor and his pretty speech. Every man gave a more lively interest to his own self-preservation than to any thought of miraculously beating back the enemy for silver.

But the new governor was at least no coward and, having made his speech, he moved along the parapet offering grim-faced encouragement and helping with the cotton bales to shore up the battered walls. He also went to the yard below to urge the soldiers who lurked under cover there to return to the fray upon the walls (for the inebriates among them, I offer neither reason nor excuse – though most of those were Dutchmen).

How we held the Moors off till nightfall I know not. But there was no sleep on the walls that night, for we were much reduced in our numbers and there was a fear of a Moorish escalade in the darkness. Several times in the night there were shouts of warning and musket-shot, but the Moors made no attempt to throw their ladders up against the walls, nor was there any general assault.

When morning came I looked at the soldiers about me and there was not a face among them had anything of hope in it. And then the Moorish cannon opened upon us. Their infantry attacked across the open ground. But for each Moor that we killed now, there were ten to replace him, whilst within the fort every mortality and injury was a loss irreplaceable.

At midday the Moors, as was their custom, desisted from the battle to refresh themselves and the raking fire which galled us suddenly ceased. I went wearily to the bastion overlooking the river. It had been an ever-decreasing hope for the ships' return, or the arrival of the *Prince George* from the northward, that had kept us at our stations throughout the morning. But on the river by the fort there was not one vessel. There was an angry despair now among the soldiers on the bastion, for they saw the evidence of our abandonment written upon the water's empty face. Some talked openly of hanging Drake and the ships' captains. But as many talked of surrender, and of trusting to God as our last shield against the barbarities of the Moors.

With a heavy heart I came down from the bastion and went to seek out the Reverend Bellamy.

The room where the surgeon washed was now more like to a charnel-house. I did not go inside, but stood at the door till Bellamy saw me and came out to the verandah. We stood by Edward's palanquin.

'There is a boat waiting at the Saltpetre Ghat,' Bellamy said to me at once. He reached into Edward's palanquin and to my astonishment drew out first a bandolier, and then a Dutch artilleryman's hat. 'You are a deserter now, a Dutchman, going to join the nawab's artillery. Have you any Dutch?'

'No.'

'Then use French if you are stopped. But not a word of English. You will take these letters to Mrs Watts in Chandernagore.' He drew a package from the palanquin where he had secreted it. 'The boatman expects a European. You must say to him "Richmond".'

'Richmond,' said I, struck by the strangeness of it and by these careful preparations he had made.

'He will know by this you are to be taken to Chandernagore. You may trust the boatman for your carriage there, but nothing beside. Keep the letters always about you. And you can take no weapon.' He indicated the pistol in my hand and, seeing my doubt, said, 'You must pass through the nawab's line. They will either have the pistol from you or they will kill you for it.'

I set the pistol down by the palanquin. 'What of Edward?' said I.

'What of any of us, Mr Douglas?' Bellamy went down the steps, urging me to come with him now. Edward was sleeping now, and with a last look and a silent prayer, I left him.

We crossed to the stables and into the blacksmith's forge. Bellamy spoke briefly with the smith and then turned to me.

'Put on the bandolier now. Godspeed, Mr Douglas.' He gave me his hand and then left me in the smith's care.

I followed on the smith's heels through the stable-yard, where the press and confusion of the Armenian and Portuguese women and children was very great. Once clear of them we crossed the square to where a number of storehouses were set hard against the fort's western wall.

Going after the smith into the last of these, I saw that there were small anchors in there and rope and all manner of things for the boats. These goods were tight-packed and the air very foul, so that no one had taken refuge in the place. We clambered over the pieces and then the smith got down on his knees and opened a trapdoor in the floor. There was a storage chamber beneath. I followed him down into it and found there a tunnel going from the chamber. He told me it went under the west wall and out to the Great Ghat. The tunnel was lit by daylight from its west end, for at that end was a stout grill of iron bars through which could be seen the ghat and the river.

'Wait here,' said the smith and crawled along the tunnel and did some operation to the bars with a tool he had there, and then he removed them and came back to me. 'You will be straight onto the ghat. And the Moors are now in position to fire at you there. Get yourself to some protection and quickly.' He laid his broad hand upon my shoulder and thrust me down on my knees and into the tunnel.

The Dutch hat bunched in my hand, I crawled forward. I stopped by the opening and knelt there for some while, listening to the musket-shot and the cannon.

Then behind me the smith said, 'I must re-fix the bars, lad. And you must either come back now or go on.'

I took a breath for courage. And then I clambered out, turned toward the Saltpetre Ghat and ran.

*

I was shot at almost at once, from both before and behind, but it was not a heavy fire and my fear gave me wings, though the fifty yards from the fort's wall to the first house seemed like a thousand. But halfway across, I sensed the Moors had ceased firing upon me, having seen the Dutch hat that I waved with great vigour to signify myself as a deserter, and they now turned their fire upon our soldiers on the parapet to safeguard my escape. When I reached that first house, I dived in with the Moors to take cover from my fellows in the fort. The Moors there laughed and congratulated my bold escape, and I took advantage of their temporary good humour, gesturing back through their lines as if I must now seek out my Dutch countrymen. They turned me about to confirm that I carried no weapon, then set me loose. I went north-east past Mr Tooke's house, the Moors there paying me no mind, taking me now for one their European mercenaries.

From Tooke's house I went to the Saltpetre Warehouse, which was burning, and from there down to the Saltpetre Ghat, where a solitary boat was tied. There was no boatman and I wondered if I should simply take the boat and flee, but then the boatman came out from his hiding place, clearly in some terror.

'Richmond,' said I.

'Yes, yes.' While he hurried to untie the rope, I got in and lay down beneath the arched awning at the bow. Then he shoved off and leapt aboard. From beneath my cover, I saw him take up the oars and commence to row us rapidly out into the river.

After some minutes and our vessel not having been fired upon, I ventured to raise myself.

And the first dreadful sight I saw was the *Prince George*. She was aground on the east bank, and burning, keeled over so near to the shore she was hid from the fort and her smoke mingled with the smoke rising from the warehouses. For all they knew in the fort, she was still afloat and still their last hope of rescue. From my place of safety, I now watched that last hope burning to the waterline.

Shouting and screaming then erupted from the fort, and I turned and saw the Moors swarming along the Great Ghat and into the fort through the wide-open river-gate. Other Moors leaned scaling-ladders against the walls and climbed onto the parapets.

They had beaten like breaking waves against the fort for days, and at last they had forced a fatal opening. There was shooting and our men fell from the parapet like fledglings from a nest. The East India Company flag was struck. The nawab's colours were raised. The shooting increased for a minute, and the cries, and then the musketshots slowly died to nothing.

Our boat found the current and we turned upriver. The captured fort and the burning town fell away and soon there was only the black smoke to mark them far behind us.

Calcutta was lost. I can say no more.

CHAPTER TWELVE

'Will you have cake, Mr Douglas?' said Mrs Watts, and, when I declined the plate she held out to me, she hesitated before putting it aside. 'You will say if you require anything. I trust that you will ask me.'

'Truly, it is enough that I am here,' said I and thanked her again for her concern and the kindness she had shown to me. Knowing very well that she was in some anxiety to open the Reverend Bellamy's package, I told her that I was no invalid and that she might leave me and go in to peruse the reverend's letters in privacy. But she would not go till my urging of her a second time, and then she rose at last and touched my shoulder and left me upon the balcony.

I was not the first to arrive in Chandernagore from Calcutta, for there were some had escaped Fort William and fled overland before crossing the river here. My own belated arrival was a circumstance for which I was now exceedingly thankful, for I had thereby been spared the probing inquisition to which Mrs Watts had told me the French governor, Renault, and his second, Monsieur Law, had subjected the early-arriving refugees. As to myself, I had simply disembarked at the ghat below Fort Orleans and made myself known to the nearest

French officer. He it was who had escorted me to Mrs Watts's temporary apartments within the fort.

Now I sat upon her balcony and drank the tea that her servant had brought for me, and everything that had happened in the past few weeks, since I had last seen her in Cossimbazaar, seemed a nightmare from which I was but newly awoken. Her daughter Amelia played with a doll at the far corner of the balcony, but the girl did not speak with me. It was as though I still carried in my person some evil vibration of the horrors I had witnessed and that by some deep and healthy instinct the girl kept her distance from me, which she was not wont to do before.

It was some while before Mrs Watts returned. She sat then at the far side of the small table from me and watched her daughter pensively. After a time, she said, 'You may go in now, Amelia. Ayah has a treat for you.' Amelia rose without demur and looked at me glancingly and went in. Then Mrs Watts turned to me. 'I would not press you, Mr Douglas, for that you would not wish to remember.'

'It would be very little, then, that I might tell you.'

'The French have been very good to us. I have sent to ask Monsieur Renault to allocate some suitable quarters for you.'

I tried to thank her but the words caught in my throat and tears unaccountably rose in my eyes. It was exhaustion, I suppose, and she feigned not to notice, but turned away a moment and looked down at the fort's yard while I recovered myself. I said, 'Mr Watts was very well when I left him. But that is three weeks now.'

'William and Mr Cole are held hostage with the nawab's army. The Dutch governor in Chinsurah had communication with William as the army went down to Calcutta.'

'Then he is alive.'

'He was alive then. Since that time, I have heard nothing.'

'I am sure that he is safe,' said I, though in truth with little certainty of it after what I had witnessed

She smiled weakly and I saw what slight comfort my words had given her. I told her of Edward then, of how I had met with him on my way to Calcutta, of his injury and of how I had left him.

Then Mrs Watts told me of what had passed at Cossimbazaar after my quitting of it. She began with the worst – Lieutenant Eliot, believing himself dishonoured by both the surrender of the fort and his subsequent ill-treatment at the hands of the enemy, had blown his own brains out with a pistol. Hastings and Marriot, two writers like myself, had been out at the *aurangs* (which are the native weaving-houses) when our factory was seized. They had managed to find refuge in the French factory at Cossimbazaar, but this only after running the gauntlet of the nawab's troops in the town, who had robbed them of all they possessed but their clothes. Batson and Sykes had escaped the factory and been given refuge by the French. But Chambers had been sent to the public prison in Murshidabad, there to be incarcerated with the city's common criminals for some two weeks before the chiefs of the French and Dutch factories had stood surety and taken him into their care. He was now being nursed back to health in Chandernagore, not a mile from where we sat.

Harry Khan, alas, still languished in the nawab's prison.

It is a measure of the mark Calcutta's fall had made upon me that this dreadful litany from Mrs Watts filled me with something very like relief. I had not dared to hope that, the nawab's wrath once unleashed upon Cossimbazaar, so many should now survive.

Mrs Watts, well perceiving my want of strength, had upon my arrival set her cooks to prepare something for me, which was now brought out to us. She took herself a small plate that she might keep me company as I ate and, by such considerations and by her sympathetic ear and a little French wine, she began to draw from me – without my knowing it to begin – the story of all that had befallen Calcutta. But once I had begun in earnest, I could not stop myself from speaking, and I own that it came from me with all the candour and force of a first confession and the food unfinished and put aside.

By the time I was done, night was falling. Bats flitted over the fort's walls from the river and temple music drifted up from the black town. For some while she sat silent and stared at nothing, for I had spared her but little of the tale.

At last she said, 'You will please to write this all down in a letter to my husband, Mr Douglas. In the morning, once you have rested.' I nodded, and she said, 'Mind that you do it before you have spoken with the others who have come up from Calcutta. They will not all of them agree with you.'

'The truth will not change.'

'The tellings will change. There shall be such a rich mud of lies from this that you shall hardly understand that you were there. Some will attempt the truth, but the truth is never unmingled. Before you speak with any others, write down all that you have been witness to.'

In obedience to Mrs Watts's request, I spent all the next morning in penning my recollection of the events I had witnessed, which was a melancholy task, and at midday took the papers to her apartments. Upon my being announced, she came herself to the door and received the pages into her own hand, but she did not invite me inside and I saw that she was very much distracted.

'It is not for myself,' she said in reply when I voiced my concern. 'But have you not spoken to anyone this morning?'

'At your request I have spoken with no one but the servants of my billet since I left you.'

'I fear there has been a terrible incident. I am at pains now to discover the truth of it. There are reports – but this must wait. Monsieur Renault is with me even now.'

I enquired, in some perplexity, as to the nature of the incident.

'They say there has been a great slaughter in Fort William. But please, I know no more than this. I must go now.' She folded the pages I had written and withdrew.

My billet was in a house belonging to a captain of one of the French Compagnie ships in the white town, so that in coming to Mrs Watts's apartment inside the fort, I had first passed through the settlement. And there by the settlement's main church I had seen many refugees from Calcutta gathered, though I had not stopped to speak with them. I now returned to this place and sought among the topasses (which was most of them) for any with good English, who had recently arrived from Calcutta. Presently I found a fellow who answered, and, as I spoke with him, two others pushed their way to me and now all three broke out with their stories of what they had seen the evening of Fort William's surrender, when I had escaped.

And among the confused recountings it seemed there was scarce one plain fact that stood uncontradicted. Every European on the walls had been killed. No, that was not true, those had been spared. The Armenian women had been taken by the Moors first. No, that was a lie. Hardly was one claim made but it was straightaway refuted by another. The three agreed only in a general lamentation that most of their own women and children had been stolen by the Moors. They demanded to know of me what was being done by the British to recover these stolen people to their families.

'I am sure they will be well. I am sure that everything is being done,' I said, but when I saw the hollowness of my words in their eyes I was ashamed. For truly, I was sure of nothing in this regard and I had no wish to make false promises or hold out cruel hope to people so desperate. 'You must ask Gouverneur Renault,' said I, but as I tried to get by them, I saw distrust of me now on every face. They had seen Drake and the others abandon them. And though from several remarks I knew they recognized me as one who had been on the walls till near the end, yet, as a servant of the company, I was not excused the general opprobrium. Some in the crowd jostled me and muttered against me and a mischief might have been done to my person had a Jesuit priest not then appeared on the church steps with a distribution of clothes to distract their attention.

He signalled to me with his eyes and I moved quickly away.

Chastened by this ugly encounter, I repaired to the bazaar near the river. Under Edward's tutelage I had learned how quickly information might move with the trade on the river, the price of opium in Murshidabad being almost instantly known at every bazaar all the way down to the Bay of Bengal. I expected, then, to discover from the traders what had happened, but on arriving at the bazaar I saw two French soldiers of the garrison standing by several carts and the market people pressing in upon them with all manner of vegetables and foodstuffs. The two soldiers were buying steadily and many coolies were at work there loading the carts. It was a quite prodigious quantity they were loading, and this, and the unusually late hour for a trade conducted by custom in the early morning, made it seem a very copy of our own company's preparations in Calcutta before the nawab's descent upon us. I confess, the likeness to it somewhat unsettled me.

One of the soldiers, then noticing my observation of what they did, called out in French to know what I did there.

'I am seeking a friend,' I answered, to which he replied, very surly, that he believed I should not find any such person there. His companion continued to buy, and I knew I should have no joy of the market-men for the present.

So I went south then, first along the ghat and then a long way beyond, past the moored boats and half a mile further on to where the crossing point was, below the town. Here barges plied to and fro linking the town of Chandernagore to the village on the other side and to the broad track there that led down to Calcutta. And here, now, were refugees from Calcutta and in plenty, both on the far side awaiting barges and nearer to me in an encampment beneath the trees.

But though I waited at the place for some hours, not a single European came over the river who could give me an account of any such incident as Mrs Watts feared had happened. From the topasses and Hindoos of the encampment I heard only an absurd tale, to which I gave no credence, of the captured Europeans having been imprisoned in the Black Hole together and turning one upon another like ravening beasts, and so I returned to the town.

I went to the river the next morning also, but by then the tide of wretched humanity fleeing the nawab's depredations was at the ebb. I learned no more and soon returned to my billet at the captain's house. This captain I never saw, for he stayed out at his ship and I was alone in the house and very glad of it. In the afternoon, much enervated by the heat, I did myself down upon a stone bench in the captain's garden. A servant brought me water and I sipped it from a beaker while I considered, for the first time since leaving Fort William, what my own personal position was and what was my duty now as a servant of the company. And whether, indeed, there was any future remaining for either myself or the company in the province of Bengal. Our greatest pride, Calcutta, the richest of all the European settlements here, was lost. The factory at Cossimbazaar was taken. I had no doubt but that the other company factories at Dacca, Jaglia, Balasore and Bulramgurry must soon fall prey to the nawab, if they had not done so already. In short, the turn of fortune's wheel had been so sudden and of such a degree as to reduce us from being the greatest European company in Bengal to the least, not only lower than the French but lower than the Dutch and Danes. Even the single Prussian Agent, Mr Young, might be deemed above us. Though the height of our fall seemed scarcely credible, to all outward appearance we were now upon an equal footing with the Armenians.

And from several unguarded remarks I had heard about the town, from the French traders and soldiers I met in going about the streets, it was clear that whatever hospitality and sympathy the French might extend to individual ones of us, they found the whole of the British actions in Calcutta very blameable. They truly believed that we had arrogantly provoked the nawab's ire. And from the reports they now had from the refugees, they were fully convinced that we had thereafter played the part of knaves and despicable cowards.

It was while turning these unhappy thoughts through my mind that I heard a bold step come across the hard earthen path toward me. I sat up. A young French officer stopped before me.

'Monsieur Douglas. You are invited to attend the Gouverneur Renault.'

I had the impression he had learned the line by heart, for his English was heavily accented and when I asked him, 'Pourquoi?' I received no answer but a shrug and an open-handed gesture toward the steps.

Governor Renault was not alone. He had with him Monsieur Law, the chief of the French factory in Cossimbazaar, whom I had met. I knew him to be a man both liked and respected by all the nations that traded upon the river and also the Hindoos and Moors. I had conversed with him during my brief time in Cossimbazaar, and now we exchanged some pleasantries in French, though much stilted by the unhappy circumstances of our meeting. There was also an officer who had lost one arm, and Law introduced this fellow to me as the garrison's chief of artillery, Terraneau. My escort, the young officer, took up a place at Renault's desk and brought quill and paper to hand. Renault addressed me in French.

'We have some questions regarding the dispositions of the nawab's forces. You will understand our concerns. I have asked Adjutant Cordet to take notes for our later reference.'

'Sir, I am no soldier.'

'Soldiers I have and in number. It is proper information as to the nawab's mode of warfare I am in need of.'

'Mrs Watts has suggested that you could assist us,' said Law. 'If you would prefer, I shall call her here.'

I knew that Law would not lie. And I knew also that their need was real, for the nawab was but a few days' march to the south of them.

'There is little I can tell you. The fighting was very confused.'

'What guns were used against the fort?' asked the artilleryman, Terrneau.

I told him how musketry had been employed in the investment of the town, and then continually thereafter to overwhelm our outer defences. He asked how long the outer defences held. I told him. When he expressed surprise, I said, 'They would have fallen more quickly yet, but for the actions of one of your own countrymen, Le Baume.'

Now Renault and Tourneau glanced at the young fellow, Cordet, who kept his eyes fixed on the paper in front of him. There was meaning in their looks, but a meaning to which I had no key.

'Did they use no cannon?' enquired Law.

I told them of the French artilleryman doing service on the nawab's side. 'He appeared to have no want of powder or shot,' said I, but none of them made any reaction to this, which made me doubt now those rumours we had heard in Fort William of the French having sent both powder and shot to the nawab's aid. When they enquired about this Frenchman, I said, 'He was a marquis.'

'The marquis de Saint-Jacques?' queried Law wearily.

I said yes, that I believed that was the fellow's name.

'He is not a marquis,' said Renault. 'He is a renegade. A deserter. He is no more a marquis than is my footman.'

'We had two eighteen-pounders at a battery outside the fort. We were forced to abandon them when we withdrew inside the walls. They were not properly spiked. This fellow – the marquis – he was able to turn them on us to some effect.'

He asked me who worked the cannon. I told them that we suspected it was French deserters and Dutchmen.

'The shot breached your walls?'

'They did not need to. Once the Moors were in the church and the higher houses without, they shot down on us. Their flame-arrows were a continual harassment.' Law remarked that I had seen the church here in Chandernagore, to which I replied that I believed it was not as tall as St Anne's in Calcutta. 'But you would know better than I what command it has of the parapet.'

'You believe it should be razed?'

'I am not a soldier.'

'More a diplomat it seems,' remarked Law with a smile.

On the desk, a large sheet of paper was now spread, upon which Cordet drew a quick and broadly accurate sketch of Fort William and the river, and then he handed me the quill. Under detailed questioning then from Terraneau, I attempted to recall the exact disposition of our guns on the bastions and the emplacements of the Moors that had wrought the greatest havoc with us. I marked them all down on the sketch. After several minutes of this, there came a pause. We all of us thoughtfully studied the annotated drawing. And then Cordet placed his finger upon the line marking the river by Fort William.

'You have not mentioned the cannon aboard the ships.'

'The women went aboard early in the siege.'

'Yes. But what use was made of the cannon?'

'They did not dare to fire here for fear of striking the fort.'

'But here' – he touched the sketch – 'where the enemy also attacked from. The ship's line of fire was clear.'

'I understand that the ships came under fire from the enemy. I expect their captains thought it prudent to withdraw themselves out of range, downriver.'

'Once Governor Drake was aboard,' murmured Terraneau.

'There were women aboard also.'

'The ships did not fire at any time?' pressed Cordet.

'I believe there may have been some musketry.'

The feebleness of these answers was apparent even to me, and I felt a flush of shame that there should be no better defence of my countrymen's actions. There was a silence while all these Frenchmen considered the sketch, and the part played – and not played – by our ships.

Law at last took pity on me, remarking lightly that we were none of us there sailors. He suggested that as my own post had been in the fort, it was pointless to now pursue any further 'la question nautique'.

Their enquiries returned to the artillery in the fort. After some minutes more I could give them no further enlightenment, and Renault and Law then thanked me most graciously for my attendance upon them, whereupon I took my leave.

I had not yet reached the fort gates, nor yet quite overcome the embarrassment and shame I had felt before my French questioners, when the adjutant, Cordet, hailed me. I stopped and he came quickly across the square to me.

'Gouverneur Renault invites you to take a room inside the fort while you remain in Chandernagore.'

'I am settled where I am. But I would be obliged if you would thank him for me.'

'The gouverneur asked me to tell you also that we expect the nawab's troops to pass through Chandernagore very soon. We are informed he returns to Murshidabad with the greater part of his army. We are in preparation for some disturbance.'

'They would not attack you.'

'We have given him no reason for it. But his soldiers are drunk with the joy of war. Who can say what they may do? We are advising all our Compagnie people to keep to their houses while the nawab's soldiers pass.'

'Then I shall do the same.'

'The room in the fort is available to you.'

'I pray that the gouverneur will not think my refusal uncivil. But I have seen what safety may be expected within a fort.'

Cordet assured me that no offence would be taken, and we were about to part when he said, 'Your praise of Le Baume, Monsieur Douglas. Was that to flatter us?'

'Had every one of us in Calcutta fought as bravely as Le Baume, we had not now found ourselves in our present unhappy situation.'

This answer brought a thoughtful cast to Cordet's face, the reason for which I was still puzzling on after we had bid each other good day and gone our separate ways.

CHAPTER THIRTEEN

*T*hat there was some good reason for the French apprehensions was proven the following morning when the first of the nawab's triumphant soldiers, returning north from Calcutta, crossed the river below the town and began to despoil the villages to the south and west of Chandernagore. At the height of the alarm Cordet called on me briefly to inform me of the state of affairs and to ask if my name might be added to the list of volunteers ready to stand to the defence of the town.

'Or I can add your name to those requesting a place out on the ships,' said he.

'I will assist in the fort.'

'But of course.'

He added my name to his list and bade me listen for two cannon shots from the south-east bastion, for this would be the signal to come into the fort to be armed. He seemed very eager for the action, as if the prospect of an investment of the town did not trouble him, but that he almost welcomed it. His ignorance, in fact, reminded me of my own before the Calcutta besiegement.

But the signal was never made and, though there were some envoys rode back and forth between Gouverneur Renault and the nawab's temporary encampment a few miles beyond the black town, the alarm soon passed. The worst that happened in the settlement was that a troop of the nawab's cavalrymen rode through it, behaving very haughty and uncivil toward all they met, both European and native, and leaving after them a most unpleasant air of threat.

Within days, the nawab had broken camp and marched northward. And though it was not at first generally known exactly how much Renault had paid to buy this peace from the nawab (it was, it transpired, four lakhs of rupees, which is four hundred thousand) it was universally and immediately understood throughout the town that the extortion had been no trifling matter. In consequence the mutterings against the pusillanimity and arrogance of us British, at whose door they laid the blame for their loss, became much increased. And I believe it was at least in part to oil upon these waters that Mrs Watts made up a small party of the French women to go with her down to the garden by the river, south of the black town, and there spend some time at leisure, with no thought of the nawab. She decided that I should join them and presented me with a sketchbook, that I might amuse them with my drawing. I did not like to go, but knew not how to refuse her.

'That is very pretty, monsieur.'

'It is the sitter.'

'Madame Gordonne is handsome. It is your picture that is pretty.'

I continued with my work, seated propped against a tree with my sketchbook upon my knees. It had been, I own, an enjoyable morning, both from the company of the ladies and from the sketching, which two things lifted my cares almost equally. There was a pavilion on the bank near to the river and Mrs Watts was now directing the servants as to where the table for our refreshments should be unfolded. The mademoiselle, who had joined us, now pointed at my sketch.

'What is that?' Her brow creased as she looked from the portrait to the sitter to find the blemish. It was a small ant and I brushed it from the paper. When I glanced at her, she frowned very prettily and spread her skirts and knelt by me.

121

She conversed with Madame Gordonne for a time then, the small gossip of the town, and I continued with my work, and when I had finished the sketch I leaned the pad for the mademoiselle to see. Upon her admiring it and praising the likeness, the sitter, Madame Gordonne, rose from the bench and came to see. She had a more critical eye than the other, but after studying it a minute, she asked if she could have it, which pleased me and I gave it her.

Then the mademoiselle asked if she might sit for me, and at my agreement she went promptly to the bench.

'Shall we not first take some refreshment?' I wondered, for the others were now moving toward the pavilion and the unfolded table. But she would not hear of it, saying that nothing in Bengal ever happened when it should and that it must be some good while before the servants had made everything ready.

Spoilt, thought I, and wilful. For my drawing master had taught me to seize first upon the character, else there be no truth in the likeness.

And indeed, the portrait grew very easily beneath my hand, though she turned her head often and tried to draw me in conversation. When I told her that if the sketch was to be finished that hour she must expect my silence, she continued to question me regardless.

'And what is in this Orkney?'

'Very little.'

'Did you like to live there?'

'Well enough.'

'But not well enough to stay.'

'Mademoiselle—'

'Antoinette.'

'Unless you wish for an inferior likeness, mademoiselle, I must ignore you. Please do not think me uncivil.'

'Uncivil or only English?'

'Orkney is not in England,' said I beneath my breath, and I continued with her eyes and got them very well. But after fifteen minutes more and the sketch not quite done, she grew bored with her sitting. I noticed her glancing frequently toward the other women who were now taking their refreshment by the pavilion, and she soon spoke of joining them and returning later to the sitting. But not wanting to break from it and liking what I had done, I spoke again that she might be distracted from the others and stay at the bench and so let me finish.

And it was now, with me very intent upon the sketch, and half-speaking with her and less than half-listening, that Cordet arrived at the pavilion. I saw him from the corner of my eye and thought no more of it, but continued with my drawing. But then the mademoiselle quite suddenly stopped in her talking. I glanced up and saw that she had seen Cordet and that she was watching him now as he strode toward us from the pavilion. And I saw also that there was some consternation in her.

'Mademoiselle?' said I.

'Antoinette,' Cordet called to her sharply.

'You are not my keeper,' she said very low, so that the ladies might not hear it.

'Come away,' said he.

I stood now and began to explain that we were together here only that she might sit for me, for I saw at once that he had misunderstood our being apart from the others. I stepped toward him and held up the sketchbook. He was much vexed though and could not immediately calm himself.

'You are wanted with the other ladies,' he told her.

'You are a fool, Sébastien,' she replied, rising, and she turned very pointedly and thanked me and hoped that I might bring the sketch to show her. She looked at him in scorn and then went past him and on to the pavilion.

He looked from her to the sketch and then to me. My sketchbook was still held out to him and now at last he saw the drawing. And I saw from the change in his face that he immediately knew that he had wronged her.

'I have made four other likenesses already.'

'I did not – I had not seen—'

'She has a strong face. But I do not think I have quite got her chin,' said I, and stepped up to him so that we might inspect my work and he be relieved of his confusion. I made some further remarks on the picture and he was soon in command of himself. He bowed his head over the picture now that I might not see his embarrassment. But then he seemed to wish to explain himself to me and, upon my remarking the fineness of the nose, he said, 'Yes, it is like all the women in our family.' He looked up at me. 'Antoinette is my cousin.'

'Ah,' said I.

And as we walked to join the others at the pavilion, he was sufficiently recovered to remark ruefully to me that the sharpness of Antoinette's tongue was likewise common to all the female line of Cordets.

I had thought the incident unnoticed by the others, but as I escorted Mrs Watts back to her apartments in the fort some time later, she remembered it to me and said, with amusement, that she had feared for a moment she might have to play the part of a second in a duel.

'It was a misunderstanding.'

'And what duel is not? But do not take it ill, Alistair. God knows, there has been little enough to make us smile these past weeks.'

But I was not inclined to dismiss the small incident as lightly as she, for it seemed to bespeak the great mistrust that the French had of us in the town. Not liking now to endure either their contempt or their pity, I accepted none of the invitations that came to me thereafter, though they were for simple hospitality's sake offered me, but confined myself instead to the captain's house and its gardens and wrote letters to those in England I had promised. My father and mother were both gone now, but I knew of some that would fear for me when they heard of Calcutta's fall. Apart from these personal letters, I wrote also to a young schoolfellow of mine, William Jones, a boy several years my junior, but of such prodigious linguistic gifts (as all the world has come to know) that he had been able to tutor me in some Persian phrases before I left London and he, I think, not ten years of age. To him I had promised report of any noteworthy thing in his line that fell under my notice. This was now a particular blessing, for with Jones I felt no need to linger on Calcutta's fall, it being a subject that would excite his interest to a much lesser degree than would the small manuscript of

Hindoo tales that I had purchased for him from a scribe in the Chandernagore market.

Also, there was a small library in the captain's house, and so I spent many quiet hours there, over several days, with Voltaire and Molière and Rabelais.

And it was also while I was in this library that a peon brought me a note from Mrs Watts. I read it once and then a second time with just as much bewilderment as the first, for it was an invitation to come and dine with her and Mr Watts.

'The nawab released them at Hugli,' said Mrs Watts, leading me along the passage. 'A Dutchman brought them down.'

'And they are well?'

'They have not been treated well. William may tell you.'

She showed me in to the drawing-room of her apartments and the two gentlemen rose to greet me. We shook hands warmly and there were many glad words said, for they were as pleased as I to find ourselves gathered together and all alive. Since parting at the nawab's camp we had each of us had fair reason to suppose that it might end quite otherwise.

Cole was the more wasted of the two, and he apologized to me now and said that he found himself a little weaker than he had supposed. Mrs Watts called a servant for him and Mr Cole then left us to go to his room.

'I have read your pages on the siege,' Watts said to me. 'You show no knowledge that Mr Cole and I were for the while prisoners in the nawab's camp out by the ditch.'

'I never heard of it. I am sure no one of us did within the fort.'

'We heard the guns and much talk, but saw nothing. We had supposed the fort's surrender must be the worst of it. Your account suggests we were mistaken.'

'I wrote only what I witnessed, sir. I cast no aspersion on any man's character.'

'Character, yes. There will, no doubt, be much talk of character before this is ended. Letters must be already drafted and awaiting packet boats to Madras and London. But you wrote nothing of Sri Babu or Omichand.'

'Once I came to Calcutta I had no more dealings with Sri Babu. Omichand I never met with.'

'We have asked Alistair here to dine with us, William,' said Mrs Watts.

'All in good time.' He turned to me again. 'I may tell you I have come to doubt the good intentions of Sri Babu's master, Coja Wajid. We have heard his name connected too often with the French. And have you formed any notion why Mr Drake imprisoned Omichand?'

I related as much as I knew of the affair – of the boat taken on the river and the coded messages that were talked of in Calcutta before Omichand's arrest. Also I told him of the guns found in Omichand's house, the fire and the vile murders done there by the *jamindar*. 'Many suspected this *jamindar* took word of our dispositions to the Moors when he escaped.'

'You did not write this down.'

'It was but a rumour, sir. And there were so many rumours there had been no end to the writing of them. On the last day of the siege Mr Howell asked Omichand to write a letter to the nawab, requesting a parley. I believe this was done.'

'It was. And after the siege, Omichand came to the nawab's camp and saw us privately to offer his effusive commiserations. He did not seem inclined, however, to forgive Mr Drake.'

We spoke then for some while of various people caught up in the Fort William siege, and all too often, to the hopeful mention of a name, I had to answer with the terrible reply, 'He too was killed.' I asked after Edward, of course, but Watts had heard nothing. Edward was but one more of the nawab's victims as yet unaccounted for. After a time, Mrs Watts absented herself from the room, and only then did Mr Watts lean forward in his chair and with lowered voice ask me what I knew of the horror in the Black Hole prison.

I confessed that I knew nothing.

'Then I will spare you such dreadful details as I have heard. Sufficient to say that the night the fort fell as many as two hundred

Europeans were locked in the Black Hole prison. By morning, not thirty were left alive.'

'But that is not possible. The Black Hole could not hold so many. It is a space no bigger than this room.'

'We have had the report from several quarters, Alistair. And Gouverneur Renault has heard similar reports from his people. For myself, I am certain there was the foulest murder done that night. Not once only, but many times over.'

I remembered now the talk among the refugees at the southern encampment – the incredible tale of Europeans turning upon one another like beasts.

'Have you no names?' said I.

He turned his head sadly.

The air in the room seemed suddenly stifling to me then. The many deaths I had witnessed at the siege had been horror enough, but a wanton slaughter of prisoners was a barbarity beyond warfare. My mind went to those men and women I knew whom I had left behind at my escape.

'Had I stayed—'

'Then you had most certainly joined them in the Black Hole and become yourself another wretched victim. You have done good service, Alistair, both in your going to the fort and in your coming away. And you may do some further service yet, should you be willing.'

What useful service I might do the company was very difficult to see, the whole of our enterprise in Bengal having been so thoroughly broken now and plundered. My several days of reflection had discovered no improvement to either the company's prospects or my own. Indeed my expectation now was that there would be an undignified scramble by the Bengali survivors, such as myself, for any vacant positions in the Madras and Bombay presidencies. Those failing to secure a place must then be sent on the earliest passage back to England. And my own lack of seniority and connection must certainly mark me out as one of these first-leavers, so that I would be returned home within eighteen months of my sailing and nothing to show for the time between but the humiliation of defeat and the ignominious surrender of the company's best jewel.

'May I call upon you, then, Alistair?'

There was now in his eye an unsettling gleam of determination and a stern fixity of face. It was a look I had seen before, and often, in the Highlands. The iron had entered Mr Watts's soul.

'In what capacity, sir?'

'That is yet to see. But for now I must know only if I may depend upon you.'

With some hesitation, and no certainty of it, I heard myself answer him, 'Aye.'

Fort Orleans was set back from the river somewhat further than Fort William in Calcutta, so that there was a broad apron of ground between the walls and the ghat. It was while walking across this ground the next morning that I spied Cordet, calling instructions to a lascar (that is to say, a native sailor) on the sloop that was tied there. I went over to him and he congratulated me on the safe return of Mr Watts and Mr Cole. He asked me if they were now quite comfortable and I assured him that they were and very grateful of the gouverneur's hospitality. He nodded and turned to give further instructions to the lascar now dragging a sea-trunk across the deck.

'You are not leaving us?' said I and, upon Cordet's admitting that he was, I asked him then if all the European boats now moved freely upon the river.

'All but you British. As you know already, Monsieur Douglas.' He nodded toward the Dutch pilot with whom he had seen me speaking. 'I expect he also told you that Governor Drake and his friends have stopped at Fulta?'

The pilot had told me that precisely.

'Is the man reliable?' said I.

'He is a Dutchman,' said Cordet with a shrug, and then he called in a local dialect to a lascar on the sloop. The man answered at length and Cordet faced me again. 'These have come up from there. This fellow thinks the British have three ships and a schooner. He has heard that the others foundered on their way down from Calcutta.'

I was curious to know where Cordet might be bound.

'France?' said he to my enquiry. 'And what would I do in France now but plot against you British?'

'Which you may do well enough here,' said I, and he laughed. 'You are for Pondicherry, then.'

'I am. And there I will grow sleek and fat, if I do not first die from boredom. But you will excuse me now, Monsieur Douglas.' He went to speak with the sloop's captain and I did not wait, but went at once to seek out Mr Watts.

I was a stranger to the discussions between Mr Watts and Mr Cole that followed my report of our ships being at Fulta and a stranger also to the nature of the other information Watts received from the express couriers, the *cossids*, who had brought him letters from the south that morning. And so it was with no little surprise that I saw the palanquin arrive a few hours later at the gate of my lodgings and Watts stepping out from it and advancing toward the house purposefully with a large sealed packet in his hand.

I embarked for Fulta the same evening.

CHAPTER FOURTEEN

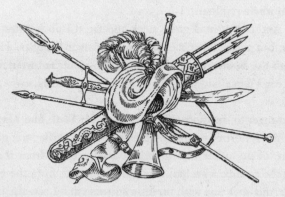

*A*t dawn there was a great stillness on the river and only the pilot
and I awake when our sloop came to Perrin's. I saw Kelsall's Octagon
and the ruin the Moors had made of it, and also the redoubt where
Thoresby had died. There was a small encampment of the nawab's
troops still at the place and, as our sloop went by, the Moors watched
us, but without interest, and soon turned away to rake the coals of their
fire. There was not a breath of wind, only the tide carried us, and up
ahead a heron rose with heavy wings from the river.

Cordet then came up from below.

He joined me at the rail but did not speak, for which I was thankful. The sloop moved slowly now around the river-bend and Calcutta
and Fort William came at last into view. From a distance, nothing
seemed changed, but as we drew nearer we saw the terrible devastation done by the Moorish burning all along the shore. Hardly a house
but had lost its roof, and everywhere there stood the blackened stubs
of trees and posts that had burned. There was no smoke now coming
from the buildings, but in the air there lingered the sharp smell of wet
ash and a worse smell that I could not at first identify. Cordet pointed

to the lumps beached at the high-water line upon the bank near the fort.

'They are not cotton bales,' he said to my suggestion, and very soon we could make them out clearly, and with a silent horror, for they were bodies, mostly women, the remains of them held together only by the Portuguese dresses in which they had drowned, the dresses but poorly protecting those remains from the vultures.

At the Great Ghat under the fort a fleet of small boats was tied, and one of these now cast off and cut across our bow before turning upriver. Upon its deck, amidst much other plunder, stood the harpsichord that Mrs Holwell's niece had played for us in Reverend Bellamy's drawing-room.

There was little movement else nearby the fort. The nawab's flag hung limp above the river gate. The Moors at their guns up on the bastions watched us. As we continued to fall slowly downriver we saw to the south of the fort that the Company House had been near to lev-elled and not only by the fires, for there had been some further demolition done there, quite singular.

We passed below the fort and beyond to the line of devastated build-ings along the southern shore, and then there were yet more burned-out hulls near the great blackened ribs of the *Prince George*. We moved steadily on and the beached bodies and the fort and the town passed from view behind us and last of all the Moors' outpost at Surnam's Garden. Then the riverbank was clear again and the sun fully risen and shining on the water and no sign that there was any human blight on the face of God's first creation.

Below Tanner's Fort, I brought out my sketchbook from my trunk. My charcoal moved quickly, and soon I had made a passable likeness of the bow and the broad river ahead of us.

'It is very fine,' said Cordet.

'It is trifling.'

'Most would be very happy to produce such a trifle.'

I turned the page and held out the sketchbook and charcoal, but he protested his own want of skill in the art and left me to go and speak with the pilot. I scanned the riverbank for some simple subject, but nothing took my eye till I noticed one of the lascars asleep near the anchor rope and curled like a cat. I then sat myself in the shade of the gunnel and commenced, with little hope of success, to attempt to capture the likeness. But I soon became absorbed in the labour (and no doubt it was a welcome diversion of mind after the sights of Calcutta) and I did not notice the time pass till the shade finally moved off the lascar and he awoke, screwing up his eyes against the sunlight.

'You would do well to keep that from him,' said Cordet quietly, and he reached over my shoulder and closed the sketchbook on my knees. I had not been aware of his standing there, nor could I guess how long he had done so. His look bade me to silence, but when the lascar was past us, I asked Cordet what he did – or what I had done. 'These are superstitious men. And your hand is too good. He could not mistake the likeness. It would not please him.'

'Had I known, I would not have begun it,' said I, and I opened the sketchbook and tore out the picture. But when he saw that I would throw it overboard he stopped me. He asked if he might keep it for a souvenir.

'It is yours.'

Taking my charcoal, I wrote the date on the sketch and he asked me then to sign it, so I marked it A.D.

'It is Alistair, is it not?'

'It is.'

'Sébastien,' said he, and gave me his hand and with a smile to himself murmured, 'As I believe you first heard from my cousin.'

The sloop being no great size and the air below deck stifling, we found ourselves for much of the day seeking refuge in that shade made by the mainsail. We neither one of us spoke for mere speech's sake, but made sure to find repose each in his own way and with no hindrance to the other. Mrs Watts had secured for me several volumes from the generosity of Mrs Renault, and I was now able to relieve my mind, to some degree, by a careful reading of the thoughts of Pascal. Cordet for his part kept some military manual to hand and interspersed his reading with frequent wanderings to the bow, where he would stand with his spyglass to his eye and scan the banks and the river south-ward.

The French flag at our stern had kept the Moorish boats clear of us, and when we came to Buj Buj, where stood the last of the nawab's forts above the delta, we had no trouble from them, though there were many boats tied near the fort showing the nawab's colours.

Some hours after, in the late afternoon, the captain called to us and directed our attention to the horizon up ahead. The mast-tops of the several ships were barely discernible to me. Another fifteen minutes and the pilot took the wheel again to get us safely over the shallows near Fulta.

There was no proper fort at Fulta. It was only a small town, a meagre Dutch settlement bearing no comparison with their stronghold at Chinsurah. Here were independent Dutch traders of small means and the houses of the Dutch pilots who hired themselves out to the ships of all nations upon the river. But it was not the poor settlement that drew our eye as we neared, but rather the British ships lying at anchor close in to the shore. For the British vessels formed a separate flotilla from the Fulta boats, and upon our approach there appeared at every rail a line of people – men, women and children – so abject that they neither hailed us nor waved but only stared at us like wraiths. Our captain did not like their appearance, nor yet the pestilential air that came out to us from landward, so he cut short our approach and dropped anchor. He had earlier told me that he would lie up at Fulta for the night, but now he would send me across to the British ships directly, for his intention was not to remain here, but to go further downriver before nightfall.

'You need not stay here,' said Cordet, who was standing beside me and regarding the British ships with a dismay almost the equal of my own. There was a filthy scum lying on the still waters near to the hulls and several of the women held up their children to us and, by pitiful gestures, made us understand their want of food. A boat was coming out to us. 'We will pass near to Ballasore,' he said. 'We shall put you down there or at some other place of your choosing.'

But our factory at Ballasore, though Cordet was not aware of it yet, we had already abandoned from fear of the nawab's violence.

'I must get down here, at least for a while,' said I, and I asked if there were provisions he might spare. Cordet consulted with the captain, who looked askance at me, and the invitation to sail on with them was repeated. 'Give me an hour upon the ships. If am not returned to you by then, do not wait for me.'

They gave me some sacks of rice to take in the boat and I bade them farewell and the boat took me across to the *Dodaly* (which was the vessel upon which I saw the most women and children).

The sacks of rice were hauled up after me, but I ordered my trunk to remain in the boat. The sacks were taken into the charge of an officer and two seamen who disappeared toward the foredeck with many desperate people trailing after them. The scene upon the main deck was truly dreadful. People had taken station on every part of it, with only some small gangways left clear. Clothes and old cotton had been strung up to provide shade, and there were people lying near who did not even turn to see my arrival, so deep were they lost in their fevers.

And then I saw Le Baume stepping over and around the wreckage of people and coming toward me. 'I cannot say that I am glad to see you here,' said he, taking my hand. 'It is a place to keep away from, as you see. But who has brought you?' He looked out to the sloop and the French flag on its stern.

'They are going further downriver tonight.'

'It would be my advice also,' he said quietly.

'It is a French officer by the name of Cordet.'

He started and looked at the sloop again, but in such a way now as made me think him no particular friend to the other Frenchman. Then he led me to see Manningham, who insisted upon my going across to the *Fort William*, which was the ship upon which Drake had taken up residence. And once there I found myself in the midst of those others who had abandoned us at the siege. Drake was there, and Frankland and Captain Grant, also the secretary Cooke. These, with Manningham and Le Baume, made the full complement of those who now heard the bare narrative of all that I had seen since their flight from the fort. Much they knew already from the natives, but much was new matter to them, and after hearing me, and reading the letters I now delivered from Mr Watts, they had many more questions for me. Several times we were interrupted by the noise of heated argument and bickering outside, for the *Fort William* was like to the *Dodaly* in the crowd of unhappy life strewn haphazardly across its decks.

Drake, though he might pretend otherwise, could not help but feel the near-inconceivable change that had happened since our last standing together in his room at the fort. Full of pride of his station, he had then been the undisputed governor of the Bengal presidency and ready to take umbrage at any slight. Indeed, by his actions, he had all but dared the nawab to descend on Calcutta and fight him. His fall from that lofty position had been brutal and swift and, I am sure, very chastening. He several times made mention to me (as though in passing) of the circumstances that had made him believe the fort lost and of his assumption that his own flight must serve as the proper signal for a general retreat. I could not tell how much of this he truly believed and how much was but a tale he had told himself that he not be convicted of cowardice in the court of his own mind. But that he felt the need for some defence was clear. Frankland and Manningham had some words to say to me too, upon their concern for the safety of the women-folk at the time, and their consequent failure to return to the fort during the siege. Cooke and Captain Grant said nothing. Cooke, I think, because he thought it impolitic, but Captain Grant because he must know I could not doubt his courage and because he believed any such excuses that he might make to be contemptible. Le Baume, who had been evacuated after his wounding, also kept silence.

In truth, all the remarks I heard then were really but a rehearsal for the answers they must soon give to the council at Madras and the directors in London. It is possible, too, that their tongues had been loosed by having before them, for the first time, one of those whom they had so singularly abandoned. But when I declared an intention to go on to Culpee on some private business for Mr Watts, this was met with all the indifference Watts had told me to expect. Indeed, I was nothing to most of them, but only an unhappy reminder of their actions at the siege.

Le Baume accompanied me from the cabin. As we re-crossed in the boat to the *Dodaly*, he asked me if Mr Watts had any genuine hope of the company's return to Calcutta, to which I replied that, at the very least, Mr Watts had not given up such a hope.

'I wonder if this might change his mind,' said he, gesturing to the wretched ships about us.

'But what does Mr Drake intend to do here?'

'Wait. See what comes.' He shrugged, as though almost in thrall himself to the lassitude of the place.

I asked him why they had not all gone ashore and why there was such a want of provisions with the Dutch settlement so near at hand. He told me that the nawab had ordered the markets to be closed to the British and there was an injunction laid on the Hindoos here to give us no aid. 'We keep to the ships for shelter. And from a fear that we may need to sail from here at the point of the nawab's sword.'

'You cannot live like this much longer.'

'We may stay a while yet. We still expect Major Kilpatrick and his men from Madras. Heaven help them. The air here is pestilential.'

'And will Major Kilpatrick fight the nawab?'

'With two or three hundred men? Drake has sent a request to Madras for more soldiers. But in Madras they will have their own concerns.' He lifted his chin towards the sloop and enquired how I had been treated.

'Gouverneur Renault has shown all of us Calcutta refugees a great courtesy. They have opened their private houses to us. We are much in their debt.'

He seemed pleased to hear that for, though he held a company commission, he was a Frenchman still. When the rope ladder came down for him at the *Dodaly* we bade each other farewell and, as he grabbed the ladder, he winced from the pain in his arm. He saw that I had seen it.

'We did not all run, Alistair.'

'I know it,' said I. He nodded unhappily and climbed up from the boat.

The sloop set me down at Culpee the next morning and three days later I took passage on a Dutch vessel south to Madras.

CHAPTER FIFTEEN

'*L*ieutenant Harding departed for England with his fiancée last month.' Colonel Clive glanced up from the papers I had brought him from Mr Watts. 'Why do you ask?'

'It is nothing, sir. A personal matter.'

His eyes stayed on me a moment longer, then returned to the papers. 'Do you know what is in these?'

'I have not read them.'

'You have written one of them. Mr Watts has included your account of the siege. And I make no doubt of your honour, Mr Douglas. I enquire only after any understanding you may have had from Mr Watts.'

'I believe he proposes an attempt at the retaking of Calcutta.'

Clive glanced up. 'Were you party to any discussions on the like with Mr Watts?'

I assured him I was not.

'But you would have your own opinion on so bold a proposal.'

'I expect it would be no easy matter. But something like it is necessary, sir, if we are to remain in Bengal.'

Clive lifted an eyebrow and then returned to reading Watts's papers.

He was not much past thirty – about the same age as Watts – and he had all the confidence and bearing to be expected of a man with so considerable a reputation He wore the uniform of a king's officer (he held commissions from both the king and the company), and his neck was somewhat full about his jacket's stiff collar. Though there was nothing of softness in his manner, had I met him in repose, and out of uniform, there would have been little to distinguish him from a thousand other young English gentlemen, except only his eyes, which were hooded and watchful. And also, perhaps, his slight fleshiness of face, which seemed no proper part of him, but an addition he had acquired in London that would soon be put off now that he had returned east. He had been much fêted after Arcot and, though he had been sent now to be governor of Fort St David to the south, the common expectation was that he had returned to the Carnatic to replace Pigot in the Madras presidency. It was thought that this would be a sinecure to him. But as he intently read the letters I had brought, and his interest became increasingly engaged, he looked ever less to me like a man fitted for the purpose of idleness. He leaned back now as he studied one particular letter. Its contents seemed to intrigue him. At last he put it aside, saying, 'Mr Watts recommends you to me as a young man of discretion. And you speak the French of a Frenchman, he says.'

I nodded, and he appraised me with the same judicious eye he had given the papers. I made bold to ask him then if any news had come down of the Calcutta survivors.

Clive searched among the other papers on his desk and finally handed me a list of names. 'These are those reported dead by Mr Holwell.'

'Mr Holwell is alive, then.'

'He has endured great trials if we may judge by the report. But he is alive, yes. This past week we have received all manner of communication from your superiors in Bengal. Not only Mr Holwell, but Mr Watts and Mr Cole have sent letters overland by the *cossids*, as have Governor Drake and the other gentlemen at Fulta. The discord among them is quite apparent. Mr Holwell blames Mr Watts that no proper defence was made of Cossimbazaar. Mr Cole blames Governor Drake that he failed to negotiate terms with the nawab before the siege. Governor Drake blames the various misinterpretations placed upon his actions. Tell me, Mr Douglas – who do you think to blame for the calamity?'

'No single man could have prevented it, save only the nawab.'

He pursed his lips. 'What do you know of these gentlemen – Mr Manningham and the Frenchman Le Baume?' I told him that Manningham had been the senior warehouseman in Fort William and that Monsieur Le Baume was a French officer come into the company's service from Chandernagore.'

'Nothing else?'

'Le Baume fought very bravely at the siege.'

'And Mr Manningham?'

'I cannot say. He was aboard ship taking care for the safety of the women.'

Clive gave me a shrewd look but pressed me no further. He explained then that a *pattamah* had been received from Drake informing the Madras Council that these two gentlemen had been sent from Fulta to bring a full accounting of the catastrophe to Madras. I told him that they had both still been at Fulta when I had left there, but that I had been at sea for several weeks since then.

I looked down the list of the Black Hole dead. And Fairborough's name, to my immense relief, was not on it. But the Reverend Bellamy's was, and many others that I knew. I returned the page to his desk. Clive rose now and went to the window. It was open and a welcome cool breeze blew in from the sea. I saw that he thought more than looked, and that the papers I had brought to him from Mr Watts were very much on his mind still.

'I saw the squadron as we came in,' said I.

'Yes. Very handsome, as their captains will be the first to tell you.'

I went and stood by him and looked out to the ships lying at anchor half a mile off from the shore. Apart from two Indiamen of the Company and several local packet-boats, there was a small naval fleet the like of which I had not seen since my departure from England: four ships-of-the-line, second and third raters, five frigates and as many sloops-of-war.

It was certain the French had no such fleet anywhere on the coast and perhaps nowhere east of the Cape. Clive now told me that they had come around with him from Bombay, where they had dealt with a pirate stronghold that had interfered with the company's trade. I remarked that when I had first seen them I had thought it meant war again, between us and the French in Pondicherry.

'There is nothing decided yet,' said he. 'But you may believe I am far from sorry that they, and the 39th, are by good fortune with us at such a time.'

Whether it was Pondicherry or Calcutta he thought of, I cannot say. The swell was light and the ships rode easy at anchor, but just to the north of us the small waves broke in a steady rushing foam upon the beach.

He asked me where I had taken quarters then, and upon my telling him I had taken none, but had come to him directly from the ship, he went back to his desk, saying that his secretary would see to a place for me among the Madras 'writers'. I do not know how it was I had the courage to say it, but I spoke then what had been in my mind almost since the first day Watts had given me those papers to bring to him. 'Sir, though I have no notion how it may be done, is it possible I may make application to you, that I might take a commission with the company regiment?'

His looked at me in some surprise. He remarked that Mr Watts's letter had mentioned no such thing.

'I did not tell him of it. It was very evident to me he had far greater concerns.'

'And you suppose I do not?'

'Sir, I only thought that as you are – that is, if you would consider—'

'Do not fret, Mr Douglas. The desire is not blameworthy. I am surprised only that you did not see fit to advance your cause through the patronage of Mr Watts. Have you family in the regiment?' I admitted that I had no such good fortune. 'Well. Let us leave this for another time. You may remind me of it. For the present you will remain with the other "writers" here.' He dismissed me then, but as I was going

140

from the room, called after me, 'If any fool recommend to you the dancing girls there at the Trichy temple, take no heed of him. Avoid the place. They are full of the pox.'

'Thank you, sir.'

'Good day, Mr Douglas.'

And so I returned to the life of a writer, which in Madras was a life of the utmost tedium. In Cossimbazaar the company servants were not so many and a natural ease had, in consequence, existed among us. But in Madras there were sufficient of every rank that each might make its own small society, and so writer stays with writer, factor with factor and junior and senior traders likewise stand apart one from another.

Every few days I went into Fort St George and made application to Clive's secretary and every few days was turned away again. But the longer I stayed among the other writers, with no Edward Fairborough to buoy my spirits, the more determined I became to break free of it. For the writers in Madras shared common quarters, ate in a common room, shared a common ambition (which was to become rich by their trade) and worked frequently with their ledgers open upon a common table, so that it struck me I had been removed halfway around the world merely to take up again the life I had led as a schoolboy, with the supplemental diversions of intoxication, gaming and fornication. And though, from boredom and a general dissatisfaction with my lot, I took to these last three with as much enthusiasm as any, waking often in the black town with a reeling head and an empty purse (though I had taken Clive's warning to heart and so stayed clear of the Trichy temple), the whole of my thoughts remained in Bengal.

The senior traders, far from restraining our youth, winked at our exploits, as well they might who had served their own time as writers and now had all the young European women of Madras to choose from (for these would not look at us writers, as being too poor and too far yet from our return to England).

The only check I remember on our actions came when one of our number – a very innocent fellow – contracted the pox, which covered him in rancid pustules before it killed him. I will not say we took the

141

proper lesson from it, but neither did we leave off, after that, from a regular attendance at the church.

How long it might have continued like this I do not know, but that I had little wish to remain in the life is evidenced by my repeated applications to Colonel Clive's secretary. Then came a day when two noteworthy things happened, the first of which was the arrival of a letter addressed to me from Mr Watts. I withdrew into the privacy of my room, and away from the curiosity of the other writers, before I opened it.

The note from Mr Watts said little, but included with the note was a letter which he had forwarded to me. I recognized the hand, at once, as that of Fairborough. It was dated but four weeks since.

My Dear Douglas,

I am sending this by a Jew here, Isaacson, who has some freedom on the river and may get this to Fulta.

I would like to tell you that I am in good health and that all is well with me, but that is so very far from the truth, as you may imagine, that I will not pretend to make any such pleasant deceit. Let me say only that I am fallen among the Moors and you will know the implication of it.

I am in Mr Bell's house at present, though I have been for some while in the hospital, and may be so again. (There is some Moor here pretends to something in the medical line. He is not a bad fellow, but quite useless.) I have now some use of my legs, but only for twenty or thirty yards, and with a cane in each hand, before I must sit awhile and have some relief from the pain. But I am only too conscious that without your help to me at the time of my accident, I might have no such pain to complain of, as having then no life.

And yet I must ask you to do something more for me.

I include with this letter a power of attorney, which I grant to you, that you may make use of it to gather up whatever estate I have here in Bengal, should the worst happen to me. Convey it by what means you think best (I recommend diamonds, but I will not

142

tie your hands in the matter) to a notary in London called Arkwright, who holds my will. He is by the Red Lion in Holborn. It will make a proper dowry for my young sisters. I am very loath that my years in Bengal should, through my late misfortune, go for nothing, and it is this thought has most troubled me while I have lain here. It will give me some peace to hear from you that Isaacson has got this letter to Fulta. I am much obliged to you, Alistair.

What need I tell you of the rest? The dead are too many and the Moors have made a carcass of Calcutta by their plundering of it.

The Reverend Bellamy is dead, and a hundred and more died with him in the Black Hole prison. The Moorish doctor is very emphatic that it was not done at the nawab's order, but by an idiocy of the gaolers. I do not see Reverend Bellamy and the other victims would quibble the difference.

There is a topass woman was stolen from her husband to be a 'bride' to some Moorish officer. He stole the tailor Campbell's lad also, to be a slave to him. But the Moor threw the pair off for some reason and they have got back to Calcutta now, but the woman quite mad and the poor lad castrated and too ashamed to show his face to me. The Jew, Isaacson, feeds him.

I am very tired now and must make a stop.

If you should have need to make use of that power of attorney, I beg that you would also call on my parents and my sisters and remember me to them as a loving son and brother.

Yours in friendship and trust,

Edward Fairborough.

I read the letter once more, and also the power of attorney, and I put them away, safe in my trunk, lay down on my bed and covered my face with my arm.

It was on the afternoon of the same day that I was walking by the Capuchin buildings, where the officers had their quarters, when someone hailed me and I looked around and saw Le Baume. I hurried across to him, more glad than I can say to find him at last arrived. After our first greetings, I asked when he had come. He had arrived that morning, he said. Manningham had been with him till Uppalum, where Le Baume had left him. 'He complained of everything. Too much rain. Too much mud. He would not move, so I came on alone.'

I asked if he had seen Governor Pigot, or Clive or Admiral Watson, to which he replied that he had been with the council the whole morning, but that there was little they did not already know. He smiled as he made this remark and raised a brow to me.

'I had instructions from Mr Watts,' said I.

'Yes. He arrived in Fulta two weeks after you left us with Mrs Watts, also, and their children.' He looked at me more closely and enquired with sudden concern if I was ill.

I waved this aside, though in truth I had been drinking till the early morning and, on top of that first biliousness, I had then received that awful letter from Edward. Now I asked Le Baume for news from Fulta and the rest of Bengal and he took me over to the officers' quarters and we sat at the shaded bench there and talked. We spoke in French. It was a pleasure to me to be treated as a man again and not as a lowly writer. But the news from Fulta was as bad as I had feared.

'In Fulta they are dying. It is full of disease. Major Kilpatrick arrived as I left. I know that many of his men will die there too. The markets are open to the British now, but it is an unhealthy place. The Dutch have let us put up huts on shore, but many have stayed on the ships. There are arguments continually. You did well not to stay there.' When I expressed surprise that the nawab had made no attempt to drive us from there, Le Baume simply scoffed. 'A few score Europeans sickening on a mudbank? It cannot concern him. But here—' he gestured around the officer quarters, 'here I have been two hours and all everyone talks of is an expedition to retake Calcutta.'

'There are many rumours of it.'

'But what is wanting? The ships you have. And there is a regiment here with the ships. I have spoken with the officers.'

I knew well the cause of the council's hesitation in sending the ships and men north. But instead of the truth, which was that war was feared between Britain and France, and a consequent reopening of hostilities between us in the Carnatic, I mumbled something to Le Baume about the winds and the season being against us.

'That is all?'

'I believe so.'

'Britain will soon be at war with France, Alistair. That is if we are not at war already. And when Governor Pigot has confirmation of it the ships here, and the king's company, will set upon Pondicherry.'

'That is idle speculation.'

He smiled, amused, I think, at my discomfort and the easy way he had turned me, but he knew, as I did, that he would feel something much worse than discomfort if war between Britain and France were at last declared. And this was not a subject we either of us wished to dwell on, so we talked of other things – I very glad of his company and both of us very happy to see each other once more and to put aside, for an hour, all thoughts of a war between our two countries.

The *Chesterfield* and *Walpole* arrived from England on the nineteenth of September with the news that war was not yet declared, though many wise heads in London expected such a declaration daily. But the council in Madras could wait no longer. The war with France remained a war only in prospect; the Moorish occupation of Calcutta was a thing certain. I was at my ledger when I got word of the council's decision.

'The fleet is for Bengal,' cried one of my fellows, rushing into the room, and the others gathered round him to hear all the rest of it, which was that the king's soldiers of the 39th, and any company soldiers who might be spared, were to make an expedition under Admiral Watson to retake Calcutta. 'Colonel Clive is to lead the land force,' said he, very puffed up with his first knowledge.

I did not wait to hear more but dropped my quill into the inkpot and went out.

The colonel's secretary received my application to go with the expedition as a volunteer with an instant refusal.

'There is no call made for volunteers Mr Douglas. There are some hundreds of sepoys and company soldiers I must get room for on the ships.'

'But I have come down from there.'

'I am aware of it. And so it is a matter of wonder to me that you should wish to go back.'

'Surely there must be some place.'

'There is no place. And if you have had your head turned by talk of the spoils to be had now in Bengal, you will take my advice and put it from your mind. There will be more find graves there than riches.'

He was a wiser man than I knew and would hear no more from me, but dismissed me directly.

At the officer's quarters, I was surprised to find no great urgency, but everything very much as when I had visited Le Baume before. I had visited him frequently and always found my visits welcome, for he was not accepted by the officers here in Madras as he had been in Calcutta. It was the closeness of Pondicherry, I believe, made the difference and the remembrance of the fighting there had been between us and the French, here in the Carnatic, which had not happened in Bengal. But this day, when I came into the officers' common room, he was at cards with two captains of the 39th and a naval lieutenant and merely lifted his head to me. So I dropped into a chair near where several more officers lounged about and took up a dog-eared copy of the *Gentleman's Magazine* from the pile that the *Chesterfield*'s captain had brought out from England. I turned the pages but did not read.

The talk all around me was of the expedition and of what advancement might be expected. In my first visits to Le Baume I had been surprised to discover how the officers' conversation resembled that of the company's writers and traders, with money and advancement a subject more often to be met with than tales of military glory. But I expected it now and could almost have been amused by it, had not my attempt to join the expedition been so recently and absolutely thwarted. I quickly tired of their good spirits and their talk of Colonel Clive and Admiral Watson. I put aside the magazine and went to stand at Le Baume's shoulder. He introduced me to Lieutenant Warwick. Captain Lynn and Captain Coote I already knew. I watched a hand, and Le Baume played boldly and lost, and another just as bold, and lost again.

146

His stake was finished now, which I own I was glad of, for I thought he might come away then and speak with me privately and perhaps help me discover some way to join the expedition.

But he did not come away. Without any hint of embarrassment he asked the others at the table if he might play upon credit, which I saw Coote and Warwick were unsure of, but Lynn, who had the most of the winnings before him, would not hear of Le Baume leaving the game. And Le Baume assuring Lynn that he was to receive some payment from one of the Hindoo bankers the next day, Lynn made no hesitation but extended Le Baume twenty pounds. It was done between gentlemen, and Coote and Warwick made no remark, and the game seemed about to continue.

I spoke quietly to Le Baume in French. 'I have put myself forward as a volunteer. Clive's secretary has refused me.'

'But you must come,' said he.

'I had hoped we might discuss it.'

He looked at me and at the cards that Captain Lynn was now dealing. I saw he did not want to leave the game. And then Lynn finished dealing and I think it was from a fear of Le Baume's going with me that he said, 'It is an English mess, gentlemen. And perhaps it were better we should all speak it. You are after all one of us while you are here, Capitaine.' He smiled at Le Baume very friendly; and Le Baume decided then. He picked up his own cards and said to me in English that he would try and help me, but it must wait a better time.

But next evening when I called to see him, I found that Le Baume had been sent with a troop of sepoys to deal with the dacoits (who are bandits) then troubling the coastal road to the southward. Captain Coote told me of it.

'But when shall he return?'

'Before the squadron leaves. You are very friendly with him, Mr Douglas.'

I nodded. 'When he returns, can a messenger be immediately sent to me?'

He promised it would be done.

But with the fleet now little more than a week from sailing, all hope

147

seemed exhausted. I returned to my work with a heart like a stone and distractedly went about my business.

It was some days later that I walked through the warehouse with my tallybook, taking stock of the stacked bolts of cotton newly arrived from the *aurangs*, and trying without success to accustom myself to the notion I would not be returning to Bengal. I thought of Edward and of how I should best fulfil his request of me from here in Madras if that terrible thing should happen. The bolts had been poorly stacked and I sent two coolies up onto the racks to fix them. While I watched the work from below an ensign appeared in the doorway just near to me.

'Are you Alistair Douglas?'

'I am.'

When he came across to me, I looked at him quizzically. Soldiers did not usually come into the warehouse.

'There is an excursion arranged for the ship's officers to the Mount. Colonel Clive invites you to join them. I am to take your reply.'

CHAPTER SIXTEEN

*T*he Mount, lying several miles inland from Madras, was a place where many senior company servants kept their villas, to which they would repair with their wives during the rainy season to get respite from the harsh weather on the coast. Two of these villas had been made available to Colonel Clive and Admiral Watson. The colonel having gone the previous evening, the party I joined at the fort gates in the early morning was composed mainly of the ships' officers, with the admiral at the centre of them. They were all uniformed, most of them wearing long blue jackets, so I was quite conspicuously the only civilian of the party.

The admiral's blue jacket had the gold braid stitched onto both the broad lapels and above the broad white cuffs. The wig beneath his bicorn hat was almost to his shoulders. His hat sat at an angle now as he bent forward to hear his officers, his lean face genial but intent. He seemed almost fatherly in his manner toward them, and they on their best behaviour in his presence. He was forty or more, with the lines of experience cut deep into his brow, and I knew from the many remarks I overheard in the officers' mess that he was regarded with a universal respect, both for his seamanship and his bravery. And more than that – and which is far more rare – he had not only his officers' respect but also their affection. So there was now a quite genial air over the party as, at the admiral's order, the palanquins and the horses were brought up. The admiral put his hat beneath his arm and climbed into the first palanquin, while the officers moved severally to their places in the line. I mounted and moved off, Lieutenant Warwick riding beside me.

I was known to Lieutenant Warwick from my visits to the mess, and he seemed content that I should lead the column with him. Of all the naval officers he had ever been the most friendly with me (he assured me I bore a strong resemblance to his young brother in England), and as we rode together it came into my mind that I should myself have been pleased to have such an elder brother as he. He rode as he seemed to do everything else, with ease, and like a gentleman. His tanned face was very open and lively as he looked about him now. It was no wonder to me that the other lieutenants though equal to him in rank should treat him as they did, like their senior.

After half a mile I looked back. Behind me were a few officers, mounted, and behind them a dozen palanquins swaying on the shoulders of the bearers. At the rear were a score of servants and cooks and a bullock cart carrying everything we might need for our leisurely excursion. There was a fellow just behind me who, though in the saddle, quite clearly could not ride. His mount was growing very restive beneath his clumsy hand.

'He has had his fill of oats this morning, Mr Adams,' remarked Lieutenant Warwick with a laugh.

'Keep down, you bugger,' said this Adams and tugged at the rein, which only caused the horse to throw its head the higher.

'He is not accustomed to you yet,' said I.

'Nor I to him, by Christ.' At these words, his mount jumped forward and I pushed mine on to stay clear of him.

Lieutenant Warwick led our little expedition and, as I rode with him at the head of our caravan, he called my attention to various local landmarks, for he had been often to the Mount while the admiral had stayed at the villa. But I could be little concerned whether it was Shiva or

Ganesh or some other Hindoo deity held sway at various shrines we passed, as well the lieutenant knew. And eventually I must ask him.

'All is in readiness,' he replied. 'It is only the date of our departure to be decided upon and we must trust to the admiral and the colonel for that. They will decide it today. But we shall greet the New Year in Bengal. And with a modicum of good fortune, in Calcutta.'

'You are sanguine of success then.'

'But do you doubt it?'

'We were swept from Calcutta by a great army. You go to face that same army now with but a few ships, and only as many sepoys and soldiers as those few ships can carry.'

'You were not at Gheria,' said he. (Gheria was the pirates' stronghold near Bombay that the squadron had reduced at a stroke before coming on to Madras.)

'Calcutta is no Gheria,' said I, but he did not seem to hear me.

He stood in his stirrups now and pointed with his whip. 'There is the Marmelong Bridge. Do you see?'

A mile further on we came to the famed thirty arches, which spanned the wide and almost dried-up river course. We stopped to admire the Latin inscription put into the stone at one end by the Armenian merchant who had paid for the bridge, and the date, which was some decades before. When the whole party had arrived, Lieutenant Warwick imparted what he had learned of the place, and when each had admired the inscription we returned to our horses and palanquins and filed onto the bridge. All eyes were now directed toward the Little Mount which was our next destination. Lieutenant Warwick was rehearsing to me the little information he had collected concerning the veneration of the Little Mount by the Hindoos and of how some credulous Armenians thought a cave there had been the home of St Thomas, come straight from the Holy Land.

'That would be Doubting Thomas,' said I.

He smiled and then, behind us, a cry went up and we turned to see Midshipman Adams's mount rearing and Adams' arms flung about the horse's neck. The horse came down on four legs again and bucked. Adams now lost his stirrups and the horse bolted toward us. We were at the narrow waist of the bridge. I was caught on the wrong side of Warwick's mount, so there was nothing for it but I must stand and await the oncoming rush of horseflesh. I waved my whip and shouted 'Huzzah!' in fear that I should be knocked headlong into the dry riverbed.

But there was not sufficient distance for the brute to gather any real speed, else the incident had ended very badly. As it was, Adams began to slide down the horse's neck and the horse slowed and was almost at a prancing walk by the time I reached out and grabbed its bridle. Adams fell in a heap upon the stone floor of the bridge.

He was not hurt, only bruised, and soon on his feet and stiffly testing out his limbs. To the general merriment of all the others, and at the admiral's own particular order, Adams now changed places with an officer in one of the palanquins. This officer leapt spryly into the saddle and I saw that we should have no more trouble.

Lieutenant Warwick congratulated me as we set off again, to which I replied that I had done nothing. 'But Adams is a favourite of the admiral's,' said he. 'You may trust me upon it. You could not have done better had you saved the colonel himself.'

We spent an hour at the Little Mount, inspecting the cave and the Armenian church above it, then proceeded to the Mount proper and climbed the hundred and thirty-three steps to the Portuguese church at its summit. From this place there was a splendid view afforded across the plain back to the coast and spyglasses went from hand to hand, as each officer took his turn surveying the scene. And then Lieutenant Warwick remarked the half-dozen small figures approaching the steps at the base of the Mount far below us. All agreed that the colonel was among them.

'Hurry the galley up, Mr Warwick,' said the admiral, with a nod toward the cooks and coolies arriving with their burdens now at the top of the steps. 'Let us give the colonel no reason to doubt of our competence ashore.'

There was something of a game and challenge made of it among them now, to have everything in readiness before the colonel's arrival. The officers hurried the coolies and opened the camp-chairs themselves. Two fires were set and an awning slung as a canopy between the trees near the church. All this was done, and the food already in the pots, when Clive and his party arrived at the summit less than fifteen minutes after our first sight of him. A jesting cheer broke from the naval officers when Clive, hands on hips and breathing hard, appeared at the head of the steps. He smiled and paused for breath and went to where the admiral sat beneath the shade cloth. Behind Clive came the others of his party, his aide, some Hindoo servants and two Europeans. The banter among the naval officers died.

'It is Rémy,' said Lieutenant Warwick quietly to an officer beside me. 'The deputy governor in Pondicherry.' The officer asked Warwick who the other fellow was, the cocky-looking French officer. Warwick did not know. But to my own considerable surprise, I did.

'He is from Chandernagore. His name is Cordet.'

Admiral Watson and Colonel Clive sat at the solitary table and the two Frenchmen as their guests, while the rest of us sat on cloths spread upon the grass. The servants came among us with the dishes and we ate with no formality, the officers seeming very content to be ashore with the usual shipboard etiquette a little loosened. Colonel Clive, at the table not ten yards from me, I overheard mixing poor French with his English, so the Frenchmen felt the more welcome. Admiral Watson spoke French very fluently and so there was no awkwardness among them.

Around me, the ships' officers talked in a general way of the fitting out of their vessels, but the expedition to Bengal none mentioned with the Frenchmen seated so near. By the meal's end, Clive and Cordet had found their common subject and, while the admiral and Rémy drank port, Clive marshalled the pewter mugs and clay dishes upon the table. Cordet studied this marshalling with an admiring concentration and listened while Clive described to him the details of the Siege of Arcot.

I confess I felt an unexpected stab of envy. Cordet's uniform, though French, had given him an immediate footing with Clive I could not hope for. Cordet was a part of the universal brotherhood of arms, and

I was not, and in that moment I felt the difference with all the misery of wretched exile.

After we had eaten there was a general taking of ease and some, like me, made sketches, some read, while others wandered about the hilltop or inspected the relics of the church. But after a while Clive had finished talking Cordet through Arcot and he now suggested a target be put up and a trial made of the naval officers' marksmanship. Clive offered his own pistol for the purpose and his aide (accustomed I suppose to Clive's ways) had powder and shot ready.

'Forty yards off, by the plantains, if you would, Mr Douglas.'

Clive gave me a few clay dishes from the table. Cordet gathered up some more of the dishes and came with me.

'You are very far from Bengal.'

'Nor is this Pondicherry,' said I.

'Today I am aide to Monsieur Rémy. He meets with your colonel to find a solution together to the dacoits.' He hesitated, and then said, 'We have heard there have been many deaths at Fulta.'

'It is an unhealthy place.'

'I am surprised they have not left there. Either that or retaken Calcutta.' When I kept silence he said, 'In Pondicherry we would be grateful for such a fleet as the admiral has brought you.'

'So that you might attack us?'

He laughed. 'So that we might defend ourselves from you.'

By the plantains we used the heels of our boots to dig up several small mounds. And against each mound we put a clay dish. As we walked back to the others, Cordet asked me if I would remain in Madras or return to Bengal.

'I have not yet decided.'

'If I had your freedom I would return home. There is no honour to be won in the Indies.'

'By which you mean to say you had rather be in Europe and at war with us.'

'I rely upon your countrymen to provide the opportunity. I am sure they will not disappoint me.'

We set our last targets and returned to the others.

154

Each officer took a shot and three of the shots were hits, one of them by Lieutenant Warwick. And then Rémy shot and missed and Cordet shot and hit. When they congratulated him he took his purse from his jacket. I thought at first it was to make some wager, but he opened a kerchief on the ground and knelt and tipped out the coins from his purse. They were silver *siccas,* a coin not much seen in the Carnatic. While all the officers looked down in curiosity, he searched among the coins and then found what he looked for. He held it up – a *sicca* coin with one side coloured white.

'Who hits it may keep it,' said he, gesturing to Warwick and the other two successful marksmen. Warwick remarked the smallness of the coin. He suggested none would succeed. 'If you fail, then I will try it,' said Cordet and he gave me the white *sicca*, scooped up the other coins and repocketed his purse. I walked with him down to the mounds by the plantains.

He said, 'They must practise more before they leave for Bengal,' and he looked at me, but I ignored him. 'They are careful not to speak of it, but it is the talk of every bazaar, Alistair. They leave within the week to retake Calcutta.' Still I said nothing, for he was not speaking in jest now, but in very earnest. 'We will know the truth soon enough. A plan is easier to hide than a fleet.'

'You must debate that matter with the admiral,' said I and walked on the faster.

He set up the coin with the white side of it facing the officers. We stood away from the mound while Warwick and the others took their shots. Each one hit the mound, but each time Cordet checked the coin he called a miss.

After the last call, Cordet looked at me, and then he went back to the officers. I reset the coin and wiped the dirt away so that he might see it. The thing was not the size of a gaming counter. I stepped back.

Cordet took Clive's pistol and set himself. He put his left hand behind his back. He turned his head and closed one eye and smoothly raised the pistol. He held steady a moment and fired and the earth kicked up from the mound. Going forward, I knelt and found the coin. I picked it up and walked back to where the others were now gathered about Cordet.

I put the unmarked *sicca* into Cordet's hand and went to find my sketchbook.

The two Frenchmen had gone down to Clive's villa below and Admiral Watson and Colonel Clive had now repaired to the table where wine and water were brought them. No officer approached them, but they were left alone, and every one of us knew that they now made their final plans for the squadron's departure.

Lieutenant Warwick came up by me where I sat on the steps to the church. He asked me how I knew Cordet and, when I told him, asked me what Cordet and I had spoken of here today.

'He wished to know something of the business of the fleet.'

'And what did you say?'

'I referred him to the admiral.'

'That was well done. Though the French cannot stop us, it is but prudence to keep them sailing in the dark.'

'That was my thought, sir.'

He laid a friendly hand upon my shoulder and went up into the church.

It was an hour more before the admiral and the colonel were done with their parley, and by then the day's heat was very full upon us. Admiral Watson let it be known that he would wait till the heat had passed before returning to Madras. The colonel was intent on descending at once to join his French guests at the villa.

With a courage born of desperation now, I intercepted the colonel at the head of the steps.

'Sir, forgive me, but I have had no reply to my letter of last week.'

'I am wanted below, Mr Douglas. You may accompany me if you wish.' A servant went ahead of us and I went down at the colonel's shoulder. 'I regret I do not recall the letter. May I assume its contents were of a likeness with the others?'

'I believe I may soon have sufficient to purchase a commission. It would be a question of days.'

'And I would not be too far from the mark in supposing it might also be a question of a very substantial debt?'

'My prospects are—'

'Your prospects are not such as will spare you from incurring a ruinous financial penalty for any debt you now undertake. You will forgive my bluntness, Mr Douglas. I have seen others tread that road.'

'You do not question my credit, sir.'

He checked in his course down the steps and looked back up at me. His gaze made me feel the foolishness of my remark. 'You are aware that I was once a "writer", just as you are.'

I nodded.

'There is only one lesson I ever learned in my life as a "writer", but it is a good lesson and one well worth the learning. Shall I tell it you?'

I nodded again, though warily.

'The man who buys low and sells high is on his way to riches and the man who sells low and buys high is on his way to ruin. A fellow can want a thing too much, Mr Douglas.

'You did not stay a writer.'

'Do not congratulate yourself overmuch that you have found out the weakness of my own position.' He turned and descended. 'The general lesson stands.'

'Why was I invited here today, sir?'

'I thought I might have need of your French. Rémy's English is poor, but his aide is quite capable. There is no need for you to come down with me, Mr Douglas.'

'Cordet means to find out your plans for Bengal.'

'As would I in his position. But I thank you for the notice of it.' He touched his hat to me and turned his back and continued his descent and my last hope gone down with him.

For their amusement, the officers had, by the time of my return, set up mangoes on the mounds of earth and took now pots at the fruit with their own pistols. They invited me to join them in their sport, which I did, and, in the smell of powder and the general good cheer and surprised remarks that I might have taken the white *sicca*, I found some shallow relief from my bitter disappointment.

Admiral Watson and a few senior officers played at cards and dozed in their chairs beneath the awning till past four o'clock. The cooks then descended with all their implements, the shade-cloth was taken down and the chairs folded, and the coolies brought our baggage down behind us from the Mount. Lieutenant Warwick rode off alongside the admiral's palanquin, talking with the admiral through the window. The syces were slow to ready the horses and so it was twenty minutes before I mounted, and by then the palanquins had passed out of sight. I did not catch them again till I entered through the fort gates in Madras at sunset. Lieutenant Warwick then rode up to me and said I must thank the admiral for the day. Together we rode across to where the admiral was just alighting.

'You must not think of it, Mr Douglas,' he replied to me. 'A change of company can only be a pleasure to us.' He made a pleasantry in French and I answered him in French and he said, 'Yes, Mr Warwick told me you had some facility. I see it was no exaggeration he made of it. And I owe you thanks too, that you saved the neck of young Adams.'

'It may be best, sir, he keeps himself from the horses.'

'You may be sure Mr Warwick will tell him.'

'Good evening to you, sir. My best wishes go with you to Bengal and my thanks again upon the pleasure of the day.'

I touched my hat to him and he to me. I rode across to the barrack stables, where the syces were washing down the other horses, and there I dismounted. I did not wish to linger near the officers' quarters, for their expectations of the coming expedition could now only crush my spirits the more. And so I handed the reins to a syce and unbuckled the saddlebag. The saddlebag slung across my arm, I turned my step toward the writer's quarters and I own there was some savage thought in my mind of losing myself in some night-time depravity in the black town. But as I crossed the yard I saw Lieutenant Warwick just now parting from the admiral. He rode straight across to me.

'Mr Douglas. If you would hold a moment.' He came and stopped by me. 'If you wish it, you will sail in the *Tyger*. It is no commission, you will understand. You are merely a cargo that the admiral carries at his pleasure. You will have a berth with the midshipmen.'

'Do I understand you right, Mr Warwick?' I said, quite stupefied.

'A midshipman's berth is the best we may do. You must take it or nothing.'

'I would not care if it were a berth in your bilges.'

'You would had you ever been in them. We depart on the sixteenth. And you will have no room for a trunk. But you will see me in the morning and I will enter you in our books as a supernumerary to Bengal.'

CHAPTER SEVENTEEN

*A*ll the first week of the voyage I was ill, scarce leaving the midshipmen's quarters. And so baffling and contrary were the winds of that first week that by the time I came above decks the fleet was dispersed and I saw now, at every corner of the compass, only a vast ocean and an empty horizon.

'You have missed your breakfast,' said Lieutenant Warwick, much amused to see the poor state I was in. I gripped the gunwale tight and fixed my eyes upon the empty horizon. 'It is as fair a wind now as we have had,' said he.

'Then you may thank me, if you will, for the many prayers I have said while your ship churned me like rancid butter.'

'You will get your legs now.' He called sharply into the shrouds where a pair of seamen scuttled about like Bengal monkeys. It seemed an ability almost miraculous to me at that moment, but to look at them made me giddy.

I returned my attention to the horizon and remarked to Warwick on the fleet's evident dispersal, for the *Tyger* had sailed with four other of the king's ships – the *Kent* which was Admiral Watson's flagship, the

Salisbury, the *Bridgewater* and the *Cumberland*, and besides these came the company ships, the *Walpole* and *Marlborough*, the last of which carried most of our munitions. Warwick answered me that the seas had not been so high as to cause any true concern for the other ships, and that we should all certainly be reunited at the mouth of the Hugli.

'Though when that may be is now a matter for some conjecture among us. We have been at sea seven days and we are not yet a hundred leagues north of Madras. The smaller ships may have made less headway than ourselves. We are fighting the wind, Mr Douglas. It is the season.'

His easy acceptance of our situation was a fine example to me, if I had but the sense to see it, for there is no defying the sea when her mood runs contrary. But I had not then the understanding in my bones, and so every day and every week of our voyage became a slow unfolding torture to me, for I would have us always further on. To while away the many hours that hung so heavy upon me, I sketched, and spent much of my time as a solitary, both above and below decks. The quarters of the sepoys, below decks, were cramped and the air fetid, but they seemed to prefer to stay there in the companionship of their fellows than to come much above deck. They had some superstitious feeling about the sea and at sunrise and sunset each day a few of their number made sure to perform a Hindoo ceremony up near the bow, chanting and throwing a lit paper into the waves. It was an odd thing to see done by men in uniform. I sketched this and made sure to include the sailors, who often watched over this ceremony in silence from the yards.

The ship's officers and the officers of the 39th treated me with courtesy, but I had no part in this society (excepting for the particular consideration given me by Lieutenant Warwick and Captain Coote), and so while we made the voyage I found myself mostly dependent upon the midshipmen for conversation and companionship. There were six of these fellows, including Adams, from fourteen years of age up to seventeen. During that illness of my first week aboard, I took them for brutish tormentors, with their comings and goings from the cabin at every hour, their talk and their card games, their arguments and laughter, all the while that I lay in abject misery. But once recovered from my illness, I found them to be much of a likeness with my old schoolfellows at Harrow, only with rather more of the quality of manliness and a little less the veneer of education.

They each of them had but a simple ambition in life, which was to rise ever upward through the ranks of the Royal Navy, an institution whose mysteries so enfolded them that they could conceive of no higher calling for a man. I was several times exasperated to find some discussion with them run suddenly aground by the words, 'It was the Captain's order', or 'It is a lashing offence' or even 'It would not do aboard', and no attempt by me to reason beyond these sacred barriers ever drew one of these midshipmen after me. When it was discovered that I might help them with their books (Lieutenant Warwick tried them weekly upon their trigonometry) I took my place as a scholar among them, and never had a tutor more willing pupils, for without trigonometry they would never be officers.

I made one further connection on the voyage worthy of mention, and that was with the rear-admiral of our small fleet, Admiral Pocock, who seemed to have a suspicion at first of my attaching myself to the expedition for a pecuniary motive. But once he had put this by, he several times called me to take a turn with him about the quarterdeck, and got from me what information he could regarding the fall of Calcutta and our people now in Fulta. He was a man slightly older than Admiral Watson and, though respected by the officers, his stern manner inspired no affection. It was he (so Lieutenant Warwick told me) first advised Admiral Watson that the contrary winds and our consequent slow progress necessitated an early reduction in the rations. We were dropped to three-quarters, but as we made no improvement with our speed northward, by mid-November we were put on half-rations throughout the fleet. Shortly after this, Pocock transferred to the *Cumberland.* I cannot say that he was missed.

I never heard any seaman make open complaint against the cut in rations (I think because they were accustomed to such usage, rather than from any fear of the lash), but the dozen company artillerymen we carried complained bitterly. It was the sepoys, I believe, suffered the worst, for they would not eat the salted meat that made much of the half-ration. And it was among the sepoys our surgeon noticed the first cases of scurvy. After this, navigational trigonometry ceased to be an abstraction to me and I was as avid as any of the midshipmen to hear the report of our latitude from the officers coming off the watch.

On the last day of November we sighted Point Palmyra, which was the first land we had seen for weeks and the final promontory we must round before arriving at the Ballasore Roads and the mouth of the Hugli. And, on the first day of December, before we had rounded the point, the *Cumberland* struck hard on the Palmyra Reef.

'She is aground, sir,' I heard Lieutenant Warwick report evenly to the captain. They were up on the quarterdeck and I had been at the rail, watching the land, which was the most wonderful sight after our interminable weeks at sea. The *Cumberland* was not a league off from us, and I could see that she was stationary and her sails strangely loosened and sagging in the wind. I did not immediately understand the peril she was in.

'Signal the *Kent*,' ordered the captain. '*Cumberland* aground. We are sending two boats to her aid.' Warwick passed on the order, then volunteered himself to command the boats. The captain told him he might take twenty oarsmen in each and Warwick was instantly down from the quarterdeck, with a sharp warning to me to stand clear, and going along by the boats and bellowing the oarsmen to their stations.

The rush of men about the deck was like the movement of eels in a barrel, for they crossed and re-crossed, tight-packed, but order quickly unfolded. The boats were lowered, the seamen scrambled down the ropes and then Warwick went down, and the men bent their backs to the oars.

Young Midshipman Adams came up by me. Upon my asking what would happen now, he said, 'The lieutenant will tie his boats up to her, sir. Look there, the *Cumberland* is lowering two of her own now. They will tie up to the *Cumberland*'s stern. She may be hauled off if they are lucky.'

'And if she cannot be moved?'

'Then she is for the deep, sir.' Catching some bellowed orders from on high, he pivoted and hurried to obey.

The *Tyger* and all the rest of the fleet with us now tacked away from the dangerous reef, but then we came round again and dropped mainsails and awaited, in safety, the fate of the *Cumberland*. Many of our sailors climbed onto the yards, some up to the topgallants, for a better view. I stayed where I was and watched the *Cumberland* while I listened to our captain and his officers up on the quarterdeck, for it was only by their talk I could make any sense of what was being done to save the grounded ship.

The *Cumberland*'s sails had been struck now and she had a look of helplessness about her. But she had got some of her own boats lowered and now these, and the two from the *Tyger*, moved with some purpose about the edge of the reef. After an hour, the tone on the quarterdeck above me changed and I understood that apprehension was turning, at last, to hope, though my own unpractised eye continued to see only that same scene at the reef of a grounded ship and a swarm of boats about her stern. Half an hour more and a sailor cried from the rigging above me, 'She is afloat, sir.'

And now I, too, could perceive the *Cumberland* moving, the boats at her stern drawing her off with a painful slowness. The captain immediately ordered that the *Tyger*'s carpenter be taken across to lend a hand in the *Cumberland*'s repair, then the captain retired to his cabin. By ones and twos the seamen came down from their vantages in the rigging. The change of the watch was called. With hardly a look towards the *Cumberland* now, the seamen went about their usual business.

It was over, the *Cumberland* saved, and nothing more impressive to me about the whole operation than this final easy acceptance of their success. And what a shaming contrast there was between this and our so-called defence of Fort William. Here was a proper preparedness and men, not inviting danger, but ready to face her with a calm and steady purpose. I still did not share the midshipmen's certainty that the arrival of the Royal Navy in Bengal would set the Moors to flight. But I began now to see the reason of their firm-held faith, for it must be allowed, they worshipped at no mean altar.

But the bad luck of our voyage dogged us to the last for, upon finally rounding Point Palmyra, we found ourselves in the company of only the *Kent* and the *Walpole*. Some of the fleet we had not seen for a week and more. Other ships we had been parted from by the winds on the Point. But for all that, there was a palpable relief felt when we at last anchored at the Ballasore Roads and took on board the Dutch pilots who would steer us over the shoals and up into the Hugli. And the pilots were doubly welcome to us, bringing with them as they did a supply of rice which we were much in need of. And, to me at least, triply welcome, for the passenger they brought.

'Have a care there, Mr Adams,' said I to the midshipman who helped our guest aboard. And when he turned sharply to look at me – and that with a gratifying astonishment – I put out my hand to greet Mr Watts.

CHAPTER EIGHTEEN

'You have been well out of this place, Alistair,' said Mrs Watts, taking up her parasol from by the door, 'and I very much hope you will not have cause to regret your return.'

'I do not regret it.'

'There have been so many die here. One's heart protects itself after a time.' She asked if I had seen the graveyard and I said that I had passed it in coming up through the settlement. Indeed, I said, there were graves being dug even as I went by. 'It is nothing remarkable to us here,' said she. 'Major Kilpatrick has watched his men go into the ground almost daily since he came. A vale of tears. I never knew what the words meant till these past few months. Disease and death – they have become our very familiars. But so long as my children are alive, I thank God. And William. That is all that I have dared to pray for.'

She opened her parasol and put a hand on my arm and we came down the steps from her verandah, across the small dirt yard of the bungalow, and turned down toward the river.

Mr Watts had sailed up in the *Kent* from the Ballasore Roads, in parley with Admiral Watson and Colonel Clive, so I had not seen him since our first meeting on the ship till I came ashore at Fulta. But upon my arrival here, he had taken me by way of the British encampment and the graveyard, and up through the settlement, to the bungalow where he was quartered with his family. He had left me to wash and eat, with an instruction to bring Mrs Watts at midday to the British encampment down by the river, where there was to be a ceremony of Governor Drake's devising. I now made bold to remark to Mrs Watts as we walked to this ceremony that I had almost expected to hear of some mutiny against Drake's authority while I was in Madras.

'You were not alone in the thought. But Major Kilpatrick's arrival gave Governor Drake's authority a new lease. Yet you may be sure Mr Holwell, and certain others, have not concealed their unhappiness. You have not seen Mr Holwell?'

'No.'

'The nawab kept him in chains. I understand there were other indignities. He arrived here scarce alive – and the report he has given of the Black Hole, I cannot tell you.'

I offered her my commiserations on the Reverend Bellamy's death and she looked down at her feet.

'William has some communication with Calcutta. Omichand has used his influence to keep the bazaars here open to us, though I do not doubt that he takes himself a profit from the trade.' We went on through the main square of the town and palanquins were offered us, but Mrs Watts refused them and as we came from the square, she said, 'I do not mean to speak with bitterness, Alistair. It is from disappointment that this adversity has exposed a weakness in us that I had not suspected. God forbid the French should see us so plain.'

'There are many good men in the squadron.'

'Yes. And Major Kilpatrick has taught us all to hope in Admiral Watson and Colonel Clive. But we have waited a long and bitter time. I am almost afraid now to hope that we may soon leave here.'

The river was before us now, and upon it those ships of our fleet which had safely arrived – the *Kingfisher*, the *Delaware* and the *Protector*, which we had not seen since Madras, were arrived here before us. Beside these now lay at anchor the *Kent*, the *Tyger* and the *Walpole*.

And all of these were at some slight distance from the *Dodaly* and the *Fort William* and the other vessels which had disgraced their flags in the abandonment of Calcutta. Taken together, it was as substantial a fleet of fighting vessels as had ever been seen on the Hugli River, and with yet more of the squadron still to arrive.

The sepoys we had carried from Madras were now ashore and they had made their camp beyond the town and near to the water. And just by this camp, below us, Admiral Watson, Mr Watts and Drake, Colonel Clive and Major Kilpatrick and the other officers and members of the revived Bengal Council were now gathered at a flagpole, newly erected. Behind these were the European survivors of Calcutta, much wasted from their travails here in Fulta, yet their faces were lit with a pathetic hope for the restoration of their fortunes. I led Mrs Watts down there and we took our places by the flagpole.

'Drummer,' called Drake's secretary, Cooke, and a black drummer of the sepoys came forward. At the beat of the drum, Cooke then stepped to the flagpole. He presented the British flag to the two soldiers there and they attached it and raised it in fine military style. As it reached the top of the pole, a salute sounded from the *Kent*, twelve guns, amidst a cheering from the Fulta survivors. I looked at Mrs Watts and she did not cheer, but stood together with her husband and the admiral and colonel, all of them in silence.

Then Drake stepped forward, who had led the cheers, and gave an address of welcome to the admiral and the colonel. This he followed with a recitation of our grievances against the nawab and a general proclamation of the renewed authority of the Bengal Council into which both the admiral and colonel were now formally inducted. It was pomp, pure and simple, and I daresay those who had been marooned in Fulta took great heart from it. The rest of us, however, had an eye only to the dark clouds gathering overhead. And when a thunderclap suddenly sounded, there was a hasty end brought to proceedings and a hurried search for cover as the heavy raindrops began to fall. I found myself with Mr and Mrs Watts, and the colonel and his aide, all of us sheltering with some tethered horses beneath a canopy of dried palm-fronds the sepoys had put up beside their encampment.

'This is a welcome to Bengal indeed,' said the colonel. Mrs Watts remarked that the rain was, at least, more welcome than further speeches and Clive smiled at this. There was more banter of the kind, but after a minute the rain was so heavy that it extinguished all other sound. We stood unspeaking and looked to the flag, clinging now like a wet rag to the pole. The rain came in a deluge and for some minutes the ships were almost hid from our view by the heavy veil of falling water.

The sepoys huddled in knots about the field. Three artillery-men, who had been moving a gun carriage when the storm broke, were now in some trouble with their horse, which was losing its footing on the wet ground. Though two men had their shoulders to the carriage and the third pulled at the horse's reins, they could make no proper headway. Clive watched them a long while, then he took up a stick, reached out into the deluge and thrust the stick into the mud. With-drawing it, he read the depth of the mud, and then he tossed the stick aside and folded his arms and watched silent as the artillerymen continued their futile struggle.

His look was very black now and no one of us dared to say a word to him.

'Both the admiral and the colonel have sent letters to the nawab,' Mr Watts told me as we rode a short way along the river, north of Fulta. 'They have invited him to surrender Calcutta to us and to pay proper restitution for his depredations, or to suffer whatever consequences may follow.'

'When I think on the size of the nawab's army, sir, and of the small number of men who serve under Colonel Clive—'

'Keep your silence on it. The colonel's men will see the force against them soon enough. And, I have no doubt, the admiral will have an easy mastery of the river. That may be worth any number of troops.' It had been more than a week now since our arrival in Fulta and yet the *Bridge-water*, *Cumberland*, *Salisbury* and *Marlborough* had not yet entered the river. But Watts now told me there was a report received that morning of two ships arriving at the Ballasore Road, just outside the river-mouth. 'I am sure the admiral will not wait longer for the others.

Some of his men are already sickening. He is as anxious as any to put the fevers of this place behind him.'

'I am at a loss to know why the nawab has suffered us to remain here these past months.'

'The nawab has had greater concerns. He has been fighting north of Murshidabad to protect his throne. He goes on as foolishly rash as he started. He has gone so far as to strike Jagath Seth across the face in open *durbar*.' Upon my expression of amazement, Watts assured me that this scarce credible fact was indeed true. Jagath Seth, the greatest banker in Bengal, a man whom the young nawab might have been expected to befriend from a motive of mere prudence, really had been struck by the nawab. Such an outrageous insult would not be easily forgotten. 'It is our great good fortune that the young nawab has a capricious and vicious temper. And a peculiar genius for creating new enemies.'

He turned his horse onto a sidetrack toward the river and I followed him. After a short time I saw the mast of a small pinnace that had, till now, been hid from view by the riverbank. There were two men sitting on the riverbank, one of them wearing the cap of a Jew.

'Is that Isaacson, sir?'

'It is.'

'He must know if Fairborough be still alive.'

Watts stopped and dismounted, but when I made to do the same, he said, 'You will wait here.'

'But I must speak with him.'

'You will not speak with him,' said he and left me and went down to speak with Isaacson and the other. I saw he received from them a letter which he took to one side privately and read. He then gave to them a packet like to the one I had delivered to the colonel in Madras. They did not wait but went down into their boat and shoved off from their mooring and immediately set sail. Watts came back to me and remounted and turned up the track.

'The other fellow is an Armenian,' said Watts. 'Their trade in Calcutta has been destroyed, but they continue to live near to Fort William.'

'They are our friends, then.'

'They may profit by our return to Calcutta. As to friendship, I do not believe they think on it. And in affairs such as this, you would do well to follow their example.' We rode on a little further, and then he said, 'They tell me Mr Fairborough is alive. You must not rely upon it.'

The *Bridgewater* and the *Salisbury* at last arrived and the sepoys they carried came immediately ashore. Everything on land was now supervised by Major Kilpatrick, as the colonel had been stricken low at this time with a fever. There was a quickening of anticipation among the men, for none now expected the arrival of the *Marlborough* or the *Cumberland*, but all plans were made in the knowledge that the part of the expeditionary force that might be relied upon was now here assembled, and that an advance upriver must happen within days.

And indeed Mr Watts soon heard rumour of such an order and straightaway took me with him to Major Kilpatrick's quarters, which were in the bungalow neighbouring his own. Between Watts and Kilpatrick had grown a friendship while they had stayed here in Fulta. And, as Watts had given me a room in his bungalow, I found myself, in these days, frequently in Kilpatrick's company, so that he had come to speak to Watts in my presence with an ease he would not have done otherwise. This day we found Major Kilpatrick, who was the most even-tempered of men, very unsettled by the order he had received from the admiral.

'I cannot conceive what advantage we will have by it,' he told Watts, laying a hand upon the map. 'All the sepoys must march, he says, and only some of the king's men be carried in the ships. The admiral might as easily carry us all in the ships beyond Mydapore and set us down half a mile below the Buj Buj fort.'

'Have you told him so?'

'Aye. And the colonel has written so from his sickbed. The admiral will not be swayed.'

'Surely the march cannot be so difficult.'

'It is the easiest stroll in the country if there be no rain. But what chance of that in this season? But you must think me a churl, William.

You have heard nothing from me these past months but my determination to retake Calcutta. Now we are ready to advance and you hear me complain of all the trouble it may cause me.'

'The track will turn to mud.'

'It will not stop us I suppose. Though the sepoys will be more concerned to sleep than fight when we arrive at Buj Buj. Let us not mention it more. You have not come to hear my troubles.'

'Mr Douglas has expressed a willingness to serve with your officers.'

'Has he indeed?' Major Kilpatrick turned to me. 'You will not take it badly, Mr Douglas, if I refuse you. It is better you know it at once than that I should give you any false hope.'

I was too stung by this blunt and unexpected rejection to answer him.

'You are aware,' said Watts, 'that he served at the siege of Fort William with great credit.'

'I am. And, were it only a question of my own inclination, he might serve with my officers and very welcome. But I tell you plainly – and in confidence – there has been too much time spent already in settling the apportionment of the spoils. Now that the admiral and the colonel have reached an agreement that it shall be an equal division between the naval and land forces, we have been able to make a prospective settlement with the officers. To introduce Mr Douglas among them now must result in a diminution of the agreed shares. There would be strife.'

'I ask only to be made use of, sir,' said I.

'Nevertheless, there would be strife. And I am sorry for it.'

While I was still reeling from the bitter disappointment of this rejection, Kilpatrick's aide announced Mr Scrafton, a young company man who had been the Third in our factory at Dacca. He was a young man, not yet twenty-five, and Kilpatrick asked him at once how the colonel fared.

'He bids me tell you that there should be no delay made now on his account, sir. He has risen from his bed.'

Kilpatrick thanked Scrafton for the welcome news and Scrafton then added that the colonel now sought to know the state of the preparations.

'I will call on him,' said Kilpatrick.

'He expects that I will bring him your report, Major.'

'I will call on him directly, Mr Scrafton. There is no reason for you to trouble yourself,' said Kilpatrick, and I saw now there was something less than warmth between Kilpatrick and this fellow Scrafton. (Watts later explained to me the reason of it, which was that Scrafton had spent much of his time at Fulta ingratiating himself with Drake, and, since the squadron's arrival, with forming a connection to Colonel Clive and Mr Walsh, the paymaster to the soldiers. Kilpatrick distrusted these manoeuvrings. 'If everything is to your satisfaction aboard the *Bridgewater*, Mr Scrafton, I will not detain you longer.'

'The captain makes some difficulty of my taking my own man aboard. I would be obliged if you would speak to him, sir.'

'If the captain refuses your man, it is not for me to overrule the order. I have just now received application from Mr Douglas here for a place on the ships and was obliged to disappoint him. If the captain cannot take your man, you must bear the hardship as you can.'

'My man would be aboard to serve me, not to grasp a share of the spoils.'

I started at this, which was an almost open slur upon me, but Mr Watts, standing beside me, put his hand upon my arm to check me.

'You will tell the colonel I shall call upon him within the hour,' said Major Kilpatrick tersely, and summoned his aide to show Scrafton out. After Scrafton was gone, there was a look passed between Watts and Kilpatrick, and the latter remarked that Mr Scrafton seemed to have a very confused appreciation of his place in the expedition.

'He will apply now to the colonel to get his man aboard,' said Watts.

'I have no doubt of it. Nor would I be surprised if he succeeded in the application.' Kilpatrick was much annoyed by this, which was my good fortune, and the best deed that Scrafton ever did for me; for I believe this annoyance was the reason Kilpatrick now turned to Mr Watts, saying, 'You have a berth in the *Salisbury*, William. If Mr Douglas wished to go aboard with you, I believe he might do some good service there.' He turned to me then. 'May I call you a marksman?'

'I can hold a rifle, sir.'

'You are a marksman then. And I will be sure the *Salisbury*'s captain hears of it.'

He was as good as his word, and when the ships some days later moved off in a slow and stately line from Fulta, I was at the rail of the *Salisbury* with Mr Watts. There was no salute of guns, nor any high display from the people who came down to the shoreline to see us off. I saw among them Mrs Watts and her children, and Mr Watts saw them too. His eyes did not leave them, nor did his wife and children leave the shore, till Fulta slipped at last from our view.

CHAPTER NINETEEN

*T*he ships rode slowly on the incoming tide, with our lookouts in the topmasts keeping in sight the sepoys who marched north on the track by the river. There was no impediment thrown in the way of our sepoys by the Hindoos of the place, but quite otherwise, for trailing after the column came a number of bazaar people from Fulta, their bullock carts laden with provisions and all manner of things which they might trade with our sepoys and soldiers, either for coin or in return for any spoils or plunder. Our lookouts watched also for any sign of ambush by the Moors, for it was certain they had heard of our advance. Mr Watts was not the only one with spies upon the river.

But there was no ambush and we travelled slowly but peacefully till we came to Mydapore, which was the last proper landing place below Buj Buj, though still several miles distant.

Here we set down the company's soldiers to join with the sepoys, and the boats carrying the artillery train likewise disembarked their cargo of men and guns. Colonel Clive and Major Kilpatrick both went ashore now and mounted their horses, which had walked up with the sepoys, and all this I watched with Mr Watts from the *Salisbury*. As we observed the soldiers struggling to get the field guns across the muddy bank to the harnessed bullocks, and falling themselves in the mud, and rising to shove and pull the gun carriages again, Watts said to me, 'You would not be with them now, Mr Douglas.'

'I would,' said I, at which he smiled sadly and said that he would ask me again after Buj Buj. And after his saying of it, when I looked at them again, it came to me that many of those who laboured there in the full vigour of life would in a short time lie dead at Buj Buj by the chance of battle. The strangeness of it unsettled me and I could not watch them longer, but went down to the armoury to get shot and powder and make ready.

When I came on deck again it was dusk and the last of the sepoys and company soldiers moving away from the landing place, commencing their night march toward the Buj Buj fort. The *Salisbury* and our other ships weighed anchor and we went upriver to a point not far below the Buj Buj fort, but hid from it by the river bend and the onset of night. There we dropped anchor again to wait for the morning's attack.

An hour later it came on to rain.

'Clear the decks! Clear the decks!'

I woke with a start and sat up. The sailors scurried by me and up through the hatch, through which I saw the grey sky of morning. A lieutenant of the ship appeared just by me.

'I am told you are to be one of our marksmen, Mr Douglas.'

'I am.'

He tossed a seaman's trousers and shirt on my pallet. 'Wear these. You will not then often so fine a target.' When I tried to thank him he cut me off with a sharp command that I should report to the lead marksman at the bow.

I quickly changed, a confusing noise and commotion all about me, as the guns were run out, the officers called orders and the sailors moved to their stations. I was about to go up when Mr Watts came from his private bunk nearby. I thought he had not recognized me in the dim light, but then as he climbed the ladder he said, 'Good luck to you, Mr Douglas.'

'And to you, sir,' said I, and I picked up the musket, powder and shot that I had kept by me all the night and climbed after him and went to the bow.

The deck, at such a time, is no place for any but a sailor, and though I tried to keep myself clear I did not escape the sharp tongue of the bosun, who swore at me several times before I found a place beyond the bow-capstan where he was glad I should remain.

The guns, lashed to the gunwales, were now set free. They swung out on their pivots and aimed landward, while panel walls of the fore-deck cabins were removed, so that the cabin floors became now a part of the deck. Between mizzen and mainmast a great net was spread, tied fast to the stays (which was to protect the men below from the danger of falling masts and rigging).

I saw Mr Watts standing back with the captain and the other officers on the quarterdeck. Like me he appeared to be at some pains to cause them no nuisance.

The sun was now rising over the land to starboard and there was an abundance of trees there, and bushes, so that we could see no sign of any men, neither ours nor the nawab's. Ahead of us were the *Kent* and the *Tyger* and I could see their men moving purposefully about. Several times I caught the sound of a shouted order across the still water. There were but three other marksmen with me at the bow, one a midshipman whose advice to me was to fire only once our guns had opened, to cease when the guns ceased and to take care not to hit any of our own people. He added, unhappily, that unless the Moors sent out boats from the fort to attack us hand-to-hand, it was very unlikely we would play any real part in the coming action, for the bigger ships to the fore of us would certainly settle it before we came up.

A flag now went up on the *Kent* and our midshipman read it. 'It is the signal to weigh anchor. We are at them.' As he spoke, our captain gave the order, the capstan turned and a light morning breeze caught the mainsail.

We rounded the river bend a few minutes after the others and sighted the Buj Buj fort at once.

There was no hurry now, nor any rush about the decks, but every man was quiet at his station and those of us up on the main deck watching the *Tyger* and *Kent* lead us in. The fort grew as we neared, but we seemed to move by inches, the slow minutes rolling by. And then came a cry from our topmast.

'It is the colonel a hundred yards on, sir!'

From the deck we could see neither Clive nor his men, but only the trees and the squadron continuing onward.

The *Tyger* was a half a mile under the fort when the Moors began to fire upon her. A puff of smoke from the southern bastion, a boom, and a splash of water near her bow and soon another shot from the fort, then another. She sailed on a few minutes more and then, at last, replied with a brisk cannonade and the smoke cleared and she fired again. In reply a more steady fire came now from the fort.

The *Kent* semaphored that we should hold back, the midshipman by me reporting this signal to me with some annoyance. Then the *Kent* moved up nearer the *Tyger* and joined in the cannonade.

In the *Salisbury* we were mere spectators, and a most curious thing it was to sit quiet and watch the exchange play out before us. The accuracy of the Moorish fire soon increased. One shot appeared to do some damage to the *Kent*'s mast, but there was no pause in her fire. After half an hour of this the *Kent* and *Tyger* both dropped anchor and swung broadside-on to the fort, and now they opened on the fort with a will.

We saw the shots going into the southern bastion, with much whooping of our men at the sight, and soon after that the signal was given for all ships to send ashore the king's troops to assist the colonel in the landward attack. Three boatloads of these soldiers went ashore from us and upwards of a hundred of our sepoys now appeared on the bank there to meet them. The admiral then raised the red flag on the *Kent*.

'It is a general engagement,' cried the midshipman by me, very excited, but anxious too, lest we miss our chance to blow the Moors to Kingdom Come.

I own there was some reason for this anxiety, for the firing of the Moors' heavy guns was much diminished since those opening broadsides from our ships. But they had increased their small-fire, both musket and pistol, and when we came up with the *Bridgewater* nearer to the fort, we received no shot from their cannon but a considerable hail from their muskets, which made us keep our heads down at the bow. Our captain now brought our guns to bear, giving cover for our sepoys, who were now attacking a Moorish battery just near to the river.

The part played in all by me and my fellow marksmen was so slight as to be barely worthy of mention, though I believe we may have hit some hapless Moors on the parapet. Other than this, my chief impression of the next hours was the terrific din made by our ship's guns, the quaking of the deck and my need to be continually wiping my eyes clear of the tears that the powder-smoke put there. There was so much of it in the air that, at times, I could hardly breathe. That the men in their confinement below decks should continue to work their guns with such ferocity was a matter of amazement to me. Satan's sprites could scarce have endured it.

By noon the musketfire from the fort had become sporadic and, in the lulls between our own firings, we now heard the sounds of a heavy skirmish among the trees to the south of the fort where the colonel and his men must now be engaged with a considerable number of the Moors. We could see none of this battle, but only the coming and going of the sepoys at the riverside battery, from which they had now struck the nawab of Bengal's flag.

The red flag on the *Kent* was lowered in the early afternoon and so we left off our cannonading and fell down from the fort a short distance, to give cover to our men at the battery.

'They are sending the guns ashore,' my midshipman told me, and he pointed to the flatboat carrying the two guns in. We were close enough in to watch our men set up the guns on the captured battery, and soon they were cannonading the fort from the south. A number of times the sepoys attacked the fort under the cover of these guns, but as many times the sharp musketry from the fort pushed them back. Nor did the Moorish musketry neglect us on shipboard, though at the distance we stood off from them now, it was more a harassment to us than any lethal danger.

In the late afternoon I went below deck to have my share of salted pork and bread and water; and while I sat upon my pallet, eating, Mr Watts came and sat by me.

'I could mistake you for a tar,' said he.

'I have been called worse today, sir.'

'There is not one of the ship's men so much as scratched by the day's work. The captain is very pleased.'

'It was the *Kent* and *Tyger* took the heat of it.'

'I would not announce it here. Did you see that boat come out from the shore to the *Kent*?'

'Some said it was Colonel Clive.'

'It was indeed he. It is reported that his men suffered some ambush. They have taken losses, but inflicted worse on the Moors. It is possible the Moors have retreated.' He looked about him to be sure that our conversation was not overheard, but of absolute privacy there was none in that place, for many of the sailors sat about, eating and throwing dice and waiting upon another call to the guns. So speaking quietly now, Watts said to me, 'There is to be a party sent ashore. It is believed a reinforcement from the ships will bolster the soldiers. It is hoped that jointly they may carry the fort – please, do not leave off from your eating.'

'Will they ask for volunteers?'

'I do not believe these navy men have a mind for such niceties as volunteers. The captain will send whom he wills. It so happens that his will is that you will make part of the shore party – if you have no objection? I have some information for the colonel and I must be sure he receives it.'

'I have no objection, sir.'

Watts patted my knee and he rose and went to the ladder, saying that I might find him in the captain's cabin and, his eyes falling on me again, he added, 'You will go in your own clothes.'

'That will not keep me from any fighting, sir.'

'Enough if it keep you from mistaking yourself for that which you are not, Alistair.' And so saying he climbed from my view.

There were two hundred or more sailors rowed ashore under cover of darkness and we were met on the riverbank by Captain Coote, who told us that the colonel was resting in the camp nearby and that we must await his command before making any attack upon the fort. But Captain Coote being himself very eager to lead such an attack, he added he would go at once to inform the colonel of our presence, so I took this opportunity to accompany him.

The camp (which was but an assortment of tents and huts and houses occupied by Clive and his officers) was not a quarter of a mile inland and the sepoys who escorted us carried lit torches by which we discerned the bodies of the many Moors they had killed in the skirmish, now lying in the road. There was also a dead elephant, killed during the day's battle, and the sepoys stopped to show it to us before we went on.

There were several torches lighting the verandah of the house which Clive had commandeered and, once arrived there, I waited outside while Clive's aide went in with Captain Coote. I had no business to hear the exchange which shortly followed, but a window of Clive's room evidently opening onto the verandah, I heard every sharp word of it.

'Admiral Watson may go to blazes.' This was Clive, and in no very good temper.

'Sir, the sailors are here now. May we not use them?' asked Coote reasonably.

'I asked for them several hours past. What does the admiral mean, to send them now?'

'There is little noise from the fort. Should we attack now—'

'We will attack in the morning. Good God! We have marched through mud all night because the man would not carry us. We have fought all through this day. And now when we might rest, he goads me with their belated reinforcement.'

'He will expect them to be used, sir.'

'They will be used in the morning when I am ready. You will tell him so.'

'Yes, sir.'

'Wait. You will go aboard yourself. Ask the admiral if he would prefer his sailors to return to their ships till the morning or to sleep ashore. But you will leave him in no doubt that there will be no attack till the morning.'

'Sir, there is a young fellow come to you from Mr Watts. He waits outside.'

'At what hour of the day do these people suppose I sleep? Send him in if you must. Send him in.'

'Good night, sir.'

'You will thank the admiral on my behalf for the reinforcement. And be sure to rest yourself before the morning.'

When the colonel's aide showed me in, I found Clive lying upon a low couch, with a lamp burning on a small table to one side of him. He had his eyes closed when I entered and his fingers interlaced and resting on his undershirt. His boots were by the foot of the couch. His belt and pistol were on the floor, within his reach. He opened his eyes and looked at me and then closed them again.

'I have brought a letter from Mr Watts, sir.'

'You should have stayed in Madras, lad.'

I placed the letter on the table by the lamp.

'Does he expect a reply?'

'He did not tell me so, sir.'

'You had best stay a moment. I have forgot your name.'

'Douglas, sir. Alistair Douglas.'

He sat up and drew the lamp to him and then he read Watts's letter. The light gave his face a ghostly cast. His eyes seemed leaden with tiredness.

'I am sorry to disturb your rest, sir.'

'Information on Calcutta is hard to come by at the present. And Mr Watts is almost the only man who can get it. For this I do not mind some disturbance.' He glanced up from Watts's note. 'Mr Watts writes here that a servant brought this report to him.'

I explained that the fellow had preferred to slip away to the far side of the river. Clive finished reading, folded the letter and put it down by the lamp. Then he stretched out on the couch again and closed his eyes.

'Shall I go now, sir?'

'I lost an officer today and nine soldiers, Mr Douglas.'

'You killed many more of the nawab's men.'

'That does not signify.' I did not know what reply to make to his remark, or whether any reply was expected of me, and so I said nothing. After a time he said, 'Yes. Yes you may go now,' and I left him.

Returning to the riverside, I found that Captain Coote had gone already out to the *Kent*. The sailors waiting ashore were sitting about idle, with their weapons ricked, and swapping stories with the soldiers about the deeds of the day. There was no fire lit, for we were not two hundred yards from the fort and, though it was an accepted thing that the Moors would not attack us at night, it was but prudence not to offer clear targets for their muskets. But, out on the river, the ships' lanterns burned brightly and there were lanterns on the bows of the smaller boats that went between the ships and across to the far shore.

'Is that you, Mr Douglas?'

'It is,' said I, peering into the darkness.

'No need to stand alone there, sir,' said he, and now I came closer and recognized that young midshipman, Adams, with whom I had shared quarters from Madras. He was sitting with some other midshipmen of the shore party and two ensigns, all awaiting the return of Captain Coote. I sat with them and they offered me brandy from a flask, which I took, and soon tiredness stole over me and I stretched myself out on the earth with my jacket for a pillow. I own I was aware of the drink passing among the sailors, as were all the officers about me, but it seemed then a matter of no consequence, for the men had fought throughout the day and now the day was ended and tomorrow they would fight again. Who would trouble now to keep them from their rum? The junior officers who sat by me certainly had no such inclination.

I drifted on the edge of sleep and the voices of the officers and the nearby sailors murmured over me, and I thought of the day and also of Colonel Clive and Mr Watts, and of the wretched state we should be in now if it came on to rain. Finally I did sleep, though it must have been an hour only, and then I was snapped into sudden wakefulness by the harsh and urgent whisper of one of the ensigns.

'Who is that bloody fool?'

'It is Strahan, sir,' came the answer from a sailor. 'He is drunk.'

'Get him back here.'

'He is in the ditch, sir.'

There was movement among the sailors, a low murmuring, and then some quiet laughter. Turning my eyes toward the fort I then saw that fellow Strahan emerging from the water on the far side of the ditch. He was immediately beneath the lowest wall of the fort. The sailors saw him too and some now took up their muskets and went after him. Their purpose, it seemed to me, was to bring Strahan back, but at their going, others now rose and these others fixed their bayonets, and then still more, and within a minute the whole body of men was up and armed and moving toward the fort, where Strahan was visibly making a surprising headway in his drunken scaling of the wall.

'Come back. Oh Christ in heaven,' muttered the ensign in angry despair, for he could not now raise his voice for fear of alerting the Moors and bringing a rain of musketfire upon the heads of his men.

'I will warn the others,' said young Adams with a great presence of mind, and I rose and went with him down the track toward where the king's soldiers were encamped nearer the fort and resting themselves in preparation for the next day's battle.

We had not quite reached them when a shot rang out. We stopped and looked toward the fort wall. A man, whom I took at first for a Moor, was alone upon the parapet. But then the fellow raised his arm and cried, 'One and all, boys. One and all,' and then there came another shot and a general cry broke from the sailors and now the crackling fire of muskets sounded from many quarters.

A drum suddenly beat the call to arms among the king's men up ahead of us. There was a general confusion in the darkness and much shouting, both within the fort and without. And in the midst of the confusion, Adams said to me very evenly, 'Sir, I fear I have been shot,' and so saying, his legs folded beneath him and he sat upon the ground. The action was so strange that I had no doubt that something had really happened to him. I crouched by him.

'Where have you been shot?'

He raised his hand to his chest but kept his eyes on mine as if he feared to look down. His shirt, I saw now, was dark with blood.

'Can you walk?'

He could not answer and so I put my hand beneath his arm and helped him up and we moved off the track and into a hollow where we might be safe from the musketshot which was spitting through the bushes all about us now. He sat with his back against a rock and I opened his shirt, and some piece of the cloth stayed in him. I inspected it as best I could.

'It was like I was punched.'

'You are having no difficulty in breathing?'

'Some.'

By the look on his face, I surmised that it was not the shot causing this difficulty, but his evident fear of what might come of it.

'I am going to touch the wound.'

He closed his eyes and turned his head aside. When I pressed my fingers lightly on his chest he made no murmur. Then I took my hand away, and he raised his own hand and touched the wound.

'Is it the shot?' he said. 'Can I feel the shot?'

'I believe so. It is lodged in your sternum.'

'I will not die, then.'

'Not tonight.'

His eyes closed and his lips moved now in silent prayer. He was but a boy and not yet ready for death.

I could not leave then, but sat with him and the shooting increased and with it the confusion and the shouting. Some cried that the Moors were advancing upon us, others that the fort was being abandoned and that we must attack, at once, through the gates. Over everything the sharp crackling fire of the muskets sounded and the powder-flashes flared in the night.

185

Within a quarter of an hour it was over and with as little warning as it had begun. The firing died and we heard our men celebrating and shouting merrily from the ramparts. We got up from the hollow and I supported Adams in our own belated advance upon the fort. Inside the gates we found a captain of the company soldiers lying dead (we discovered, after, that he had been shot by one of our own in the confusion). But he was our only fatality. There were four of the king's soldiers lying badly wounded just inside the gates and these, with Midshipman Adams, made the full price of the work. (We learned later that most of the Moors had abandoned the fort at sunset. Had they not done so, we would have paid much more dearly for our unplanned assault.) As it was, only a few Moorish bodies lay now in the central square where they had fallen. The excited soldiers and sailors lit torches and went freely about the quarters of the fort in search of plunder and set fire to any building they found empty.

Adams sat with his hand clutched to his chest and I saw he was bitterly disappointed to be so unfortunately cheated of his first chance at plunder, so I went and took a dagger and its sheath from the body of the nearest Moor and Adams was very pleased when I gave him this small prize.

'You are a gentleman, Mr Douglas,' said he. And he then spent much time appreciatively examining the carved hilt by the light of the burning buildings while we awaited the arrival of the surgeon.

CHAPTER TWENTY

'Do not come aboard,' Mr Watts called down to me, and he climbed over the side of the *Salisbury* and joined me in the boat below. 'We are for the *Kent*.' As he spoke there was an explosion ashore and we looked toward the fort. A cloud of brown dust and debris billowed out from under the south bastion, and as we watched there came a second explosion and the bastion now toppled, the rampart crashing down into the mud and the water. Watts took his seat in the boat.

'I am told the Moors left us their powder.'

'There were forty barrels, sir.'

'It will not take fifteen to level the walls. The colonel shall count that a profitable day's work.' Watts gave his orders to the boatman and another explosion came from the Buj Buj fort, and more of the walls turned to useless rubble in the mud. As we crossed to the *Kent*, I gave Watts my account of the night's battle and, though he had certainly had some report of it from the *Salisbury*'s returning sailors, he listened now with something very like amusement in his eye.

'Captain Coote is very unhappy at the manner of it,' I told him. 'I heard him say to the colonel that there could be no honour to anyone in the taking of Buj Buj by a drunkard.'

'And was the fellow drunk?'

'The sailors all believe so. It is very likely he was, sir. Captain Coote was for reprimanding the man. The colonel would not have it.'

Watts smiled. 'Yes, I see the dilemma. But success in an enterprise must forgive any faults in its execution. I daresay Colonel Clive has the right of it.'

'May I ask, sir, why we are for the *Kent*?'

'Council business,' said he, and with no sign of amusement now, but a single line of worry across his brow.

Governor Drake, Mr Holwell and Mr Becker had been aboard the *Kent* since Fulta, and as we came aboard Watts was told these three and Admiral Watson awaited his arrival in the wardroom. Two further boats came alongside – one from the shore, carrying the colonel, and one from the *Bridgewater* carrying Cooke, Drake's secretary.

'Keep yourself near about,' Watts instructed me as he followed Clive and Cooke to the wardroom. 'I shall send if I have need of you.'

Lieutenant Warwick was on the watch and, with the kindness he had always shown to me, he invited me up onto the quarterdeck. 'And how did you enjoy your first naval action, Mr Douglas?' said he, looking from the fort and on upriver. 'Is there material enough here for your sketchbook?'

I remarked that I was now better acquainted with the form and substance of smoke than I had ever thought to be.

'You were below deck?'

'No. Nor ever hope to be during a battle.'

'There are many prefer it to the open. In truth, my inclination is like your own.' He looked into the *Kent*'s rigging, where the carpenters were at work repairing the topmast and a number of sailors clambering about fixing new ropes to the yards. There had been no great damage done to us by the Moorish guns in the fort. 'If Tanner's Fort falls as easily as this, we shall be upon Calcutta inside two days.'

'This is a bigger fort than at Tanner's.'

'I have seen a sloop batter a frigate till the both of them went down, Mr Douglas. A well-handled gun in the smallest fort in the world may do for any ship in our squadron. For myself, I am content that the gentlemen in the wardroom should give a careful consideration to our advance.' At my remark that it was not careful consideration had taken the Buj Buj fort, he said, 'We would do well not to press our luck to the breaking.' He put a hand upon the rail and looked ashore. 'There have been a number of upcountry boats going to and from the *Salisbury* while we have lain at anchor here.'

'Mr Watts has a wide acquaintance in the country.'

'I am sure we are all very glad of it,' said he, and looked at me now with some meaning. After that we spoke little, but contented ourselves with watching the methodical levelling of the fort, and the burning of the houses.

Cooke left the *Kent* that afternoon, but the others who had met in the wardroom remained aboard and dined at the admiral's table with the senior officers. I dined with the junior officers and returned with Watts before midnight to the *Salisbury*. The squadron then weighed anchor and we went slowly upriver, shadowing the night march of the sepoys whose torches lit the darkness upon the eastern bank.

All the next day and night we made the same slow progress, pausing mid river whenever the sepoys ashore rested. But in the mid-morning of the next day we at last saw Tanner's Fort on the western bank and also several small vessels lying on the river below her. And nearer to us an Indiaman, which we had not expected, her flag at first invisible to us.

Almost at once there came several cannon shots from Tanner's Fort, but we were so distant they could be no danger to us and the squadron sailed on regardless. I was up on the quarterdeck with Mr Watts when the order came to clear the decks. We took ourselves to one side and watched with some admiration while the *Salisbury*'s officers and sailors went about their preparations.

Near to us, Lieutenant Warwick trained his spyglass upon the Indiaman.

'She is French, sir,' he reported to the captain.

From the *Kent* came the admiral's signal for the squadron to anchor again, which we did, and a daunting sight we must have made then to the lone French Indiaman which lay closer in to the shore. When her cannon fired, without warning, I was more surprised than I can tell. But then she fired a second time, and then again, and on till I had counted nine shots evenly spaced, and no movement or order came from our officers. Watts raised his brow to me and said, 'It is the first salute we have had. Let us endeavour that it shall not be the last.'

The *Kent* returned the salute with five guns, but we sent no one across to the French, nor they to us and I am very sure they were glad enough to be left in peace by us. Admiral Watson called the council to meet again, and so I went aboard the *Kent* with Mr Watts. I was still aboard an hour later when their meeting ended and the *Kent* and *Tyger* weighed anchor and advanced over the first stretch of water to Tanner's Fort.

Our sepoys were by this time advancing along the opposite bank toward the fort and, meeting no opposition to their advance, they made bold to stand upright and hurry on, keeping themselves now well to the fore of the ships.

No shot came from Tanner's Fort, neither cannon nor musket. Every eye aboard ship peered at the ramparts of the fort and at the ground and huts around about the walls, but there was nowhere any sign of the Moors, only some Hindoos at the ghats below the fort, bathing in the river.

'They have fled,' I remarked to Mr Watts as we came up by the fort walls and dropped anchor.

He said nothing to me in reply. We watched the king's soldiers rowed ashore from the *Tyger*. Still no shot was fired. Once ashore they assembled in good order and marched in through the river-gate of the fort. Minutes later our soldiers appeared on the ramparts and hailed us across the water, to a general cheering on the ships. Then the nawab of Bengal's flag was struck from the bastion and the British hoisted in its stead.

*

It being decided by the admiral that the *Salisbury* should remain by Tanner's Fort (both to stand guard against any attack from the Moors and to secure the rear of the squadron which would continue now to Calcutta), Mr Watts and I remained aboard the *Kent*. And it was to the *Kent* that the pinnace came which I had last seen in the river near Fulta.

'I will answer for these men,' I told the midshipman who was leaning over the rail and brusquely ordering the pinnace to stand off.

The Jew, Isaacson, came aboard and would make no answer to me when I asked after Edward, so I took him to the wardroom where Mr Watts was in company with some of the ship's officers. Watts rose at once when he espied the Jew and we all three went to the small cabin Watts had now been allocated. It was nothing commodious and I hesitated outside the door. 'You will stay, Mr Douglas,' said Watts, and he gestured to the sketchbook beneath my arm. 'You will make notes as I instruct you.'

I went in and sat upon the sleeping platform and opened the sketchbook on my knee. The Jew then recounted the state of affairs in Calcutta and told what he knew of the disposition of the nawab's Moors. The greater part of the nawab's army, he said, was now far to the north near the royal city, Murshidabad. Only some one or two thousand now occupied Fort William and Calcutta.

'And where have they made batteries? Make a sketch if you will, Mr Douglas. From Perrin's down to Surnam's Garden. Mark in the guns and batteries where he tells you.'

I drew a rough line of the shore and marked out the gun emplacement where the Jew showed me. While I did this, Watts questioned the fellow further, and now we learned that the new native governor of Calcutta had been with the Moorish forces in Buj Buj and had taken a shot through his turban, which had frightened him more than any loss of men he had suffered.

'They did not think you would attack the Buj Buj fort so boldly,' said Isaacson. I glanced at Watts but he gave no sign that the storming of the fort was other than the act of bravery Isaacson supposed. Isaacson remarked that in Calcutta they would be waiting now to hear the guns at Tanner's.

'The next guns they hear will be ours when we fire upon them in Fort William,' said Mr Watts. Isaacson warned us that the Moors were readying fire-boats to the south of the fort and taking care to load them with powder sufficient to hole the largest of our vessels. He had heard talk of a chain being strung across the river, though he had seen no sign of such work proceeding.

There were more questions, more information offered, not all of it certain, till at last Watts took money from his purse and paid Isaacson. I led the man away and was soon watching him sail upriver in the pinnace, and I with no better understanding of Edward's fate than before. When I returned to the cabin, Colonel Clive was there with Watts, both studying my sketchbook.

'I see you are a mapmaker now, Mr Douglas,' said Clive without lifting his eyes, but I could not make out that there was any friendliness in the words and so I made no reply. He discussed then with Watts the placement of the Moorish cannons, and the danger of their fire-boats, and they ignored my presence there.

Though they were far different men, to see them together like this was to recognize in them a commonality that had till then escaped my notice. There was a great challenge before them in the retaking of Calcutta and they were very forthright now with each other in their opinions. Though careful in their plans, I was surprised to hear from Clive an open admission of the shortcomings of his force and the part that chance must play in any victory. And also from Mr Watts. But I quickly saw how clear were their notions and how intent they were to deceive neither themselves nor each other. It put me in mind of my father at work with his colleagues in the laboratory or the discussions at our little society in Harrow, and so I was the sooner at ease with these frank admissions than I might otherwise have been.

Clive at last tore my sketch from the book and folded it into his pocket.

'I will take my company soldiers ashore here on the Calcutta side. I will speak with the admiral about the fire-boats. All being well, we will march on Calcutta in the morning.' He looked at me as he went from the cabin. 'Your determination I am familiar with, Mr Douglas.

Mr Watts assures me that you may be relied upon for an equal discretion.'

After nightfall, a party of sailors embarked in several boats and went up towards Calcutta, their lamps being doused one by one, till they were all of them lost to us in the darkness. And then we waited.

There were many campfires on the shore opposite Tanner's Fort where our sepoys were, and to the south of these yet more fires where the bazaar people who had followed us from Fulta were encamped. The *Kent* lying close in to this shore, we could hear the music of the bazaar people very clearly. It was flute and drum and very lively at first and the darkness gave it a mysterious charm. But after some hours the music flagged, faded to the melancholy of a single flute and finally to nothing. Upon the ship there were now only the night sounds – the creak of timbers, the whisper of the tide and the quiet murmur of voices about the deck.

'I had expected some sign by now.'

'Such a business will not be hurried,' replied Lieutenant Warwick, beside me on the quarterdeck. We stared at the darkness, toward Calcutta where our raiding party had gone to deal with the Moorish fire-boats. 'There is biscuit by the wheel if you are hungry.'

'I would be happy to find Fort William deserted.'

'Then I fear you will be disappointed.'

'Have you taken many forts?'

'Not many. It needs a war, and we have not had that good fortune since I became a lieutenant.' We had been standing for some while now talking together, and I had felt several times that he wished to say something to me, but held back from it.

'I hope it does not displease you, or the other officers, that I am come upriver with you.'

'You? No, Mr Douglas, we are only too happy to carry you.' He paused and at last gave utterance to that which had troubled him. 'I do not mean to make myself disagreeable to you, though, if we are speaking of it, I feel I must tell you that your close acquaintance with the Frenchman has been remarked upon.' When I did not immediately reply, he said, 'I trust I have not offended you.'

'You have surprised me. It is Monsieur Le Baume that you mean?'

'Yes.'

'He is a gentleman and an officer of the company.'

'He is not liked.'

I was taken aback. 'I do not choose my friends by the likes or dislikes of others,' said I, though I kept my voice low, for fear it might carry across the deck. 'And if I had a mind to be offended, I would be offended now.'

'I should tell you something which I would not have repeated.'

'If I may not repeat it, I would prefer you not tell it me.'

'You must know of this matter.'

'I cannot bind myself to secrecy on any matter which is yet hid from me.'

He looked upriver again, as if there might be there some answer to the quandary he was in. I regretted, then, the words that we had already spoken, for I knew Warwick for a good officer and a gentleman and I could not believe that he intended malice to any.

I said, 'Let us not speak of it again.'

'It is suspected by some that the man keeps too close a connection with the French.'

I was struck dumb by his words. In the darkness I could not properly read his face, but it was no jest he had made, for he had spoken in deadly earnest. But before I could recover myself, he pointed and said, 'The Moors' fire-ships are burning.'

Turning, I saw the distant glow of orange light very clearly. The light flared, intensely bright, and some moments later the boom of the explosion reached us. Warwick left me, with no more said between us, and went to report it to the admiral.

'You will wish me *bonne chance*?'

I looked up from the midshipmen's table where I breakfasted. Le Baume had put his head in at me the doorway, for he had come down to fetch the junior company officers to the boats which were now ready to take the soldiers ashore for the march on Calcutta.

'Good luck,' said I after a moment.

He smiled, slapped the doorframe, and went to hurry his men. I stared after him, feeling a sickness in my stomach. I was ashamed of myself that I should have any suspicion of him, for there was nothing I had seen in any of his actions but was honourable. And yet Warwick's words to me I could not shake. At last I roused myself and went on deck to find Mr Watts.

'I do not see the colonel,' said he. I pointed out the mounted figure of the colonel, just by the trees on the shore. There were most of the soldiers already arrived there from the ships to join with the sepoys. 'Ah yes.' His spyglass moved. 'Yes, and there are Major Kilpatrick and Captain Coote.' His spyglass moved again, sweeping along the bank. Our infantry were assembling there with their muskets. 'I trust it looks something like an army. And if it does not, there is nothing to be done now. And here is Captain Le Baume going ashore with the last men. Will you see?' I declined the offer of his spyglass.

Within the hour the men ashore marched. At the admiral's command, we weighed anchor. The decks were cleared and we sailed at last for Calcutta.

'You may have the use of my cabin, gentlemen,' called Admiral Watson to Mr Watts and Drake and me, for we were standing at the rail on the main deck, and it was very evident he wanted us kept from beneath the feet of his men. But we declined his offer, Drake speaking for all three of us, saying that we would take muskets to the bow and play the part of marksmen there. Once we had got our muskets, we went up to the bow, Drake looking anxiously ashore and remarking that we were already far in advance of Colonel Clive.

Mr Watts, who was but a poor hand with a musket or pistol, now asked me what stance I had found best when I had played the marksman at Buj Buj. I showed him, and recounted some advice the *Salisbury*'s midshipman had given me, which was to fire only when the natural rise and fall of the ship was at the high or the low.

'He advised me also that I should keep below the gunwales while reloading, and so have a coward's fair chance of keeping my head upon my shoulders.' This last I had meant in jest, but I saw by the sudden look Drake gave me that he had taken my words very ill. He pushed by me and settled himself on the far side of Mr Watts.

The *Tyger* was in the van and she came up fast on Surnam's Garden. The Moors at the redoubt there fired upon her, but she answered them at once and the Moorish guns fell immediately silent. The *Tyger* continued on her way, the *Kent* after her, and as we came up we saw the happy sight of the Moors there fleeing from the redoubt. The incoming tide carried us swiftly on and very soon Fort William appeared ahead of us.

There came a sudden thickness in my throat, for the sight of it called to mind the last time I had been there and everything I had witnessed at the siege.

We passed a great smouldering wreckage by the shore, which was the work of our raiding party in the night, and a moment later the Moors' guns in Fort William opened upon the *Tyger*.

The first shots fell useless in the water and she deigned no immediate reply to them but went on nearer. After a minute her starboard bow-chaser fired and then all her starboard guns and the air shook with a tremendous thunder. We saw a shot from the fort go into her. A spout of water then erupted from the river by our bow and Drake was up and fired his musket and Watts after him.

The *Tyger* was moving close under the fort now and the *Kent* not far to her stern. Our starboard guns opened upon the fort.

I clutched at the gunwale and looked at Mr Watts and he at me, for when the *Kent*'s guns opened it was like something God never intended for this earth. The air was rent, and rent again, and it was not a sound only but a physical force and the first shock of it made me reel and almost fall. Watts then shouted in my ear, but the gun nearest us had fired and I was so deafened I could not hear him. He thrust his musket at me then and took mine, and then I understood that I must reload for him.

All the first minutes of the action I was in a stunned daze and reloading the muskets mechanically for Watts and Drake. But after a time, the firing eased and when the smoke cleared I saw that we had put down the best bower and were anchored now, the tide swinging our stern toward the fort. Our starboard guns then ceased firing, but almost at once the guns at our quarterdeck and stern opened on the fort. As the ship continued to swing slowly on the anchor cable, these in turn fell silent and a hawser was put out to hold us steady. I saw now that the *Tyger* was in a like position upriver of us and just under the fort's northern bastion.

Further out in the river the *Bridgewater* and *Kingfisher* sailed on, safe from Moorish guns of the fort.

'They go to stand guard at Perrin's,' Watts shouted to me, when he saw me watching them. 'We want no Moors falling upon us from the river.' But scarce had he spoken than our larboard guns opened on the fort, and then the *Tyger*'s larboard guns joined in the cannonade, and I saw our shots strike home into the bastions. The cannon-fire from the Moors was sporadic now, but their musketshot constant.

We sat there at anchor and took their musketshot and pummelled them with our guns. All sound reached me now as through water, though my mind remained clear. And now that Watts loaded for me, I did some fair mischief against the Moors on the parapets.

We kept at them fully an hour.

And then came a noticeable faltering of even the musketshot from the fort, and soon I had no more targets, for the Moors disappeared from the parapet. A minute more and their firing ceased utterly. Our own guns fell silent, and then we raised ourselves, and I looked with some wonder upon the smashed walls. The nawab's standard still flew, though I know not how.

All now awaited the admiral's command, for there seemed uncertainty among the officers of what had happened, whether the fort had been abandoned or if some ruse was being practised.

There was no sign of the colonel's forces to the south, or even the sound of musketshot where we had expected their arrival.

'We have broke them,' said Drake, and he looked upon the fort with a bright eye. He had not stinted himself in the battle. He had braved the musketshot of the Moors as well as any and seemed in himself reborn by his actions.

The command came to lower the boats.

'Sir, I would go with them.'

'Very well. But you will not go off chasing after the Moors,' said Watts, who must have known that I had no such intention.

I crossed over to the Great Ghat with the boats and planted my feet again on the ground of Calcutta. The sailors ran toward the river-gate of the fort and I moved off alone into the settlement in search of Fairborough.

CHAPTER TWENTY-ONE

I clambered around the piles of stone and timber from which the nawab had been raising his new mosque, and when I heard shouting looked up to the parapet and saw the nawab's standard being struck from the bastion, and our soldiers raising the British colours. There had been hardly a shot fired since they had entered at the river-gate, but now I heard musketshot to the east, beyond the settlement. I had no doubt there was some revenge being taken on the fleeing Moors by those Hindoos they had hurt since our expulsion. But from the south, the direction from which Clive was advancing, there was not even the sound of a pistol.

'Edward!' I called and I got past the new mosque's foundations and ran toward Mr Bell's house, calling again, 'Edward!'

There was scarce a soul to be seen. The Moors were all fled, but the Hindoos, Armenians and topasses still kept themselves hid. Twice I saw children's faces at the windows, but they drew back in fright when they saw me. I had my pistol drawn ready when I entered Bell's house lest I be surprised by a tardy Moor.

'Edward, are you here?'

Receiving no answer, I went down the central hall and looked in at each room. I will not say the house was destroyed, but it was despoiled and there had been fires lit in some of the rooms. I had been in the place several times when Mr Bell and his family lived there and hardly a piece of their furniture now remained. The pictures were all gone. The rooms were bare, but for a single rug in each and some large embroidered cushions piled up by the walls. In a rear room, Moorish clothing lay abandoned on the floor. I went out and made directly for the hospital.

It was there, beyond the burial ground and at a safe distance from the fort, that I began to see some Hindoos of the town come into the streets – very few, to be sure, and those few very fearful. They regarded me with a deep distrust and suspicion, so that I was very glad of my pistol. I hailed one of these fellows who I saw standing near the hospital's main door and asked after Edward.

'Is the fighting finished, sir?'

'We have the fort. The Moors are fled. But where is Fairborough?'

'He was taken to the fort when the ships came.'

As I hurried back to the fort, I found the soldiers now moving out through the settlement and I made sure to stay in the open that they might see me the more clearly. But they had other thoughts now on their minds – I heard two of them debating the quickest way to the goldsmiths' quarter in the black town. Nearing the fort, I saw now that the steeple of St Anne's had been toppled and that many of the buildings near the fort had been pulled to the ground.

At the fort's main gate I found half a dozen of the king's men standing sentry.

'You may not pass, sir,' one of them told me, very firm.

'But I am come from the *Kent*.'

'I know where you are come from, Mr Douglas. But this gate is barred by the order of Captain Coote.'

'But I must be admitted.'

'They will admit you at the river-gate, sir,' said the man, in such a tone that I knew mere reason could never prevail here. The man's orders were an obstacle immovable.

On the Great Ghat there was considerable traffic of men and supplies already arriving on flatboats from the ships and passing up through the river-gate. I joined with this stream and passed unchallenged into Fort William. I went at once to the Black Hole prison. But the only prisoners in there were a handful of Moors.

'Fairborough?' I said through the bars. 'Edward Fairborough.' They showed not the slightest recognition of the name. 'European,' I said. 'A big man – dear God, this is hopeless.'

The soldier standing guard offered to beat them for me and, I confess, I might have accepted the offer had I thought such a beating might make them answer. It was while I was in this pass that I saw Mr Watts crossing the yard. I hailed him, and when he came across to me, explained my trouble. He spoke through the bars in their own tongue and the Moors were immediately on their feet. They spoke to him with a considerable excitement and it was some while before he could calm them.

'These are simple men,' he said to me after hearing them out. 'They have been told by their officers that we are in the habit of burning our prisoners at the stake. I have assured them that we would not think to do worse than shoot them.'

'What of Fairborough?'

'They have seen Mr Fairborough here in the fort.' Mr Watts turned to the bars to hear something one of the Moors was telling him.

'What is it?' said I, but Watts raised a finger, commanding me to silence, while he questioned the fellow more. When he was done, he turned on his heel, bidding me come with him. 'Mr Fairborough was not held here alone. They say he was held with a Jew.'

'Isaacson?'

'It must be. They have been taken to Omichand's house.'

We passed out through a small door in the main gate, and those same king's men who had refused me entry were still at their posts outside. But standing before them now was Colonel Clive, and behind Clive the company soldiers, and behind these some several hundred sepoys. It was evident we had arrived in the midst of some dispute between

Clive and the sentries, for he was now saying to their leader, 'I will not be refused by you, nor will I have my men so treated.' He broke off upon seeing us. 'Mr Watts. I can get no sense from these here. What is Captain Coote's business in the fort?'

'I believe the admiral has made him governor.'

'What nonsense is this? I have had twenty of my men go into the fort by the river-gate and Captain Coote's men have straightaway put them out.'

'I am sure it is a misunderstanding.'

'It is a misunderstanding by Captain Coote, as he shall soon discover.'

The company officers standing close by their colonel now looked upon the king's men standing sentry at the gate with a real belligerence. I felt that there was some mischief threatening and I think Mr Watts felt it too, for he invited the colonel to step aside with him that they might speak privately. This they did, taking a slow turn together beneath the fort's eastern wall, Clive speaking hotly and Watts trying to calm him.

The cause of Clive's unhappiness was only too clear – the ships had retaken Calcutta without him. And then to discover that his sepoys had been unceremoniously ejected from the fort and that Captain Coote had been appointed governor without consultation – the hurt to the colonel's pride was only too evident. And to me, in my need to be away from there, it all appeared quite absurd.

Then happened the lucky accident of Captain Latham's emergence from the gates. He was a friend to both the colonel and the admiral and he went now to join Watts and Clive. There was further talk till, at last, all three came back to the gate. Colonel Clive, with a face like thunder, went in with Captain Latham to seek out Captain Coote. Watts came away with me toward Omichand's house.

'Is the matter settled?'

'The management of it is now in Captain Latham's hands. I pray there is no more of this, for we cannot be divided while we fight the Moors.'

'Will the nawab come down upon us?'

'Who can say what foolishness this nawab may not sink to? Yet for the present, I am more greatly concerned for our friends.'

We came around by the ruin of St Anne's and the first thing we saw was the nawab's standard flying from a pole in Omichand's garden. In silence now we hurried on to the house.

'Edward,' I called as we entered and Watts called out, 'Isaacson!' We went on through the house, calling to them, with our pistols loaded and ready

Unlike the Bells' house, this one of Omichand's was untouched. All its furniture remained. No mark had been made upon its walls. There was no one in the lower rooms, so we went up the stairs, and all my thought now was of that previous time when I had climbed the same stairs and the dreadful scene that had then awaited me.

But in the upper rooms was no sign of Edward or Isaacson. We entered that room where Omichand's man had set the fire. The floor was still blackened, but polished smooth now, and there were papers left about as though the place was but newly abandoned.

'If this was Omichand,' said Watts, 'it appears that he does not think to be long away from here.' He picked up a few pages, glanced at them and then put them down. 'He will have left nothing of importance. I would wager he is out at his garden by the Maratha Ditch, waiting for everything to settle here. By morning, he shall be at the fort with an offer to us of his inestimable services.'

We went out to the landing, and were about to descend the stairs, when we saw through the window a person moving in the yard behind the house. But there was something very wrong in the movement and, while we watched, the fellow staggered like a drunkard and fell.

'It is Isaacson,' said Watts and he raced down the stairs and I followed at his heels.

It was indeed Isaacson, but an Isaacson scarce recognizable from the man who had come to us in the *Kent*. He had been beaten so badly that his whole face was discoloured and swollen. His eyes were little more than blackened slits and his clothes were torn and bloody. Watts knelt and cradled Isaacson's head and Isaacson clutched at him with a feeble hand.

'It is I,' said Watts. 'You are safe now. You need have no fear.'

'Gone.' said Isaacson, though very indistinct and hoarse. 'Are they?'

'The Moors are gone.'

'Where is Fairborough?' I asked him.

Isaacson attempted some answer, but then seemed to choke. He began a violent retching.

'Bring him water,' said Watts, lifting his chin toward the well.

But as I went to the well I noticed a palanquin lying near, tipped on its side. I hurried over and looked in. It was empty, but there was blood on the cushions inside. I looked back at Watts. He was calming Isaacson now and talking with him. I came away from the palanquin and crossed to the well and lowered the bucket. Putting a hand to the windlass, I raised the bucket, calling to Watts, 'There is a palanquin over here. It may be Edward's.'

'Alistair. Come back now.'

'One moment.' The bucket was up and I turned and set it on the well's rim.

'Alistair! Leave that. Come away.'

'I will bring it,' said I – and then not a word more, for I had put the wooden ladle into the bucket, and now I stared at the red water that was in the ladle. And then I looked into the well.

I was not in my right mind then – not for some while.

We buried Edward the same evening. There were others to be buried too, from the *Kent* and the *Tyger*, for the Moorish cannon and musket had not been entirely useless. There was a dignified ceremony performed and a sobriety observed by our small party in the graveyard, while the *Kent*'s chaplain read the service and the bodies went into the ground. But from the fort and the settlement there drifted over us the first music of the night's celebration, for the living must live in spite of death, which none knows better than a British soldier. Nor did I weep at the graveside, though I had cried like a child when we first raised his body from the well. It is no small thing to see a friend so used and brought to an end that a man could not wish upon a dog.

'You will not stay in the writers' quarters,' said Watts as we came from the burial ground.

'I cannot stay on the ship any longer, sir.'

'You will accept the hospitality of my house here, Alistair. No – say nothing. I will not debate it with you. My servants have nearly all returned. They are preparing a room for you even now. I am summoned to the *Kent* to dine with Admiral Watson. But I will make sure my cook will not let you go hungry.'

'Please do not trouble yourself.'

'It is no trouble to me. Indeed, it may spare me much trouble, for I would not have you fall ill.' I said nothing, but I felt him watching me now. 'I would not intrude upon your private thoughts but, if I may make so bold, I would ask that you keep it before you that war is no respecter of persons. We can none of us expect to be always in safety. And we must all look to God's mercy at the last.'

'God is in heaven, but I am upon the earth,' I murmured, and Watts begged my pardon, that he had not heard me. 'I will accept your kind offer of a room, sir. And you need have no fear of me falling ill.' He patted my arm in solace and I saw that he watched me very closely, for he had most certainly heard what I had said.

His house was close by the north wall of the fort, overlooking the river, but it had not suffered the same despoliation as most of the houses in the settlement. His servants told Watts that an official of the nawab's had occupied the house. That was why the doors and shutters had not been torn from their hinges and used as firewood, which had been done in those houses where the Moorish troops had been billeted. Much of the furniture, though, had been taken, so there were few comforts there, saving only the greatest one of privacy.

When Watts was gone out to the *Kent*, I sat upon the verandah steps and picked at the flat bread and the spiced mutton his cook had prepared for me and watched the small boats moving between the ghat and the ships. The deep peacefulness of it all seemed very strange to me when I thought on the fearsome battle there had been out there in the morning. And not that morning only, but during our own besiegement in the fort, when on the same riverbank had lain the many topass women who had drowned. Nor could I get my mind free from Edward, or from what they had done to him. At last I went down the steps and along the Great Ghat below the fort, but I could not throw off my troubled thoughts. Some sailors playing at dice there hailed me and I stopped by them in the torchlight.

They were as intent now upon their game as they had been upon their fighting, and I was glad, for a while, of their company. A flagon of rum passed among them and when it came into my hands I drank some of it down, which pleased them, and they carried on with their game and paid me no mind now. I stood with them till they, with rough courtesy, invited me to join the game and then I took my leave of them.

By St Anne's, the sepoys had made their camp, the officers taking up quarters in the houses near at hand and the common soldiers setting down their sleeping rolls in any sheltered place they could find. Several campfires burned on the street there, and that same music played which I had heard downriver at Tanner's Fort, but it gave me no pleasure now and I did not tarry but went up the steps into church.

There had been considerable destruction done inside the place – the pews were all gone, and the altar, and great piles of rubble from the fallen roof now lay across the broken floor. Nor was I alone there, for up near where the altar should have been, there was a man and a woman kneeling. After a minute they rose and came by me, the man nodding to me as he passed. It was Mr Hatherley, one of the company's senior traders, whose only son had died in the Black Hole. Mrs Hatherley did not look at me, but clutched a kerchief to her mouth, and her husband supported her now across the rubble and out from the church.

I picked my way across the fallen stone and tiles and finally found the clear place where they had knelt. I did not kneel, but sat upon a stone and thought of Edward and of the good man that the Reverend Bellamy had been, and of the other victims of the Black Hole and those who had died at the siege. It was almost too awful for contemplation. I closed my eyes and then came to me the words of the Psalmist, 'O Lord God, to whom vengeance belongeth. O God, to whom vengeance belongeth, shew thyself.'

I sat there in quietness and the words echoed in my soul.

CHAPTER TWENTY-TWO

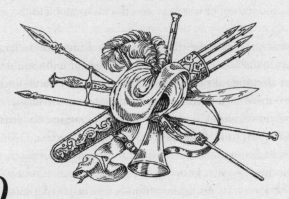

'Open the gates!'

The river-gate fell open at the order and Drummer Fredericks played in the admiral and his party of naval officers from the ghat. A line of the King's 39th came to attention as the admiral and officers crossed the square to the flagpole. The council waited there with Captain Coote and the colonel. And all about the square and at every vantage were the other soldiers and sailors. It was a very fine scene, which I might have sketched, had I the heart for it.

That fellow Cooke, with an obsequiousness fit to turn a man's stomach, bustled about the admiral and Clive and Drake with needless instructions on how the ceremony was to proceed. Colonel Clive finally stepped forward to formally present the keys of the fort to the admiral. Each of them made a pretty speech in praise of the other's valour and then Cooke ushered Drake forward. Then the admiral made another brief speech before at last handing Drake the keys to Fort William.

Between Watson and Clive there had been a formal correctness, the key passing between them as a token of that honour each man claimed for himself in the reconquest of Calcutta, but Drake, upon receiving the keys, was quite visibly affected. He was governor once more, and no surer proof than the keys in his hand, and when he now made his speech of acceptance his voice quavered. He closed his speech by reading out a formal declaration from the council, which he said the council had unanimously agreed upon the previous evening.

It was a declaration of war between the company and the nawab of Bengal.

'I will post this upon the gate,' he said, holding the declaration up for all to see. 'And I am informed that the admiral will soon post a like declaration alongside it on the behalf of the king. I need not rehearse to any here the unjust treatment we have had at the nawab's hands. That time is at an end. We must be free to exercise our lawful rights as bestowed upon us by legal treaty with the emperor in Delhi. And if the nawab continues to interfere with those rights, or obtusely seeks to deny them, then he must know that we now have the means to maintain them by force of arms against him or any other. We will be trifled with no longer. God save the king!'

An echoing chorus of 'God save the king' answered him from the whole crowd about the square.

The drummer boys started up again and escorted Governor Drake, Admiral Watson and the council to some private place in that small quarter of Government House which stood undamaged. The midshipmen standing by me began to speculate how much further the squadron might now range upriver and the extent of the plunder to be had there. I had meant to return at once to Mr Watts's house, for he had asked me to await him there, but as I turned from the midshipmen now I overheard a remark that stopped me.

'The admiral should not wait, but knock the French out of Chandernagore directly.'

I listened now and heard many similar sentiments expressed. I quickly found out Adams, who was fully recovered now from the shot to his sternum, and drew him aside.

'What is this of Chandernagore?' I said quietly.

'It is the French stronghold on the river, sir.'

'But what is it they speak of? I have just heard your colleagues here speaking as if we should fight them.'

'That is their opinion only, sir. For myself, I would sooner trust the admiral's judgement.'

'But the declaration of war was against the nawab, not the French.'

'We will fight the nawab and the French both, sir. That is the belief in the squadron.'

'I never heard of this belief before now.'

'It was not commonly spoken of before now. But certainly it was thought of, even in Madras.' I fixed him with a stern eye. I knew that he hid something from me. And because he did not like to deceive me, he at last relented. 'Yesterday in the evening – you must not repeat where you heard this—' I assured him I would not. 'Yesterday a conversation was overheard between the admiral and Lieutenant Warwick. It is a certainty we are at war with France, sir. We have been at war with them for some months.'

'But the admiral did not fire upon the French Indiaman below Buj Buj. Nor did they fire upon us.'

'He is a fox, sir. And they are cowards.' He begged leave to rejoin the other midshipmen, for they were now returning to the river, and so I released him.

At war with France. And it says much that I did not for a moment doubt the truth of it. Such rumours had been rife in Madras and, though I had heard less talk since our sailing, the possibility of it had been there all the while. But once in Fulta I had thought only on Buj Buj, at Buj Buj on Tanner's and once at Tanner's my every thought had been turned toward Edward's fate in Calcutta. My only wonder now was at how well the secret had been kept, for I could not conceive that Admiral Watson and Lieutenant Warwick were the sole possessors of it. Mr Watts must certainly have known and also the colonel – and how many others? And me, like a blind man in their midst.

Lieutenant Warwick was standing with some of his fellow officers by the flagpole. They were taking their ease and talking with the few European women who had come upriver already from Fulta behind the squadron. The lieutenant removed himself from them at my approach.

'I never saw your Governor Drake look more cheerful,' said he. 'He waved that declaration very fiercely, did he not?'

'Are we at war with France?'

He never faltered, but only touched his fingertip to his hat as one of the two women departed the group just by him. 'If we were at war, it would be for the admiral, and not one of his captains, to declare it.'

'I have my answer,' said I. And then, 'But you are not a captain, Mr Warwick?'

'Others have had the good manners to conceal their surprise.' He told me he had received his commission from the admiral that same morning. 'I had not even the time to put on my new buttons before we came ashore. And now I must not stand here idle.' We went toward the river-gate with me offering him a belated congratulation. I asked him what ship he would command. 'The *Thunder*. She will be a bomb boat, if only I can get the powder and men.'

'You may take me as a volunteer.'

'You do not know what we are about.'

'You mean to go further upriver.'

'Your business is here.'

'There is no business here.' I gestured around the fort. 'It will be months before the company has rebuilt. And the company has declared war upon the nawab. Every servant of the company is surely now a soldier.'

'This is not the Inns of Court, Mr Douglas.'

Passing out through the river-gate, we went along to the President's Ghat, which was the only pier that had not been burnt by the Moors. The idea of going upriver with the squadron had now taken hold of me, though I had not thought of it till this same minute. I would be out of Calcutta and away from the scene of horror and Omichand's house and I would get a weapon into my hand. By the time Warwick got down into his boat, I had from him the time of his sailing, which was before dawn on the next morning's tide, and the destination, which was the nawab's stronghold at Hugli.

'I will come out to you in the morning, before the tide.'

'You must speak with Mr Watts,' he called back, and his boat shoved off toward the *Thunder*.

Had I let but one word fall of my intent, Mr Watts would certainly have forbidden it and so I made sure to keep myself clear of him for the rest of that day. In the evening he dined with the council in the fort and I slept early and rose before he awoke the next morning. I left a note for him to find when he breakfasted.

And by sunrise I was aboard the *Thunder*, and moving upriver with the tide.

It was not the whole squadron, but only three ships, the *Bridgewater*, the *Kingfisher* and the *Thunder*, that the admiral sent on this raid upon Hugli. And the largest of these, the *Bridgewater*, we almost lost in the first hour of the journey, for she grounded upon a sandbank by Perrin's and could not be got free. Lacking the means to assist her, we in the *Thunder* carried on up to the Dutch settlement of Barnagore, where we anchored to await the others. We waited both that day and the next before they came and then there was a meeting of the three captains held aboard the *Bridgewater* to determine how they might proceed safely in these higher reaches of the river. If a grounding like the *Bridgewater*'s should again happen, and near to the nawab's soldiery, it must end in our own certain slaughter.

There were one hundred and thirty of the king's men embarked on the ships, three hundred sepoys under Major Kilpatrick's command and many sailors who had volunteered from the *Kent* and the *Tyger*. Our hostile intent could not be mistaken and, though there several Dutch vessels lay at anchor nearby, they sent no boats to us in the two days we waited there, nor did the Hindoos come out to trade with us.

Captain Warwick did not invite me to his bridge (I think from a feeling that he should commence in his post as he meant to continue, without favourites, but with a firm and just command). So I kept company with Captain Coote and some of the other officers and it was from them that I heard we had finally been refused all assistance by the Dutch, who feared the nawab's wrath against them. Our captains had, in consequence, determined to send a party of sailors to the Bataviaman which lay near us and to steal away her pilot by main force, which act was being done even while the officers told me of it.

Within the hour, and no shot being fired, there was a very frightened but quite serviceable Dutch pilot aboard the *Bridgewater* and we all weighed anchor at last and proceeded toward Hugli.

The three towns of Chandernagore, Chinsurah and Hugli (which was the Moor's stronghold on that part of the river) all lay in extreme proximity to one another, with Chandernagore, the French stronghold, being the southernmost, just two or three miles short of the Dutch stronghold in Chinsurah. After Chinsurah there was but little open ground before Hugli.

'That is Fort Orleans,' I told Adams as we came up toward the first town, Chandernagore. 'And gentlemen there will surely know that we are at war with them.'

'If they fire upon us, sir, we will make them regret it.'

Captain Warwick ordered the guns on the main deck to stand ready. Several of the French Indiamen lay at anchor close in to the fort and we saw their sailors lined up at the rails. They were not thinking to fire upon us, but gazed over the water with no small curiosity. Up on the ramparts of Fort Orleans, the artillerymen stood at their guns. There came from them no salute to our passing flag, which we should have had by the friendly custom of the river.

And so we passed slowly by Fort Orleans and Chandernagore, and I could not help but think of Monsieur Renault and Monsieur Law, who must certainly be in the fort, and of the hospitality they had given to us after Calcutta's fall.

'The admiral will not like it that they did not salute us,' remarked Adams.

'It is not the worst they might have done.'

'There is no excuse for them, sir,' he said darkly, for a dislike of the French was in his bones. 'The admiral will not like it when he hears.'

We lay up that night abreast of the small and worthless Dutch fort at Chinsurah, and in the morning we spied Moorish troops on the eastern bank.

'They are the remnant of the Moors we drove from Calcutta,' said Captain Coote, peering through his spyglass. 'They will try to cross the river to go to relieve the fort at Hugli.' As he finished, the *Bridge-*

water fired into this remnant, a short cannonade, but uncommon accurate. The Moorish column broke in several places and fled at once to safety, away from the river.

Our three ships moved now with no haste, but much menace, till we were abreast the town of Hugli, just a few hundred yards below their fort. We anchored, and straightway opened with our guns upon the town.

Though the heavy walls of a fort may take a hundred shots and still stand, the walls of a house are another thing entirely. The buildings of Hugli now shattered and collapsed like dolls' houses under the terrible rain of our shells. There was some feeble musketshot came back at us from the shore, but after an hour even this fell away. Unopposed we shelled the place mercilessly, taking care to spare only the few warehouses near the shore.

At midday, those remnants of Moors from Calcutta were spied again. They were now on the bank opposite the fort, collecting boats there and making ready to cross. The *Bridgewater*'s guns fired into them again, but they did not run and so four flatboats full of armed seamen were sent over. They rowed right up, near to the bank, firing their muskets and throwing the Moors into a great confusion. The seamen torched the Moorish boats they found there.

'You will not stay with the bomb, Mr Douglas?' said Captain Warwick, when he saw me going over the side with the king's officers. The firing of our ships had ceased and now the soldiers and the sepoys were going ashore to wreak that terrible destruction ordered by Admiral Watson and Colonel Clive.

'I am familiar with the place,' I told him. 'Captain Coote has requested that I take him to Coja Wajid's house, which is known to me.'

'I have no desire to answer to Mr Watts for your loss.'

'I shall remember it, sir.'

I went down into the boat with Captain Coote and some others and we crossed over to the nearest ghat, and already the soldiers ashore had started the great burning.

CHAPTER TWENTY-THREE

Those warehouses we had spared from our shelling were now unguarded, and the sailors had battered down the doors and commenced their plundering by the time we came ashore. The flatboats were already being loaded with the plunder.

'There is an avenue further on,' I told Coote as we went up by the warehouses. 'It runs to the east of the fort. Coja Wajid's house is before the fort, but on the far side of the avenue.'

'Is there cover from the fort's ramparts?'

'There is a walled garden behind the house.'

He commanded a junior officer to stay with the plundering sailors till they had finished there. Coote then led the rest of us up through the town.

There was hardly a shot fired at us till we came within range of the fort, but then the Moorish defenders opened on us and Coote and his men were only too glad to hurry after me into the safety of Coja Wajid's walled garden. Within minutes the soldiers had broken in one of the rear doors to the house and were rushing inside. I sat and rested a moment by the fountain, in that same place I had once rested with

Edward. At the far side of the fountain, Captain Coote dipped his kerchief in the water.

'You must not judge the men hard,' said he.

'I do not judge them.'

'The order is to despoil. It is sharp revenge for the Black Hole.'

'It is a wild justice. And you may believe me, sir, when I say I do not judge the men. They may destroy this town and all its people and none better pleased than I.'

Another officer called him away and I was left alone by the fountain. In the next minute two Moorish servants of Coja Wajid's were dragged from the house and shot dead in the courtyard just by me. I got up from the fountain and walked by the bodies and went into the house.

All through the afternoon and night our ships pounded at the fort walls, attempting to make a breach. Sailors were sent ashore with scaling ladders, and I was with the officers when they gathered in a room of Coja Wajid's house to hear Captain Coote's final instruction. 'It will be a diversionary attack upon the main gates while the greater part of our force scales through whatever breach the ships have made in the walls.'

'And if no breach is made?'

'There will be a breach.'

'How many are in the fort, sir?'

'We believe there are one or two thousand.'

The officers were silent, each making a private calculation of our chance of success. But none seemed daunted.

'The diversionary attack will itself need some cover.' Coote looked about him. 'Mr Douglas, you will keep three men in the house here. The upper windows have a clear view of the fort gates.'

'Yes, sir.'

'Very good. Then we only await the breach.'

The breach was made at two o'clock in the morning.

We fired upon the fort's gates and ramparts from the upper rooms and the Moors, with increasing ferocity, returned our fire even as our soldiers on the street below advanced toward them. We had but forty soldiers committed to the diversionary attack, but these now made such a din with their cries and their muskets that the Moors brought ever more men onto the ramparts for fear of being suddenly overwhelmed. And while this was doing, the ships' cannon fell silent and our main force, down nearer the river, rushed as one and broke in through the breach.

Our diversionary force broke off now and sped around to the southern side to join their fellows. And now from our place in the upper room we could see the sailors scaling the fort's walls.

'Let us get down there,' said I, and the other three rose and raced on ahead me. When we came from the house, the others ran to the south of the fort, so they did not see the main gate come suddenly open. 'Wait!' I cried, but they were already lost in the darkness, running to get some share of the spoils.

The first Moor came from the gate and ran northward, away from me. And then another. I went onto one knee, raised my musket to my shoulder and when the third man appeared through the gate I shot the fellow dead. Very calmly and deliberately, I then reloaded. When I raised my musket again, the Moors were spilling from the gate not in ones and twos, but in a rushing stream. I shot into the stream. There was no pause in them, but they rushed on, driven like frightened cattle from the fort by our soldiers. I reloaded and shot into the stream again.

Though I was exposed all this while, I do not boast of it, nor count it any mark of courage. I felt nothing in these moments, neither anger, nor fear, nor any nobler thing. They ran in panic from the fort, thinking only of escape, and I shot into them because they were Moors and our enemies. But the stream ran thick and fast and the fort was soon drained of them entirely. Soon it was our own soldiers came out the gates and fired after the fleeing Moors and then I left off my firing.

But my heart was set on destruction now and there was a wild recklessness in me. I went into the fort and fetched a torch in my hand, and the loosed spirit of vengeance became part of me, and I ran with the others and set the buildings all aflame.

What use to tell every detail of what we did that night and on the days and nights that followed? Enough to know that we destroyed. We put aside our humanity and wreaked a blood vengeance on the Moorish stronghold. At daylight we left the dying conflagration within the fort and spread like locusts through the town. We burned the granaries and sacked the houses and moved on and killed any Moor that we found. That first day, each man said to his fellow, 'Remember the Black Hole' and suchlike phrases, but by the third day each fed his own appetite freely, whether for plunder or destruction or some worse thing (for there were women taken).There were no justifications made, nor judgement given, and it was not only the sepoys who did the worst acts as some officers afterwards claimed, but each did that for which he must one day answer to his Maker.

And once Hugli was laid waste, we overspilt the boundary of Hugli and entered into the black town of the Dutch stronghold of Chinsurah. The Dutch soldiers were too few to match us and so stayed within their fort, while the Dutch governor sent desperate letters of protest to our ships, some of which came into the hands of Captain Coote, who showed them to his officers and to me. For after the third day, the flame of vengeance being quenched in me, I kept close by Captain Coote, who had not for a moment lost his reason in the midst of all the destruction. But the forces at work in those days were not such as might be constrained by any officer and Coote could only wait for the demonic flame to destroy itself.

It took fully seven days. On the eighth day, when the men, in exhaustion, begun to gather down at the ghat, Captain Warwick ran up a flag to call his sailors back to the ship.

When I went aboard, the *Thunder*'s deck was crowded with bales of cloth and all manner of crates and boxes bearing the personal marks of the seamen. And when I looked below-decks it was equally crowded with both men and plunder. The press of my fellows was intolerable to me at that time and so I found myself a small private space up on the main deck, squeezed between the gunwale and a bale of silk, and there I rested my head on my jacket and slept the sleep of the damned.

*

We did not go to Fort William directly, but anchored two miles north of the Maratha Ditch and close to the shore, for just inland of this place the colonel had established a camp. We now learned that the nawab and his army were marching toward Calcutta, though they were not expected for some days yet. Clive had set up his camp here to meet the nawab's advance. We set ashore those sepoys and company soldiers that we carried and while I watched them disperse into the camp, Captain Warwick hailed me.

'Mr Douglas. I am sending a boat down to Calcutta with Captain Coote and his officers. There is a place in it for you.'

'I thought I might go ashore here, sir.'

'There is a place in the boat for Calcutta and you will take it.' His look was severe, but as I went to where Coote and the officers were waiting for the boat to be brought up, Warwick lifted his chin toward the bales and boxes on the deck. 'Point out what is yours, Mr Douglas and I will see that it finds you in Calcutta.'

'There is nothing.'

'Nothing?'

'No, sir.'

I turned from him and he said, 'I hope you do not think yourself a better man that you made no gain from the plundering of Hugli.'

'I had not thought on the matter,' said I, though in truth I was much discomfited by his words.

I begged my leave of him and he bade me pay his respects to Mr Watts. And so we parted.

Our boat drew up to the Great Ghat and there were many coolies at work there, some repairing the stonework in the fort's walls, others mixing a thick mortar, and others labouring to replace the wooden piers which the Moors had destroyed. All of this made a considerable contrast to the dreadful scene we had left behind us at Hugli. We got from the boat and, as I walked behind Coote and the others up to the river-gate, someone called, 'Mr Douglas!' and I turned found that fellow Sri Babu approaching. The others went on without me.

'Where is Omichand?' said I when he reached me, for my heart was very bitter against that blackguard and against everything which had been done at his house.

'He is not in here. He is detained by the nawab.'

'When he returns, Mr Watts will speak with him.'

'I must see Mr Watts now.'

'I am sure you many find him at his house or within the fort. Good day.'

'I am refused entry to the fort.'

'The security of the fort is not in my charge. If the guard have denied you, I expect they have an order for it.'

He did not reply to this, but his dark eyes stayed fixed on mine a moment. I believe he sensed the change there had been in me since our last meeting. At last he stepped close to me and from his loose-hanging sleeve produced a packet. 'I will wait at Omichand's house,' said he.

I slipped it discreetly into my coat and went then in search of Mr Watts.

Drake's secretary, Cooke, told me that I must wait.

'But I have that for Mr Watts which touches directly on the council's business.'

'So you say,' said he.

'Do you question my word?'

'This is not a military camp, Mr Douglas. And it will do you little good here to mount the high horse of your honour.'

'I pray you will tell Mr Watts that I have for him those papers which he commanded me to bring for him.'

'You did not say so before.'

'I say so now,' said I very evenly.

Cooke appeared to consider whether he might still dismiss me and finally decided that he could not. He rose reluctantly and went into the council chamber. Presently Mr Watts came out alone.

'I understand you have those papers I sent for.' He raised a brow.

'Forgive me, sir.'

'It will be some time before I forgive your flight to Hugli, Alistair. Pray God, what were you about?'

I took Sri Babu's packet from my coat and gave it to Watts, explaining how I had come by it. Watts tore open the packet immediately and went to Cooke's table and sat to read the letters.

'We had some of the injured from Hugli arrive here yesterday,' he said as he read. 'They seemed well pleased with the havoc they had caused there.'

'Yes sir.'

'Where is Sri Babu now?'

'He waits at Omichand's house.'

Watts kept his head bent over the letters. I was grateful now that Sri Babu had met me, for the letters had deflected Watts from all other considerations, most particularly from my own unsanctioned journey to Hugli. I watched in silence while he read, but after a minute there came a sharp jangle of metal on the stone stairs behind me. I turned, expecting to see an officer. And so it was. I stood bolt upright.

'Monsieur Cordet,' said Watts. 'I think you know our enterprising writer, Mr Douglas.'

'We are acquainted,' said Cordet. He did not shake my hand, but dipped his head to me in a formal manner. Watts asked him to go straight into the council chamber and Cordet rested a hand on the hilt of his sheathed sword and went in.

Watts refolded the letters now and regarded me. My gaze rested on the chamber door where Cordet had disappeared.

I said, 'The fort at Chandernagore gave us no salute as we passed. Neither in our going up, nor in our coming down.'

'Cordet is here as a second to Monsieur Sinfray. They have been sent to us by Gouverneur Renault.'

'To seek a neutrality with us?'

'The French have offered to act as intermediaries between us and the nawab. And these letters you have had from Sri Babu make a similar offer from Omichand and Coja Wajid. It appears that everyone is, of a sudden, very anxious to intercede on our behalf.'

'Renault fears our guns.'

'We must presume the presence of the admiral's squadron has played its part in the gouverneur's calculations. But that is by the bye. Your room at my house is as you left it. My family have now taken up residence, so you will not find it so quiet as before.'

'I can move to the writers' quarters, sir.'

'You will stay where I tell you. And for the moment that will be in my house.' He rose and put the letters into an inner pocket. At the council chamber door, he paused. 'I would be obliged, Alistair, if you were to leave no more such foolish notes on my breakfast table.' He went in and closed the door behind him.

There was a hip bath brought to my room. I stripped and got into it and then a Hindoo servant poured cold, clean water over me, from a pail. I sent him for more water and then flannelled off the grime and the dirt while I watched young George, Mr Watts's son, attempting to catch a green gecko which moved along the wall of my room. He reached, and missed, and reached again.

'What shall you do with it if you catch it?'

'Keep it. May I put a chair on the bed?'

'Will you fall?'

'No.'

'You will not cry for your mother if you fall.'

'No.'

I pointed to the chair at my table and he went and fetched it back to the bed. He put it up by the pillows, and then clambered onto the bed. The chair was unstable, and so he rested a shoulder against the wall and snatched at the gecko quickly, and got it. He came down carefully, the gecko trapped between his hands. He went and slipped the thing into a small box he had left on the table.

'Yesterday I caught a spider. Do you think they would fight?'

'I should think the lizard might eat the spider.'

'Did you go to Hugli?'

The question caught me unguarded. But I answered yes, that I had.

'How many Moors did you kill?' He was not looking at me. He had

221

edged his box open a crack and was peering in now at the trapped gecko.

'I cannot say,' I said.

'I killed sixteen flies. I fed them to the spider.'

'That is your mother now, calling for you. Tell her that I shall be along presently.'

When George had gone, the servant came with more water and I finished my bathing. After I was dressed, I took the chair down from the bed and caught my face in the glass a moment. And then I quickly looked down and fixed my coat and went out.

While I had been with the expedition in Hugli, the people in Calcutta had not been idle. And now, as I walked out with Mr Watts and his wife to take the evening air and to pay a visit to the injured in the hospital, I had the opportunity to see what was being done in the way of rebuilding the settlement. The debris of battle had been cleared from the streets around the fort and the stone and rubble of the fallen buildings had been gathered into large heaps. There was a scaffold of bound poles rising up the sides of St Anne's and also up the sides of several other tall buildings which had lost their roofs. The coolies went to and fro with baskets of stone balanced upon their heads and many carpenters now worked to replace the doors and shutters which the Moors had stripped from the houses and burned.

Those Europeans who had kept premises in the settlement had reclaimed them immediately upon their return here from Fulta, but, though they had set them again in good order, it was very apparent to me that it would be many months yet before the life of the settlement was properly re-established. But a fair beginning had been made, at least, which was more than I had expected from the way our people had languished so miserably in Fulta.

'Hope,' said Mrs Watts, upon my remarking the change in our people. 'In Fulta, they had surrendered it. Restored here, they are restored to hope.'

A woman then called to her from along the street, and her face fell. For it was Governor Drake's wife with another wife of the council, and with them a company officer. Mrs Watts said to me quietly, 'You may flee whilst you can, Alistair,' and I would most surely have done so had not the officer been Captain Le Baume. He smiled broadly when he saw me and came and shook my hand while Mrs Drake fell to conversing with Mr and Mrs Watts. Le Baume had heard of my joining the expedition to Hugli and he was eager now to hear the details of it directly from me. I put him off with a meaningful glance at the ladies about us.

'But have you seen the Frenchmen here?' said I. 'Messieurs Sinfray and Cordet?'

'I heard that they were here.'

'Have you met them yet?'

'Why should I need to meet them?'

'I only thought, as you must know them—'

'I am not of the council. They have no reason to ask after me. Nor I after them.'

I saw very well then that he had as little inclination to discuss the Frenchmen as I to talk of Hugli. And so I asked why he was not out at the camp beyond the Ditch with the colonel; but by Le Baume's look, I perceived that this was a subject no better than the first. He told me briefly that it was necessary for a company to stay in the settlement and that he had been deputed by Clive to be that company's commander.

'So you are our last line of defence,' said I, to cheer him.

'I am put here to be out of the way. But you must join us. We can defend the gaol together again,' said he, and he seemed amused now at the thought that we should be so strangely returned to the place where we had begun.

But then some mounted men came down the main avenue towards us from the fort, and as they neared we saw that it was the Frenchmen and their sepoy escort. Cordet lifted his hat to Mr Watts and the others and he inclined his head to me as he went by, but to Le Baume he gave not the slightest acknowledgement.

There was less comment on the two Frenchmen than there might have been had it not been for the presence among us of Le Baume. And Mrs Drake having by this time decided that our two parties should join together and that we should now all go on to the hospital, we then turned out of the main avenue and went up by the destroyed arsenal. I stepped up with Le Baume by Mr Watts and mentioned to him Le Baume's offer that I join with his company inside the settlement.

'That is a gentlemanly offer, monsieur,' said Watts, leaning forward and looking across me to Le Baume. 'Unfortunately I cannot make Mr Douglas available to you.'

'But I will be here, sir,' said I.

'You will not,' said he. 'There is some work you must do for the colonel.'

CHAPTER TWENTY-FOUR

'*I* requested an assistant to copy the accounts and the Return.'

'That is why Mr Watts sent me, sir.'

'It is drudge-work for a scribe. He should not have sent you.'

I stood beside the colonel on the earthen wall of the tank, looking down at the company soldiers being drilled across the level ground below us. It was almost the first time since the outset of our troubles with the nawab that I had seen anything that answered to my imaginings of real soldiery, and I was very glad I had not taken Scrafton's advice to await Clive's return down by the tents. Clive spoke with Major Kilpatrick, who stood to the other side of him. There was some discussion between them concerning the poor handling of one of the field guns below.

'And are the councillors still at each other's throats, Mr Douglas?' said Clive, watching an ensign run an order down to the artillery officer.

'I could not say.'

'Because you know not? Or because you would not?'

'Neither know, nor would, sir.'

'I will have a wager with you,' said he, with his eyes moving continually over the drilling men below. 'I will wager you have brought for me a letter from the Fort William council. They will remind me that it is by their authority only that I have command over these men.'

'There is also a letter from the admiral. And one from Mr Watts.'

Clive paid me no heed, but gave order for the sepoys to be brought onto the drilling area. As the sepoys took up their formation, their chief officer, the *subadar*, came up and I moved aside that he might stand by Colonel Clive while the sepoys were put through their drill. At the *subadar*'s command, his junior officers set the sepoys in motion below us and from the sepoy's wearing of the company uniform, and from their well-practised movements, there was nothing from that distance to tell them apart from the regular company soldiers, but only their turbans. After another half-hour of advance and retreat, the late-morning heat came on and Clive then ordered the *subadar* to rest the sepoys and to choose a dozen among them to go north and bring back report of any Moors having crossed the river yet up near Hugli.

As we came down from the tank (which is like a small reservoir filled with water), I noticed a number of soldiers standing sentry by the heavy forest nearby, and when I expressed surprise to Captain Coote that they should expect attack from such a quarter, he repeated my remark to the others, at which they found some amusement. The *subadar* then told me that the sentries had been placed there after wild buffalo had attacked and badly gored two sepoys who had gone to the forest for their daily ablutions.

Clive led me into his tent and unlocked the wooden chest there. 'Take up your quill, Mr Douglas, and look your last upon the daylight.' Inside the chest lay a prodigious disorder of papers – receipts and bills, notes of payment, banker's drafts, and a hundred things beside. 'I have not had time to go through all this since Madras. You may believe I am a better soldier than ever I was a writer.' He gave me the key to the chest, saying that I should begin immediately, for the sloop *Syren* was to leave within days and the Return must then be ready for the directors in London. 'Mr Scrafton has looked at some of it. He may wish to check the Return when you have done.'

So commenced my short service with Colonel Clive. Once he had ordered that a desk and chair be brought for me, he took from me those letters from Calcutta and retired to his bunk at the rear of the tent. His own campaign desk was set up near to the tent's opening and, having read the letters, he went there and took out paper and ink. 'How many were in this French delegation?' he asked me over his shoulder.

'Two, sir.'

'And were they well received by the gentlemen of Calcutta?'

'There is no good feeling toward the French at the present time.' I glanced across at his back. 'It is a common belief in the settlement that we are already at war with them, sir.'

'Civilians are always too free with their speculations.'

'It is spoken of in the fleet also. It was talked of very openly while we were in Hugli.'

He craned round. 'You were in Hugli?'

I hesitated and then nodded.

'It is not a matter for shame, Mr Douglas,' He turned his back on me again, and took up his quill. 'If it succeed in bringing the nawab to reason, I had ordered a hundred Huglis.'

All that day and the next I spent at the ledger, drawing up the accounts and bringing some order to the paperwork in the chest. For the most part I did not move from Clive's tent, for I frequently had to put before him unexplained pages that he had signed that he might clarify my understanding of them. On some few occasions he had need to speak privately with Major Kilpatrick and Captain Coote and the other senior officers and then I was sent from the tent to make a survey of the weaponry and powder and men in the camp, that the Return for the directors in London be accurate. In the course of gathering this information from the officers and men, I found them in almost universal good spirits, and not in the slightest perturbed by the reports of the nawab's advance toward us. The only cause of any trouble among them was a certain envy directed at those who had been up at Hugli, for the spoils were by this time sold on to the bazaar people, who had their own lively encampment two hundred yards east of us, nearer the river.

To Scrafton I applied but once for some assistance. He raised himself on his elbow but did not get up from his bunk.

'If you cannot do it,' said he, 'you should not have come out here.'

'It is merely these two numbers.' I showed him the paper. 'I think that is your signature. But the reckoning of the two numbers seems to me incorrect.' He did not like to hear it. He waved the paper away. 'You will make no objection then, Mr Scrafton, if I alter the reckoning.'

'This is a trivial matter.'

'Then you make no objection.'

'It is to decide such trivial matters that you have been brought here, Mr Douglas. Do with it as you will.'

I did not apply for his assistance a second time.

When the tide came up from Calcutta, then the admiral would send a boat up with his letters for the colonel and, on the ebb tide, Clive would send his own letters in return. It was this continual sending and getting of messages that most surprised me while I was in the colonel's tent, for scarce ten minutes of the day passed uninterrupted and Clive was ever at the centre of it, not wearied by it, but, to my estimation at least, much enlivened. He seemed almost a different man than the one I had spoken with when he had lain as if stricken after the skirmish at Buj Buj. Even in the matter of the accounts he was not so slovenly as I had first assumed (and he had pretended to me), for he had a private cipher with which he had marked many bills, and after he had shown me his method I was able to work through the chest more quickly than either one of us had expected. I was almost to the bottom of it when Major Kilpatrick came one afternoon to the tent in the company of a sepoy.

The sepoy made his report. A part of the nawab's army had crossed over the river and these Moors were at Cowgutch, thirty miles north of us. Clive questioned the sepoy a minute more and then dismissed him.

'Do you credit the number?' Clive asked Kilpatrick.

'Ten thousand infantry? It does not surprise me.'

'Shall I leave, sir?' said I.

'Stay and finish it,' Clive told me. 'You are almost done, and I have sent for a boat to take you with the Return and accounts down to Calcutta.' I did as he ordered, and he fell again to talking with Kilpatrick so that I learned, even before most of the officers, that Clive fully meant to meet the nawab in the field.

I finished the papers that same hour, and while Clive's officers gathered in conference at his tent I went around by the tank, to the place where the sepoys had their camp, to find out the exact number of *sowdars* that had returned from the northern patrol. Once that number was finally entered, the Return would be complete and I might then leave for Calcutta. The *subadar* directed me to the drill-ground and there I found the returned *sowdars*, playing a mounted game. Amidst a cloud of dust, they were in full cry, so I climbed a short way up the earthen wall of the tank to a place of safety from whence I might count them all. After I had tried and failed to tally them amidst the movement and dust, my eyes settled upon one bold figure who, though continually pushed aside, continually returned. I studied him a moment more and, certain now, cupped my hands to my mouth and cried, 'Harry! Harry Khan!'

I hurried down the bank and called again from the side of the ground and he, at last, heard me and cut from the game. He rode over and dismounted.

'I had not thought we should meet again,' said I. 'We were told you were a prisoner.' He held out his arm and showed me his wrist. A deep scar, the breadth of a manacle, encircled it. 'Mr Watts is in Calcutta. I am returning there, you must come with me.'

'You are not *subadar* here.'

'I shall speak with the *subadar*.'

He brought the reins over his mount's head, turned from the drill-ground and I walked at his side. It seemed no great pleasure to him that I had discovered him there. I had many questions for him and it was some minutes before I understood the reason of his reluctance to answer me. He did not want to speak of the prison. And yet that prison in Murshidabad was where he had mostly been since the last day that I had seen him. He was thinner now, certainly, but there was another change in him, visible only in his eyes, and I wondered at what horrible cruelty had been done to him there. He told me that he had been released from the prison seven weeks past, on a Moorish holy day. Some friends he had in Cossimbazaar had taken him in and nursed him. He had started south just two weeks ago and met up with our sepoys from the *Bridgewater* above Hugli.

'But you need not remain with the sepoys here, Harry.'

He stopped at the rail and tied his horse there. He undid the girth and took off the saddle. 'Tell Mr Watts we need bullocks to pull the guns.'

'Come with me and you may tell him.'

'The nawab brings fifty thousand. Mrs Watts and her children should go onto the ships.'

'No one here speaks of so many. You must come with me,' said I. He looked around at the sepoys and the company soldiers. They were not a tenth of fifty thousand. He shook his head. 'Then I cannot persuade you?'

Again he shook his head.

The boatman then found me. He reported to me that the boat was standing ready at the river, under the colonel's orders, and waiting to take me with the accounts and the Return down to Calcutta.

'He would not come.'

'I am glad enough that he is alive. I confess I had hardly expected it,' said Watts.

'He was concerned that they had no means by which to draw the field guns.'

'The council has the colonel's note on the matter. Tell me – did the news of the nawab's army crossing the river cause the colonel no alarm?'

'It did not seem so. He and Major Kilpatrick appeared very sanguine of it – if anything, in some eagerness to join battle.'

'No talk then of a retreat to Fort William.'

'They regard the fort in its current condition as indefensible. And they have no expectation that the nawab will be foolish enough to bring his army within range of the ships. But there was no fear in the camp.'

'The men take their confidence from Colonel Clive. From what source he takes his, God alone knows. Forgive me, Alistair, a glass?' His hand hovered over the tray and he then poured a glass of Madeira for each of us. Since my return to Calcutta, and Mr Watts's immediate invitation to me that I should repair with him to the privacy of his drawing-room, I had found his manner rather strained and distracted. I had thought at first that the fault was mine, that I had done that – I know not what, except it concerned Hugli – for which I must now in the privacy of his drawing-room, receive his considered and just rebuke. Several times he seemed on the point of coming to the matter, and as many times he veered from it with further questions on all that I had seen out at Clive's camp. But now when I took the glass from him, he came to it.

'Alistair, I find that I must ask of you that which I have no proper right to ask.' His face was expressionless and all the strain now was in his voice. 'There has been a deal of unpleasantness within the council. There has been all the business of the siege played out again. Accusations have been made. I have found my own character impugned over the loss of our factory at Cossimbazaar.'

'Your character, sir?' I broke out in some surprise.

He set down his own glass. He dropped into a chair.

'The *Syren* departs in the morning. She will take a number of letters to the directors in London from individual members of the council. I tell you no secrets if I say that Governor Drake and Mr Holwell have quite contrary reports to give on various incidents during the siege. The time that we have wasted in council discussing the matter – I am ashamed to think on it. I had thought we had done with contention when we left Fulta. How very wrong was I.' I felt dismay at this, for a divided council could do much harm to us with the nawab again ready to come beating at our door. 'I speak now in confidence to you, Alistair. As I would not speak but from the press of circumstance and time. The *Syren* will take their letters, whether I speak or no.'

'I understand.'

'You do not understand, but that is no matter. To be plain, I find myself compelled to do what I would not, which is to meet my fellow councillors upon the squalid fields of contention. I must compose my own letter – which is to say my own defence – to our directors in London. And that before the *Syren*'s departure.'

'Surely the directors will not be swayed against you.'

'That you may be the judge of yourself.' He rose and beckoned me to the table, and upon my going there he took a bundle of handwritten pages from a satchel and placed them into my hand. 'Here is a copy of the governor's recounting, from the surrender of Cossimbazaar till our retaking of Calcutta. Mr Holwell, I understand, has written his own account, but has refused to supply me with any copy.' He then took out another bundle and placed it on the table. I saw at once that these were the pages I had writ myself, at Mrs Watts's bidding, when I first arrived in Chandernagore after Calcutta's fall. 'If you are agreeable to it, I would have you read the governor's account and make a note of any assertion you feel unwarranted by those facts you were witness to. Your own first account may supply any lapse of memory.'

'But how may this help you?'

'You will understand when you have read the governor's letter.'

I drew up a chair. There was quill, ink and pages, ready upon the table. I thumbed the pages Drake had written. 'The governor has spent no little time over this, sir.'

'Alistair, you may refuse me, and I will say no more on it.' I did not reply, but turned the first page to make a start. Watts's hand came down upon mine. 'There is council business in the letter. I have not removed it, lest I be tempted to spare myself. But it is a great trust I am placing in you.'

'I know it, sir.'

'You shall,' he said, and he then lifted his hand and withdrew himself from the room. I took up the first page of Drake's letter.

The two hours that followed I account a watershed in my education, for in the first hour I read and reread Drake's letter. Once I had recovered myself, I referred to my own account and made a note of anything I would question. In the second hour, I called Mr Watts in to join me. I showed him the notes I had made and he talked to me very freely then of all the matters to which Drake's letter pertained. It was an opening of the curtains behind which the affairs of the company were hid, and I own I was child enough that it was a flattery to my vanity.

Yet this was nothing to the deepening shadow that moved over me as I came to understand the great care that had been taken over Drake's mingling of truth with lie, so that fair actions were traduced as blameworthy, brave actions seemed cowardice and good men became but agents bent on the governor's destruction.

The tone of the whole was set at the very outset of the letter. Here Drake, with supreme effrontery, reported the advertisement he had made in Fulta, by which he had requested those who slandered him privately over the fall of Calcutta to make a public declaration of their accusations against him. None, he wrote, had done so. Having thus established himself as an upright man among vipers (and the directors having no means of knowing the scorn felt toward Drake over this advertisement, which none dare answer for fear of the governor's power), the remaining part of the letter made sure to justify Drake in all his actions. And every stage of the whole disaster leading up to the siege and fall of Calcutta was made to seem the result of decisions made by other members of the council, most particularly by Mr Holwell and Mr Watts.

Yet against these calumnies, there was also some measure of truth in the letter, sufficient, at least, to give some credence to the whole. And I saw very plainly now why Mr Watts should need to send the directors a letter of his own.

And beside those intrigues with the native people of which I had been dimly aware, there was in the letter considerable mention made of the activities of the merchants Coja Wajid and Omichand and, most astonishingly of all, a bald assertion from Drake that he believed Omichand had been responsible for first calling down the nawab's troops upon us, though this last being joined with Drake's self-exculpation over the imprisonment of Omichand in the Black Hole, I was at a loss to know how I might read it.

There was much mention of the man Rajaram, the nawab's chief spy, and also of Sri Babu.

Watts went very carefully through the notes I had made and asked me many questions. He sat at the table now and, as we talked, made notes of his own in preparation for the drafting of his letter.

'I cannot believe that you can take this so calmly, sir. I have never liked Mr Drake, but I think now that I despise him.'

'It was not to have you take my side against the governor that I showed you his letter. And you may trust me – there are many worse men in this world than Governor Drake.'

'He has traduced you.'

'A man who has been called a coward will rarely respond with temperance.' He saw that I was not persuaded. 'Answer me this then, and truthfully – do you believe him a coward?'

I had reflected on this matter frequently. I had seen Drake flee the fort. But I own, there was something in the reasons he had since given for the action. And while he had been in the fort, he had not played the part of a coward. And I had seen him wield the musket in the fort's recapture. 'I believe that he is base. But no, I do not believe him a coward.'

'No more do I. But he must live all his life now in the shadow of the word. Put yourself in imagination beneath the same shadow and you will perhaps understand him the better.'

'Shall that excuse him?'

'What shall excuse me, Alistair, that I now answer with a like letter of my own?' He bent his head over his notes. 'Let the blameless judge. I am not of that party.'

'You may send to the directors all that I have writ there, sir. I will put my signature to it.'

'I thank you for the thought. But you must know that as a writer your words will carry no weight in London. Worse, the inquiry into this affair will be a snare for the innocent. Be advised, you must not put your name or signature to anything in this business.'

'My offer stands.'

'As does my refusal of it. And I must now have some privacy, if you will.'

CHAPTER TWENTY-FIVE

*T*he nawab approached and all Calcutta waited. Yet it was very much different from those days before our besiegement the previous year. For on the river now were the admiral and his squadron, which we might with full confidence rely upon, and to the north of us lay the encampment of the colonel and his men. And in the settlement the people who had been so long at Fulta, and in such straits, knew well now the price of defeat. So there was not now that air of negligent complacency there had been before, but each man now stood ready to do his duty.

While we waited, the Frenchmen, Cordet and Sinfray, returned to continue their parley with the council.

'Gouverneur Renault will support the nawab against the British,' Le Baume told me when I called upon him at his quarters in the settlement to tell him of the French envoys' return. He was in his garden with a sepoy officer standing on the open ground nearby, sword in hand. 'Pondicherry has sent him no reinforcement. He has seen what you have done at Hugli.'

'They were Moors we fought at Hugli.'

'They were your enemies. Gouverneur Renault will expect no better treatment at your hands. He must make a neutrality with the British or ally himself with the nawab.'

Le Baume drew his sword and went forward, calling the armed sepoy onto the bare ground. I sat myself on the verandah steps then and watched the thrust and parry of their swords. Le Baume had the advantage of the other fellow and several times paused to give the man some instruction, but it was not ten minutes before Le Baume halted the proceedings and took the sepoy's sword and sent the fellow away in disgust.

'I cannot find a single one of them with a hand for it,' said he.

'May I?' I rose from the step, indicating the spare sword he held.

In some surprise, he gave me the sword. I went down and crossed to the patch of bare ground. There I took my stance and then went through those exercises Jean-Claude had taught me. I had not practised for some considerable while and I faltered at first. But Le Baume, watching my efforts, called out, 'Less shoulder. It is not an axe.' I tried again. He called more advice to me and encouragement. After a few minutes I began to move with more ease, though far short of my expectation of myself.

'Your father is a soldier,' he called to me from the steps.

'My father is dead. And while he lived, as far from being a soldier as any man may be.'

'But an officer has taught you.'

'A Frenchman,' said I. 'Perhaps that is why I wield it like an axe.'

He laughed. 'If you show the colonel, he will surely grant you a commission.'

'One broadside from the *Kent* will cut down any number of perfect swordsmen,' said I, slicing the air and thinking of what I had seen on the ships.

'I have heard artillerymen boast of it. But they are, in every army, the men with the least conception of honour.'

'But they are right.'

'They may be as right as they please. You will not find a single gentleman among them.' It was what Jean-Claude would have said. Le

Baume asked the meaning of my smile, but I shook my head and continued my exercise and now he came across to me and gave me some proper instruction. But while he instructed me, he asked what I had seen at Clive's camp. It was a question I would never have hesitated to answer but for Lieutenant Warwick's warning to me that night of our approach to Calcutta. Nor was it lost on me that the colonel might have had some reason he had left Le Baume in the town and not taken him out to the camp. Now I made some innocuous remark about the men's spirits being high and added, 'If the nawab attacks, you will certainly be called up to reinforce the colonel.'

'It is possible. Till then I am only Omichand's gaoler.'

I stopped. I rested the point of my sword on the ground.

'I had thought Omichand was with the nawab.'

'He returned to his house this morning. Till the council know the true reason for his return, Omichand may not move freely about the town. I have set a guard there. I am no officer now, but only a gaoler.'

Being now acquainted with the many suspicions held by the council concerning him, I was only too glad to hear that Omichand was watched. But upon my remarking that this might be a duty as important as any other, Le Baume shrugged as if my words meant nothing, for he was convinced already of the slight being done to him. He took the sword from me now and sheathed it, promising to continue the lesson at another time.

As we crossed the garden toward his bungalow, I took the invitation from my pocket. It was the reason I had come to see him. 'You are invited to dine with Mr and Mrs Watts.'

'That is very kind.'

'Cordet and Sinfray shall be there.'

He continued to the steps in silence.

'Melchior?' said I, and I held up Mrs Watts's card to him.

He looked back. 'You will ask Mr and Mrs Watts to accept my apologies. I find that my duties do not allow of my dining with them tonight.'

Before the Frenchmen and the other guests arrived, Mr Watts called me out to take a glass with him upon his verandah and now we sat there quietly and watched the red clouds of sunset across the river. Out on the *Kent* and the *Tyger* the first of the night lamps were being lit and a *syrang* steered his small boat past the ghat in front of us and upriver. The *Syren* had departed and taken with it the strain that I had felt in Mr Watts. He was relaxed now and was not in the least troubled by Omichand's reappearance, and when I asked him, he spoke to me openly of the reason for the French envoys' return to us.

'There is no mystery to it, Alistair. They are in fear of us. They see our good fortune in having the admiral and the colonel with us at this moment.'

'We share a common danger in the nawab.'

'They see it. But they have been very careful to let us know that their General Bussy has an army prepared to enter Bengal at their summons.'

'But that is to threaten us.'

'It is to warn to us that they are not quite so helpless as they appear. And they have offered again to stand intermediary between us and the nawab. We have rejected their offer. And if you know that we have asked again if the Chandernagore council will put its seal to a neutrality with us, you know the whole business.' He turned and called for a servant, who presently came out with a lamp. The lamp was set farther down the verandah, where it might draw off the insects. Then came from the house his children to bid their father good night, which made a most charming picture as they bent to receive his kiss upon their foreheads. Next they came to me and George shook my hand and then his sister. George had from me then a promise to sketch the serpent that their cook had killed, and from his father a gruff admonishment to let me alone. After the children were gone inside again, Mrs Watts came out to join us and she made no mention of the council's business or the nawab or the French, but she spoke of her children and of some small affairs in the settlement. I saw that it was very agreeable to Mr Watts to listen to this awhile and put aside the great affairs that he was caught in. And I marked again the perfect amity and understanding between them, with sometimes a glance or an expression doing the work of many words.

The surgeon, Dr Forth, arrived first and then some others of the town, and at last the Frenchmen, who at once begged Watts's pardon that they must be on the road from Calcutta before nine o'clock.

And so we went inside to our supper.

'Pray, how does Madame Sinfray?' Mrs Watts asked.

'Very well,' Sinfray replied.

'You will not forget to pass on my best wishes.'

'No, madame.'

'Madame Sinfray was good enough to bring me her dressmaker when I first arrived in Chandernagore,' said Mrs Watts, turning to me for some assistance, for I had proven a more willing conversationalist all through the meal than had the sullen Monsieur Sinfray. 'I am sure I departed Chandernagore more in the fashion than ever I entered it. And all by Madame Sinfray's kindness.'

'I am sure we many of us will echo the sentiment,' broke in Dr Forth. 'For I think we all here have some reason to be grateful of the hospitality shown us in Chandernagore.'

There was a general murmur of agreement around the table. This was, indeed, the reason Mrs Watts had arranged the supper – that there might be some gratitude shown to the French by those of us to whom they had given refuge in Chandernagore. Unfortunately, Sinfray had shown little inclination during the meal to acknowledge the effort she had gone to in arranging the supper, but had rather behaved as though he were with us now on sufferance and would very much like to be gone.

But now that Dr Forth had spoken, others of us around the table asked to be remembered to various ones in Chandernagore. As did I, saying that I hoped I might one day call on the French sea captain who had given me the freedom of his house and library

Monsieur Sinfray could not hold out entirely against this general, friendly assault. 'My wife will be touched that her kindness is not so easily forgot, Madam Watts. Merci.' He raised his glass and offered a toast. 'Gouverneur Renault,' said he.

Mrs Watts glanced uncertainly at her husband, as did I and most of the others at the table. But Mr Watts never hesitated, he raised his own glass and we all now followed his example.

'Gouverneur Renault.'

The dishes were taken away, and more wine poured, but neither Cordet nor Sinfray indulged themselves. Cordet sat opposite me and, though we had not spoken, I had seen that he had made some effort at civility with both Mrs Forth on his right and Mrs Armstrong on his left, the wife of the engineer. Now Cordet looked past Mrs Armstrong and asked her husband what progress he was making with the re-building in Calcutta.

'It goes on. It goes on. They tell me I am too impatient, monsieur. Well, if I am, it is Bengal has taught me. I have been patient before. My reward for it was to have nothing done by those who had earlier prom-ised me the world.'

'Spoken like one of the company's own traders, Mr Armstrong,' put in Watts genially.

'Truly, Mr Watts, I cannot get done in a month here, what was the work of a day in London.'

'I see you are rebuilding your church first,' said Sinfray. 'When you are done, you must come up to advise us.'

'But it is only your steeple is down,' said I.

Cordet dropped his head to one side. He asked me how I should know that, of the steeple.

'I saw it.'

'But when?'

I would have given much at that moment to be saved by any other at the table, but Mrs Watts was busy instructing the servants and Monsieur Sinfray was remarking to Mr Watts the lateness of the hour and the Armstrongs and the Forths were now talking together, so I could only sit pinned beneath Cordet's steady gaze.

'I saw it as we sailed by Fort Orleans.'

'No Indiaman of yours has come up.'

'No.'

His eyes narrowed. 'The *Bridgewater*?'

'I was in the *Thunder*.' He looked at me now without speaking, but with such a look that I felt I must answer. 'You have seen what the Moors did here in Calcutta.'

'Yes. And after your ships left, I went up and saw what you did in Hugli.'

'War is not pretty.'

'That was not war.'

'Gentlemen,' said Watts. 'If you will raise your glasses with me. Let us drink to the prosperity of all the settlements in Bengal. And to those who have befriended us in times of trouble.'

'A Christian toast,' said Dr Forth.

The toast was drunk, but afterward Cordet did not speak to me and it was not long before he and Sinfray took their leave of us.

The next morning Mr Watts sent me into the black town to discover what truth there was in the reports of the Hindoos fleeing Calcutta in fear of the nawab's imminent arrival. I spent two hours wandering about there and stopped by the temples to speak with the Brahmins and in the markets to speak with the local merchants. Nor did I neglect to speak to our *chowkays*, who knew of every camel and bullock cart that came and went from the town.

'Many who came back with us are now leaving again,' I told Watts upon my return.

'There is no great panic I trust.'

'It is very orderly, sir. Is it true that we have encouraged their departure?'

'Who is it says so?'

'It is a general belief among the *chowkays*. And by my own observation, those I saw leaving were not in any fear. They leave as people expecting to be but a short time away.'

'Then let us work to make it so.' He appeared very content with the news that I had brought him. And this it was that decided me.

'If we are calling the nawab down to do battle with us, sir, I am very clear that my place is among the soldiers. If you will release me, I will go up to join Colonel Clive.'

'Do not goad me, Alistair.'

241

'I am not a boy, sir.'

'Have you learned nothing from Hugli?'

'This will not be another Hugli.'

'You do not know what it will be. No more does the colonel, nor the admiral. If the nawab means to make to make war upon us, very well, we must answer him. But once the guns open, we are all of us playing at dice.'

'Colonel Clive is greatly outnumbered. He will be in need of more men.'

'That is not your affair.'

'Sir—'

'Listen to me. If you join the colonel, you will be but a soldier, which is to say one who may be cut to pieces with grape-shot and two days after forgotten.'

'I do not fear that.'

'Then you are a fool. And I had never thought you one till now.'

We were both of us silent then and both much out of temper, for these were the first words ever exchanged between us in anger.

'Then you will not release me to join the soldiers?' I said at last.

He bent his head over the papers. 'The women and children will be taken out to the ships. You shall make part of their escort.'

I was in sudden alarm now. For this was the same shameful duty that Frankland and Manningham had done at the siege. The soldiers would fight the Moors, while I was hid in safety behind the skirts of the women.

'Will I then return to the fort, sir?'

'You will then put yourself at the disposal of your ship's captain. It may be he shall find some fitting work for you. And I trust that you will do it, and well.'

CHAPTER TWENTY-SIX

*I*t was with no great alacrity that I rose from my bed, and then dressed and went out to wait on the ghat in front of the house for Mrs Watts and her children. I heard the children's voices inside. There was neither fear nor anxiety in them, but only excited laughter, for they were happy at this small adventure of a temporary removal to the ships. After a time Mrs Watts came out and called down to tell me that they would not be ready for some while.

'Will you ask Dr Forth which ship we must go to? You may tell him that we will go out there directly.'

'I shall ask him.'

'Alistair,' she called and I looked up. 'I am very glad you will come with us.'

I could not answer her. I turned away and went along the ghat and then around by the fort and up to St Anne's, where Dr Forth was overseeing the muster of the women and children before their removal to the ships. There were many coolies still at work there on the church walls, and also their wives who broke stones for them. And on my approaching the church, I had thought that it was this breaking of stones beneath hammers that made the loud reports that I heard. But then the European women on the church steps there began to point to the northward and I turned and saw plumes of smoke rising in a distant quarter of the black town, somewhere out by the Maratha Ditch. A moment more and I recognized the cracking sounds as distant musket-shots.

Veering from the church, I hurried to Omichand's house, where I saw Le Baume standing with Omichand, both of them looking north-ward toward the smoke and the musketshots.

'Captain,' I called and Le Baume beckoned me up.

'I hear no cannon,' he remarked as I came to them. 'Have you heard any cannon?'

'No.'

'What can I do?' cried Omichand. 'In my own house, in my own town, I am a prisoner. Were I free, I could go then myself to the nawab.'

'You are held under Governor Drake's order,' said Le Baume. 'And you will go nowhere.'

'Drake? He has fled already to the ships. Drake is among the women.'

Le Baume looked as if he might strike the impudent fellow, but he restrained himself and we stood and watched the new plumes of smoke now appearing out to the north-east, by the ditch. I knew well what Le Baume felt, for I felt the same thing myself – that the proper place for a man was out with the fighting. But his orders were to remain here and mine to go with the women. We discussed briefly what we saw and heard, which was but to distract ourselves from our miserable duties. At last Le Baume turned unhappily from the sight of the smoke and strode across to the steps and went down to speak to his soldiers. Omic-hand then clutched my arm and whispered urgently, 'Send Mr Watts to me,' and I at once pulled my arm free and hurried away from him.

'It is not the nawab's whole army,' I told Mrs Watts as I went quickly up the steps. She was waiting there on the verandah with her children and their *ayah* and the children stood on their trunk and leaned on the rail, hoping for a better view of the smoke. 'At least by the estimation of Captain Le Baume.'

'Even so, let us get to the ships directly.'

'I must first see Mr Watts.'

'He is not here. He is met in council within the fort. What ship are we given?'

'The *Thunder*. But I must see Mr Watts before we go.'

'The fort is closed now to all but the soldiers.'

'Then I must write.' She looked at me with exasperation, but then I bent toward her and said, 'It concerns Omichand.' Her look changed and she glanced at her children, but they were safe there with the *ayah*, and she bade me come quickly inside.

She had paper and ink immediately to hand. 'What you write may not reach him. Tell me what it is and I will write it.' I suggested that if she only addressed the letter in her hand, I might then write it. 'I have not time to be coy with you, Alistair. It is not politic that any private communication between William and Omichand be discovered. You will tell me the message you have from Omichand and I will write it so that none but William may understand.' She poised her quill above the paper.

I told her how I had observed the distant smoke and heard the musketshots, with Le Baume and Omichand. 'And then Omichand spoke to me out of Le Baume's hearing. He said, "Send Mr Watts to me."'

'Nothing more?'

'He spoke it as a matter of great urgency.'

She sent her quill dashing across the paper. It was but a few brief lines that she wrote, nor did she conceal them from me, and in them was no mention made of Omichand, but she wrote of her departure to the *Thunder* and of some unexpected domestic trouble that had arisen with her servants. The servants were named and, having already the key to the message, I quickly perceived that one stood for Omichand, another for Mr Watts and a third – to my astonishment – stood for me. She put a blotter to the letter and sealed it.

'We will pass it in at the river-gate,' said she, rising. 'And it is unattractive to stare so.'

'When came I by that new name?'

'There is nothing meant by it. It is safer for everyone.' She went out and called to the bearers, who fetched the trunk down to the palanquin. And then the children and the *ayah* went down and Mrs Watts took my arm, as though she might need some support to her feminine frailty, and so I brought her down the steps to the ghat.

Captain Warwick greeted Mrs Watts and me as we came aboard and he did not hesitate to offer her the use of his cabin. Neither would he listen to her protest that she had no wish to inconvenience him, and so the trunk, the children and Mrs Watts were soon established in their place beneath the quarterdeck. For myself, once I had seen the family settled, I renewed my acquaintance with the midshipmen's quarters, and who should I find there but Adams. He rose to make a loud proclamation of my virtues to those fellows newly arrived from the *Marlborough* who did not know me. He was somewhat taken with grog and began to show off the livid scar above his sternum and this with a muddled recital of how he had got it. I advised him to pray sit down and keep silence, which he did at once and with the obedience of a lamb. Once I had stowed my small sack of belongings, I returned above deck and stood with the seamen at the landward rail.

Smoke still rose to the north-east of the black town and there was a deal more musketshot, though very distant from us and hid from our view by the town.

Captain Warwick called me up to him. He enquired what I knew of the smoke and the musketshot and, when I confessed my ignorance, he pointed along the shore, saying, 'And what of those fellows?' He gave me his spyglass. And training it where he pointed, but a half a mile north of the Watts house which we had so recently vacated, I was taken aback to see a small troop of Moors. They were putting fire to some topass houses there.

'To my best knowledge the officers ashore are unaware of them.'

'That is no matter. They shall be aware of them just as soon as the *Marlborough* gives them the signal.'

The *Marlborough* lay to the north of us, a cable off from the shore. And a minute later the *Marlborough*'s rear guns opened and the shells exploded like hellish fury in the midst of the Moors. The firing then continued very sprightly, with the Moorish remnant in sudden pell-mell retreat and the seamen on the *Thunder*'s deck calling and making a shrill whistling in appreciation.

'That is gunnery, Mr Douglas,' remarked Captain Warwick.

'That it is,' said I, though I own I took not the same pleasure in it as did he and the sailors.

'I only wonder that the colonel should have let them come so far,' said he. I told him that I believed there was some parley to be made with the nawab. To that Warwick said, 'Let the nawab keep his Moors from the town and he may parley all he pleases.'

When the Moors were at last fled from sight and the *Marlborough*'s guns fallen silent, we saw the natives of the black town emerge from their hiding places and commence to douse the fires the Moors had made.

'There is a boat going in to the fort, Mr Douglas. She will not wait.'

'I am to remain here, sir.'

'We are well able to keep Mrs Watts and her children in safety.'

'I am instructed to remain here by Mr Watts. He said that I was to place myself under your orders.'

'There is little use you can be to us here.' Warwick looked at me a moment and saw, I must believe, that the situation was very far from my own choosing. 'Then we shall both have to make the best of it. Perhaps you might assist the midshipmen with their books while you are aboard.' I nodded unhappily. 'There is no shame in obedience to an order, Mr Douglas. You might ponder on that while you are about the instruction of Adams and the other young blockheads.'

It was a curious and uncomfortable thing to be confined aboard the ship, with the fort and town so close to us and the enemy present, but out of our sight. Nor was I the only one to feel it, for when I set Adams and his fellows to their trigonometry the next morning there was no concentration to be had from them. They talked among themselves continually and speculated endlessly on their chance of being sent ashore, for there was then a rumour throughout the squadron that the colonel was in want of more men.

But I had learned, since Madras, how these rumours were always moving about the ships and what little credence I should give them.

On going above in the late morning, I found the greater part of the main deck made over to the women and children, and the seamen could move about only awkwardly. So great was the press of children that there had even been a part of the quarterdeck surrendered to them, which was a circumstance that could not continue if the *Thunder* were to be moved from her station.

Above the river-gate of the fort, I saw our colours fluttering in the warm breeze that was coming down with the retreating tide. There were a few wisps of smoke rising out by the Ditch, but there had been no sound of any fighting in the night, nor was there any now, only a regular though distant musketry, which sounded like a practice or a drill. The door to Mrs Watts's cabin was propped open. She was working at her needlepoint, and beside her young Amelia did the same.

'I had almost thought you had abandoned us, Alistair.'

'Is there any news yet from Mr Watts?'

She turned her head and urged me to patience.

'Where is George?' said I.

'So long as he is not overboard, I do not ask. He cannot be far.' She continued with her needle and I came in and sat down. I stared out of the cabin door to the shore. 'Have you no sketchbook?' she asked me.

'I have. But I am not inclined to it at present.'

'You are distracted.'

'I am.'

'You fret to be left aboard with us.'

'It is not from any aversion to your company. I had rather be ashore, that is all.'

'The sailors do not mind to be out here.'

'Mr Manningham and Mr Frankland did not mind to be out here either.'

She studied her needlepoint. 'They also serve who only stand and wait. Now you begin to know what it is to be a woman.'

I looked at her and I thought on that *sadhu* who had died when we hunted by Cossimbazaar. I thought on the Reverend Bellamy and the Jew and a hundred smaller things besides. She leaned forward now to help her daughter with the needle.

I kept myself from Mrs Watts's cabin for the rest of the day, and the rest of the day was an age, for there is no lassitude like the lassitude aboard an idle ship. But shortly after nightfall there was much movement of the smaller boats, for I heard them knocking against the hull from my place in the midshipmen's quarters. I had been reading by the lamplight one of the few books they had, but the knocking of the boats continued and was now joined by several raised voices and the sound of boots up on deck. I at last put aside Dampier's *Voyages* and sat up. And as I did so, Captain Warwick put his head in at the hatch.

'Are you going with the volunteers, Mr Douglas?'

'I am,' said I, though in some confusion at the question and knowing nothing whatever of the matter afoot.

'Then look lively. The boats will not wait for you.'

He disappeared as suddenly as he had come and I, with haste, after him.

CHAPTER TWENTY-SEVEN

W e shoved off from the *Thunder* and our oarsmen struck out for the *Kent*. By the time we came alongside her, I had learned from my companions that we were to muster on the *Kent* only as a prelude to going ashore to join forces with the colonel. 'It wants only the admiral's "yea",' declared the oarsman nearest me.

There was no stealth in our movements, nor in those of the other boats which we found already tied to the *Kent* when we reached her. Many seamen called to one another and some climbed aboard the *Kent* and some climbed down again. All the talk now was of the nawab and of the admiral's intention to best the colonel in the fighting of the Moors.

I found the *Kent*'s main deck crowded with the waiting seamen and all the women and children aboard her either below decks or huddled together up by the bow. I enquired of the watch officer whether he knew when we were to go ashore.

'Just as soon as the admiral shall give Captain Warwick the order.'

'We are to be led by Captain Warwick then.'

'So you are.'

'But what has happened?'

'The *Salisbury* has gone up to cover the colonel's camp from the river and you fellows have all swarmed here from the other ships. That is all I know of it.'

And indeed when I made enquiry of the other officers, there was not one of them could give a more definite answer. After an hour Captain Warwick came out from the admiral's cabin and called the officers to him and they all disappeared with him inside the cabin again. A further hour passed, and every eye drawn now impatiently to the admiral's closed door. When the door finally reopened, a short order of rum was ordered for any who wanted it, which was most of the seamen. Muskets were then distributed, though there were not sufficient for every one of us, there being five hundred men and more, both up on deck and down in the boats. But Adams made sure I got one of the muskets.

Before midnight, we shoved off from the *Kent*. Once we had drawn away from the ships, the lamps of the other boats were scattered like fireflies in the darkness around us. The men grew quieter and, as they grew quieter, we heard the Moorish music drifting over the town from the east where we reasoned the Moors must be now encamped in readiness to attack the settlement. That we should attack them was I think a notion that had not occurred to them.

We disembarked by Kelsall's Octagon, for there was a stone promontory jutting into the river there and the officers formed us into small companies for our better management in the darkness. With a lamp at the head and the tail of each company, we set off in the direction of the colonel's camp, our march made easier by reason of the new track made by all the coming and going there had been of Clive's men to the river. Also, there were some Hindoo guides whom Clive had sent down for us.

We arrived at Clive's camp at two o'clock in the morning.

The camp was already under arms. A number of large fires had been lit to see by and the officers carried torches as they hurried about giving orders and uttering loud oaths. Captain Warwick, who had gone on ahead of us, now came and told us how the attacking column was to be formed and of our place in it, which was to be immediately behind the van of the king's soldiers. All was well till he revealed the nature of our service – there would be no more weapons issued, for the unarmed seamen were to be now put in harness to draw Clive's guns – six field pieces and one cohorn (which is a small mortar).

From the ranks someone called Clive a name unrepeatable.

'Who spoke? Who was that?' demanded a lieutenant, but none would answer him.

'A word is easily mistaken in the dark,' said Warwick. 'We will say no more of it. Take the men to the guns.'

The artillerymen who waited there gave us warm welcome, which did much to calm the ill-feeling of the seamen. And it was from these artillerymen that we got our first account of what had brought us to the camp (I was surprised in those days, as I have since learned not to be, at how little a man at the front line is ever told). Our part of the column being a neighbour to the sepoys, I went and sought out Harry Khan. He confirmed to me what the artillerymen had told us, that some of the nawab's men had passed within sight of Clive's camp two days before.

'After them came the army. We saw them passing. They are camped now at the ditch.'

'But they did not attack you?'

'Messengers came from the nawab. Coja Wajid sent his dog Sri Babu. Yesterday the colonel sent his dogs, Scrafton and Walsh, to the nawab.'

'Is the nawab himself now in the Moors' camp?'

'Walsh and Scrafton say it. But parley is finished,' said Harry, very satisfied. 'Now we fight.'

'When we are through this, Harry, you must return with me to Mr Watts.'

He stared into the flames of the campfire and did not answer me. There was a look in his eye most terrible, and so I came away from him.

The ropes were by this time fixed to the field pieces and the cohorn and also to the carts where the munitions were loaded. Those of us with muskets were divided into two parties, half to the front of the train

252

and I, with Midshipman Adams and sundry others, to the rear of it. Captain Warwick went among us with a few words, very sober but encouraging. When he mounted, there was a steadiness among the seamen as if they were aboard ship and awaiting a familiar command from the quarterdeck.

I spied the colonel not far to the rear of us, mounted with his officers close by the company troops. He did not bluster, but occasionally a man rode from him taking commands along the column, so that there was no doubt but that Clive directed all. Nor was it by any great fanfare that our column was launched, but just by one of those commands, for we suddenly heard ahead of us Drummer Fredericks of the king's soldiers and then the tramp of the soldiers' boots. A shanty then started up among the sailors as they hauled at the ropes to move the guns, and then we were all following after, and behind us Clive and the company soldiers, and behind them the sepoys.

'We will box their ears and no mistake,' said Adams, who was at my side. 'But by God sir, there was enough marching from the river to the camp.'

'Four miles and we will be on them.'

'A soldier is a donkey.'

'It will but warm you.'

'I was warm enough on the *Thunder*. Let the nawab get himself some battleships and fight us like a gentleman.'

After less than an hour's march, there was some adjustment made to the column, the colonel bringing his company soldiers to the fore of the seamen and artillery, and he also sent two hundred sepoys up in advance of the king's men. This halt gave some respite to the seamen who by their exertions had kept the whole train moving forward at the same rate as our march. They had been working in teams, much like the native palanquin bearers, with always two men walking alongside their labouring fellows, regathering their strength before retaking their places at the ropes. But in truth it was work for bullocks, not men, and when the column moved once more there were some sharp orders needed to get several of the seamen from off the ground where they rested.

At this time also, an order came along the whole column that there should be no unnecessary noise made lest we give the enemy undue warning of our advance. And here we fixed our bayonets.

It was another hour or more of marching before the darkness began to lighten somewhat above the hedges which we now descried faintly to the right of us. And in the dim light of the dawn I looked about me at the faces of the seamen and they were pale like ghosts and watching, watching everywhere, for they sensed, as well as I, the enemy very near to us. But there was a heavy morning mist in the air all about that screened us and I understood then how carefully Clive had chosen the hour of our march, and, was very glad of his care.

Then suddenly came musketfire to the front of us. We judged it to be our sepoys by the hubbub that followed, but the column kept its forward motion with the Drummer Fredericks now sounding our advance. A strange minute followed in which we had our muskets ready while the officers rode in the mist alongside us, that first hue and cry of our sepoys faded almost to nothing and the shouts of the enemy came out at us from the mist on both sides.

Then Captain Warwick cried out, 'Cohorn to the starboard side! Fire upon loading! We are in their camp!'

'Jesus Christ,' said Adams at my side, and he fired his musket aimlessly into the mist, as did several others about me.

A lieutenant from the *Salisbury* soon took charge of us and we quickly formed into ranks either side and held our fire and waited for the order. It was as we waited thus that I heard a sound as of birds on the wing passing over, but thought little of it till a fellow in the ranks, two men off from me, fell on his back screaming with an arrow buried deep in his face. The lieutenant gave the order and we fired and the Moorish cries that then rose from the mist gave us fresh heart.

The Moors shot their fire-arrows then. They came arcing at us through the mist and we knew them at once to be a very great danger to the munitions in our train. We heard Captain Coote bellowing at the king's men and they soon let fly two volleys and the flame arrows ceased. Then our cohorn fired and then the column moved forward again.

'How can we fight in this damned fog?' shouted Adams to me.

'Where is that fellow hit by the arrow?'

'He is dead. Watch where you step.'

I looked down at the ground in front of me where he pointed and there was the lifeless body of a Moor who must have fallen in the first skirmish with our sepoys in the van. The heavy wheels of our field guns had mangled him.

The flame arrows flew through the mist again, though fewer than before, and again the king's men quieted them with a volley. But one lucky archer survived their volley and a single flame arrow now sliced through the mist and fell among the grenadiers, whereupon an explosion rent the air and a bolt like lightning flashed through the mist.

The sound of it had barely died when Captain Coote's voice rose up, calling for a gun from the train to advance up the column. The confusion among us was considerable now, but nothing to that into which we had thrown the enemy by our violent irruption into their camp. Our field guns now fired grape to left and right, almost level with the ground, and several times we saw through the mist the Moorish tents shredded to rags and Moors stumbling about in confusion. It took little skill to drop them like partridge.

The Moors then made a cavalry charge upon the van of the column. We heard it and felt the thunder of hoofs through the ground, but we did not see the charge. We heard also the tremendous volley that stopped it and after that the screaming of the Moorish horses, which almost drowned out the cries of the men. At this dreadful sound the nawab's elephants took fright and began to trumpet, but the mist hid them from us, which made them seem everywhere about us, though we knew it a thing impossible.

'Fire and advance! Fire and advance!' called our lieutenant, though we did not need the order, for to be parted from the column was certain death to us and to leave off firing was an action we never thought of.

The Moors harried us now with musketshot through the mist and we returned their fire tenfold. Whenever our column came upon their tethered animals, whether horse or camel or bullock, we gave no quarter, but slaughtered them where they stood, and set fire to every tent, and in our wake was a bloody tail of destruction.

A camp of fifty thousand Moors is no slight thing, and we fought and marched and fought an hour and more before the thick morning mist began to clear. The whole of our artillery train was then for the first time visible to us, strung out in front. I looked about for Adams but could not see him. As the mist lifted further, I perceived to our right flank, by the Ditch and at no great distance, a thick cluster of Moorish tents and some very large like to the *durbar* tent of the nawab. Clive himself now rode back to the field guns.

'Fire upon those tents. Give them what shells you have,' he cried. He spoke with Captain Warwick then, whom I was very glad to see still among the living. The entire column stopped now and with one in ten of us set to defend our backs to the eastward side, we turned our whole fire upon the tents and the redoubts that the Moors had made upon the Maratha Ditch.

For the first time in the battle, they returned our fire with a brisk cannonade, which seemed to convince Clive that this was the place of the nawab and his generals. So Clive stayed by the artillery with Captain Warwick and gave the gunners much encouragement.

After half an hour the Moors had re-gathered sufficient of their cavalry to make an attempt to come around the column. But we saw them off easily, for we had put the fear of God in them by our bold march into their camp and a few accurate cannonades and volleys was now all it took to set them retreating in some haste to the cover of the Ditch. Their fear was worth an army to us.

But when the Moorish muskets began to gall us to some good effect, the colonel left the artillery to Captain Warwick's care and went himself to the van, where Fredericks was soon drumming us forward again. The field guns ceased their cannonade. The sailors, who had been helping the artillerymen with the shells and shot, now took up the ropes and bent their backs to draw the guns after them.

I found myself briefly at Captain Warwick's stirrup and called up to ask what we were about, for no order had come to us, but only the beat of the drum.

'We will keep south till we may cross the Ditch into town.'

'How long will that be?'

'Have you some more urgent business you must attend to, Mr Douglas?'

'If there is no better place found,' I told him, 'you may go in at the Bread & Cheese Bungalow. It is where Lal Bazaar meets the Ditch.'

'I will be sure the colonel hears of it.' Putting heel to horse, he went forward to confer with another officer.

There was a splitting of our artillery now and the cohorn and three field guns were drawn smartly forward to the van. At the sight of these guns going forward and feeling the first heat of the king's muskets suddenly upon them, the Moors to the front of us soon made a lively hurry to disperse. The van now moved more quickly than we could follow, for there were fewer sailors now to draw the rear guns, and many of these already at the point of exhaustion. And though the Moors to the front were dispersing, those following behind us were steadily increasing in number, and the sight of us moving out of their camp and turning our backs upon them gave these Moors the spur. Very soon, and for the first time since the battle began, their infantry were making some real attempt to advance upon us and our sepoys at the rear found themselves suddenly and unexpectedly hard pressed.

Two of the sailors drawing the guns then fell in quick succession and the remaining sailors shouted at us, their protectors, to rid them of the deadly Moors at the rear. We stopped to fire, but our sepoys fell back upon us.

'Hold!' cried our lieutenant at the sepoys. 'Hold where you are!' but they did not comprehend him and so there was an entanglement between us and them that the lieutenant was trying to undo with loud oaths when he took a shot through the throat. He dropped onto his back not ten paces from me. I went and knelt by him and his face was already deathly white and his lifeblood pooling on the ground beneath him. His eyes were wide open but I knew at once that he did not see me. His heels kicked sharp circles in the ground and I took his hand and a moment later his whole body jerked violently and the life went suddenly out of him. When I let his hand fall I found Harry standing at my shoulder, taking steady aim at the Moors.

'Who is next in command?'

'The officers have gone ahead. It is your *subadar*.'

'He is killed.' Harry discharged his shot and then told me, as he reloaded, that I must send up the column for help or the guns here would surely be lost.

I sought out Adams and sent him with the message, which he seemed only too glad to take. The Moors stood off from us, but their numbers continually increased. Harry brought some order to the sepoys and I tried to give encouragement to the sailors and soon we moved again, but slowly, and then an accident happened that stopped us entirely – the axle-tree of one gun carriage broke. The cursing sailors inspected it from above and beneath, but there was nothing could be done for its repair.

'It must be spiked and left,' said I and, none seeing any better plan, this was done and we continued forward till a second accident soon after occurred. Another of our guns being briefly stopped to return a Moorish cannonade, it fired several shots in quick succession and split its own barrel. This gun too we must abandon and then onward again, but very slowly now, for we were all of us greatly fatigued with the fighting and in some dread of the Moors closing behind us.

Then a sailor cried, "Thank Christ,' and soon we saw Adams returning to us from the van with Ensign York and a stout reinforcement. Their arrival, and Ensign York's bold command, put fresh heart into us.

'Stand and fire! Fire!'

The Moors to our rear withdrew themselves a way after our lead went into them, and we then rallied ourselves and got the last gun up to join the rest of the column.

The Moorish guns continued a desultory and ineffectual cannonade, but we swung wide of them and soon came to that place on the Ditch which I had before mentioned to Captain Warwick. And Captain Warwick was himself there by the Bread & Cheese Bungalow, still mounted, as we brought our gun into Lal Bazaar, where the front of the column was already disbanded, the men lying collapsed in the shade to either side of the road with their coats and shirts open, and some emptying flasks of water onto their own heads.

'Where is your lieutenant?' Warwick called to me.

'He is killed.'

Colonel Clive then rode over from near the Ditch, very pleased to see Ensign York returned with the gun. He ordered the gun onto the bank, though there seemed little fear that the Moors should attack us now.

'The bastard colonel has enjoyed this,' murmured an unhappy sailor just by me whose shoulder was bloodied from the chafing of the ropes.

Some men from the settlement then rode up Lal Bazaar toward us. I recognized one of them as Le Baume but I did not stay to speak with him. I went instead behind the bungalow where I knew was a hidden water butt, and there I wet my head and drank my fill. I could not put from my mind the sight of that lieutenant shot through the throat. My body trembled strangely from fatigue and exhaustion, and I went across to a banyan tree nearby and there lay down in the shade by my musket. I was very tired and closed my eyes and our cannon now started, though sporadically, from up on the bank. And it was while I was lying there, recovering myself, that the colonel and Le Baume came mounted around the side of the bungalow, away from the men, to speak privately. They did not see me.

'I will make a new assault.'

'You will make no assault, Monsieur Le Baume.'

'My men are not tired.'

'That is nothing to the purpose. You will lift your guard now from Omichand's house. Let the man at liberty. He may go where he pleases and you will show him every courtesy.'

'But he will escape.'

'You will do it, and at once. And if this be an example of your obedience, I am not surprised Monsieur Renault put you out from Chandernagore.'

No more was said between them, and when I sat up I saw their horses moving off from the bungalow.

Some artillerymen were left with the guns near the bungalow, but most of our weary force went down Lal Bazaar to the fort, where we stopped outside the gates and rested while the wounded were taken directly to the hospital on carts and in palanquins. The soldiers who had been confined to the fort throughout the action now came out to hear the tale of it, and also Governor Drake and some other members of the council. But after half an hour Captain Warwick roused his sailors and led them around the fort and down to the ghat, there to embark for their ships. Ten minutes more and Clive with his officers came in from the bungalow, put the soldiers and sepoys in some order and set them to march back out to the camp whence we had all started in darkness that morning.

And then only Harry and I remained, and we went to find Mr Watts.

CHAPTER TWENTY-EIGHT

*T*he Jewess, Isaacson's wife, showed me in to her small front parlour. Through an open door, I saw Mr Watts in the next room seated by Isaacson, who was propped up in his bed, his face recognizable now and the swelling gone. Watts had been speaking quietly with Isaacson, but he rose at once when he saw me and came out to the parlour. He knew by my appearance that I had not come from the ships.

'Where is my wife?'

'She is safe on the *Thunder*, sir. I was called to serve with Captain Warwick ashore. We have marched through the nawab's camp.'

'You yourself have marched?'

'Yes, sir.'

'How came you to be here?'

'A servant at your house saw you leave with an Armenian. I came to the quarter and asked after you.' He looked at me askance and I said, 'Harry Khan is with me. He is waiting outside.'

Watts went and took his leave of Isaacson and came out into the street with me. He was very pleased to see Harry, and Harry to see him. But Watts made no personal question of him and asked only after our attack upon the nawab's camp. Harry gave him an estimation of the nawab's strength, which was forty thousand.

'I am sure I must be grateful to you for getting Mr Douglas back to us in safety,' said Watts. He then told Harry to return to the house by the river, where he might get a proper meal from the Wattses' cook. 'We shall be along presently,' he said, turning on his heel and calling me after him. We had gone but a short way on when Watts said to me, 'Harry is much changed.'

'I believe it is the time he spent in the nawab's prison.'

'Did he speak of it?'

'Not a word.'

'I expect you are right.' I asked if he had seen the scars on Harry's wrists and he nodded, saying, 'But that is not the worst the nawab has done. Not even the worst, I suspect, to Harry.'

'Isaacson appears much recovered.'

'Yes.' He glanced at me. I know that we both thought of Edward. 'Harry seems certain that your attack has put the fear of God into the Moors.'

'It was a bloody business, sir.'

'An attack may be very bloody and yet no great success.'

'The Moors know that we have been among them. But Harry must know the effect of it better than I.'

'That is true.'

'Colonel Clive has set Omichand at liberty.' At this news Watts smiled and I said, 'I had thought you would not like to hear it.'

'Omichand has his liberty at my request, Alistair. While you have been about your bloody business, I have spent an hour and more over breakfast with Omichand. The sound of your guns caused him no little indigestion, I may tell you. He will now take the council's demands to the nawab.'

'He does not seem to me a man to be trusted,' said I, which was but a very mild expression compared to what I truly felt.

'He is very useful to us. We will go up this lane here.'

Watts led me through the byways of that quarter, as one very familiar with the place, even to the edge of the black town where the Aligarh temple was, a place famous in Bengal for its dancing girls. Now we saw no dancing girls but only a few white-robed Brahmins, lounging upon the steps as though they had no concern for the nawab's army out by the Ditch, nor any other thing but only their own leisure. We stepped around the cows that were feeding upon some flowers dropped from an offering plate on the lower step and, as we did so, one of the Brahmins made a distinct and quite singular gesture with one hand, looking all the while at Mr Watts. When I looked at Watts, he appeared not to have noticed the fellow, but then I saw Watts's hand, as he walked on, give a quick answering signal in return. There was no doubt in my mind, but that some message had passed between them.

I said nothing. Mr Watts soon after turned away and led me then from the black town and as we came into the settlement, he said, 'You will go out to the *Thunder*, Alistair, and escort my family back to the house.'

'Were it not better that we should wait?'

'How so?'

'For their own safety.'

'They are now as safe ashore. The nawab's army is withdrawing as we speak.'

By the late afternoon the nawab's withdrawal was a fact known throughout the settlement. And another fact was also known, which was that the place where the nawab had planted his own tent and standard, before we dislodged him, was in Omichand's great garden out by the Ditch. It was from Le Baume I learned this, for once the Moors had withdrawn their whole force, it was he who was sent along the Ditch with his company to recover any guns and munitions that had been abandoned there. To have had no part in the battle, but after be called upon to sweep up the leavings, was a thing very bitter for Le Baume, and I think that he had now begun to suspect the feeling that there was against him.

The next morning it was discovered that the Moors had withdrawn as far as the Salt Lake and Watts had it from Omichand that the nawab, very much shaken by our bold assault (we knew now that we had killed over a thousand of his men), was now ready to hold some serious parley.

*

Mr Watts, in the two days that followed, was very often from his house, most frequently at the fort with Governor Drake and the council, but sometimes out in the *Kent* with Admiral Watson, and once paying a visit to Colonel Clive in the camp to the north. During this time I was kept occupied by Mrs Watts in the sketching of portraits of her children, by which means she kept me near at hand in the house for those times when her husband should have need of me. Though not privy to the particulars of the treaty being made, I quickly understood by remarks between Mr Watts and his wife that the colonel and the admiral had been deputed by the council to deal with the nawab on their behalf, their reason being, I suppose, that the nawab might be most amenable to the wishes of those he most feared. But the letters from these two were not the only ones going out to the nawab's camp, for I took a number of letters from Mr Watts to the house of the Jew, Isaacson, where that Armenian who had been Isaacson's companion in the pinnace, Coja Petrus, also stayed. These letters were addressed to Ranjit Rai, who was the agent of Jagath Seth the banker. Ranjit Rai was present in the nawab's camp out by the Salt Lake. What was in the letters I neither knew nor asked, and Mr Watts was firm that I not mention them to any but himself.

'Better yet, if you should forget them entirely.'

'Isaacson is up from his bed, sir.'

'I am pleased to hear of it. You will take him my compliments with this last letter,' he said, sealing it.

'By "last", do you mean that the treaty is now signed?'

'Very nearly.'

'How came that Coja Petrus to be living in the same house with Isaacson?'

'Isaacson has given him shelter since the Moors burned him out. Are you surprised that a Jew should be capable of charity?'

I said that I was not.

'But you are unsatisfied.'

'It is only that I have a feeling I have seen them together at some other place.'

'You saw them in Fulta, in their pinnace.'

'Did I not see them also when I first came to Cossimbazaar?'

'It is possible, but any knowledge you have of those two, I would prefer you not speak of.' I saw that he wanted no more questions on it and he then gave the letter into my hand and nodded me toward the door.

On the 9th of February the treaty was signed. There was no ceremony performed at the signing, but it was done as a final act to the passing of the messages and letters that had proceeded ever since our bloody march through the nawab's camp. I was working on my sketch of young George, his mother sitting nearby, when Mr Watts came in and announced to us that the business was done.

'Thank God,' broke from Mrs Watts. 'Thank God it is over with.'

He put a hand on her shoulder, and she her hand upon his, and I rose to offer my congratulations to him.

'Is the nawab beaten then, Father?' asked George.

'I do not think he will trouble us again here in Calcutta. You may go and tell your sister so.'

When George had left us, Watts dropped into a chair and extended his stockinged legs out before him like a man greatly fatigued and in need of rest. Mrs Watts offered to have a servant bring refreshment, but he shook his head and told her that he would not have the servants called. He produced a rough copy of the treaty from his coat and gave it to Mrs Watts. She read it and passed it to me.

There were seven main points to it, the primary ones being that all the rights and privileges previously granted the company by the emperor in Delhi (such as his grant to us of Calcutta) should hereafter be properly respected by the nawab, and also that any losses we had suffered till now must be made good. In addition Mr Watts had extracted from the nawab rights for the company to fortify Calcutta, and to mint coin, and sundry other privileges.

'It is everything,' said I when I had finished my reading of it.

'It is everything and more,' remarked Watts. 'And by other signed letters we have the nawab's assurance that our enemies shall hereafter be his.'

'By which we mean to say France?' said I.

'By which we mean to say France and the nawab means to say nothing,' rejoined Watts. 'But we now have his signature to it. And Governor Drake will today make a public announcement of the state of war now existing between France and England. We will see what follows.'

'Then it is not over with,' said I.

'Calcutta is secure. But only while Admiral Watson and Colonel Clive remain to enforce the terms of the treaty. Once they are gone from Bengal, I think you know, Alistair, what trust we may put in the nawab's good faith.'

'Then what purpose has the treaty?'

'You may discover the purpose of it at first hand, if you will come with me as my secretary to Murshidabad.' While I was still recovering from my surprise at this invitation, Watts turned to his wife. Her joy at the signing of the treaty was now gone. 'My dear,' he said, very placatory, 'it is necessary some one of us from the council now represent the company at the nawab's court – both to ensure the nawab's compliance with the treaty and for those other matters.'

'And Drake and the council have asked you.'

'I know the nawab's court. And I have the language.'

'And you have the courage, and they have not.'

'My dear—'

'I am so very tired of those men.'

'It will not be much longer now. You will be safe with the children here.'

'But you will not be safe.'

'I shall have Harry with me – and also Alistair, if he agrees to it. We shall make ourselves secure in Cossimbazaar and, from there, conduct our business in Murshidabad. Omichand shall make smooth our way in the court.'

'Omichand?' said I in astonishment.

'There is no security in Cossimbazaar,' said Mrs Watts.

'Omichand is useful and that is sufficient. You need not be his friend, Alistair. But you have not answered me. You have been very willing to put your hand to the sword. What say you to diplomacy?'

'This is very sudden,' said Mrs Watts.

'Alistair may refuse me if he wishes. He knows it.' He looked at me. 'You may stay here in Calcutta and take up your duties as a 'writer' and you will have my blessing on it.'

'Do not press him, William.'

'I am not pressed,' said I and, hesitating no longer now that I knew my alternative, enquired of Mr Watts the time of our departure.

Captain Warwick was at the hospital when I found him, moving along the line of bunks with Lieutenant Brereton and stopping by the wounded to give some words of comfort or encouragement. With certain ones he even sat awhile and shared a word in privacy, and sometimes drew from them a quiet, gallows laughter. The surgeon saw me watching from the hallway, and said, 'Do you leave with Captain Warwick for England, then?'

'No.'

'Nor I, more's the pity.' And at my remark that a surgeon was as much needed here as in London, he replied with some asperity that it should remain so for as long as the colonel saw the chance of some profit in Bengal. Captain Warwick completed his round of the injured men and came out with Lieutenant Brereton to join us in the hall. There was some money to be left for the injured sailors, and while Brereton went to settle this with the surgeon, Warwick came with me outside. I said that I had no notion that so many had been wounded.

'When we left Madras, I feared the expedition would be costly.'

'Do you take the expedition as completed?'

'The expedition will be completed only at the admiral's command. For myself, the admiral's command is that I bear the tidings of our exploits here to the Admiralty in London, which I am very glad to do.' He turned toward the fort and I walked with him.

'Because they will give you a proper ship there?' said I.

'They are as like to give me an old tub. But I had rather captain such a tub than be lieutenant on the finest man o' war. What of you, Mr Douglas? Does the colonel look now more kindly on your request for a commission? I will write him of your steadiness under fire if it should help your cause.'

'I have not applied to him again since Madras.'

He was surprised by this and asked me if I had considered a more honourable service, by which he meant, of course, the Royal Navy. 'You know navigation better than any midshipman. This war with France will thin the ranks of officers ahead of you. If I were to speak with the admiral—'

'Forgive me, I mean the navy no slight. But I am not bred to her ways. It would end unhappily.'

He was about to protest, but saw in my eye a conviction unshake-able. 'Perhaps so,' he said. 'You must know your own mind best.'

We walked on by the burial ground, and there were many fresh-filled graves there after the previous day's fighting. We were silent as we went by.

'It is about Captain Le Baume that I wished to speak with you,' I said when we reached the far side and, Warwick not answering me, I added, 'You have seen now how he has led his men. Has he not behaved as honourably as any English officer?'

'He is not English.'

'No more am I.'

'Do not trifle with my words. The matter does not allow of levity.'

'But were there no other grounds for the suspicion harboured against him. It cannot be only that he is a Frenchman.'

'Some would consider that sufficient.'

'You are not one of them.'

'The sailors beneath my command do not like any Frenchman. Nor do I think the less of them for their dislike. It is a healthy instinct.'

'I believe you know something more particular of Le Baume, else you never had spoke a word to me.'

'It were perhaps better I had not.'

'When you are departed Bengal, I will be here still with Le Baume. Unless I have good reason to do otherwise, I must then treat him openly and in full confidence of his loyalty to us. If that be wrong, pray tell me so, and why.'

He grabbed my arm quite suddenly and drew me into a doorway. 'It is as well we are not aboard my ship, else I would have you in irons. It may be I should have answered you, but you will not speak to me so.'

At this moment Brereton, very fortunately, called out to Warwick – I think only to give us warning of his approach from behind us, for he had surely seen Warwick grab me. Warwick let go my arm. 'Thank you, Mr Brereton. I will see you at the ghat.' Brereton touched his hat to us and looked at us curiously but carried on by.

I said to Warwick, 'Sir, I am to go with Mr Watts to Murshidabad to treat with the nawab – and possibly with the French. When I told Le Baume of it this morning, he volunteered to go with us.'

Warwick looked at me unhappily now. He saw that I had some very good reason for my questions. 'Let us walk,' said he. We came from the doorway and set off slowly after Brereton toward the ghat. 'I will tell you, but I would not have it repeated. Not to Mr Watts. Not to Le Baume. Not to anyone.'

I nodded. I saw how hard it went with him to speak it.

'You will recall all the time the ships' officers spent idle in Madras and the many card games there were in consequence. Le Baume had a great avidity at the table, but he played with more enthusiasm than skill. He ended by owing a considerable sum. He had not the funds to pay the debt at first. But he then found a Hindoo banker to make him an advance in specie. Or that is what he said.'

'But the debt was repaid.'

'The debt is immaterial. Captain Lynn found himself in a like need and applied to Le Baume for an introduction to the accommodating banker. Le Baume would not give the banker's name. An argument followed but, very fortunately, nothing came of it. I made enquiry in the bazaar after the banker who had taken Le Baume's paper. I had a notion there was a pirate's rate extracted or Le Baume would not have been so coy as to the name. I could find none who would own to having taken Le Baume's paper.'

'Bankers are secretive fellows.'

'The next day we went out to the Mount. You will remember it.

Those two Frenchmen were with the colonel. One set up a coin to be shot at.'

'I remember it.'

'He had a purse full of them – silver *siccas* – a coin not seen in Madras from one year to the next. It was just such coins Le Baume had used to repay his debt.'

'That may have been coincidence,' said I, though much doubting of the possibility.

'There is nothing proven against Le Baume, Mr Douglas, or he had not remained now among us. And I say again, I would not have the tale repeated. The officers that know of it have kept it close. It goes to the man's honour. You must make of it what you will. But, by my advice, you must not take him with you to Murshidabad.'

CHAPTER TWENTY-NINE

Mr Watts and Omichand travelled each in his own palanquin, whilst I went mounted, for the motion of the palanquin was disagreeable to me, except it be over some short distance. It was no short distance we set out to travel, but as far as Murshidabad, whither the nawab and his army were also journeying, though several days in advance of us. Melchior Le Baume was not of our number, nor had I needed to lift a hand to prevent it, for Mr Watts had evinced a definite wish that our caravan not be mistaken for anything other than a peaceful delegation. So we left Calcutta with no officers, but only the palanquin bearers, Harry Khan, Omichand, twenty sepoys for our protection and also a small number of Hindoo camp followers with our provisions. I was spared, therefore, from any difficulty in the matter, which might have been considerable, for it was not only what we did in Murshidabad that should be kept from the French, but the mere fact that we must pass by Chandernagore on our way there. Mr Watts had told me that he suspected the French there of intriguing with the nawab against our interest, and the possibility of the colonel and the admiral going up to attack the French at Chandernagore was now a matter of public speculation in Calcutta.

And so I was not sorry to be leaving Le Baume behind us.

The first part of our journey northward was uneventful, though I could not help but deplore the great changes that had happened in the countryside since my journey south from Cossimbazaar with Edward and Sri Babu. Since that time the nawab's army had crossed and re-crossed the territory and most of the villages near to Calcutta had now been burned and all their grain stores emptied or destroyed. The village people that we saw gave us no greeting, but looked on sullenly as we passed. Neither could we buy from them eggs or milk or any fresh meat, for they had none and ate only the rice they had had from the Moors. We were very glad of our own provisions.

I rode with Harry and half the sepoys at the head of our column, then was a gap left for the dust, followed by Mr Watts and Omichand in their palanquins and behind them the camp followers and the other half of the sepoys and Coja Petrus at the rear. Occasionally I fell back to ride alongside Mr Watts and converse with him, though it was apparent these were but interludes from the extended discourse he was almost continually engaged in with that devil Omichand. Mile after mile their palanquins moved on side-by-side, with their interminable discussion going back and forth between their open shutters.

At the beginning Omichand was careful to fall silent at my approach or else commence some badinage of no consequence, but as he came accustomed to see the familiarity of my conversation with Mr Watts, Omichand too, became less guarded with me. I think he saw me as something of a servant to Mr Watts, for in truth he was of a type that can scarce conceive any other relationship between men, but they must be either master or servant. This made him very shrewd in the ways of the nawab's court and also in matters of trade, but once I had trav-elled in his company, shared meals with him and heard his conversation, I own I found him the very shallowest of men. To the finer feelings of the heart and the higher faculties of the mind he was the most distant of strangers. His understanding was swift, but it went no deeper than what could be turned to his own advantage, and of the world beyond that narrow compass I never heard him make any intelligent enquiry. His face was plump and, for a native face, quite pale, framed as it was between his blue turban and a beard dyed the deepest of blacks. His habit was to comb his fingers through this beard while he talked, his mouth ever smiling, and his eyes ever busy to confirm the lies of his tongue.

We crossed the river onto the western bank below Chandernagore, and here Coja Petrus and one of Omichand's servants parted ways with us and went into the town, while we skirted wide of it. They were sent to find out the truth of the rumours we had heard concerning the nawab's dealings with Gouverneur Renault after the Moors' retreat from Calcutta. But the servant rejoined us on the track two hours later with no definite information but only more rumours of some accommodation between the nawab and Renault, and so we proceeded some miles further on and made our camp a short distance from the town of Hugli. Here Omichand left us to go into the town and meet with the *faujdar* (who is, to the Moors, like a governor), for Mr Watts considered that this *faujdar* was very likely to have some certain knowledge of the nawab's rumoured dealings with the French. For my part, I was not sorry to stay clear of that town, for it could not be that they had repaired a tenth part of the destruction we had wrought there. The very name of it now was sufficient to call up in me a disquieting sickness of spirit, a feeling I was loath to face directly, and which I could not yet fully own for remorse.

While we awaited Omichand's return, Watts rested in the shade of his palanquin and read Tacitus and dozed, whilst I went among the sepoys with my sketchbook. It was almost evening before Omichand returned and I was, by then, seated with my back propped against Watts's palanquin, putting the last touches to the sketches I had made. Omichand got out from his own palanquin with an energy I had never seen in him before now. The loose folds of his long jacket flapped about him as he hurried across to us.

'I had begun to think we had lost you,' said Watts, setting aside his book and swinging his legs out from the palanquin.

'You shall hear, sir. You shall hear.' Omichand snapped several sharp orders to left and right of him, but his servants were already about their business and putting a cloth and cushions on the ground near Watts's palanquin. Omichand was hardly slumped down upon these cushions when a small jug of water was given him and he drank it in that strange manner of the Hindoo, without the jug touching his lips, the stream of water pouring from a height straight into his mouth.

'You have seen the *faujdar*?' Watts prompted.

'Yes, yes.' Omichand tossed aside the empty jug and called over to the men at the campfire. The sepoys there did not stir (for it was not Harry had given the order) but several servants there moved to do his bidding. 'The French are very clever. And Gouverneur Renault? Very cunning fellow.'

'Has Renault treated with the nawab?'

Omichand slapped his thigh theatrically and swayed forward with a finger raised. 'One lakh. The nawab has returned to Renault one lakh of the money he took from them last year. And who has brought it to them from the nawab? Coja Wajid's man, Sri Babu.'

'And what does the nawab think to have in return?'

'Wait, wait. The French are permitted now to build their fort in Chandernagore how they please' – he rubbed his finger and thumb together – 'and mint coin. The same gift the nawab has made to the English.'

'Are they indeed?'

'He is very clever, Gouverneur Renault. You have beaten the nawab, but the French have shared in your victory.'

'Is the *faujdar*'s information reliable?'

'He is afraid for his position. He is not confirmed as *faujdar* yet. He fears the nawab's weakness. I have made a small gift to him, a few hundred rupees.'

'The company shall repay you.'

'That is nothing. I think no more on it. But hear – with Sri Babu came a message from the nawab – if the English attack the French in Chandernagore, the *faujdar* must assist the French.'

'That is contrary to the treaty.'

'But also, if the French attack the English, then the *faujdar* must assist the English. The nawab fears both of you. If one overcomes the other, there will be left only one great European power in Bengal. And the nawab has learned from Colonel Clive and Admiral Watson what Europeans may do.'

'The French would be fools to attack us.'

'If you attack the French in Chandernagore now, you will defeat them.'

'We shall see.'

'The *faujdar* has made a proposal, sir. Will you hear it?'

'Say on.'

'If the company pay him twelve thousand rupees, he will be sure to send no assistance to the French in Chandernagore. He will delay sending a reinforcement to them while you attack. After you have won the victory, he asks that you be at peace with him and use your influence to keep him as *faujdar* in Hugli.'

'Very white of the fellow,' Watts remarked. 'But if he thinks to extract such a sum upon his good word, he is much in error.'

'I have said to him there would be no payment from the company until his word was proven by his actions.'

'Or by his inactions.'

Omichand laughed and clapped his thigh, his whole manner very false.

'Sir?' said I, lifting my chin to indicate to Mr Watts the Hindoo, a stranger to us, now standing at the edge of our camp. The sepoys had seen him as well as I, but none had accosted him, for by his white *shalwar* and the red thread across his shoulder and bare midriff, he was a priest of high caste. He stood there silent and motionless, and watched us. But the Brahmin was no stranger to Omichand, who called him over to us. The fellow came and squatted on his haunches. 'He will take a message to the colonel if you wish it,' Omichand told Watts. 'This one knows nothing of the matter. But if the colonel says to him "*Golaub que foul*", this one will bring word to the *faujdar* that the offer is accepted. And he will then hold off from reinforcing the French.'

'Rose flower,' said Watts, translating from the Persian.

'But not in English. Only "*Golaub que foul*" or there will be confusion.'

'You have been rather busy in Hugli,' said Watts to Omichand, and there was that in his tone which pleased me, for I saw now that Watts was not altogether taken with the forwardness of Omichand's dealings on our behalf. Whether Omichand sensed it too, or whether he merely thought his main point won, he continued now in a less urgent vein, talking of other matters he had heard of in Hugli – of the growing dissent among the nawab's generals and the large loans the French had taken from the mighty banking family the Seths, and many things besides. The Brahmin waited, silent.

Some time later, night already fallen, Coja Petrus came into our camp. He reported to Watts that the French were moving their valuable goods and treasure out of Chandernagore and into the safekeeping of the Dutch at Chinsurah. Watts then retired with a lamp into his palanquin, composed a letter to Clive and put it into the hand of the Brahmin.

At Cossimbazaar the nawab's sentries were at the gate of our factory. Harry rode on ahead of us and spoke with them, and when we came up they surrendered all the keys to the gates and the warehouses to Mr Watts very peaceably. They told us that the nawab had been returned to Murshidabad for several days now and that Monsieur Law, the chief of the French factory in Cossimbazaar, had been at the gates that very morning to make enquiry of us, for we had been expected for some while.

Harry pushed upon the gates and I said to Watts, 'It has been a time we have been away from here,' to which he only answered distractedly, 'Monsieur Law has the start of us,' and walked by me and into the factory.

After the despoliation and damage inflicted by the Moors on Calcutta, we were prepared to find the Cossimbazaar factory a ruin, but we found it, instead, very much as we had left it, with only the smaller items of value taken from the bungalows. All of the furniture was still in place and a fair quantity of cloth and trade goods remained in the warehouses, for the nawab of Bengal's seal had been put on many doors, which had secured them more than any locks. Omichand did not stay with us, for he was impatient to be in to Murshidabad, there to meet with the banker Jagath Seth, and discover what intrigue Monsieur Law was working against us at the nawab's court.

Once Omichand had left us, Watts bade me go with Harry to the bazaar and make a public pronouncement of our return (though the fact of it was certainly known already in the town) and thereafter summon back to the factory all our servants who had been turned out by the Moors. There was a considerable commotion at the bazaar upon our arrival and Harry was hailed from all directions, for he was a figure well known to them. He pushed his knuckle over his moustache and smiled and looked almost the Harry of old, for he was much gratified by this happy reception. He climbed onto a bench and hauled me up beside him and when he had quieted them somewhat, he addressed them for a minute. When he was done, I asked him if it were necessary that I should speak. He whispered a few native words in my ear, urging the rightness of them for the occasion. He repeated the phrase to me and I, fool that I was, puffed out my chest and proclaimed the words very boldly. There was a moment of stunned silence and then a laughter, quite appalling, swept the bazaar. Harry, shaking his head in mirth, got me down from the bench.

'What the devil did you have me say?'

'Only that you English fellows have returned,' he said, scarce able to contain himself.

I made no further enquiry, for I perceived there was no harm meant by it (though it was not a liberty he would have taken with Mr Watts). No young woman in the bazaar would meet my eye now, but they covered their faces as I passed and the old women laughed at me very openly.

'We need not mention this to Mr Watts.'

'No, sir,' said Harry.

At the factory, I resettled myself in that same bungalow I had shared with Hastings and the other writers before the nawab's army had first appeared with menace at our gates. And, once settled, I took myself across to Edward's bungalow, where I set about the melancholy task of gathering up what remained of his personal possessions and papers. The accounts of his personal trading he kept in a small ledger in a secret compartment of his bureau and I found it still there, untouched. So I bundled it with his other personal effects and made a small packet.

From there I went down to the counting house, broke the nawab's seal and went in.

Everything was in its proper place. Even the ledger lay open on the desk. I sat and remembered the morning we had learned of the withdrawal of the native boats, and how angry Edward had been. I considered also the many other days when I had sat there benumbed with the tedium of it, while Edward with relish had negotiated a few rupees off the price for the silk we were buying, or uncovered some ruse by which the Hindoo middlemen were cheating us, or solved some dispute with the weavers at the *aurangs*. His absorption in the life had been total. And as I sat there now, with Edward's small bundle of personal effects on the desk before me, in a room where I had once sat each day with him, I felt how unforgivable was the act that had robbed him of his life.

'Mr Douglas!' called Watts from across the yard, and I closed the counting house ledger, took up the packet of Edward's things and came away, I confess, with some small hope of vengeance now stirring in my heart.

CHAPTER THIRTY

'*Y*ou will not come with me into the audience chamber,' said Watts, after we alighted from the palanquins into the courtyard of the nawab of Bengal's palace. 'Speak nothing within these walls but with an expectation it will be repeated to the French.'

'Yes, sir.'

'You will be taken to the palace garden. You may wait for me there.'

There were two very fierce-looking Moors, with scimitars at their sides, standing guard at the main palace door. And out from between these two now came a palace eunuch, his head shaven, in the blue robes of his caste. I had heard of these fellows but never seen one, for they stayed always within the precincts of the palace and this was the first time that I had ever been within the royal walls. Finding me with Mr Watts, which he had not expected, the eunuch called out to one of his fellows to take me to the palace garden.

This second eunuch took me through further courtyards until we came at last into the garden at the north side of the palace. Here were vines climbing on trellises, several fountains of no great size, but very pleasing, with a rill joining them and many plants in bloom, their scent hanging heavy on the air. There was soft music coming from a far corner of the garden, and voices. When I stopped to admire the first fountain, the eunuch would not give me peace, but urged me to that far corner. I followed him again and, coming around the last wall of vines, found myself almost immediately upon the party gathered there. The music of the flute continued, but the voices all stopped at the instant of my arrival.

Here was another sight that I had not seen before: the Moorish ladies. There were several of them there, richly robed, lounging upon silk cushions, with a number of their maids and eunuchs kneeling or seated about them. Behind these were the musicians and above the musicians a canopy of vines. And then my eyes stopped suddenly, for now I saw the two Europeans who had been to one side, partially hidden from me.

'Monsieur Douglas,' said Law, stepping forward, with a smile, to greet me in French, saying, 'But you are alone.'

'You cannot have expected me here, sir.'

'We knew of your return to Cossimbazaar. It could not be long, but you would come here. You know Monsieur Cordet.' He gestured to Cordet, who now came forward.

'Monsieur,' said I to Cordet. 'Monsieur,' said he, with a nod to me.

'But where is Monsieur Watts?' asked Law, looking toward the garden gates.

'He is gone into the palace. I believe he is paying his respects to the nawab.'

'Of course,' said Law and, by his tone and his look, he made sure I understood that he knew exactly what Watts did with the nawab (which was to blacken the name of the French). He took my arm then and introduced me to the Moorish women, who were the wives of several nobles of the court. He spoke to them in Persian, which he knew as well as Watts. I was surprised when there were some small phrases of French in their replies to him, for it bespoke an acquaintance I had not expected. 'But you arrive just as the ladies grow weary of our company, Monsieur Douglas,' said Law. 'Perhaps you will walk with us below. There we may take in the fair prospect of the river.' He had soon guided me from the women and down to the lower part of the tiered garden, where a number of Moorish arches made windows in the walls overlooking the river. It was indeed a fair prospect, with many boats moving on the water or tied at the ghats, and many fine houses on the bank opposite, facing us. 'These gardens are the best rooms in the palace. I have often enjoyed walking here in the evening with the nawab.'

'Now that he has returned from Calcutta, he may have time to enjoy his walks with you the more,' said I.

Law smiled. 'That may be. It is true that we had not expected his return so soon.'

'You may thank the colonel for the nawab's company.'

'I am sure we are very grateful to him. And you, no doubt, have heard of the nawab's generosity toward us in Chandernagore?'

'It is not my concern, sir.'

'That is my thought exactly, Monsieur Douglas. How the nawab is disposed toward one of our two nations is no concern of the other.' Law asked then after our factory in Cossimbazaar. He offered to send us anything that we might have need of which might not be got from the bazaars.

'I am sure we are quite comfortable.'

'And Omichand, I have no doubt, will busy himself to make you even more comfortable than you are.'

'We shall not rely upon it.'

'Shall you not?' said he.

'No more than you upon Coja Wajid's good offices,' said I, knowing well of Wajid's sympathy with the French.

My reply seemed to amuse Law, but I was only too conscious that he had led me further than I had meant to be drawn and that Mr Watts would, perhaps, not have liked to hear me speak so. To get out of my difficulty, I asked after some people we had both been acquainted with in Chandernagore and Law was very pleasant in his answers and content not to press me on any greater matters. He was a gentleman. But it was not long before he found some reason to excuse himself and left me with Cordet and went, himself, into the palace to find Mr Watts. Neither servant nor eunuch accompanied him, which I took as no good sign for us British, for it was clear he was very familiar there and trusted.

With Law gone, Cordet propped himself in one of the arches overlooking the river. I noticed there was no sword in the sheath at his side and he saw that I noticed. 'Only the nawab's guards may have their weapons within the palace or the grounds,' said he. When I nodded, he continued, 'It was a bold stroke of your colonel's to march directly into the nawab's camp.'

'There was a heavy fog. We were very fortunate. I am surprised to find you here.'

'I go where I am ordered. Is it true there were more than a thousand Moors killed?'

I remarked that I was too busy with my own self-defence at the time to count them.

'But you were not there?' said he in surprise.

'I was there. And you may be sure it was not like Hugli.'

'I have not forgotten Hugli.'

'Neither one of us has forgotten. And I have thought often of your saying that it was not war. I do not know that you were right, but neither am I proud to have been a part of it.'

But, though Cordet had not forgotten Hugli, it was this latest battle that now captivated him. 'And is it true you British were only two thousand?'

'It is possible. We were not many.'

'And the colonel was with you?'

'He commanded the column.'

'You have done that which you shall remember.'

'Yes,' said I. 'I shall remember it.'

There was no mistaking his admiration of what Clive had done, nor his envy of my small part in it. But it seemed to me that my martial daydreams had suffered a harsh collision with the world, which Cordet's, till now, had not. And, when he questioned me on the tactics of the battle, wanting to hear every part of it, he took my reticence for a kind of dissimulation.

'An infantryman has no view of the battle but his own,' said I at last.

'You must wait to speak with Colonel Clive if you would know more of it.'

'I shall,' said he. 'Only let it not be at Chandernagore.'

We looked at each other and I could not read him, and neither he me. I said, 'You have not enquired of Le Baume's part in the battle.'

'Le Baume is not my concern.'

'What business had you with him in Madras?'

'What has he said?'

'Nothing.'

'Then that is the extent of the business I have had with him.' He pushed away from the arched window and talked of rejoining the Moorish ladies in the upper garden, and started at once up there, so I could press him no further on Le Baume.

The women chided him for his absence and ordered their eunuchs to bring us refreshment and we each of us sank onto his own seat of cushions in the shade beneath the vines. Cordet had almost as little Persian as I and he spoke with the women in the local tongue, with an admixture of French. It was clear he was a very great favourite with them, for they laughed often, which I had not expected of them. They were more free with him, and at their ease, than they would have been with any Moor of similar rank. In the midst of his talk with them, he turned to me and said, 'It would amuse the ladies if you would do a sketch for them.'

'I have no materials.'

'The ladies are not accustomed to any refusal,' he said and commanded a eunuch to bring charcoal and paper. 'And you will remember not to draw their faces. It is not their custom.' When the paper and charcoal were brought, the women held some discussion among themselves and at last decided upon a subject for me, which was a white rose, framed by the iron trelliswork against the garden wall.

They ignored me then, or seemed to, and I began to work the first lines. All was languor in the garden, for the music was stopped now and the only sound was the water running in the rill and the faint cries of the town, beyond the garden wall.

I said to Cordet while I sketched, 'Either the ladies are very quick in their learning or you have been frequently in this garden with them.'

'It is the pleasantest place in the city.'

'You contrived to tear yourself from it to go with Sinfray to Calcutta.'

'Would that I were my own master,' said he. Then he got to his feet. 'I might then have had the leisure to remain with you now. As it is – I will see you again, I expect, in Cossimbazaar.'

'I expect you will see me as frequently in Murshidabad. Perhaps even here in the palace.'

He bade me good day and took his leave of the ladies. Unlike Law, he did not leave the garden alone, but one of the eunuchs shadowed him. I saw, of course, how neatly Cordet had tied me to the place with my sketching, keeping himself free to go to whatever intrigue proceeded in the palace. In truth, I was more amused than annoyed, for I knew that, in my ignorance, I could do no service for Mr Watts yet, but perhaps might cause some harm by inept meddling and so I was content, for now, to remain with the noble ladies.

When I had completed the sketch I presented it to that lady who, by her manner, seemed the most senior and she showed it to the others, who admired the work and spoke to me directly for the first time, saying, 'Belle, belle,' and a few Persian and Portuguese words besides. But shortly after that, they signified to me with both gestures and their little French that they must retire for their midday prayer. I returned to the lower garden, with a eunuch watching over me. There were a great many boats on the river below and, on the ghat opposite, a Hindoo funeral pyre burning. And when a Moorish priest commenced to call his people to their prayers, Mr Watts hurried down from the upper garden to fetch me.

'Let us now to Lombard Street,' said he.

The palace of the Seth family, though imposing, was smaller than the nawab's palace, and not by the river but in the merchants' quarter. And here Watts felt no need to leave me at the door, so I followed him to the central courtyard and thence into an antechamber and, at last, we were ushered by a servant into the room where Jagath Seth himself held court.

Omichand was there before us and did not rise at our entry. But Jagath Seth rose from his cushioned bench and greeted Watts very warmly and acknowledged me with a nod when Watts made mention of me, and was in all ways a very gentleman to us. Though I had before been in some outer quarters of this palace on company business, I had never laid eyes on any one of the Seths, for they kept themselves very private and worked their will across Bengal through agents such as Ranjit Rai. Now, while Watts spoke with Jagath Seth, I studied the man's face, which was clean-shaven, and noted the attentiveness with which he regarded Watts's words. Jagath Seth's eyes were very still, nor did they move from Watts when he asked some question. But there was nothing severe in his regard, and he seemed to listen in order that he might understand, and not from any baser motive (which is a thing could not be said for the crafty Omichand nearby). Nor was his manner of dress extraordinarily lavish, but he wore a white *shalwar-khemis* (which is a loose shirt and trousers) such as was common with many of the wealthier Hindoo traders. There was a single band of gold about his wrist, and on his forehead the red mark of his religion.

At last Mr Watts expressed the company's gratitude for Ranjit Rai's assistance in drawing up our treaty with the nawab, and also for an advance of credit to the company (which I had not known of). Jagath Seth brushed these aside as matters barely worthy of mention between friends.

'What peace have you made with the French?' said he, in perfect English. 'Or will you fight them?'

'That is very direct.'

'I am sure the nawab asked you the same.'

'And I must answer you as I have answered him – that though we must acknowledge that our two countries are at war, yet our council has proposed to Gouverneur Renault a neutrality here in Bengal. We have been awaiting his answer for some days now.'

'Monsieur Law fears the British will attack Chandernagore.'

'There is no such order given.'

'Monsieur Law has also been very careful that the nawab should not forget the French army that is by his border in Orissa.'

'We have heard much of this so-called army and of this General Bussy who commands it. For myself, I do not regard either one of them. By the reports I have received it is a weaker force than Monsieur Law and Gouverneur Renault claim. And it seems to me very convenient for Monsieur Law's purposes here that this army of Bussy's be ever on the point of crossing into Bengal, but ever delaying. The threat is without cost and can never be tested.'

'It is very real to the nawab.'

'Then Monsieur Law has done his work. I trust in the coming days I may do mine equally well. But you will have your own reports of this Bussy.'

'They are no different from your own,' Jagath Seth admitted.

Mr Watts continued very direct. 'You will have your own reports, too, of our force under Admiral Watson and Colonel Clive. What strength they have is no secret, but a plain fact known in every town and village from here to the coast.'

'It is known in Chandernagore at least,' said Omichand, and Watts glanced at him in warning.

'You may be assured, sir,' said Watts, addressing Jagath Seth, 'that it is not our intention to destroy the trade of Bengal. The furtherance of trade is our whole purpose here. It is very clear to me after my audience with the nawab that Monsieur Law has planted in him a deep suspicion of the Honourable Company and all its actions.'

'The colonel and the admiral have done more than ever did Monsieur Law,' remarked Jagath Seth (and with some justice, I thought, though Watts made no such acknowledgement). 'As to the trade in Bengal, it will not improve while there is war.'

'We have offered the French a neutrality.'

'Not only war between you and the French, Mr Watts. This nawab raised an army almost the same week he came to power. It has not left the field since: first against you British, in Calcutta, but also against Sanjit Kaung in the west. Now there is talk of the nawab marching his army to the aid of the emperor in Delhi. War. Endless war. How can there be trade?'

'That is very true,' Watts lamented. He had caught Jagath Seth's rather false tone of worldly-wise regret and now echoed it back to him. 'It is a question we have had ever before us very often in the council since the nawab first fell upon Cossimbazaar.'

'You have discussed this very question, then?'

'We have,' said Watts and his gaze met Jagath Seth's now with a stillness quite remarkable.

'And have you an answer?'

'No certain answer,' said Watts, 'but only Colonel Clive and Admiral Watson.'

He kept his gaze upon Jagath Seth and Jagath Seth upon him. I saw that there was understanding that moved between them. Then at last Jagath Seth made a gesture to the turbaned boy who had been seated by the door all this while (he was a deaf boy, as were several others the Seths kept about them). The boy fetched chai and sweetmeats and now Omichand talked, making very free with the reputations of the nobles in the nawab's court, the factions among them and the bribery practised there by the French.

There were some names of the Moorish nobles which I had heard before, but as many more that were new to me. But the one name that caused them the greatest consternation was that of Mohan Lal.

'He was with the nawab even now in the audience chamber,' remarked Watts.

'Every word that he speaks is a poison to the English,' said Omichand, and he turned to Jagath Seth. 'Is it not true?'

'I could not say.'

'It is true,' Omichand affirmed. 'He keeps as close to the nawab as a new bride to her husband.'

Jagath Seth leaned towards Watts. 'Mohan Lal would not let a cargo of Omichand's opium pass down the river last season.'

'That? That is nothing,' broke out Omichand, but Jagath Seth only smiled and gestured for the boy to pour more chai for us.

The talk became general for a while, of the poor harvest, the coming rains and some holy festival soon to take place in the city. Though Watts and Jagath Seth both appeared quite content with this turn, Omichand's impatience was very apparent to me. But after a time the leisurely survey returned to the politics of the nawab's court and Jagath Seth remarked that the nawab feared the English kept their warships in Calcutta in expectation that the rains would soon flood the higher reaches of the river. It was the nawab's belief, Seth said, that the river would then become navigable to our squadron and so bring all Bengal, as far as Murshidabad, beneath the range of the admiral's guns.

This was a thing I knew impossible, owing to the deep draft of our ships. But Mr Watts did not say so, he sipped his chai and remained silent.

CHAPTER THIRTY-ONE

*E*ach morning Watts made the short journey from Cossimbazaar to Murshidabad and each evening returned to read the letters and messages that had arrived in his absence, and also to write his reports to Admiral Watson and Colonel Clive. I did not go with him always, for he gave me charge of gathering that information we needed concerning the reparations owed to the company and to our private people under the terms of our new treaty with the nawab. The reluctance of the nawab's officials made this a task almost impossible for me, but when I complained of it to Watts he seemed unperturbed and said only, 'There will be time enough when I am done,' and suchlike phrases, by which I came to understand that our efforts to hold the nawab to the treaty were but a secondary reason for our coming up from Calcutta.

Certainly Watts himself spent no time over it, except to now write a letter, on my behalf, to Drake and the council, giving a full account of the losses we had suffered by the Moorish seizure of our goods and looting of our factories. I own that my carefulness over the task diminished when I understood it was but a cover for the more urgent business being carried forward by Watts and Omichand. The nature of that business was not long hid from me, for when I remarked on the loans advanced us by the Seths (the record of which I kept in the factory ledgers), Mr Watts told me quite baldly that he needed this money for the bribes he dispensed daily in the nawab's court. Without these loans, he said, we could make no headway against Monsieur Law and the French faction in Murshidabad. We were in the study of his bungalow at the time. Watts had made sure of the locked door before he spoke to me.

'It is an evil necessity, Alistair,' he concluded, though with less sign of shame than I might have expected.

'But what value can they have who may be bought? They can never be trusted.'

'They may be trusted so long as our bid for their services exceeds that of the French. Omichand knows the weakness of every one of them. As to their value – you have seen the old Brahmin who is so often at our gate since we returned.'

'You gave orders that the sepoys should not chase him away.'

'From that you will have surmised that he is a spy for the company. Just as his fraternity in Calcutta.'

'I have not spoken to him.'

'I do not accuse you. Nor do I think you would be so foolish. But it may alter your opinion of the value of bribery in this place if I tell you that the fellow is not ours but rather the creation of Rajaram, the nawab's chief spy.'

'The fellow spies upon us?'

'No.'

I reflected and then said, 'It cannot be that he spies upon his own master.'

Watts smiled. 'It is not the servant I have bought, but the master. It is Rajaram who sends this fellow to me with reports of the nawab's treacherous dealings. I see you do not quite believe me.'

'Sir, if you say it is true—'

'I thank God, that it is! Else I had not known what small weight there is in the nawab's word. He will join his force with the French against us just as soon as the colonel and the admiral are withdrawn from Bengal.'

'But that is contrary to our treaty.'

'He will not be bound by his word, but only by his fear. We must move boldly against the French while we yet have the opportunity. I have recommended to the colonel an immediate attack upon Chandernagore. My fellows on the council continue to negotiate with Gouverneur Renault for a neutrality between our two nations in Bengal. If they succeed, they shall have – by their blindness – destroyed us.'

'You are very sanguine of it.'

'I am so very far from sanguine, Alistair, that I have considered returning to Calcutta, where I might argue in person the necessity of an immediate attack upon the French in Chandernagore. But that would leave Omichand with the sole direction of our affairs here. You may imagine that is a circumstance I must be at some pains to avoid.'

'But if you have need – that is, I feel I might do more to assist you, sir.'

'By a constant harping on all the points of the treaty and a steady probing to discover the extent of those spoils they have had from our factories, you are doing me an indisputable service. While the nawab thinks we depend upon words he will practise to deceive us with words. In the meantime, there is an undermining of his courts now proceeding beneath his feet. You do better service than you know.'

How much of this was merely soothing balm to a young man's pride I could not tell, but it succeeded at least in returning me to my task with new purpose, for no man works well but with some good reason for it. And while I confronted the evasions and duplicities of the nawab's officials and attempted to extract from them some reasonable accounting of what company goods they still held, what they had sold and for what price, Watts continued to work his own sinuous purpose in the court unregarded.

It was in the first week of March and Mr Watts in his bungalow deep in conference with Omichand, when we received the nawab's peremptory and unexpected summons to join him in a hunt the next morning on the open plain behind the black town.

Several of our greyhounds had survived the Moors' seizure of Cossim-bazaar by reason of Harry's placing them with a keeper in an outlying village that distant day when we had returned from the pig-sticking. The keeper had now brought them back to us and we suffered no embarrassment from lack of them, but went out to the plain with the hounds loping at the side of our horses. Harry and a few sepoys led us, making altogether as bold a show of it as we had ever done. Mr Watts had been very particular about the appearance of our party before we issued out through the factory gates, and when we came to the appointed meeting-place on the plain I was very glad of his care in this matter. For not only was the nawab there, but also his senior courtiers and with them Monsieur Law and Cordet and several others from the French factory, and all of them turned out very fine, and their horses. There was an elephant there also, with a headpiece of colourfully embroidered cloth and on its back a canopied box called a howdah, wherein the nawab would ride.

'You will keep your wits about you today,' Watts warned me as we neared.

'Say nothing,' Omichand told me from his palanquin on my other side. 'You must speak only with the French.'

'Mr Douglas will speak with whomsoever he pleases,' said Watts in mild rebuke, for it was most assuredly not Omichand's place to instruct me. 'Only have a care, Alistair. It is clear we have not been brought here for the chase.'

We dismounted and left our horses with Harry and the sepoys while we joined those other Europeans and Moors gathered before the nawab's tent. When we came there we saw that the face of the tent lay open and inside was the nawab with several noblewomen and a number of young boys, who were not servants but dressed in silks and playing about the tent very freely. When I remarked on them to Omichand, he told me they were the sons of the nawab's senior courtiers and that I should look no more into the tent, for one of the ladies in there was the nawab's wife and the nawab would be sure to take offence. Leaving Mr Watts with the Moors, I went to stand with Cordet, who was alone but for the single hound lying at his feet.

'Monsieur Law told me that we should not be the nawab's only guests,' said Cordet. 'It did not seem likely we should have the field to ourselves.'

'I am sorry we have been obliged to disappoint you,' I answered in French, for so he had spoken to me.

'For myself, I am only too pleased that you have come, Monsieur Douglas. Almost as pleased as I am to be from that infernal palace for a day.'

'I had thought it agreed with you very well.'

'My hounds are more agreeable to me still. And yet if should I stay with them overlong, I must surely come away with their worst fleas upon me.'

This allusion to our Moorish hosts was spoken very quietly, though it was perhaps better it had not been spoken at all. At least Cordet, by his glance at me, seemed to say so, for there was a quick regret in his eye and he immediately talked of other matters, as if to draw a curtain across the briefly opened window of his mind. At the same time I sensed that he watched me, as if I might be drawn to follow his indiscretion with an unguarded remark of my own. Indeed, I might well have done so had Watts's warning to me not been so very recent. I determined to be more on my guard of him.

The nawab was very soon in the howdah and his old counsellor, Mohan Lal, lifted up there with him. When the elephant had risen from its belly we all mounted and our sepoys went wide, joining sepoys the French and Dutch had brought and the nawab's mounted huntsmen, to make a great arc of men toward the horizon and so gather in the game to the centre.

As we rode, Watts and Law moved easily among the Moors, each conversing very readily in the Persian tongue, though I noticed that no Moor would remain with either one of them long, for there was ever a reason to call him back to his fellows or to the Dutch chief whose nation had not meddled with the court. The reason for the nobles' wariness was not far in seeking, for though they rarely lifted their eyes to the nawab in his howdah, he had no such scruple and ran his gaze over them all continually while Mohan Lal whispered in his ear like the very commonest harlot.

It was my first sight of the nawab since we had, those many months ago, been summoned to his durbar tent from the Cossimbazaar factory. Those months between had put deep lines in his brow and dark shadows beneath his eyes and he looked no longer like a boy. What he had unleashed upon us – either by his own will or as the pawn of another – had now returned upon him, and he had no answer to it but to withdraw to the palace and the intrigues he had been raised in and there abide the storm. While we had been in Murshidabad rumours had come to us that the emperor in Delhi might bring an army down the Ganges to chastise the nawab. Others had told us that there was neither security nor safety for the nawab in any quarter of Bengal, but that he must have guards always in readiness about him. The nawab had not suffered yet as Fairborough, and so many others, had suffered at his hand. If he no longer looked like a boy there was good reason for it and there was a low satisfaction to me in the sight of him so uneasy in his golden howdah, his face very strained and his eyes at once troubled and weary.

'You have not called upon us, Mr Douglas,' said Law, bringing his horse alongside mine. 'I hope you do not think you would be other than sincerely welcomed.'

'At present, sir, I am at the mercy of the company's affairs.'

'Whenever they shall be concluded—'

'I shall most certainly call upon you,' said I, though it seemed a prospect very distant.

'Monsieur Cordet is greatly taken with your many exploits on the battlefield.'

'I have done no more than what was required of me by duty,' said I, quite sufficiently full of myself.

'Let us hope that duty has no further need of your services in this regard. We should be very sad to lose you.'

'You should be sadder still to lose Monsieur Cordet,' I remarked, at which Law smiled and began to talk of the hunt, for he saw that I would not be drawn on more substantial matter. And nor, to give a true gentleman his due, would Monsieur Law be so discourteous as to press me.

Soon we had come to that place where we must await the driven game. We Europeans had brought muskets only, but the Moors had both muskets and bows, for archery was a great delight to them and they practised it constantly. And now there was a small trial of skill among them while we waited there. The nawab dismounted from the elephant, a follower presenting him with a bow and a quiver of arrows, while gourds were hung on bushes at varying distances from our party. The Moors took turns to shoot at the gourds with their arrows, and though two of the fellows were very skilful, they were also very careful to fail on any gourd which defeated the nawab. The nawab saw this as well as any, but his vanity would not let him withdraw from the contest and so he won his empty victory over them. Yet he had no pleasure in it, but became the more irascible and displeased with those about him. When he returned to his howdah he was smiling, but with a fierceness quite discernible, and I noticed that Mohan Lal desisted awhile from his serpent-like whispering.

Nor did the nawab's temper improve when his troops and our sepoys at last drew their wide arc close upon us with loud cries and huzzahs, for the game they put up was very unequal to our fair expectations, being but a solitary goat, which by the broken tether around its neck was escaped from a village. Once this was slain with the first arrow that was shot, we waited a minute more and then came a jackal, which Cordet dispatched at once with his musket. After this the Moorish troops and our sepoys arrived, and Harry came to where I stood with Watts.

'There is no living thing on the plain,' Harry said quietly, but with some anger. 'The villagers are robbed of their grain by the nawab's soldiers. They must hunt now to feed themselves.' Upon Watts's asking if they had seen any villagers, Harry replied that the villagers had run from them. 'Some threw stones at the nawab's huntsmen.'

'We will speak no more of it here,' said Watts, but I saw the impression made on him by Harry's report; for a peasant would not stone any man of the nawab's except his own situation be utterly desperate. To be caught at such an act, and by the current nawab, the peasant must surely forfeit his life.

The nawab held no converse with his huntsmen, though I saw that a few of the Moorish nobles listened now to the reports of these men just as we had listened to Harry. They received these reports with faces impassive and when the nawab's elephant rose and moved off, his nobles followed, as did we, with no show of outward care but the hunt. The slain goat came with us, and a haunch of the jackal, as food for the Moors' hawks in the city, and we made a wide circle on the plain – for an hour and more – but saw no further animals worth the killing and so returned at last to the place where we had left the Moorish women.

There was by now a second tent erected at the place, to which we men repaired while the women remained in the other, with only the children, the servants and the nawab having the freedom to move between the two. The goat was cut up and grilled upon skewers, and then laid out on platters with other food the servants had brought from the city. The nawab settled with his nobles and Watts and Law sat on cushions near to him and the rest of the Moors and Omichand around the platters. Cordet and I sat together, below the salt, at a far distance from the nawab. Yet at the end of the meal, when the bowl of rosewater was passing around and each of us dipping his fingers into it, it was to Cordet and me that the nawab made some gesture of nomination. He spoke then to Watts and Law and after a moment's discussion Watts looked down to us. 'Gentlemen. You are invited by the nawab to watch him fly his hawk. There will be no further hunting today.'

Cordet was no less surprised than I, nor did the nawab give us time to gather ourselves, but he rose from his place and went by us out of the tent. What must we do then? At a sign from Monsieur Law we two rose together and followed after the nawab.

'The nawab asks if you have seen such a bird before,' said the translator, speaking French to us.

When we confessed that we had not, the nawab, in his palanquin, seemed very gratified by our answer (his vanity was truly that of a child). Far behind us now we saw the Moorish noblemen leaving the camp and a line of palanquins departing with them, carrying their ladies. One tent had been struck, but the other awaited the nawab's return, along with that half of his troops and guard which were not trailing immediately behind us as escort. The keeper of the royal bird rode before us, the hooded hawk perched on his staff which was itself propped in some special casing of his saddle. Having yet no notion of the reason behind this private excursion with the nawab, or indeed if there be any such reason beside his want of youthful company, Cordet and I were quite sparing of our conversation. (And also from my new-found wariness of the Frenchman.)

'We will stop here,' said the nawab's mouthpiece at last and the palanquin settled and the nawab alighted. He went and took the hawk onto his gloved wrist, while the keeper lodged the staff into the ground. This done, the hawk leapt from the nawab's wrist to the staff again. The nawab talked, as if to himself, while he studied the bird, but his translator looked at us while he spoke.

'It is the finest hawk in Bengal. It will always return to me. Other birds would tear him with sharp talons, if they could. But they cannot. He is watchful.'

The nawab pushed a finger through the feathers at the hawk's throat and took the bird onto his glove.

A number of our escort had gone ahead of us and wide, and now the nawab went forward. He spoke over his shoulder to the translator who went with him and the man beckoned us urgently to go forward also. After a minute there was a peculiar whistling made by the escort hidden up ahead and the nawab stopped dead at the sound. He whispered to the bird then and with a swift, expert motion slipped the hood from the hawk and at once raised his gloved arm. The hawk rose, its wings powerfully beating, and the nawab's gaze went after it. There was a shining clearness in the nawab's eyes in those moments, for his mind was with the hawk and outside his own troubles and I could imagine him, almost, a man.

The hawk mounted and mounted, as we watched it dwindle and then, suddenly, another bird rose from by the stunted trees to the left of us.

'*Achah*,' said the nawab quietly and the hawk seemed to pause in the sky far above and then fell with the speed of a musket ball.

Its prey neither turned nor dived and the hawk hit it directly and hard. In tight entanglement they fell from our view.

'It is a fine bird indeed,' remarked Cordet and the nawab seemed to understand, for he smiled, which was a thing I had not seen all that day.

The keeper went into the scrub ahead to fetch the broken prey and also the hawk. With the hawk returned to his gloved wrist, the nawab whispered to the bird while he stroked the tufts of its breast. As the nawab walked toward the trees, the translator indicated that I should come also, but that Cordet should remain behind.

'You are favoured,' said Cordet.

'You must allow me to doubt of it,' I returned, and went ahead with as much apprehension as curiosity to join the nawab.

The translator walked between us, but one pace behind. Once we were out of earshot of Cordet, the nawab began to speak, keeping his eyes straight ahead, as if expecting another whistling signal from our escort. There was nothing in the nawab's eyes now of youth, but all his weariness and troubles had returned to find lodgement there. He evinced an unexpected forwardness now, as if it were beneath his dignity to attempt any subtlety upon a European as lowly as me.

How far would Admiral Watson come upriver?

That was a question, I told him, that I doubt even Mr Watts could answer.

Why was I always with his *zemindars*?

I explained that those men must assist me with the records they had made while they were in Calcutta.

'Why?'

'Because without a proper accounting, my Lord, there can be no proper fulfilment of the treaty.'

'Who helps you?'

'None have helped me. In truth, they have been very reluctant till now.'

'You must be patient.' These were the very same words I had heard from his *zemindars*, not once but a hundred times. To the *zemindars* I had replied that our treaty made no mention of patience; to the nawab now I said nothing.

A short way further on we heard that whistling again. He stopped and launched the bird, but with no avidity now, for he seemed distracted by the thoughts his own questions had stirred in him. The hawk was still high in the air and circling when he said to me, 'You are very far from your home. Why have you come to Bengal?'

'The same reason as every European comes – for trade.'

'You have come to get riches.'

'I will not scorn to make what honest profit I may.'

'When you have your riches you shall return to your home. That is the way of the Europeans. The Armenians remain with us. Dutch, French and English, these do not like to remain here. They have wealth, they depart. You would depart.'

'I expect I shall, my Lord. In time.'

'Years?'

'Perhaps.'

'I could spare you many years of struggle. Many years.'

'It is a saying among us that the struggle makes the man.'

'It is a saying for fools and peasants. You are close to Mr Watts. If you would only agree to report to me what schemes the English plan against the French, and against me, you might return to your country a wealthy man and not in years, but in months. Or weeks.'

The crudeness of the offer was astonishing to me, as also the realization that the pretence of the day's hunt had been but a prelude to this tawdry and disgraceful advance. The nawab had his arms folded and his eyes turned upward to the circling hawk, as if this speculation in a man's loyalties was the small-change of his daily business. When I glanced at the translator, I found his face equally expressionless.

'You may tell your master,' said I, addressing the translator, for I hardly trusted myself to meet the nawab's eye without striking him, 'you may tell him that he must count me among the fools and peasants. And now if I may beg my leave, there is that which I must wash off from my boots. I will rejoin Mr Watts. I bid good day to you.'

CHAPTER THIRTY-TWO

'Your friend Monsieur Cordet has left for Chandernagore.' Watts had been holding some short parley on the verandah of his bungalow with one of the Hindoo merchants of the black town who had some connection into the French factory. The fellow was even now passing out through the factory gates as Watts came down to me. 'It would appear the nawab made Cordet an offer much like to that he had earlier made to you.'

'Then we have suffered the same insult.'

'Cordet is no simpleton. He refused the offer. But it seems Monsieur Law has now decided to remove further temptation from the nawab's way. And in Chandernagore, Cordet will not have his thoughts troubled by any further such faithless promise of riches. His thoughts will all be taken up with the threat posed by the colonel at his doorstep.'

'But Colonel Clive is in Calcutta.'

'He has crossed the Hugli to the Chandernagore side. And his force is now larger than it was. Admiral Pocock has arrived in Calcutta with the *Cumberland* and more of the king's men. There is a sepoy reinforcement arriving from Bombay. The council in Chandernagore shall not sleep easy for some while.'

Though well satisfied with this turn in affairs, Watts looked worn, as if he lately slept no better than the French in Chandernagore. It had been now two weeks since our first returning to Cossimbazaar, and in that time Watts had not rested. He had been continually between Cossimbazaar and Murshidabad, busying himself to make certain of our friends in the court and also to ensure that Monsieur Law faced endless and quite insurmountable obstacles in attempting to secure either the nawab or the Seths to an alliance with the French. Monsieur Law was a most capable man and the nawab untrustworthy and, in consequence, Mr Watts's task was no trifling one.

I had been with him now several times to the palace of the Seths and once I had sat by him while he talked with the nawab in the audience chamber of the great palace (the nawab giving me neither glance nor any acknowledgement that he had ever spoken to me). And ever, as Watts pressed forward the company interest and spiked the intrigues of Monsieur Law, that fellow Omichand hovered like a pestilence about him. Now, when Watts said that he wished me to accompany him to Murshidabad and I replied with a remark upon the unwelcome certainty of Omichand's attachment to us, he turned on me quite sharply.

'Your feelings toward Omichand are well known to me. I do not ask that you change them. I do not ask the impossible. But I demand that you do not show these feelings openly.' I lowered my eyes. Edward Fairborough was in my mind and also those women and children we had found strangled in Omichand's house. 'I more than demand it. I require it, Alistair, if you are to come with me now.'

'I cannot trust him.'

'That is not required of you, only your discretion.'

Harry approached with the syce and our horses, ready-saddled. They stopped before us in the yard, and Watts mounted and said no word more but only looked at me where I remained on the step. I despised Omichand, but I could not stay there like a sulking child. I mounted my horse and we rode in silence from the yard and on to the road to Murshidabad.

*

Omichand kept a house in Murshidabad midway between the nawab's palace and the palace of the Seths and it was to this house that Watts habitually repaired to consult with Omichand before calling upon the nawab. We went there now and found Omichand in a state of some excitement (or pretended excitement, for it was his habitual practice to exaggerate any business he was in and his part in it).

'I have made the nawab see it is the French who deceive him. I have made him see that the colonel and the admiral desired a treaty, but that the council in Chandernagore have acted dishonestly.'

Watts remarked drily that the recent letters to the nawab from Colonel Clive and Admiral Watson had undoubtedly contributed to the nawab's change of heart – if such, indeed, it be (for he was not blind to Omichand's self-serving intrigue).

'It is. It is. But the nawab's mind is unsteady. It will change again. Monsieur Law is to see him today.'

'Then I shall call upon him this evening.'

'You must go now.'

Watts looked startled to be instructed in this manner. 'It is impossible,' said he. 'I cannot intrude upon a private audience.'

'The nawab wishes for you and Monsieur Law to appear before him together. He will listen to your arguments. He is afraid the two of you will bring your war into Bengal. He is very angry that Gouverneur Renault has not agreed to a peace with Admiral Watson.'

'Renault has deferred to the authority of their council in Pondicherry.'

'I have told the nawab. Monsieur Law has also told the nawab.'

'Does the nawab understand that it is a tactic of the French? That they only await reinforcement that they might then fall upon us?'

'Monsieur Law will have many reasons prepared to show why this is not so. You must not delay, sir, but go to the palace directly.'

For once I was content that we should do Omichand's bidding, and Watts was equally convinced that no time should be wasted, for Monsieur Law would be certain to turn every moment he spent alone with the nawab to the French advantage. But as we rode through the crowded streets to the palace, I asked Watts if he would prefer me to turn aside to the counting houses of the nawab's treasury where I might continue my interminable negotiations over those reparations owing to the company by our treaty.

'Today, Alistair, we must make a show at the court. You will stay with me.' At my enquiry what I should do there, he replied, 'Keep silence. And look as much like a battalion as you are able.' We were soon through the main gates of the palace, with no further advice from Watts on the role I should play there. When the syce took our horses, Watts ran an eye over me. He pointed to my cuff, which I then straightened from my sleeve. 'The audience will be in Persian. You will understand none of it. That is no matter. Say nothing unless I address you or the nawab through his translator. Should Monsieur Law seek a word with you, you will refer him to me. Whatever your regard for him, you will remember that he is a Frenchman. Be assured, he does not forget the fact for one moment.'

'Your wig is askew, sir.'

He put his hat beneath his arm while I made some minor adjustment to his wig and then a servant came and escorted us to the inner chambers of the palace.

Though the coolness inside was very welcome, the many cloths and Moorish rugs about the floors and upon the walls gathered dust, so that there was ever a staleness in the air along with a strong and sweet smell of incense. It was here in these poorly lit inner chambers that the various personages of the court could be found at different hours of the day. And not just the courtiers, but the eunuchs too, who were plump, shaven-headed and very lordly toward the other palace servants. It was here also that Omichand spent much of his time while he was in Murshidabad. Though it was customary to await the nawab's summons here, this day we were led straight past several high supplicants and admitted directly into the audience chamber where we found the nawab waiting, with some nobles, seated upon the dais. He did not rise from his cushions, but acknowledged our bows with a nod and then we had to wait while chairs were brought for us (this the necessary price of our speedy admittance). We were hardly seated before Watts began to speak – nor did he leave off for some minutes – with a firmness and sincerity of tone quite affecting, though I understood not a word of it. The nawab then spoke privately with that old fellow Mohan Lal, who sat on a bed of cushions near to him. After hearing Lal, the nawab directed several questions at Watts, wherein the names Clive and Watson and Drake were clearly distinguishable (the name Drake uttered with a surprising ferocity).

And so it went on for fully an hour, with Watts and Lal remaining always calm and the nawab after a time showing clear signs of temper, so that he seemed almost a child between men. Sometimes Lal spoke to Watts directly, but it was never long before the nawab intervened with his voice raised in anger and the name of Drake or Clive or some other of the company upon his lips. At one point our *vaqueel* was called for (this was the Hindoo who answered for the company at the nawab's court) and the fellow was questioned closely by Mohan Lal with the nawab peering intently and with malice at the *vaqueel*, who answered as if in fear of his life. The terrified fellow was then sent away and a minute later Monsieur Law was ushered into the audience chamber. I believe it surprised him to find us there but, once he had made obeisance to the nawab, Law nodded to us very courteously and settled himself into the chair that was brought for him.

The presence of Law seemed to calm the nawab, and there passed several minutes with Watts and Law and the nawab simply conversing, as they must have done very often in the past, but then the nawab's petulance resurfaced quite suddenly and I noticed how he raised his voice now when he questioned Law and cut short Law's replies. There was some talk of the French general, Bussy, of whom there had been so many rumours, but whose army seemed always to remain beyond the horizon.

I must confess, my mind wandered. The language of the court was like a heavy fog through which I could see but dimly and the reading of the faces about me grew very trying without the accompaniment of meaningful words for a guide. And what my mind wandered to was the nawab. There he sat in a robe, silver-threaded, on silk-covered cushions, in the audience chamber of his own great palace, and before him sat the envoys of two foreign nations and he not knowing if he should expect from either one of them friendship or annihilation. It came to me then how great was his hate of us and how great his fear.

I was brought from my musing with a start. For suddenly, at some remark from Law, the nawab was on his feet and shouting and Mohan Law at once rose to calm him. Then Watts made bold to speak and the nawab seemed to give him an affirmative answer, at which Watts turned to me saying quietly, 'Come away with me now. Do not speak with Monsieur Law.' Together we rose, bowed and retreated from the chamber.

'What has happened?' said I when we were among the still-waiting supplicants.

'Monsieur Law has made an error. We must act at once.' Watts waited for no escort or eunuch, but boldly led me along a passage and into a room where was, he told me, the nawab's secretary. Upon our appearance there, the secretary immediately turned out his two scribes from their places and closed the door after them. Watts addressed the Moor in English.

'The nawab will shortly send for you to draft a letter to Admiral Watson.' Watts took up one of the departed scribes' quills. 'You will include this phrase in the letter before the nawab affixes his seal to it.' He paused for a moment and then wrote it without hesitation. I read the words as they appeared on the page.

'You have understanding and generosity. If your enemy, with an upright heart, claims your protection, you will give him his life. But then you must be well satisfied of the innocence of his intentions, if not, whatever you think right, that do.'

He then handed it to the secretary, saying, 'You shall have a thousand rupees for your trouble. But the words must be exact.'

The secretary read the words. And then he blotted the paper and slipped it under some other papers on his table for safekeeping before he hurried us out.

CHAPTER THIRTY-THREE

*I*n the palace garden we found ourselves alone but for an old Hindoo gardener who scythed the grass on the lower tier. I made very sure of our privacy before I asked Watts the meaning of the scenes I had just been witness to.

'The nawab is intemperate,' he said. 'He has no clear mind and that which he has is unsteady.'

'Our *vaqueel* seemed to tremble.'

'Our *vaqueel* has seen more than one man executed at the nawab's whim. He was questioned to determine if my own earlier answers to the nawab were truthful. The nawab has a terror that the admiral may bring his ships to Murshidabad.'

'But the river here is not navigable to us.'

'As I told the nawab. And as our *vaqueel*, very fortunately for the preservation of us all, subsequently confirmed. But the nawab, in his present state, will persist in his fear of any phantom.'

I asked then the meaning of the nawab's startling outburst against Monsieur Law.

'A happy accident. The merest trifle.' Watts shook his head and smiled in some wonder at the memory of the incident. 'The nawab was in the midst of instructing us that he would now write to Admiral Watson forbidding this, that and the next thing – to which Monsieur Law simply observed that the admiral would most certainly ignore him. Which is but plain and simple truth, I may say. But the nawab did not like it. He took it as an offence to his dignity that Law should suggest any might dare to ignore him. As you saw. The admiral will now receive a very different kind of letter.'

'Can that secretary be trusted?'

'Alistair, I do despair of you.'

'It is not "trusted" that I mean. Will he do as you bid him?'

'I believe that he will.'

'The phrase that you wrote is an invitation for us to fall upon the French.'

'It may be read so.'

'Then we will break our treaty by a ruse.'

'There are two parties entered upon our treaty. Tell me – what joy have you had of your dealings with the nawab's officials? Just so. And I may tell you there have been any number of letters from the admiral urging the nawab's prompt fulfilment of the terms of the treaty and any number of feeble excuses from the nawab as to why he cannot do so. The nawab has chosen to view the treaty in the oriental manner. We should be cutting our own throats to persist in viewing it in a manner European. But I see this does not entirely convince you.'

I confessed that it did not.

'Well then – that is, perhaps, no bad thing. You are not yet twenty. It is fitting you should have a goodly stock of scruples about you. For myself, I take Christian comfort from those wise words of King Solomon – "Be not righteous over much why shouldst thou destroy thyself; neither make thyself over wise." I do no dishonour to a much lamented friend if I say that it was the Reverend Bellamy who first directed my attention to those words.'

'You were close to him.'

'I was.'

'I have never understood his connection with you and Mrs Watts.'

He looked away over the garden and down to the river. 'Now is not the time for that. Once the nawab's letter is written, you will take it to the council in Calcutta. Harry shall accompany you.'

The way between Cossimbazaar and Calcutta had become very familiar to me and, for this reason and also owing to the good companionship of Harry, the few days that we spent on the journey passed quickly. We skirted Chandernagore, but met with several French soldiers down at the crossing-place on the river. They did not detain us, but asked after the disposition of the nawab's forces to the north whence we had come. We told them the truth, which was that we had seen none but only those near Hugli. They jested that Clive must be in desperate straits to be calling down a reinforcement of one civilian and one sepoy and then they signalled to the bargemen to take us over to the eastern side. From the barge we had a fine view upriver toward Fort Orleans and saw there the earthworks Gouverneur Renault had commenced building as an outer defence to the fort. I waited till we were safely disembarked and along the road a way before I stopped and took my sketchbook from my saddlebag and quickly sketched from memory the positions of the new gun emplacements we had seen.

The final part of our ride into Calcutta was a ride among ghosts, for we came by way of the Maratha Ditch, where our force had wreaked bloody vengeance upon the nawab's troops through the mist. Now, weeks later, the bodies had all been cleared from the field, but there remained signs of the battle everywhere about – broken planking from the carts, Moorish arrows, the tethering stakes where the Moors had been encamped and the bones of many dead horses. We did not speak but rode on till we crossed the ditch and, as we came near to Fort William, I recalled that time so many months before when I had arrived here with Edward Fairborough to report the fall of Cossimbazaar, he with his secret desire to claim a bride and return with her to England. We could not know that he would never leave this place again, but lie here among strangers in eternity. Vanity of vanities sayeth the preacher; and yet the heart will always hope. Turning my gaze from the burial ground I passed, with Harry, through the gates of the fort.

'And you have put this into the hands of Governor Drake?'

'As Mr Watts instructed me.'

'You saw him read it?'

'The colonel and he read it directly. There was a meeting of the council in progress when I came there. They stepped out to see me. Afterwards Cooke went out to the *Kent* to give the admiral the letter, and I with him.'

Mrs Watts passed her eyes again over the letter I had delivered from her husband. We continued to walk by the river, her daughter Amelia running on ahead of us, and Mrs Watts reading. 'I cannot conceive what is in the nawab's mind,' she declared.

'Pride.'

'Pride is a vice of every ruler. But this?'

'It is worse than ordinary pride. The man is blind to any but himself.' While I told her of the hunt and of the general depredation I had witnessed throughout the countryside as I travelled, she continued to peruse the letter. But when I told her what I had seen in the nawab's audience chamber and the bold means by which Mr Watts had caused the crucial phrase to be inserted into the nawab's letter, she no longer read her husband's words but fixed her gaze upon me.

'You had this from William's own lips?'

'I was at his side when it was done.'

'Does the colonel know of it?'

'He did not ask.'

'You must not tell him, Alistair. Neither the colonel nor anyone.'

'I would not betray him.'

Mrs Watts looked at me very steadily and then she stepped near to me and put a hand on my arm. 'You have been a good friend to William.'

'His life is in the nawab's palm. He is daily in some danger and yet he continues his work. I cannot believe he must play second to such a man as Drake.'

'Mamma,' called Amelia, who had gone on ahead of us along the river. 'He is here!'

It was George, Amelia's brother, for whom they had both been searching when I first met with them at the Great Ghat. Since then we had walked by their house, past the Salpetre Ghat, and a quarter mile on and here was the boy, at last, at play in a flatboat from one of our ships. The boat was tied up at a small wooden pier and as we came near to it several topass children leapt from the boat and ran, George crying after them in Portuguese to come back to their game. Mrs Watts folded her husband's letter into her sleeve, and while she went to call her son from the boat, I stood a moment and studied the ships in the river.

The *Thunder* was gone and with it Captain Warwick, but every other ship of the squadron remained here at anchor. The admiral's flag flew upon the *Kent*. The *Tyger* and *Salisbury* lay closer in, the sailors idling now upon the decks. They had been here for several weeks, ever since the expedition to Hugli. I had no doubt but that the ships were fully primed now with new powder and shot and waiting only the admiral's signal to send them upriver to Chandenagore. And I knew, as they did not, that the letter that would unleash them was already delivered to Admiral Watson's hand. But they lay calm upon the river now, and peaceful.

'Will you sail in the *Kent* or the *Tyger*?' demanded George, bounding up to me past his mother from the flatboat. 'Is it war?'

'Alas, the admiral does not consult me on such matters. And though you do not ask, your father is very well and bids me cuff you about the ears as a reminder of him.'

George laughed and dived away as my hand whipped over his head. Mrs Watts put an arm about her daughter's shoulders and we retraced our steps to their house, George racing ahead and falling back, throwing stones into the river. As we strolled now, I gave Mrs Watts a more personal account of her husband's situation in Cossimbazaar. She was very pleased to hear that Mr Watts was residing in their old bungalow and that the factory was again much as it had been before the nawab's first assault. It amused her to hear that a certain aged servant had returned to the bungalow, for the fellow was one, she told me, for whom Mr Watts had a particular and quite irrational aversion. And she was comforted to hear also of the safe arrival of the junior trader, Hastings, in Cossimbazaar, just the day before my departure, for she thought well of him, as she did not think well of some others who might have been sent. Amelia, who had listened quietly all the while, spoke up to say that she was glad Mr Hastings could be a friend for her papa, and I forbore to explain to either mother or daughter that Hastings looked only to the company's affairs at the factory and that Mr Watts, in the greater business, remained as fully alone as any man may be.

'I fear I must leave you now,' said I, as they mounted the steps of their house. Mrs Watts, in perplexity, turned to face me. 'You know that Colonel Clive's secretary was killed in that action out by the Ditch,' I told her. 'Admiral Watson expects now that the colonel will have need of someone in his further dealings with the French at Chandenagore.'

'But the colonel has no right to command you,' said Mrs Watts.

'I have volunteered.'

'At William's behest?'

'It is my own decision.'

Mrs Watts hesitated, and then sent her children into the house. When they had gone, she faced me again.

'It is a very bad decision, Alistair. You must come in now and we will find a way how this may be undone.'

'I do not wish it undone.'

She came down one step. 'Why would you choose to fight those you know at Chandernagore? You are not heartless.'

'It is not for me to choose my country's enemies.'

'It was not our country that was given refuge there. It was you and I and so very many others.'

'We were not then at war.'

'Do you suppose Gouverneur Renault or Monsieur Law would have turned us away even then? Though we are now at war with their country, we are not thereby excused the simple obligations of humanity. Among the first of which is gratitude. Or am I wrong?'

'I remain as grateful as ever I was, Mrs Watts. But now my duty is to—'

'Pray speak no more of duty. It is the cloak of cowards and you must be a better man than that.' She came down another step. She was very close to me now. 'You were at the pillaging of Hugli. You fought along-side the sailors out by the Ditch. You were here at the siege. Why have you put yourself forward again? There is none expect it of you.'

'I expect it of myself,' said I, feeling myself wronged by her with that grave charge of ingratitude.

'It is pride then. And such a pride as might shame even the nawab.'

I exclaimed against the harshness of her judgement.

'That is but a feather, Alistair, to what you will bring down on your own head by your own pertinacity and foolishness. Will you not reconsider?'

'I cannot. I have given the admiral my hand on it.'

'Oh, that is just like a man,' she said and with no kind meaning to her words.

'I am sorry you take it so,' I returned. 'And I am surprised. That I should be blamed, who will but put into effect your husband's sincerest intentions. He has striven that this should happen.'

'And were he here he would strive yet harder still to restrain you from your present course which is no good one, I may tell you. If Chandernagore must be taken, it should be taken without your assistance.' We looked each upon the other. I own that I was stung by much that she had said. But my eyes did not waver and she, at last, began to understand that I might not to be swayed by her reproaches, for she said, 'I do not mean to slight you, Alistair. You will forgive me, I hope, if I have spoken too harshly.'

'It is no matter.'

'But you will not be dissuaded?'

'I will not.'

'Howsoever much I urge it upon you?' I turned my head but kept my eye upon her. She saw now that I was resolved upon it. She came down the last step. 'Then give me your hand.' Surprised, and not knowing what was to come, I raised my hand uncertainly. She clasped it tight and placed her other hand over it. 'You must promise me that you will not be killed.'

I smiled at first, but then saw that she did not. She looked at me now almost with the eyes of my own mother.

'I mean to come back,' said I.

A moment more and she released me. She did not wait but turned and went up the steps, gathering her skirts before her and with her head bowed. And it came to me then how very much she feared for the life of a man who was beyond her touch, which was her own husband.

CHAPTER THIRTY-FOUR

*C*olonel Clive and his small army of two thousand soldiers and sepoys were no longer in Calcutta, but he had taken them across the river and marched them northward, so that had I come with Harry directly southward from Chandernagore instead of crossing over the river, we must surely have met with them on our way. As it was, we found ourselves now well to the rear of them and our progress toward them somewhat slowed by the necessity of our joining with those Bombay reinforcements who had arrived in Calcutta since Clive's departure. Of these there were perhaps three or four hundred men, Europeans and sepoys taken together, but we travelled with only a small troop of them, for there had been a sickness among them and they were now unable to act as a body but moved up to join Clive in straggling and piecemeal bands.

There was much talk among that band we had joined concerning the whole purpose of Clive's northward march. Some said it was to prepare for an attack upon Chandernagore, but as many others believed it was done in obedience to the nawab's wishes. It was spoken among them as a fact that the emperor in Delhi had been captured and imprisoned by marauding Afghans, who were even now advancing toward the nawab's territory in Bengal. None of this troubled Harry, who was certainly in no good humour, though for a different reason entirely – his horse, on the first day after our crossing the river, had been sequestered by one of the Bombay officers. Harry, in consequence, now marched on foot with the dozen sepoys of the company. On the second evening that we camped with the band I made sure to speak privately with him. Once I had served as a patient audience for his complaint over the sequestered horse, I learned that neither he nor any sepoy gave the slightest credence to this tale of our marching to the nawab's assistance.

'We go to fight at Chandernagore,' Harry said, and would hear of no other possibility. 'Now leave me in peace.'

'We cannot be far now from the colonel.'

'You do not walk.'

'I could do nothing to prevent it, Harry. I will find another horse for you.'

'You cannot.'

'I will.'

'Among these Bombay *chutahs* you are nothing. Almost as low as Harry Khan.'

He turned his face from me. I did not leave but sat by him in silence awhile, regretting that the easy companionship of our journey from Murshidabad was at an end. For myself, I felt the sadness of it, but for Harry there was that, in his heart, worse than sadness, for I saw beneath his impassivity an impotent but burning anger. At last the sepoys at the second campfire took their cast-iron cooking pot from the tripod, and when they called to Harry he rose without a word to me and went to join them.

Two days later, on the morning of the 14th March, we arrived at the colonel's camp. I at once fell in with the European officers and Harry with the sepoys of the company.

Clive's camp was not two miles west of Chandernagore and this morning of our arrival a very significant one, for at sunrise (we later learned) Clive had mustered the soldiers and read to them the king's declaration of war against the French. So by the time of our coming to the place, there was already a great busyness about the camp; and Captain Coote, very prominent among the officers, going from one quarter to another and putting urgency into his grenadiers and the other red-jacketed soldiers. To be short, the whole encampment was preparing for the first attack upon the town.

I went to make report to Captain Coote, and when he saw me lingering uncertainly behind two junior officers, awaiting my turn, he beckoned me sharply forward.

'Where is Mr Watts?' he asked, looking by me. When I explained that I had left Mr Watts in Murshidabad, Coote said, 'It is as well. He can do more good for us there than here. I never saw a gentleman less able with a pistol.'

'I have volunteered, sir.'

'Have you indeed?' He seemed amused by my forwardness, which I would not have taken kindly but that he had always treated me well. 'Then you may attach yourself to my grenadiers if none else will have you. But I must warn you, it is no sinecure. You will do proper service.'

'I would prefer it so.'

'We shall shake you off yet, Mr Douglas. Either that or make a soldier of you.' He began to move away, at which I told him I had a letter for the colonel. He pointed to a tent nearby and walked on, those two junior officers still close at his heels.

What was in this letter to Clive I did not know, except that Watts had given me firm instructions that I keep it always on me till I had put it into the colonel's hand. And now, when I had got admittance, I gave it to him directly. When he had read but part of it, he sent the others out from his tent. And when he had read all of it he told me to bring an ember from the campfire outside. I brought it and he had me set it down on the dirt. He put Watts's letter onto the ember and watched pensively as the letter curled into flame. 'Am I to take it that it was you, Mr Douglas, who took the nawab of Bengal's letter to the council?'

'Yes sir.'

'Then I am in your debt. There was considerable hesitation in some quarters until that letter arrived in Calcutta. Had it continued—'

'It was only my duty, sir,' said I and, when I heard myself, thought of Mrs Watts and bit my tongue.

'What have you seen of the nawab's forces as you came south?'

I told him I had seen not a single Moorish soldier till we came near Hugli. Then I took from my coat the sketch I had made of the half-moon earthwork to the southern side of Fort Orleans. I related the time and circumstances of my making the sketch and told him of the French battery I had seen at the riverside.

'It appeared the place where they might very likely run a chain across the river,' I suggested.

'It is more than likely, for they have done it, Mr Douglas, and for good measure, sunk a number of mud-filled vessels to block the passage of our squadron. That is not your concern. But I thank you for this sketch,' said he, while with his boot grinding the ash of Watts's letter into the dirt. 'It will be no easy matter for you to return to Mr Watts in Murshidabad. Since your coming down, the nawab has dispatched troops toward Hugli.'

'I have volunteered, sir. Admiral Watson thought I might be useful to you here.'

'Admiral Watson overreaches. I have no need of you.'

Major Kilpatrick, to my relief, then came into the tent. He shook my hand when he found me there and then turned immediately to his business with Clive. They discussed their plan of attack, Clive showing him my sketch of the French earthworks. Kilpatrick congratulated my enterprise, and when he had finally departed, Clive went to the field-desk and began to write, as though he had altogether forgot me.

'Captain Coote has also offered me a place with his grenadiers, sir.'

'You may go to him after. You will first find Captain Le Baume. I am sure he is still brooding in his tent. In his own mind he is made another Achilles,' said he, continuing to write. 'You will take him this order, Mr Douglas. He will lead twenty infantrymen a mile to the south of the fort and make an attack on the redoubt which overlooks the river there. I am writing it into his orders that that he is to be careful of his men. You will report it to me if he is neglectful of the admonition.'

*

I found Le Baume sitting by his tent at a far corner of the camp and, though not brooding, it was very noticeable that some change had come over him since our last parting. He seemed to have no role in the many preparations now under way all around him, but merely sat in his chair, his legs stretched out before him, watching with an eye of indifference the bustle of activity on every side. At my approach, he raised himself, but only a little.

'Bonjour, Monsieur Douglas.'

'Bonjour,' I returned, somewhat surprised to see him so lethargic who was always so full of life. I gave him Clive's order and, while he read it, explained that I was to join him in the attack.

'You?'

I laughed. I asked him if that was the full extent of his welcome to me.

'Why will you come?'

'It is the colonel's order. He does not need me here.'

'Ah,' said he, as if that story, at least, was very familiar to him.

A drumbeat sounded to the east of the camp, and we watched as Captain Lynn led his infantrymen and sepoys into the scrubland toward the outskirts of the black town. Around us the soldiers paused in their own preparations to watch their comrades go. Some called after their backs in encouragement and others whistled very piercingly. There were many loud and slighting (not to say filthy) remarks directed against the generality of Frenchmen. Le Baume watched in silence and with a somewhat bitter smile, till they were gone. We heard now only the drum's steady beat receding in the distance.

I remarked to Melchior that I believed the colonel had meant that we should depart the camp immediately.

'Captain,' said he abruptly, and he very forcefully slapped his hand upon the arm of his chair. 'I am Captain Le Baume and you will remember it. Your Colonel Clive will remember it also.'

'I am sure he has never forgotten it,' said I, startled.

'Everything is forgotten by the English.'

'That is not true.'

Le Baume rose, calling for his syce as he stalked away from the tent and from me.

By the time we had mounted, there was already the sound of heavy musketfire to the east of us, which we took for Captain Lynn's first engagement with the Chandernagore outposts. We rode southward, Le Baume's small band of sepoys and soldiers marching to the front of us, and we met with no delay, but came quickly within sight of the French redoubt by the river. And almost at our first sighting of the redoubt we came under fire from the enemy' muskets. We took cover and returned their fire, but it was not long before they had trained one of their six-pounders upon our position amidst the trees. One shell fell very close to us, shredding the leaves and spattering hot shards into the tree-trunks to the right of us. Le Baume gave the order to fall back. In the redoubt the French cheered to see us turn tail, though they must have known they would not be rid of us so easily.

But nor was I sorry that we should retreat so hastily, for this seemed to me an obedient compliance by Le Baume with Clive's written warning that he must be careful of the men. And I own, I was already very loath to be carrying any tales to Clive of Le Baume's actions.

'Monsieur Douglas,' said Le Baume, when he was sure of his men's safety, and then he slipped into French without thinking. 'I will go further south to the river. Keep the men firing at the redoubt. Make sure they stay apart, spread them out. If that gun finds its range again, retreat with the men further.' Upon my asking what he looked for at the river, he said, 'Another point of attack,' and he was crouching and moving away southward. My first thought was that he was become himself again, that brave-hearted fellow I had fought alongside at the Calcutta siege.

But when an hour went by and he had not returned and the fire between us and the redoubt continuing very hotly, I began to doubt of the wisdom he had shown in leaving his men in my hands. I began to wonder also why he had gone himself and not sent an infantryman to scout out a new point of attack by the river. When I thought of it (and I thought of it the more as the French fire increased) I could see no proper reason, in fact, why he had left us.

'Tell that man to be silent!' I demanded, for there was a fellow in our line suddenly gabbling like a lunatic.

'Sir, it is Jones, sir. He is hit in the guts.'

Keeping low, I made the fifteen yards to see him. Jones gabbled no longer but his face contorted strangely as he fought for each shallow breath. He held his bloodied hands against the wound in his belly. I made no attempt to prise them off.

'Get four of the sepoys here to him. They can make a stretcher from the branches. Tell them to use their jackets to rest him on.'

'He will die anyway, sir.'

'If so, it will not be of our neglect.'

'The captain won't like it.'

'The captain is not here,' I said with some heat. 'He has abandoned us. Now do as I have said.'

While the sepoys cut down the branches with their bayonets, we increased our fire upon the French. They no longer wasted the shells of their six-pounder upon us but galled us continually now with their musketshot. It was blind good fortune that some other of our number did not take a shot now like Jones.

'The stretcher is done, sir.'

'Then get him on to it, for pity's sake. Tell the sepoys to carry him back to the surgeon. And twenty rupees if they are quick enough to save him.'

At my command the soldiers sent another crackling volley into the redoubt. It gave the French pause, and our sepoys time enough to get Jones on to the stretcher and away without further harm.

It was not long after their leaving with the stretcher that Le Baume at last returned. When I enquired, with what little civility may be imagined, where the devil he had got to, he took a bridling offence at my tone.

'You are not an officer, Monsieur Douglas.'

'I know it. Just as I know that you are, which is why I wonder that you should have left your men while they were fired upon.'

He turned from me as if he would not lower himself to answer me.

'We have had an infantryman shot,' said I, and Le Baume's eyes went at once to the men nearby. 'It is Jones. He is stretchered to the surgeon. I fear he will not live.'

'It is war,' he said grimly. 'He was unlucky.'

'You bear it very well who were not here to see it.'

Le Baume was much taken aback by my words. His face darkened and, in other circumstances, I might have paid dearly for my bold impertinence. As it was, the French at that moment galled us from the redoubt and Le Baume put one hand upon the hilt of his sword and raised his pistol and returned their fire before hurrying to give new orders to his men.

The remainder of the day passed very tediously, with us staying behind whatever cover we could find, but moving constantly so that they might not set their six-pounder upon us. Sometimes we advanced and sometimes retreated and all the while harried the redoubt with our musketshot. I kept apart from Le Baume but was keenly aware of him moving among his men and encouraging them, and in truth it was very evident he was much more careful of their safety than ever he was of his own, for in going among them he was often exposed to the French muskets.

But throughout the day we heard Captain Lynn's heavy guns at work in the greater battle to the north of us by Chandernagore and we had some satisfaction in knowing that our enemies in the redoubt heard them too. An ensign came to us in the late afternoon to receive Le Baume's report for the colonel. He brought us news that Captain Coote and Major Kilpatrick had joined forces with Captain Lynn and that their joint force had now overwhelmed the outer defences of the town with but light losses to our side.

'Now we shall pin them in the fort and the squadron shall destroy them,' the ensign concluded.

Le Baume made no pretence of joy at the news. There was, rather, a look of confusion in his eyes and, to my mind at least, some measure of pain.

Once the ensign had left us, we returned our attention to the redoubt.

After an hour more their return of fire noticeably diminished and then unexpectedly ceased altogether. After a minute of waiting, Le Baume had still given us no order and there was talk among the soldiers of what trap those Frenchmen in the redoubt might be setting for us. And then one of our men cried, 'They are running!'

We put our heads out more boldly from behind our cover. The French were indeed running, the last of them soon arriving at a boat that must have been sent down to them from the fort. As the French scrambled into the boat, I rose with our men and we would have been at the enemy, but that Le Baume called to us, 'Wait! You will stay!'

He then stepped from cover and with sword and pistol both ready went fearlessly forward across the open ground to the redoubt. Any sniper waiting there might have put a shot clean through his heart. But there was no sniper. After a minute he climbed onto the dirt wall of the redoubt and looked over. It was a minute more before he was satisfied that no danger remained there and he then summoned us forward.

We hurried to cross to him and then climbed over the wall of the redoubt. Their six-pounder was dismounted and they had spiked it, so that it was useless to us. There were two dead Frenchmen, both shot through the face. And far away now on the river, beyond range of our muskets, we saw the boatful of fleeing French soldiers. They were riding the fast-running tide up to the temporary safety of the French fort and there was nothing we could now do to prevent their escape.

More than one of our men cast an unhappy eye at Le Baume.

CHAPTER THIRTY-FIVE

*A*ll the French soldiers outside the fort had been swept clear by night-fall, saving only that one battery at the riverside above the blockade and beneath the protection of the fort's guns, so that, by the time of our return, the whole of Clive's camp had been moved up into the black town. The rank and file alike took billets in the native houses, which had now been almost universally abandoned. It was in a larger one of these houses, adjoining to a Hindoo temple, that the surgeon of the 39th had established his hospital. But the casualties of the day had been so trifling, on our side at least, that the surgeon was playing at cards with a wounded officer when I arrived there. And upon my asking after the man Jones who had taken the stomach shot, the surgeon rose from his card game and brought a lamp and led me into a neighbouring room. He held the lamp over the bed so that I might see the chap, naked but for the bandages swathed about his middle. He was neither fully conscious nor yet unconscious, but lying quite still and perspiring very freely.

'If he sees the morning it is likely he shall live.'

'Can he hear us?'

The surgeon shrugged. He asked if Jones was a friend to me and I told him no, but that I had been with the fellow when he was shot.

'Had there been heavier fighting, I might not have had time for him,' said he. 'It is a bad wound. If he recovers I shall send him to convalesce in Calcutta.'

Jones's gaunt face in the torchlight looked like the face of a wraith. The fellow was not lost, but he hung suspended between life and death, and nothing I might do for him now, but will him to hold fast to the living. I knew then something of what Clive had felt when I saw him that night in Buj Buj, just after he had lost those nine men from beneath his command.

'Is there anything more?' asked the surgeon.

'No. Or only that I must thank you for your care of him.' I told him that I should return in the morning and as I left the house he resumed his play at cards in the candlelight.

Passing by the neighbouring temple I saw that there was a dim light coming from some inner chamber there and I heard the quiet chanting of some Brahmin inside. I heard too the gentle ringing of small cymbals that the Hindoos use at their prayers. It was a sound I had heard often from the temple near the Cossimbazaar factory when Bengal had been at peace. But now, even while the quiet cymbals sounded, there was yet the retort of musketry from the direction of the fort. Clive had sent troops to keep the French in alarm there through the night, his purpose now to harass the enemy continually and weary them, till the admiral should arrive with the squadron. I took it for a sign of good omen that the temple had been left undisturbed by our soldiers, for though it was done by Clive's order, I had seen now how lightly such orders could be taken by the common soldiery.

'Is that you, Mr Douglas?' The figure came up to me from the dark street and stopped by me in the torchlight near the temple. It was Captain Coote, his long face tilted back as he peered at me. 'If you are seeking a billet, the officers have taken the merchants' houses near the market.'

'I am obliged, sir.'

'We did not see you today.'

'I was to the south with Captain Le Baume.' I gestured to the temporary hospital. 'I have just been visiting one of our men.'

'It is no happy duty,' said he, and he looked at the place as one who knew that duty only too well.

I had, since arriving in the camp that morning, been troubled as to certain matters; nor had the day's fighting at the redoubt done anything to quiet my thoughts, but, in fact, quite otherwise. Captain Coote I respected, and he was not so distant as the colonel. And nor, I thought, so concerned in the particular matter that troubled me.

'Sir, may I ask why it was that Captain Le Baume's troop was kept apart from the others?'

'Are you a tactician now, Mr Douglas?' he enquired with a chaffing amusement.

'It is only that – sir, I hope I may say this in confidence to you.'

'You may speak your mind,' said he, and regarded me the more closely.

'I would not wish to pry into a decision of the officers.'

'Is it Captain Le Baume?'

'Yes sir.'

'You are quite friendly with the man.'

'I believe he finds his situation very hard.'

'We are none of us here for our ease. And I am surprised that he should unburden himself to you. If he has a complaint, Major Kilpatrick will hear it.'

'He has said nothing to me by way of complaint. But I know that he feels himself slighted by the colonel's treatment of him. He takes it hard that he is not used as the other officers.'

'Now I will speak in confidence to you, Mr Douglas. He is a man who has deserted his own flag.'

'It was not desertion, it was done in peacetime. And for reasons personal to him as a gentleman. The company has since accepted him as an officer. At the siege of Calcutta he—'

'At the siege he did not fight his own people. And as to any reasons he may pretend to as a gentleman, you may believe the officers, and the colonel, have made their own judgement on the question.'

'I know he is an honourable man.'

'Mr Douglas, do you urge Captain Le Baume's virtues upon me or upon yourself?'

His words checked me. I felt the colour rise in my cheeks. For in truth, I had for some time now been turning over in my mind the question of Le Baume's loyalty to us. It was Captain Warwick who had planted the first seed of doubt, and Clive's brusque treatment of Le Baume had shown me that it was not the naval men only who baulked to have a Frenchman numbered among the senior officers. Till now I had suppressed the doubt, recalling his great courage at the siege, and his private manner to me, which had never been less than gentlemanly. But the events of the day, I confess, had shaken me. To be plain, I had begun to wonder if it were not possible there had been some communication between Le Baume and the French soldiers in the redoubt during the time he was away from us, and I wondered also at his true purpose in staying us from an immediate advance upon the redoubt when we saw the French soldiers escaping. These were thoughts very troubling to me. And Captain Coote had evidently perceived the tenor of these thoughts, if not the cause.

'I believe I will seek out a billet nearer the marketplace,' said I at last.

Coote looked at me as though he would say more. But then he simply touched his hand to me. 'I bid you good night, then, Mr Douglas,' said he and moved by me and went up the steps of the hospital-house.

In the night Jones died. Upon my discovering the fact the next morning, I sought out Captain Coote and requested a transfer from Le Baume's troop and, with no questions asked, nor any comment made, he offered me an immediate attachment to his grenadiers.

The siege of Fort Orleans by our land force continued for several days, during which time we made batteries for our guns in their settlement, threw shells into and over the fort's walls and generally amused ourselves with a continual harassment of the enemy. Our *buxerries* (the native musketmen) took up positions in the upper floors of the taller buildings in the settlement and galled the French gunners on the fort's parapets with a fire intense and unceasing. While this was doing, a troop of sappers threw up a mud wall for protection and set to work undermining the fort's bastions and, though there was much to see in all this very interesting to me, I was little needed during this time. The most useful service I did was to write out, in French, Clive's offer to take any deserter into the company force at a rank equivalent to that the deserter held in the French army. I wrote out a hundred or more of these, and our sepoy archers tied the notes to their arrows and shot them over the fort's walls. I had little expectation for the results of this effort, however I was much gratified when it won us a handful of deserters each night, the most senior and useful of which (and much to my surprise) was that one-armed fellow Lieutenant Terraneau, who was the chief of their artillerymen, and the very same man who had stood with Gouverneur Renault and Monsieur Law and questioned me concerning the British besiegement in Calcutta.

While our land force harassed the French in the fort and gave its defenders no rest, the vessels of our squadron arrived day by day from Calcutta, anchoring just below the French chain and out of range of the fort. With the nearest shore battery now in our hands, it was a simple matter for a night sortie from the *Salisbury* to remove the chain before the *Kent* and *Tyger* arrived, and this was done without loss to us. And when the two larger ships finally did arrive and anchored with the lesser vessels, it was a very fine sight the squadron made to those of us ashore, though to the French the spectacle of His Britannic Majesty's ships anchored so near them must have made their hearts quite desperate with fear.

I stood not far from Captain Coote and Major Kilpatrick at the riverside to witness the *Kent*'s arrival. The sailors on the *Kent* were still on the yards and shouting halloos to our soldiers who had come down to the shore.

'What do you think, Mr Douglas?' called Coote happily. 'Are we enough now?'

'What help, sir, if we are not?'

He laughed and turned again to speak with Major Kilpatrick and I saw that they spoke of me, and perhaps of me and Le Baume, which I did not like to think of.

Soon a boat came to us from the *Kent*, with an order from the admiral that there should be a ceasefire declared. Major Kilpatrick passed on the order, which he had come down there to receive, and the messengers hurried away. Up in the settlement, and within minutes, the musketshot and shelling, that had been so constant, now suddenly ceased. The silence seemed itself to ring in the air. A second boat had now set out from the *Kent,* this one flying a white banner at her stern and moving toward the fort. I asked Captain Coote if he knew the business of this second boat.

'Admiral Watson sends a demand for the French surrender.' He cocked his head. 'Who has ordered you here?'

'No one, sir.'

His eyes went into me, and I returned at once to my post in the settlement.

The artillerymen of my battery now played at dice or idled their time away with sleep. And having slept but poorly myself for the several nights of the siege, I now took full advantage of the ceasefire and, finding in one of the abandoned houses by our battery a charpoy, I made a pillow of my jacket and took what rest I could. The great stillness and heat lay like a blanket over everything and the silence now was strangely disturbing after what we had grown accustomed to. And so I did not sleep, but lay with the perspiration soaking my shirt and breeches and thought on Mr Watts in Murshidabad and the danger he must be in, for our attack upon the French fort was a clear breach of our recent treaty with the nawab. Unlike Colonel Clive and Admiral Watson, Watts had no guns to safeguard him from the nawab's violent caprice.

For Mr Watts I had now a growing admiration. His courage was quieter than that of these other men, but equally dauntless. And I had seen in the past few days some acts of bravado by Clive's officers beneath the fort walls that had put me in mind of Reverend Bellamy's remark that soldiers were but boys uniformed. Nor could they keep these deeds private but, at supper with their brother officers, every part of each prank must be recounted. Though this was not true of all of them, it made me wonder, as I had not done before, how I might myself behave in such a regimental brotherhood.

On the subject of Le Baume, I had long since thought myself into a mire of confusion and weariness, so I was careful now to not let my mind wander there while I rested.

Shortly before evening an artilleryman roused me from my rest to report that the boat had returned from Fort Orleans to the *Kent* and that we might soon expect news of the French surrender.

An hour later, the French reopened their guns upon us.

'The king's men are ordered aboard the ships,' Captain Coote informed me as he passed by me at the well next morning. 'If you would come with us, we shall embark in the mid-afternoon.' He did not await my answer, but went on to the merchant's house where his officers breakfasted upon the verandah. I heard him tell them that Admiral Pocock had arrived from Calcutta and that we might soon expect to fight the French in earnest.

I hurried now to towel myself and put on the newly cleaned shirt I had just received from the *dhobi* (which is to say, from one of the camp-following laundrywomen, who tended to the officers). Up on the verandah, the officers were put in sudden high spirits by the news of the impending assault. They bolted their breakfasts, and then, with a jauntiness equal to Captain Coote's own, went up to the front lines to collect the soldiers of the 39th.

My jacket and pistol having been put by while I washed, I went now to collect them from the stone bench beneath the banyan. And as I did so, I saw Captain Le Baume coming up the street toward me. I had not seen him since first attaching myself to Coote's grenadiers, for Clive had been careful to keep Le Baume always at a distance from the main action and the fort. Nor was his billet with the other officers, but in a southern quarter of the black town, though whether in obedience to an order or from inclination I could not tell.

'So, it is here you are hiding,' said he, stopping by me as I put on my jacket.

'I have been with a battery up in the settlement.'

'Bravo.'

'I was not seeking your praise for it.'

He lifted his chin to the merchant's house where Captain Coote was calling after the last of his officers. He asked me what the disturbance was about.

'The king's men are to go aboard the ships.'

'To attack the fort?'

'Admiral Watson and Colonel Clive will surely tell us soon enough.' I put my pistol into my belt. 'Now you must excuse me.'

'I did not kill that man.'

I hesitated in my step. 'I do not understand you.'

'You understand me perfectly, Alistair. I did not kill Jones and you did not kill him either.'

'Who says it of me?'

'I know the ground to the south near the redoubt. I have walked it so many times while I lived here. That is why I did not send another.'

'You left us. My God, you left me to have charge over those men.'

'I trusted you. I trust you still.'

'I did not even understand that Jones was shot till I was told of it.'

'You could have done no more.'

'Had you remained with us it would not have happened.'

'That may be. And it may be that another had died instead. Or two men. Or three. His time came and that is all.'

'I will not debate it with you.'

He glanced away from me and up the street toward Captain Coote and I saw now that there seemed some great weight on Le Baume. Yet, standing but three feet from him and despite my intent observation of him in this unguarded moment, I am bound to say that I could not discern the nature of the weight that oppressed him – slighted pride or contemplated treachery. My view of him was clouded by my own confusion and the secret workings of his heart remained hid from me entirely.

When I said that I must go now, he faced me again.

'If there is an attack by the ships, the colonel will at the same time throw us at the fort to landward. You are very welcome, Alistair, to rejoin my company for the assault.'

'I am promised already,' said I, which was a cowardly untruth. And then I turned from his gaze, shielded my eyes from the sun, and looked over the rooftops toward the smoke now rising from the settlement. I felt that he watched me and that he watched me because he knew that I had lied. And so I let my shame turn to anger against him. 'I will go aboard the *Kent* with Captain Coote,' said I. 'For I will not serve with you.'

CHAPTER THIRTY-SIX

We boarded in the evening and slept the night upon deck, but we were too many and too expectant for any proper rest.

Two hours before sunrise a lieutenant with a half-dozen sailors took a small boat up to that place where the French had sunk their ships to block our passage. It was known to the sailors that the French work had been poorly done and that our ships, on the high tide and carefully handled, might make a safe passage of the blockade. But to be sure of the squadron's safety, the admiral had ordered lanterns to be hung from the two protruding masts of the sunken French vessels.

I stood at the rail, as did many others, and peered into the darkness up the river.

'I see you are alive, sir.' Turning, I found Midshipman Adams at my shoulder. He pushed in by me at the rail. 'They must be done very soon.'

'We cannot see their boat.'

We waited a minute more and then a small light was lit on the river up ahead. And, not long after another; but the lieutenant's boat remained invisible to us.

'Surely the French must see those lights.'

'They cannot, sir. There is a cowl wrapped all about the lanterns, except only for one hole pointing back to us.'

'The light is exceedingly small.'

'So long as the captain may see it. When the lieutenant's boat returns we will weigh, sir. Have you fed?'

'My stomach is unsettled.'

'Mine's a lime pit, but we must eat while we can. You must take a lesson from the admiral,' said Adams and he nodded toward the admiral's cabin which was completely open to the deck now, having had its wooden wall removed in preparation for the coming action. And there, at their breakfast by lamplight, sat Admiral Watson with Admiral Pocock, who had come aboard from the *Tyger*, and Captain Speke, the *Kent*'s captain and Captain Coote and a number more senior officers. Though there was little talk among them, they appeared to eat with a considerable appetite.

'I fear you must breakfast without me, Mr Adams. But I thank you for your concern of me.'

With Adams gone below decks, I moved further along the rail and watched now the many flashes of musketshot in the settlement. Clive's men there had kept up the same harrying of the Frenchmen all the night and yet no one of us had a doubt but that the French artillerymen would still meet the squadron's attack with a deadly purpose and with a determination unknown to the Moors. Fort Orleans was no Buj Buj and we knew that we should have no easy time of it once the assault was begun. In truth, I did not like to be on shipboard for this battle. The confinement of space and the hellish intensity of the guns were things set hard in the kiln of my memory – so hard, indeed, that as I stood at the rail now I wondered at my refusal of Le Baume's offer to rejoin his company. I felt, I own, quite ill with the apprehension of what must come. I seemed almost to see the smoke and smell the powder already and hear the booming guns, the wood splintering and the screams of men dying in close confinement.

We weighed anchor an hour before sunrise.

The *Tyger* had weighed not long before us and she went ahead, but slowly, riding the tide upriver and between the two small lights upon the masts. It was very slowly Captain Speke followed, and as we came nearer we saw those two masts standing like sentinels over the sunken French ships. We passed between the masts and our bottom brushed something, but lightly, and then the masts and the two small lamps were behind us. The sky was turning a pearly grey in the east. The first outlines became visible on the shore.

And then the lone French shore battery, beneath the fort, fired upon the *Tyger*. A single boom and a flash like a hundred musketshots, but the *Tyger* sailed steadily onward toward her planned position off the fort's north-eastern bastion. There was a stir on our quarterdeck, where I was posted with the marksmen of the 39th, and then an order went down to the gunnery officer. He now gave the men at the waist their target and, when they were ready, shouted, 'Fire!'

The guns answered with a shattering thunder.

Immediately came another shout of 'Fire!' from up on the quarterdeck and now the larboard guns on the quartedeck sounded.

This time I felt the jolt of the recoil through my whole body and the terrific booming clap seemed little muffled by the tiny scraps of cotton that I, under Adams' advisement, had put into my ears. Gunsmoke drifted over me and my fellow marksmen at the stern and with it the sharp smell of burned powder.

Near to us, at the centre of the quarterdeck, stood the admiral and his officers. Lieutenant Brereton and Captain Speke each kept a spyglass turned upon the shore.

'They are fleeing, sir,' the lieutenant reported. 'They have abandoned the redoubt. They are running for the cover of the fort.'

'Colonel Clive's men are now attacking,' observed Captain Coote.

'You will cease firing upon the redoubt, Mr Brereton,' said Captain Speke, and he raised his own spyglass to the fort. Lieutenant Brereton called the captain's order across the quarterdeck.

There was musketshot coming from the fort now and musketshot also from the settlement to landward, for Clive's men were in possession of every house with a vantage over the parapets. Up ahead, the *Tyger* sent her first volley into the eastern wall.

'You may raise the red flag, Captain,' said the admiral, and every eye above deck turned to see the flag hoisted to signal the general engagement.

The *Tyger* now opened her guns against the fort in very earnest and, when she got within pistolshot of the north-east bastion, she loosed sail and dropped anchor, her larboard guns firing all the while.

At the bow, our chase guns commenced firing and, as we drew near to our intended position off the fort's south-east bastion, our larboard guns, above and below decks, suddenly opened. We drew to within a pistolshot of the south-east bastion, then loosed our jib and dropped anchor.

To the stern of us the *Salisbury* had come through the blockade, but there was no searoom for a third vessel by the fort and so she stood out in the river and awaited direction from the admiral.

'Mister Douglas!' called Captain Coote very hotly. 'Your musket will do the French no harm unless you shall point it at them!'

I quickly found a place at the rail with some other marksmen and was soon busy upon that same service I had done at Buj Buj, though this time, I may say, with much greater effect. For the French gunners on the bastion were brave men and they showed themselves very frequently, in hazard of their lives, that they might find their marks upon our ship. And when they showed themselves we made sure to be ready for them, sending volley after volley whistling through the embrasures and over the parapets.

I was so intent upon this warm work that I did not notice the havoc wreaked upon our main deck till the soldier reloading by me remarked, 'There's deadly.' When I followed his gaze I saw then that some balls from the French cannon had torn through the larboard gunnel. There was a wide smear of blood across the deck and a man with shredded limbs screaming while his fellows tried to fetch him below. I quickly turned my eyes from the scene, but had some trouble to steady my hands at the next reloading.

Captain Speke had set more than half the *Kent*'s 74 guns to larboard. The *Tyger*, with her 60 guns, must have had two score of them directed at the fort. To defend themselves the French had a few guns on each bastion and singles at other points, where they must have reinforced the parapets. But their fort walls were *pucca* – stone and mud brick – while all that protected us was a few inches of oak, which was nothing. And yet if the oak could not stop their ball and grape, the French musketshot at least could not get through it. And so we marksmen rose only to fire and otherwise stayed low, though always in fear of a ball bursting through.

The wads of cloth in my ears I lost very early in the fight. After that the firing of guns on the quarterdeck set my head to ringing quite painfully and I soon became deaf to the roaring sounds about me. But I knew that the strikes of the French upon us were many, for I felt the jarring of the deck beneath me and frequently looked up in fear of falling timbers from the mast.

It was as I had imagined and worse, and I sincerely regretted now my refusal of Le Baume.

But our guns continued pounding the bastions and walls so heavily that after an hour we began to see the first signs of real difficulty among the French gunners on the south-east bastion, for they were compelled to slow their firing while they remounted one of their dislodged guns. Captain Coote strode across the quarterdeck to us and directed our fire at them, an intense hail of musketshot that sent two of their number falling like slaughtered sparrows.

I remember that as I crouched to reload Captain Speke was to the front of me, receiving a report from some lad. The admiral had gone astern and was peering up into the rigging. Suddenly there was an almighty crack, I felt myself struck and that is all that I recall, till I woke to consciousness some several seconds after to find Captain Coote knelt by me, shaking my shoulder.

'Douglas!' he cried. 'Are you with us man?'

'What—'

'He is with us,' he called to someone I could not bring into focus. 'See to the others.'

'Captain—'

'Roll onto your side that I may see your back.' When I had rolled, Coote said, 'Is there any great pain?'

'No.'

'Try to raise yourself. Sit up if you can.' There was a stiffness in my back, but I found I could do as he had asked me. 'Do not stand,' he said. 'I will send someone to you.'

He was gone then and I sat in a daze, a great commotion going on all about me. Slowly, very slowly it seemed, my wits returned to me. The cloudiness of my vision retreated and then I saw that I was no longer with the other marksmen but almost at the mast and there was smashed timber at the gunwale where I had been crouching to reload.

The guns roared continually. My eyes came to rest at last on Captain Coote and Lieutenant Brereton and several sailors. They were gathered in a knot and looking down on something just near to me.

'Captain,' said I, but who could hear that weak voice amidst the din of all the fighting? I reached and put my hand upon the mast and with this support got onto my feet. Nausea like to sea-sickness came over me. I braced my numbed back against the mast for some moments and, when the nausea had passed, I pushed away from there and went to join the knot of men. And on the deck in the midst of them I saw an awful sight. Both Captain Speke and that lad were lying there and much of their own blood ran about them and over the deck. The boy was very still and silent and the captain writhing, a hand clutching at the lad, and saying over and over, 'My boy, my boy,' in a voice most pitiful.

'He is raving,' said Captain Coote.

'The lad is his son,' said Lieutenant Brereton.

Two sailors, on their knees by their captain, tied a small rope about his smashed leg as a tourniquet. Captain Coote, then seeing me, asked if I felt myself recovered. I nodded. I know not why. 'Mr Brereton and I are needed here,' he said. 'You must see that Captain Speke and his son are taken down to the surgeon.'

I nodded again and Coote and Brereton then detached themselves to go and speak with the admiral, who had stood apart from this carnage, directing the other officers of the ship. The two kneeling sailors finished tying the rough tourniquet and then these and the others picked up the captain and his lad and, with every care possible in the midst of a battle, fetched them first down to the main deck and then below decks to the surgeon. I followed after them, groggy and useless.

Below decks were the first chambers of Hades – the stench of powder, the shouted orders and the screaming, the smoke and the press of half-naked bodies, the firing of the guns and the smashing of French shot into the hull. It was more real than any poet's imaginings and more terrifying – a living underworld, infernal and complete.

All about the surgeon's room were broken bodies.

'Here are the captain and his son,' said I, following the men in.

'I have eyes,' the surgeon growled. He had the sailors place the unmoving boy, who had lost his whole thigh, upon the floor, and the captain, who was mercifully unconscious now, upon the table. He then took a blade from a pail of water. When I turned to go he said, 'Do you return to the quarterdeck?'

'Yes.'

'Wait one moment.'

The sailors filed out by me, each one crouching to touch the Speke boy's forehead superstitiously as they went. Captain Speke being now unconscious from the loss of his blood, the surgeon pushed the flat of the blade against the open and bloody flesh and swabbed at the wounded leg with a cloth. 'There are too many injured, I cannot see to them all. How long is it expected the battle shall continue?'

'No one has said.'

'Is Mr Brereton killed?'

'No, sir.'

'Then you will tell him that the surgeon requests his attendance just as soon as his duties allow of it. And tell him also that I trust they shall allow of it immediately.' When he put his knife into the captain, I left him.

Above deck the firing continued as before, but now the topmast had fallen and broken the catching-net. The tangle of netting and splintered wood lying upon the deck made yet another hazard for the sailors. I passed the surgeon's message to Lieutenant Brereton and then returned to my place at the rail, snatching up the musket of a soldier who was already killed. The firing of all the guns was intense and too many lay injured for Lieutenant Brereton to now go below. But some while later I saw Midshipman Adams approach him and speak. And then, while Brereton consulted the admiral, who himself remained in full view of the French guns but unscathed, Adams came to wait by me. He leaned forward to my ear.

'There is trouble below.'

'Are we holed?'

'By Jesus, we are holed everywhere. But the trouble is with the men. They believe the tide will beat us.'

'The tide?' said I in astonishment that men in that hell below should think on aught but their lives.

He pointed to the waterline below the fort. 'We are falling with the tide. In two hours, the guns below decks will be useless.'

'There are guns on the main.'

'The fort will be firing down upon our main deck, and us and the *Tyger* both at their mercy.'

'Mr Adams!' called Lieutenant Brereton. 'Mr Douglas!' We hurried to him. 'Fetch yourselves a pistol each from the admiral's cabin. You will come with me now below.'

We stopped but briefly at the surgeon's room while Brereton went in, Adams and I remaining in the gangway where many wounded waited in agony their turn upon the table. There was a cacophony of cursing and crying. Some called upon God and some upon their mothers. The stifling air was rotten-ripe with pain and fear. Several bodies were as still as stone. And among these I saw Captain Speke's unfortunate boy, who had not survived the surgeon's knife, God rest his soul.

Brereton came from the room with a look very severe. We followed him along the gangway.

'Show your pistols, but for God's sake do not fire except in your own self-defence. I will try first what plain talk and the sight of us may do to steady them.'

'Does the surgeon still say they are mutinous, sir?'

'Hold your tongue, Mr Adams.'

Brereton well knew the characters of the sailors and also which of them he must boldly face down. A ship is no parliament and, in the midst of battle, no time for reasoned debate, and Lieutenant Brereton made the men feel it the moment we arrived at the guns. He went boldly among them as though he had heard nothing of their dissent. 'We will make a breach or have the French surrender within the hour. Where is your post? Then get to it man! You! Yes, you – bring up more powder and lively. No, the admiral is not dead and you would do more for his safety and your own if you ask no more questions but only stick to your guns. Strahan – what the devil is that smoke?'

The smoke was black, and not gunsmoke, though gunsmoke had hidden it from us at our first arrival. Indeed I saw now that there must be a fire there to the aft of us and the sailors with no concern of it. The sailor Strahan (who was that same drunkard who had single-handedly stormed the fort at Buj Buj) was quite insolent in his reply, saying that he regretted Mr Brereton had come too late and that nothing might be done. He began to talk of the best plan of getting the men from the ship.

'There will be time enough for that when the fort is surrendered,' said Brereton firmly. And he then ordered Strahan to fill some pails from the drinking-butts. Strahan gave Brereton an evil look, but he went to carry out the order.

'Mr Douglas,' said Brereton quietly, 'you will take charge of the three guns here. Mr Adams, you will watch for my return. If Strahan return without me, you will have him in irons. You may put a shot into him if you must.'

He then put his pistol in his belt, took up two pails that Strahan had filled and walked without hesitation directly into the smoke aft. Strahan, lest he appear a coward before the fellows he had stirred, had no choice now but to pick up the other two pails and follow the lieutenant.

The three guns near to me were silent, their men having slackened in their work to watch how matters would end between Brereton and Strahan. With these two now gone into the smoke, the men's eyes now turned to me. I stepped forward with a boldness I did not feel.

'Concentrate your fire upon the walls by the bastion!' cried I, which was but to repeat an order I had heard above deck. In the next moment

I perceived that they were in some doubt of the pistol in my hand. I put it into my belt and went to assist in remounting one of the guns that had bucked from its rail. After they saw me putting my shoulder to it, they then set to their own work, and I made sure not to give them instruction after that but only encouragement, for they knew their business very well.

After some minutes Lieutenant Brereton came from the smoke. He was alone and empty-handed.

'The fire is out,' he announced and, a sailor then asking after Strahan, Brereton fixed the men with a cold eye and said, 'He is out also.' One of the sailors at the nearest gun laughed, a sound quite remarkable at such a time. 'You will remain here, Mr Douglas. Keep the men firing till the French put up the white flag.'

He then left with Adams to visit the other decks.

How the gunners could load, reload and fire in such conditions, I know not. In that confined space they could barely stand upright, nor could they move three paces in any direction without entangling themselves with either one of their fellows, or a gun, or a powder keg, or stand of balls, or ropes, or some manner of nautical impediment. And all this in a heat and a stiflement of air that made a man gasp from the mere effort of breathing, and always with an expectation of the French shot smashing through upon us. Indeed, at different places the French shot did break through, maiming many and dismounting our guns, so that I was often called from the guns where Brereton had put me to assist in clearing the bloodied wreckage.

The battle went on now with a grim and deadly purpose, the sailors about me labouring like demons amidst the smoke and din. And, though none spoke of it, I saw how every man looked out of the gun-hatches at each reloading, across to the foot of the fort where the growing shoreline marked out the ebb of the tide. One hour and it felt like to a dozen, for the tide was an enemy we could not fight. Our guns had reached their maximum elevation and still the French fired upon us.

I cannot have been the only man almost despairing. And then

someone cried, 'There is a breach in the wall!' and the cry passed along the guns. I crouched with wearied limbs and looked out. The breach was real. I saw with my own eyes the great fall of stone.

'Continue firing!' I shouted, but my words were lost now in the thunder of guns, for the sight of the breached wall was a great spur to every flagging spirit.

Within minutes of the breach, Lieutenant Brereton was among us bellowing, 'Cease your fire! Hold!' When we obeyed there fell a silence upon the ship and every man now listened for a shot from the fort, but there was none. 'They have put up the white flag,' Brereton told us with as much exhaustion as triumph in his voice. 'They have surrendered.'

It was a strangely empty moment. No man cheered or made great show of victory, but each soon looked to his fellows at the guns and, very comrade-like, put a hand upon another shoulder. There was a great relief among us to have the thing over and be yet numbered among the living. Some dropped exhausted and others went to get water, but most of us who could stand now followed Lieutenant Brereton with wearied, aching bodies above deck, where there was air and wondrous welcome light.

CHAPTER THIRTY-SEVEN

*C*aptain Coote and Lieutenant Brereton were deputed by the admiral to receive the French capitulation. At my request, they allowed me a place in the boat that took them to the fort, though I own there was no necessity in it, but only my fierce and sudden desire to have the land again beneath my feet.

As we were rowed from her, we looked back at the *Kent* – from bow to stern she made a most melancholy sight. She was holed in so many places that I could not count them all, and her masts and rigging so badly damaged that Brereton adjudged them beyond any hope of repair.

'It is new masts or nothing,' said he, casting a professional eye back at the ship. He affected stoicism at the sight of her, but the pain he felt beneath was very plain to me. At last he turned from her, with a remark that he almost doubted she would ever again be seaworthy after the drubbing she had taken (which he was right in, for she never again left the Hugli).

The sailors who rowed us ashore were very free among themselves with their ill-feeling toward the fort's defenders. It was clear from their talk that they believed the French had held on beyond reason and that many British sailors had been killed to no purpose but only from French spite. Lieutenant Brereton made no order against this murmuring, but he talked quietly now with Captain Coote till we came at last to the ghat, where two French officers awaited us. It chanced that one of these recognized me from my time of refuge in Chandernagore and he spoke to me and assumed me of the party with the officers, and so it happened that I did not slip away along the shore to rejoin Clive's men as I had intended, but instead became included with them as they passed into Fort Orleans through the river-gate.

Within was such a scene of devastation and misery as I had not witnessed since our besiegement in Calcutta, for it had been several days now since Clive's first assault. And what his interminable harassment had left intact, the *Kent* and *Tyger* had now destroyed, so that hardly a building stood but was a ruin of itself, and likewise the French soldiery. Many dead lay where they had fallen and the wounded were gathered in a shaded place where a surgeon, who was himself wounded, now went among them grim-faced and weary.

It had not the full extremity of the horror of Calcutta's fall, for there were no women or children present. Nor was there a like terror to our anticipation of the oriental savagery of the Moors. And yet horror there was enough, for the dead were many and the stench of them inescapable. The unburied corpses had ripened in the heat and the putrid air now seemed entrapped within the walls of the fort.

While Coote and Brereton were taken to present the admiral's terms to the gouverneur, I sat upon the bastion steps and looked about me. It was very far from the childish dream of warfare that Jean-Claude had breathed into me in Orkney, and I knew now that European against European was no better or finer than European against Oriental. Jean-Claude had talked much of honour and gallantry, but nothing of how the maimed cry and the dead get no burial, nor the untold sacrifice that must be made for every victory. It was a bleak and bitter understanding to me.

And then I saw Cordet. He was at the far side of the fort and unlike the other beaten soldiers about him he seemed to move with some purpose, coming out from a small warehouse and hurrying along by the north wall.

'Cordet!' Getting down from the step, I started toward him. He looked around but did not see me. He went into the gatehouse and I crossed the yard while the defeated French soldiers on the parapet looked down at me, very hostile. The gatehouse door was open and I entered without thought. Cordet was there and in some urgent conference with two other French officers. The conference terminated abruptly at my arrival. Cordet, though much surprised, recovered himself quickly. He jerked his head toward the door and the other two went out.

'Do you seek my congratulations,' said he in French, 'or only my sword?'

'You may keep your sword,' said I.

'You came from the ships?'

'What remains of them. Your defeat was inevitable. An honourable surrender had spared much bloodshed.'

'There is nothing but only death inevitable. And a soldier's business is not to spare himself bloodshed. Is Mr Watts here with you?'

'He is in Murshidabad.'

'And Clive will now march there?'

'That is none of my affair, or yours. I believe that the admiral has granted generous terms to all the French officers. I understand there will be a parole given. If I may be of any service—'

'No,' he broke out with sudden vehemence. 'You may not be of any service to me. You may direct your charity to Gouverneur Renault, if you must. For myself, I want nothing from you. I ask nothing and I will accept nothing.' There was in his eye a look of such fierce pride and defiance he seemed almost a different man from the one I thought that I had known. But he had endured a siege, experienced a defeat and seen God knows what amount of suffering these past days, and he would not now endure the lash of my magnanimity. 'Will you set your sailors upon us now, Mr Douglas? Will you make of Chandernagore another Hugli?'

'I see you are not sufficiently your own master yet that we may speak civilly.'

'Do as you will. I wish you much joy of your victory.'

In no good temper myself now, I must then swallow the retort that rose in me. But, as I turned to depart, there sounded an explosion from some place within the fort. I stopped. I looked back at Cordet. And he raised his pistol and levelled it at my heart.

'You are surrendered,' said I.

He made no reply. Then those two French officers, who had earlier left us, hurried back into the guardhouse. They had replaced their uniform jackets with civil dress and one of them now took aim at me, while Cordet shed his epauletted jacket and put on the grey one they had brought for him. Cordet then went and put his head out the door and summoned three soldiers to stand guard over me.

'Your fort is surrendered,' said I. 'You are prisoners.'

'The capitulation is not signed,' returned Cordet. 'We shall take our chance without the walls.'

'It is a quibble to say it is not signed. The white flag is up.'

Cordet instructed the three soldiers to detain me there in the guardhouse till he and his brother officers had made good their escape. He unbelted his sword and placed it on the bench. 'They will not harm you, if you only wait quietly a minute,' he told me, without meeting my eye, and went out with his two fellow officers.

My guards were very sullen and my admonishment that they were breaking the rules of warfare they answered with contemptuous ribaldry and looks most threatening, so that I quickly saw they were not to be swayed from Cordet's orders. Nor did I waste my breath in challenging them further, for it seemed to me that Cordet and his fellows had but little chance of evading Clive's men outside the walls. After a short while my guards left me and then I picked up Cordet's sword and scabbard and went myself to the north gate and looked out. There were buildings very near and openings into many alleys, down any one of which Cordet and his fellows might have made good their escape. Clive's men were nowhere to be seen.

Hurrying back into the fort, I found Captain Coote watching unhappily the desultory French efforts to put out the fire caused by that explosion I had heard. The fire was in that small warehouse from which I had first seen Cordet emerging.

'You are very quick to get a trophy,' Coote remarked when he saw the sword, and that, not approvingly. When I explained what had happened (and the reason that I believed the explosion had been made), he said only, 'It was nicely done. I could wish many more had escaped so. I fear we may have much trouble of these fellows.'

I asked if I should take word of the escapes to the colonel.

'Colonel Clive is by this time aboard the *Kent* and, no doubt, debating with the admiral how the honour of the victory is to be apportioned.' Coote shouted then at the French soldier overseeing the dousing of the flames. The young fellow and his unhappy comrades appeared in no great hurry to save a building no longer in their keeping. Then Coote said to me, 'I suppose that Major Kilpatrick should be told of the escaped officers. You may go out from the fort by the rivergate.' And as I moved off, he called after me, 'Mr Douglas?'

'Sir?'

'Lieutenant Brereton has commended to me your actions during the battle.'

'There were many aboard did so much more than I.'

'I expect that is truer than you know, Mr Douglas. But I am glad that you should acknowledge it so readily.' He tipped his hat to me in a gentlemanly way and then turned to shout an Irish oath at the reluctant French firemen.

Major Kilpatrick had heard already of the escaped French officers, and not the officers only, for he told me that he feared fully two score French soldiers had made good their escape into the alleys and byways of the black town. Our men, he said, were hard-pressed now to discover them and he asked me to join one of the detachments he sent to the northern part of Chandernagore to intercept their retreat (for the major was in no doubt but the escapees would attempt to join with Monsieur Law in Murshidabad). But my detachment met with the same frustrations as the others the major had sent. The Chandernagore black town was a maze of alleys and lanes and then the Chinsurah black town started almost immediately to the north of it. By day's end, I believe there were not a half-dozen of the escapees recaptured (and Cordet was not one of these) and so Kilpatrick sent a small force of soldiers and sepoys to track down the escapees above Hugli, though with little expectation of success in so wide a territory.

In the night when I returned to my earlier billet in the merchant's house, it was very raucous in the streets round about, for the soldiers had found a great supply of *arrack*, or palm wine, from somewhere in the black town and also wine from the fort. They stinted themselves nothing now in their celebration of the victory. Likewise the officers, who had procured some casks of Madeira from the fort, were inclined to a rare affability and good cheer. I took more than one glass with them upon the verandah and listened to the tales of their escapades and I joined in their laughter now as I had not done before. And laughter there was in plenty, for it is the only release but for tears, when a man has passed through hell and no good woman near.

Though my head swam sickeningly with fatigue and drink, I only plied myself the more, so that I was soon scarce able to stand and ended by staggering to the rail and vomiting over it, to the sound of a general applause. Many of the officers shortly after set out to find the services of the camp-following native women. I rose to go with them and would have fallen but that Captain Coote caught my arm. He turned me about and shoved me inside, where I stumbled about for a time and eventually found my bed. I dropped into it hard and felt ill, but held my stomach down. I heard the guns again, pounding. I saw the Speke boy lying still. And I confess I gave not one thought to the absence of Le Baume from the officers' celebrations.

'But he is broken, Mr Douglas,' said one of the officers, when I asked after Le Baume's whereabouts the next morning. There were several breakfasting at the table and little talk among us, but many special potions being drunk as cures for the head.

'How "broken"?' said I in all innocence. 'Is he hurt?' There was then a palpable silence fell across the table and, when I looked about me, an unwillingness to meet my eye. 'Captain Le Baume is not hurt then.'

A shake of the head in reply. Further along the table two chairs went back and the officers there rose and took their leave.

347

Captain Coote then spoke from the head of the table. 'Captain Le Baume has been relieved of his command. This is what is meant, to say that he is broken.'

'But for what reason?' said I in some considerable surprise.

'It is at the colonel's order.'

'An order is not a reason, sir.'

At this there was a very general scraping of chairs and I soon found myself almost alone with Captain Coote, for only that fellow Scrafton remained of the others, sitting opposite to me.

'You are very welcome among us, Mr Douglas,' said Coote, continuing with his breakfast and keeping his gaze fixed on his plate. 'But if you are to remain welcome, you must take greater care of your tongue.'

'It was but a question, sir.'

'It was an impertinent and an insubordinate question. You are not a "writer" here. It is not the company rules. If the colonel has broken Le Baume, you may be sure it was done with fair reason.'

'I meant only to ask—'

'I pray you, think before you shall speak, Mr Douglas,' said Coote, lifting his eyes, and by his look I understood that he warned me very subtly against Scrafton.

'May I meet with Le Baume?'

'None may keep you from it. He has the freedom of the town till the court-martial convene in two days.'

I looked at him, appalled.

'Come, come, Mr Douglas,' put in Scrafton jovially. 'He shall have a fair trial before he is hanged.'

'Mr Scrafton,' said Coote sharply.

'What? Mr Douglas is a man who insists upon the truth. Is it not so?' he said, turning his silken smile upon me.

'Is such a thing possible?' I asked Coote.

'It is unlikely,' he answered. 'It is very unlikely.' And he shot a dark glance at Scrafton and then returned to his breakfast.

The thing was scarce comprehensible to me. Scarce credible. I pushed the food about my plate a moment, but then Scrafton leaned forward as if to speak again and I rose smartly from my place and went out.

CHAPTER THIRTY-EIGHT

*T*o the south of their settlement, the French had made a fine garden by the river. It was in this garden that I had once sketched the portraits of Chandernagore's French ladies and it was to this garden that Le Baume had now retired, having a tent erected in the midst of it, very solitary. At the garden's edge was encamped a troop of sepoys, and as I passed through them and into the garden the peacocks there scattered before me. Near to Le Baume's tent, I found a Hindoo boy casting newly washed breeches and a shirt across a leafless branch to dry. When I asked after his master, he lifted his chin toward the river.

The riverbank was high at that place where the pavilion was and, coming around the pavilion now, I discovered Le Baume lying at his ease upon the steps, his elbows propped under him and he staring out at the ships. He glanced up at me and then immediately back to the river. I knew not what to say to him. So I said nothing at first, but sat myself at the far end of the broad step and rested my back against the pavilion wall very gingerly, for the bruising was very painful still. He noticed my awkwardness and looked at me now curiously.

'I took a blow across my shoulders in the fighting. It is no more than a bruise.'

'How many were killed in the ships?'

'Twenty or more. And twice that number maimed.'

He looked again at the ships. He was not as I had expected him to be, full of wounded pride and brooding. Rather he seemed peaceful and strangely at ease with himself. I remarked that I hoped never again to be below decks during a battle.

'I have never had the pleasure,' said he.

'I may tell you, then, that it is hell.'

'*Credo*. But then the sailors did not enjoy the fighting out by the Maratha Ditch.' He continued to gaze at the ships as he asked me, 'Were there many dead in the fort?'

'They speak of two hundred. The French officers and Compagnie men have now signed a parole,' I told him. 'Most have been released and gone to Chinsurah.'

'The Dutch will be no friends to them.'

'Why are you summoned to a court-martial?'

His gaze went from the ships down to the native *dhobi* women washing clothes and linen in the river just along from us. Their children played in the river near to them.

'I am not much regarded by the colonel,' said he at last.

'No more am I. But he does not bring me before a court-martial.'

He looked at me directly. 'Very well. It is because I am French.'

'That is no good reason. You have done good service as an officer of the company. Clive did not see you at the siege in Calcutta.'

'What then is your excuse?'

'I am no part of the court-martial.'

'You went aboard with the grenadiers, Alistair, rather than remain under my command. And yet the ship was a place that you did not want to be.'

'That man Jones who died—'

'There is no explanation needed of you. The truth is, I have sometimes doubted of myself. It is only to be expected others should also doubt.'

'You did not allow those Frenchmen to escape then?'

'I did not. But if I am honest with myself, it was with some justice the colonel kept me from his deliberations with his senior officers.'

'I cannot believe that you would have betrayed us.'

He was taken aback and I saw that the thought of betrayal had never entered his mind. He gestured along the river, over the settlement and the fort. 'These are my own people. It is no easy thing to fight them.' He smiled crookedly. 'When the colonel broke me before the final attack – I admit it to you – I was relieved.' He laughed now at the strangeness of it.

But I could by no means share in his laughter. For it was very apparent to me now that those particular doubts I had of him were but chimeras of my own mind founded upon suspicions of him almost universally shared now throughout the British ranks. And, without he should now clear up those suspicions, the feeling against him at the court-martial might end in a verdict the gravity and even the possibility of which he had clearly never thought of.

'Are you certain that this is all that will be brought against you at the court-martial?'

'But what else?' said he.

I could avoid this no longer, but must broach it directly. 'When we were in Madras, you made payment of a debt to one of the officers with silver *siccas*. It was noticed that Cordet carried the same coinage about him.'

He squinted. 'You imagine some connection between us?'

'I fear it will be raised at the court-martial.'

'I had the *siccas* from Rémy.' Seeing my surprise, he continued, 'I had money in one of Rémy's ventures. When I saw that France and Britain should soon be at war, I thought it was best that I should not leave it ventured. Rémy is a gentleman and returned the money to me in coin.'

'But have you then had no dealings with Cordet?'

'I will not hear you on Cordet,' said he, suddenly rising to his feet. 'I have told you that is a private matter.'

'It is only that I fear the court-martial will make some further question of your honour.'

'I must bear that as I can.'

'If you were only to tell why you first resigned your commission—'

'It is not my honour alone involved in it. And I must bear it, because I am a man and not a woman,' said he, with an angry flourish of his hand, and turned sharply on his heel and left me.

I thought then for a certainty that he was lost unless I work some means to save him. But when I looked from the pavilion to the bench where those French ladies had sat for me, it seemed to me that, if I rightly understood Le Baume's words, the means to save him might not be so very far to seek.

Clive had set a guard at the *chowkay* kiosks on the road into Chinsurah to make a reinforcement to his order that the Dutch town not suffer any plundering at our hands. Once I had passed these kiosks I came into their black town, and uncommonly crowded it was by reason of all the Hindoos who had fled from their own homes in Chandernagore. They marked me by my dress as British and, though I had no real fear for my safety, I was very glad of Harry's presence beside me. The atmosphere of the place put me in mind of Edward Fairborough's frequent warnings to me that I should keep myself at some remove from the native people lest I stumble into some unsuspected but dangerous pit.

'We will stop by the church. The rector will know where we may find her.'

In the main avenue of the settlement were loitering a number of those defeated French officers that Clive had paroled. As I passed, they observed me with looks no more friendly than the natives. The Dutch rector directed a Hindoo boy to show us to the houses near the factory where most of the French women had taken lodgings. There were yet more paroled officers and Compagnie men in the street there. As I dismounted, Harry said quietly, 'These here would cut your throat,' to which I replied, with a jocularity I did not feel, that I must then rely upon him to recover my corpse for a proper British burial.

But the men, when they understood that I was come on some personal matter, treated me with as much strained civility as I might hope for. One of their number proved to be a friend to the woman under whose care Mademoiselle Cordet had fallen. So while Harry found shade and water for our horses, the gentleman escorted me to a park laid out after the Dutch fashion, very orderly. There were both women and men there, in twos and threes, making a slow promenade of the large central tank, the women carrying parasols, though they were shaded by the trees. My escort soon cut out Mademoiselle Cordet and her matronly chaperone from the others and brought them aside to me. The matron made no prevarication – she asked me directly the nature of my business with Mademoiselle Cordet.

'It is on a matter of honour, madame, between two gentlemen who are both known to Mademoiselle Cordet.'

'Honour?' she said, with some meaning.

'Yes, madame.'

'And you are one of these gentlemen?'

I admitted that I was not. 'I fear there has been a grave misunderstanding between the gentlemen. If I may speak with Mademoiselle Cordet, I believe she may clarify the matter.'

'Who are these two gentlemen?'

Mademoiselle Cordet stepped forward. 'Monsieur Douglas is known to me. He has travelled with Sébastien. I am happy to speak with him.'

The woman looked now to the gentleman who had brought me. But finding no guidance there, she turned to me again. 'You wish to speak privately with Mademoiselle Cordet?'

'With your consent, madame.'

'I am past the age for gallantries, Monsieur Douglas.' She looked at me a moment narrowly. 'Your word upon it, this is your only business with Mademoiselle Cordet?'

'You have my word, madame.'

She considered a moment more, and then said, 'You may walk about the park here together a minute.' I bowed my head to her. And as we two stepped away from her, she added, 'You will find, Monsieur Douglas, that she can walk very well without your arm.'

'You must excuse her. These past few days—I need not tell you.'

'Mademoiselle. I think you know which two gentlemen I mean.'

'This is a strange concern you have at such a time. What will happen to the fort? How long will you stay there?'

'Admiral Watson will decide. I have come here to ask you—'

'Your sailors have stolen from our officers. You must know how wickedly our servants have been misused by your people.'

'I cannot answer for every man of us. Nor can I excuse whatever has been done in the heat of the battle. I have not come here for that.'

'When you fled to us from Calcutta we gave you refuge. All of you. You have nothing to say?'

'I am conscious of the obligation.'

'It is a despicable way you have shown it.'

'No one regrets more than I, mademoiselle, that our two nations should be at war. But we must each of us accommodate ourselves to the hard fact as best we may.'

'Which is only to say that you have beaten us.'

'You do not enquire after your cousin,' I remarked. At this she glanced at me quickly and then looked ahead again. 'I take it you have heard that he escaped the fort?'

'What is your business here, Monsieur Douglas?'

'The two gentlemen I spoke of – they are Captain Le Baume and your cousin, Sébastien. I see that you are not surprised.'

'I have heard nothing yet to be surprised at.'

'Something caused Le Baume to resign his commission here. It is not a common action.' Her eyes stayed ahead and I continued, 'I have had some acquaintance with Monsieur Le Baume. I have found that he is a gentleman very careful of his honour.'

'He is prouder than a Spaniard.'

'It strikes me that Sébastien would likewise not lightly bear any slight. I can well imagine that two such, if there should come some matter of honour between them – mademoiselle?' She continued silent. 'Captain Le Baume has kept the reason of his first coming to us in Calcutta very close. You should know that his reticence on the question has brought a suspicion against him.'

'If he keeps silence, that is the right of a gentleman.'

'His silence is kept to his own harm, his very great harm.' When she looked at me now, I saw that she did not like to be told that. 'I will be open with you, though I know Le Baume would not thank me for it. He is to face a court-martial.'

Her astonishment was plain. 'Melchior? That cannot be.'

'There is a belief taken hold among the British officers that it was to spy upon us that he resigned his commission. I do not share the belief. But I must have some better evidence than just my regard for him, if I am to help him now.'

'My God, the English. Melchior is a good man.'

'If I can convince our officers that he is, at least, not a bad man, it will count much in his favour. It is of the greatest importance that this suspicion of him be now lifted. And I am right, am I not, in supposing that you are acquainted with his real motive in leaving Chandernagore?'

She asked me when the court-martial would be held and, upon my telling her, gave a start of surprise.

'They will not delay it, mademoiselle. And I may not have the freedom to come here again.'

'What is the worst they may do?'

'He may be hanged.' She stopped as though struck. 'And that he shall be stripped of his rank and disgraced is certain, unless he be helped and quickly – your chaperone watches us, we must walk.'

When we reached the far side of the tank, she said, 'Melchior left Chandernagore for my sake. Because I asked it of him – but you have guessed as much.'

'You asked this at Sébastien's urging?'

'Melchior was a friend to me. That is all. But it came about through some misunderstandings that Sébastien thought our friendship unsuitable. He made this known to me. Unfortunately he also made it known to Captain Le Baume.'

'And they argued.'

'It was worse than argument. Sébastien meant to challenge Melchior in defence of my honour. Men are such fools. Melchior promised me that he would not fight a duel. Sébastien would not see the truth, he made it impossible. It was for the good of all that Melchior left.'

'He might have gone to Pondicherry. He need not then have resigned his commission.'

'Sébastien made Pondicherry impossible also, by his closeness with the gouverneur. And if Melchior keeps his silence, you may believe it is from no base reason. He is a good man.' She turned on me with a sudden imploring anger. 'You must not let them hang him. Dear God, you must not.'

'Major Kilpatrick is with the colonel aboard the *Kent*,' said Scrafton in reply to my enquiry. 'And you and I are for Murshidabad. You must take what you may hold. We leave within the hour.'

'I must first speak with the major.'

'A sloop will take us up on the tide. You have been looked for all the day, Mr Douglas.' He made no hurry in his movements, but directed the coolie very languidly in the carrying of the trunk down the steps. Having no such luggage of my own, I dashed quickly inside and fetched my knapsack. Scrafton, from the next room, now informed me that the colonel was sending him upriver to Murshidabad for the purpose of assisting Mr Watts in his negotiations with the nawab. This surprised me very greatly, as I much doubted that Mr Watts would welcome his assistance. But I kept the thought to myself. My larger concern, for the present, was to communicate with Major Kilpatrick, who was president of the court-martial. My knapsack once packed, I went out past Scrafton, down the steps and beyond his waiting palanquin and ran on through the black town and down to the river.

I could find no boat there, only that one waiting to take Scrafton and me out to the sloop. The oarsmen were under strict orders from the sloop's captain and nothing I could say would turn them. Ten minutes later, Scrafton's palanquin arrived and his trunk. I got into the boat after him, with the thought that I might pass easily from the sloop to the *Kent*.

'It may be that I shall follow after you in a few days,' said I to Scrafton, as the boat rowed us out toward the sloop.

'I think not. It is the colonel's order that you should be my escort,' Scrafton replied without so much as a glance at me. 'It may be I shall want you as a messenger or some such. You shall most definitely ride upriver with me now.'

'Then I must first go aboard the *Kent* to speak with Major Kilpatrick.'

'I do not see that you will have the time for that.'

'I must see him.'

He fixed me now with a look very imperious (and, I may say, quite absurd on a man of but twenty-four years). 'It is not for you to challenge my instruction, Douglas. You are a servant of the company. I hope that you have not been spoiled for the company's service by the officers' indulgence of you.'

I did not know if I should strike him or laugh in his face. I met his look very directly and he finally turned away, saying that the tide would not wait for us and that I must study to adapt myself to circumstance like any other.

Aboard the sloop we found the preparations for our departure well advanced and, while Scrafton was busy about claiming some comfortable quarters for himself, I explained to the captain my need of communication with Major Kilpatrick. He was sympathetic to my request and quite ready to let me have oarsmen and a boat to ferry me to the *Kent*; but before the men could be called, the admiral's barge was to be seen making its way from the *Kent* to the fort. The captain raised his spyglass.

'It is the colonel and Major Kilpatrick,' he said, and handed me the spyglass to confirm it. 'They will be ashore before you are started. And I cannot miss the tide, Mr Douglas.'

'Not for an hour?'

'Not for thirty minutes. I rely upon it to get me over the shallows above Hugli. But if the matter is so urgent, you must come to my quarters and write a letter for the major. I shall send a boat across to the *Kent* with it. I daresay it shall reach him before he sits down to his supper.'

He turned at once to his quarters, though I stood in some hesitation. It had been no part of my intention to do other than to speak personally to Major Kilpatrick and lay open before him the truth concerning Le Baume, for I knew that the major would hear me. But finding myself quite suddenly and unexpectedly thwarted from my purpose and with no time to properly consider of the course I should take, I was thrown into confusion. In the midst of my confusion, Scrafton emerged from below and, being certain that he was no friend to me and equally certain that he would attempt to hinder the captain's aid of me, I hesitated no longer but followed quickly after the captain and sat down at his table.

Urgency and high feeling sent my quill like quicksilver over the pages and the captain at once had my sealed letter rowed across to the *Kent*. When the boat returned, we set sail past the squadron and on upriver towards Murshidabad, and I very unsettled in heart and not only from the near presence of Scrafton.

CHAPTER THIRTY-NINE

*T*he rains had not yet come. The river above Plassey proving, in consequence, unnavigable for the sloop, the captain had Scrafton and me (and the supplies Mr Watts had requested) put into boats and rowed the last part of our journey to Cossimbazaar. Now, and almost for the first time since our departure from Chandernagore, Scrafton unbent a little toward me and began to make some enquiry of the company's affairs at the nawab's court and of the central role played there by Mr Watts. I say enquiry, though in truth Scrafton's questions served mostly as preludes to the recitation of his decided opinions on political matters in which his ignorance exceeded even my own. I could not mention a name – whether Jagath Seth or Mohan Lal or some other – but Scrafton would immediately give me chapter and verse upon the character of the fellow, though where he had come by his doubtful information I was at a loss to discover. In truth, it seemed but scraps gathered from company dinners at our factory in Bengal, scraps which he had then reheated to serve as a dish of his own making. The few remarks that I ventured he greeted with the condescension of a wise old sage, and I soon understood that he wanted no discussion but only an audience, after which I let his words flow over me, unremarked, and sketched the passing houses and the temples on the riverbank.

We suffered no obstruction from the few Moorish boats we met upon the river, and came the next morning to the ghat below the Cossimbazaar factory. The trouble between Scrafton and Watts began almost at once.

All the time I had been away from Cossimbazaar, Mr Watts had kept up a daily diplomacy to the nawab's court in Murshidabad, while Monsieur Law had been no less active on behalf of the French side. The court being thoroughly corrupt, silver was the natural currency of this diplomacy, and our coffers being somewhat fuller than those of the French, Mr Watts had won many powerful Moors to our interest. But this had been but a shadow-play till the news arrived there of our defeat of the French at Chandernagore.

'You may be sure, I have pressed our case against the French remaining in Bengal,' Watts told me and Scrafton when we all dined together that first evening. 'And you may be just as sure Monsieur Law contends for their continuance here very ably.'

'I am at some wonder that you have been unable to remove him,' remarked Scrafton. 'I confess I had not expected it.'

'He is the French voice at the court,' said Watts, somewhat startled by the impertinence. 'He is not at my command. And the French are not so feeble-minded as to withdraw him.'

'I am told that he has taken into his factory a number of French soldiers who escaped from Chandernagore.'

'That is no great matter.'

'I am surprised that you should think so, Mr Watts. If it were come to a battle between our two factories, those soldiers might prove of the utmost importance.'

'A battle, Mr Scrafton?' said Watts, who had been irked by Scrafton's manner all through our dinner, but had avoided to confront him till now. 'There shall be no battle in Cossimbazaar.'

'Our business, as you have so rightly said, is to expel them.'

'As I recall, I said it was our business to have the nawab expel them.

And I think you will find that the colonel's methods, though very necessary, have not the universal application in Bengal that you expect. To fight the French here in Cossimbazaar – on the nawab's own doorstep – would be a foolhardy action. And we would suffer for it.'

'But that is too timid, sir,' said Scrafton, smiling, as though he meant only a jocular rebuke.

There was a silence of some moments. I looked from one to the other uncomfortably. And then Watts said, 'You will come with me in the morning to the palace perhaps, Mr Scrafton.'

'I am at your service.'

Scrafton dipped his head to Watts and then quaffed the Madeira, well pleased to have gained this honour so quickly. Mr Watts drank too, but unsmiling. It was very evident to me that he meant to keep Scrafton very close beneath his eye.

While Watts and Scrafton made their daily journey into Murshidabad I was kept busy in that same manner I had been before, which was the reconciling of the account of our losses in Calcutta against the reparations promised us by the nawab under the treaty. The business was little further advanced than when I had left it, but I was much aided now by the list of losses which Scrafton had brought from the council in Calcutta. Nor was I confined to Cossimbazaar for this work, but made several journeys into Murshidabad, where I met with Jagath Seth's agents (who acted now on the nawab's behalf) and also with some officials of the nawab's treasury.

Upon returning to Cossimbazaar from such a journey one evening, I met a bullock cart which was so heavily laden that its axle had broken. It lay stopped in the road before me and its load of cotton bales was being moved by a coolie onto the ground so that the driver might effect some repair. My horse jinked as I went by, else the coolie had not stumbled and, had he not stumbled, I had not seen the cannon that was hid beneath the bales in the tray. The coolies covered the thing quickly and, either by presence of mind or confusion, I did not stop but rode on as if I had seen nothing. Only when I passed the driver did I gesture with my whip to the bales in the tray and ask carelessly,

'John company, hai?' to which he shook his head and looked innocent (which is to say sly) and replied to me, 'Law.'

I did not take my usual way through the Cossimbazaar black town, but went around to the east and came down that avenue where the French factory lay. And in spite of some talk I had heard the previous day among our servants, I was very much surprised to discover the extent of the works that Monsieur Law had put into motion there, for outside the factory walls were forty or fifty coolies hard at labour to raise an earthen bank, and at the gates some heavy reinforcement being made by the French carpenters. One of these, when he saw me surveying the scene from horseback, taunted me with a cheerful Parisian vulgarity. But when I answered him in French that I was grateful to him that he should take the trouble to make such a fine door for us British to go in by, he was so angered at my words and spoke to me then in such a ferocious manner, that I knew him for a Marseillais. I would have departed then, but for the emergence through the gates of a French officer. Some camel carts then passing between me and the fort, I did not see him clearly at first. It was only after he had spoken to the carpenters and turned towards me that I recognized him for Sébastien Cordet.

I put my horse forward. He came out to meet me in the road.

'I see that you are making considerable good use of your parole,' said I.

'And you are a spy now, Monsieur Douglas?' returned he, not the slightest abashed.

'This is a public place. And the work you are about here' – I signified the coolies and the carpenters – 'it is work difficult to keep hid.'

'It is no secret.'

'The right of fortification is a privilege the nawab is very jealous of. As we learned in Calcutta, to our cost.'

'You will find that he knows of it.'

'I had the pleasure to pay a call upon your cousin in Chinsurah,' said I, and his look changed on the instant. He fixed me now with a wary eye. 'She is a more sensible girl than you described her to me.'

'You had no business to trouble her.'

'Le Baume is before a court-martial. And you have put him there.'

'Le Baume is with Clive.'

'He came to us for a reason you know very well. I am undeceived.'

'Her reputation was in my care. And if he is before a court-martial I do not see how that it is my doing.'

'Is it not?'

'Upon my honour.'

'Honour? You are a soldier escaped beneath the cover of a white flag.'

'There was no capitulation agreed.'

'Oh for pity's sake,' said I, turning my horse.

'Alistair,' said he, which checked me. I turned to him again and he said, 'It may be that we shall next meet under arms. We should not now part in anger.' He raised his open hand, for all the world as if I should take it.

I spurned the hand contemptuously and, with thoughts very dark, rode away from there.

The house in Murshidabad where Watts and Scrafton were lodged was a very fine one and but a short walk from the main gate of the nawab's palace. At the centre of the house was a courtyard, richly planted, and at the centre of the courtyard a pond filled with scores of small red fish. Watts had brought me into the courtyard when I arrived that we might have some privacy from the servants, none of whom he fully trusted. He looked down at the pond and threw crumbs to the fish all the while that I made my report. And I made it to him very quietly, as he had requested of me.

'And it is a commonplace at our factory that the French have now taken in some hundreds of their soldiers who fled Chandernagore,' I concluded.

'That commonplace is incorrect,' Watts remarked placidly. 'They have taken in no more than fifty.'

'They have thrown up the earthen walls very speedily.'

'They shall find no protection there. Monsieur Law must do what he can, but his hand is almost played out. The earthen walls are but a sign that he knows his own weakness. I have made a formal application to the nawab that all the French factories in Bengal be now passed into our hands.'

'Will he grant it, sir?'

'It would be but to acknowledge the true state of affairs. In losing Chandernagore they have lost everything. And Monsieur Law knows it very well.'

I remarked that they had not yet lost their Cossimbazaar factory at least.

'It is precisely to drive them from their factory there – and from Murshidabad – that I am about, Alistair. Only it shall not be done by arms, in spite of anything you may have heard from Mr Scrafton. Does he continue to write to Cossimbazaar?'

'We receive his missives two and sometimes three times in a day.'

'Dear God, the man cannot leave off from meddling.'

'Sir—' said I and turned my head in warning, for Scrafton himself had just come from the house and into the courtyard. And immediately behind him Omichand, like a blighting shadow. They crossed to us at the pond, Scrafton's step very deliberate, as if there might be some important news to impart.

'I was not told you were here, Mr Douglas.'

'Mr Scrafton,' said I.

'You will please to leave us,' said he. 'We have some private business with Mr Watts.'

When Watts nodded to me, I withdrew, though not without chagrin, for I found that Scrafton's incivility rankled the more each time that I met with him. As to Omichand, I believe that he hardly noticed me at all.

Inside the house the servants were very attentive of me and brought me figs in a bowl and a pitcher of cool water. Though content at first with their solicitude, I soon became weary of their attendance upon me, for, even by the generous standard of Bengal, they were too many and too close about me. When, after fifteen minutes, I found that to send one of them away from me was merely to summon another, I took the pitcher of water and went outside to sit upon the verandah overlooking the street. Though shaded, it was hotter there than inside and I knew that the servants would not follow me.

The long dry season had turned the city's roads to powder, but the house was favoured by a small garden to its front, just wide enough to take the worst of the dust put up by the several bullock carts now passing. There was a mounted Moorish troop went by also, the walkers upon the road shuffling aside in some hurry to make way for the cavalrymen, resplendent in their bright tunics. But once these had gone the road was quiet, with only the barefoot Hindoos going to and fro and the occasional palanquin or *dooley* (which is a small covered carriage favoured by the Moorish ladies) going by. I went down and got my sketchbook from my saddlebag and returned to the verandah and sat with my knees raised and my boots upon the rail. I proceeded to draw the outlines of the mudbrick buildings opposite and the minaret jutting from the tiled roofs further back and the arched tower rising from behind the palace wall.

We were to gather the French factories to ourselves and we were to push the French out from Murshidabad – and what then? While the admiral and the colonel remained with their men in Bengal, we might hold fast to what we had won. But at their leaving, which must surely come soon (for our council in Madras was much in want of them, from fear of the French in Pondicherry), what measure of justice might we then receive from the nawab? The French would be certain to return and just as certain to make common cause with him against us. And yet if I could see this, so too could Watts, for by his communication with the councils in Calcutta and Madras and with Clive and the admiral and also from his dealings at the nawab's court, there was not a man in Bengal had a deeper understanding of our situation than he. I own, I could not puzzle it out. Watts seemed a captain on some course that his crew might hope for but not clearly see, while they worked at their peril on the pitching deck. And what the devil might Scrafton be at in snatching at the tiller? And what of Omichand, now so close at Scrafton's heel?

The sketch was spoiled and I tore it sharply from the book. As I rose, Scrafton and Omichand came out and Watts after them. The bearers, who had been crouched all the while in the shade of the walls opposite, now brought the two palanquins across to the garden.

'Mr Scrafton, you will remember to make for me a copy of any letter that you shall send to the colonel.'

Scrafton continued down the steps, only raising a hand to signify that he had heard Watts's instruction, and got into the first palanquin. Omichand paused and spoke with him, while Watts and I looked on from the verandah.

'Mr Scrafton seems displeased,' said I.

'You may believe I have given him some reason for it,' said Watts. 'I trust he has not inveigled you into his scheming.'

'I am almost beneath the notice of Mr Scrafton.'

'It is an obscurity you must be thankful for. But should he stoop to take some notice of you, I trust I shall hear of it.'

Le Baume was not hanged. I got word of it from my fellow writer Hastings, who made several journeys at this time up to Cossimbazaar from the squadron, bringing secret supplies of muskets and powder to us. There had been two men hanged, but these were soldiers who had attempted to sell captured guns to the Moors. Le Baume's fate was to be 'unbroken', though the particular reason of his reprieve was unknown to Hastings. I felt an enormous weight lifted from me upon hearing the news, but I wrote no letter to Le Baume, for fear it should give rise to some fresh misunderstanding (and I knew not whether he should feel kindly toward me that I had made public his private affairs). But, at last, I could apply my mind fully to the aid of Mr Watts, which I did in the first instance by storing the muskets and powder come up from the squadron in secret places about the factory, in accordance with his orders. The French factory received no such supplies, though it was reported to me by our servants that Monsieur Law took in daily a few more stragglers from those escaped soldiers of Chandernagore. Also the nawab of Bengal's flag was raised above their gate, as though Monsieur Law and the nawab should jointly warn us against any attack upon the French factory.

What passed in the nawab's court during this time I learned only from rumour, of which there was much, and the only clear thing was that the contention between Mr Watts and Monsieur Law was being brought to some final trial. That Mr Watts had now the stronger hand was proven when one of our sepoys reported to me that the earthen banks and other fortifications recently made at the French factory were now being pulled down by the French soldiers at the nawab's order. I went there immediately to confirm it with my own eyes and then wrote a prompt report of it to Mr Watts.

Some days later I received his order that I must attend upon him in Murshidabad on a matter of the utmost importance to the company. He required of me that I dress in a manner suitable to be received in the nawab's audience chamber.

'It shall be different than before,' Watts told me as we crossed the palace courtyard behind our Moorish escort. 'Monsieur Law shall not take the news of his detention with any pleasure.'

'Is he here?'

'He is summoned by the nawab. He has been given no warning of what is intended.'

We had come directly from the house near to the palace gates, but in that short distance the perspiration had broken out very freely beneath my shirt and tightly buttoned jacket. Watts dabbed at his own brow with a white handkerchief. It was not the heat only, but a certain excited apprehension that gripped us, for if the nawab should detain Law as he had promised to Watts, and put both Law and the French factory in Cossimbazaar under Watts's charge, then the final blow against the French in Bengal had been struck and this by skilful diplomacy alone, without recourse to any nefarious scheme of Omichand or Scrafton. (These two, Watts had told me, were presently in a distant quarter of the city, held in conference with Jagath Seth, who had obliged Watts by calling them away there upon some pecuniary pretext.)

'You shall remain silent, as before. Speak only if I order it. And you are certain the sepoys are properly instructed?'

'They will not enter the palace grounds, sir.'

His head was bowed and his shoulders weighed down by the heavy care that was on him. For many weeks he had borne the weight of the company's affairs in Murshidabad alone, and he had done this, and remained here in the lion's den, while his countrymen had busied themselves in visiting an unexampled violence upon the territory of a prince so capricious that even the court nobles enjoyed no proper safety from his dangerous whim. And Watts was worn by it and it showed in his face, which was leaner now than I had known it, and in his eyes, which were tired and ever watchful.

In the inner chambers, the slaves and servants and courtiers who moved about gave no sign of recognition to us, but carried on their business as though untroubled by any thought of disturbance or change in their fast-enclosed world. We were not kept waiting (which is a courtesy I had never heard of being extended to a European in that court) but were ushered directly through to the audience chamber where the nawab was seated already upon the *musnud* (which is the royal cushion) on the dais.

There were no chairs prepared for us and, after giving the nawab our salaams, Watts set forward one stockinged leg and, in a manner very confident and gracious, offered up some short speech in Persian. The nawab, I must confess, was quite inattentive to Watts's words and turned first to one of the noblemen sitting by him and then another, in a fashion most distracted. His chief adviser, Mohan Lal, was not about, which I wondered at. (We heard later of a rumour that Lal was ill. A sickness, it was said, caused by a poisoning ordered by Omichand.) But whatever the reason for Lal's absence, it was plain that the young nawab now felt the lack of his chief adviser, so that when Watts left off speaking there were but a few desultory questions asked by the nawab and then we were dismissed from the chamber.

'He will not face Law,' Watts told me quietly when we were alone. 'We must wait here and do the thing ourselves.'

'Shall Law acquiesce?'

'It will be done by the nawab's authority. Coming from my lips, Law will challenge it, but there is no help for that.'

'Can the nawab be afraid of Law?'

'The Moors feel the obligations of hospitality very keenly. It is a trust the nawab is loath to be seen breaking by giving Law into our hands.'

Then came out from the audience chamber one of the Moorish nobles and we fell silent at his joining us. We three then retired into a vestibule where refreshment was brought us, and Watts and the noble had some conversation now while we waited. It was very plain that this fellow had been sent by the nawab to watch over us and over our coming meeting with Monsieur Law.

After some while the French party arrived with Monsieur Law at its head and Cordet at Law's right hand. There were also a few more French officers and a number of the nawab's courtiers as escort. When we came out from the vestibule there seemed some surprise among the French at our being there. The noble who had waited with us now addressed Law in French, enquiring if Law had something to tell Monsieur Watts.

'I have no manner of business with Monsieur Watts. I have come here at the nawab's summons and would be grateful of his being informed of my arrival.'

'But you have something to say to the British.'

'Unless it be "good day", I have nothing whatever to say to them.' Law dipped his head to Watts to show that he meant no personal offence.

'Then you will listen to what they shall tell you,' said the noble, and he stepped aside so that Watts now faced Law directly.

'Monsieur Law, it is the nawab's wish that you shall surrender the Cossimbazaar factory to me and that you and your men shall then go down peacefully to Calcutta, where you will be under the same conditions of parole as the other French prisoners from Chandernagore. You will forgive me that I cannot make this matter any easier.'

At hearing these words from Watts, Law's head went back. Cordet and the other French officers looked at Watts very fiercely.

'You cannot demand my surrender,' said Law. 'My men and I have as much right to our liberty as any here. If the nawab shall himself require me to surrender our factory into his hands, very well. He is the nawab. But that will be no affair of the British.'

'You have no ground to stand upon, sir.'

'You will allow that I must judge of that question for myself.'

Watts turned to the Moorish courtiers and spoke to them in Persian, but the substance of his words was plain enough – Monsieur Law was defying the nawab's will and must now be arrested. The courtiers, however, appeared alarmed to be called upon to take any decided action. While they debated the matter with Watts, Law boldly seized the chance offered by their irresolution.

'It is the nawab has summoned me here and I will see him. I will answer to the nawab and so will you.'

Already alarmed at the turn the interview between Watts and Law had taken, the courtiers had little stomach to withstand this veiled threat, for they well knew their master and the fatal blow that might fall upon them if they erred. They consulted together, and in the midst of their consultation came word that a troop of French grenadiers had forced their way into the palace grounds.

'Some signal must have passed to them,' Watts said to me quietly. 'Monsieur Law has been forewarned of our intention.'

'They cannot fight the nawab's men.'

'Neither can we now arrest him. We have no firm support from these fellows.' Watts was, I saw, momentarily at a loss as to what he might do. But calm, withal, which impressed me as much as the admiral's quiet demeanour when he had stood upon the *Kent*'s quarterdeck throughout the full heat of the attack on Chandernagore. At last Watts reached some decision and stepped in among the conferring courtiers and suggested that they take word of Law's obstinacy to the nawab. They agreed to this and Watts then sent me with them that my presence might keep them to the task.

The nawab was upon his feet when we entered the audience chamber. He had come down from the *musnud* and was walking by the wall, with his head bowed. The hem of his crimson coat dragged upon the ground behind him and when he faced us it was with no eagerness to hear the report of what had passed between Watts and Law in the outer chamber. But when he had heard it, he spoke immediately and vehemently and one of the courtiers went out and returned a minute later with Law and Cordet, but of Watts there was no sign.

The nawab returned to his place on the dais. It was a very sombre look he had at first and a very sombre tone he adopted when he first spoke to Law. Law answered in Persian and their conversation continued in that language almost as though they were alone in the chamber, for the nawab's counsellors kept silence and nor did Cordet move or speak a word.

The manner of the nawab and Law towards one another was most affecting. The nawab frequently lowered his gaze as he spoke, as one almost ashamed at what he did, while Law's tone moved quickly from importunity to regret once he saw that the nawab was not to be swayed. After a time there was mention between them of the names of some towns and then the nobles around the nawab suddenly roused themselves and seemed to protest at what it was Law had said. The nawab, however, quickly silenced them. There followed another exchange between Law and the nawab. Then Law received the betel from the nawab's hand, bowed and began to withdraw. The nawab spoke one final time.

Law answered him in French.

'Send for me again? Rest assured this is the last time we shall see each other. We shall never meet again. It is impossible.'

I followed Law and Cordet into the outer chamber and rejoined Watts while the Frenchmen all departed. A courtier then hurried out from the audience chamber to bring report to Watts of all that had passed between Law and the nawab (it says much about the corruption of the court how open and thoroughly shameless was their spying upon one another). From this fellow we learned that the nawab had ordered Law and all the Frenchmen to leave Cossimbazaar. The protest from the nobles which I had witnessed concerned the direction Law should take, for they had desired him to go south (where he must inevitably surrender to Clive's force), whereas the nawab had finally granted Law leave to take his men north-west, further upriver toward Patna, where they might be safe from us British.

Watts waited till we were through the palace gates and away from the many keen ears within the palace, before he spoke to me.

'Monsieur Law has had a reprieve. We have too few men in our factory to make any challenge to them upon the road. It seems we must be content with half a victory.'

'But can we be certain that he will leave?'

'Cossimbazaar is not Calcutta and Law is not Drake. There will be no futile and bloody sacrifice made. He will take care to leave while he yet remains under the nawab's protection.'

And so it happened, for two days later, Law, with some hundred men (both Compagnie and soldiers) and cannon loaded upon bullock carts, came out from the French factory in Cossimbazaar and started out on the road to Patna. I went out to the edge of the black town to witness their leaving. And when Law and Cordet saw me sitting there quietly on horseback in the shade, I instinctively – and quite thoughtlessly – touched my hat to them. Law, though unsmiling, nodded in return. Cordet averted his gaze and raised a kerchief to his mouth against the dust of the carts.

CHAPTER FORTY

*S*ince the first day of Scrafton's arrival in Cossimbazaar, there had existed between him and Watts an uneasy peace; but upon the departure of the French this peace turned, on Scrafton's part at least, into an almost open hostility. Scrafton made no scruple to deride Watts's judgement in my presence, relating to me in tedious detail all the ill consequences we might expect from allowing Law to slip from our grasp. Upon my suggestion that Mr Watts had achieved all that could be expected by the Calcutta Council, and more, Scrafton became quite heated with me, as though he felt any praise of Watts as an odious slight against himself. He moved like a gadfly between Cossimbazaar (where I stayed) and Murshidabad, where Watts remained now in that house near to the palace. The purpose of all Scrafton's movement was very far from apparent to me, though it troubled me to see Omichand so often in his company on these journeys. He was at pains to cloak his comings and goings in secrecy, but there was not a sepoy or even a cook at the Cossimbazaar factory unaware of Scrafton's arrivals and departures and so I was closely informed of his travels, though I paid these little heed. I continued to work at the restitution due the company by the nawab under the terms of our treaty. It was not me, then, but Harry who first sensed our danger.

I was in the counting house when Harry came to me, sitting at that same desk where Edward had once sat before the start of all our troubles. I had with me two Moorish officials, whose whole intent was, as ever, to keep the truth of the Moorish pillaging in Calcutta obscure. To this end, they had brought me any number of tallybooks and ledgers and these now lay piled in confusion about them where the fellows sat cross-legged upon the floor. Harry stopped in the doorway, ran a contemptuous eye over this pair, then said, 'You are wanted at the ghat, Mr Douglas.'

It being already the late afternoon, I bade the Moors return the next day and then I rode with Harry from the factory. He had temporized when I had first asked him who it was wanted me at the ghat, and so now, as we rode, I asked him again and was surprised by his answer that we would meet there the sepoy Bhaskar, who was Harry's second among our native soldiers. He would not tell me the reason of this meeting, and knowing Harry for a man who made no unnecessary mysteries, my curiosity was very high by the time we dismounted.

We passed the moored boats and several fishermen's huts and came at last to a hut that stood solitary, with fishing nets hung upon poles all about it. An armed sepoy stood like a guard at the door. Harry spoke to him as we approached and the fellow unbolted the door for us. Inside, there were two more armed sepoys, and when my eyes became accustomed to the darkness, I descried a third figure lying upon the earth floor beyond them.

'There,' said Harry, lifting his chin to the prone figure. He called to the fellow sharply, ordering him to rise. The fellow, with some considerable trouble, pushed himself to sit upright and set his back against the wall. The small square of light from the window now fell upon his face and upper body.

'My God,' said I, aghast. 'What has been done to him?'

Bhaskar it was, and now he managed to open one swollen eye to look up at me. His turban had been stripped from his head and his black hair hung lank about his shoulders. His shirt was torn and bloodied, and his company jacket was a rag beside him on the floor. He had been so badly beaten about the face that his eye closed now from the evident pain in struggling to keep it open. It was a beating such as Isaacson had taken.

'But this is your man,' said I to Harry, stunned, for I could not conceive what had happened that Harry should have beaten the fellow so savagely.

Harry ordered the two sepoys from the hut. When they had gone, he said to me, 'He is not my man. He is only for himself.'

'What has he done?'

'Bhaskar is a dog. Dog!' He lashed out at the man with his boot.

'Harry!'

He kicked the terrified Bhaskar twice more before I got hold of Harry's arm and pulled him away. The target of his fury rolled into a ball and lay still.

'For Christ's sake, what are you about? You will kill him.'

'Let him answer you.'

'He cannot answer anyone. Look at him. Look at what you have done to him.' Harry looked, but with no sign of remorse. I called for the sepoys outside to bring water.

'He would cut the throat of his mother.'

'If you cannot abide the sight of him, if you cannot control yourself, you will wait outside.' When Harry made no move to go, I said, 'What in the name of God has the man done to you?'

'Let him tell you.'

'If he lives, he may. Till then I would be obliged if you would yourself give me some reason for this – barbarity.'

'He has made the younger sepoys swear loyalty to him.'

'But he is their officer.'

'It is an oath to a dog. He is bought by Omichand.'

There came a coldness over me. I asked Harry if he was quite certain of it.

'He would not confess to it. But I am certain.'

I looked again at the figure upon the floor. The name of Omichand hung over him now and I found that this Bhaskar, for all his abject helplessness, was a little less the object of my pity.

'To what end?' said I, but that was a question Harry, in spite of all the pain he had inflicted upon the fellow, still could not answer.

Watts, in fear of the eyes and ears of his own servants, had given me a sign that I should make upon our first meeting, that he might then understand I had some secret matter to convey to him. And so now I made the sign upon my arrival in the courtyard of his house, where I had surprised him in the company of the banker Jagath Seth and the wretch Omichand. Watts appeared not to have seen the three fingers I had laid across my forearm and he continued his perambulation a good while before the others finally left him, but then he came immediately to fetch me.

'If you would take the air with me, Alistair, pray get your hat.'

We were soon riding through the city in two palanquins, Watts directing the bearers on a twisting route through the street stalls and past the markets and temples, till at last the press of people and wandering cattle abated and then he called up my palanquin to travel beside his.

'You must be patient a little while longer,' said he, and gave me a look of warning, by which I understood that it was not safe to speak – even if it be in English – in the presence of the bearers.

We were set down at last by a *medan*, that is to say by a great square, which lay to the front of the Iqutab mosque, which was the largest mosque in the city. The square was treeless, with small patches of grass scattered thinly over the brown earth, and a small lake at its centre. As we walked across to the benches by the lake, I saw that we were much remarked upon by the Moors, who tarried there in expectation of the midday prayer. The expulsion of the French having happened so recently and a British army being in the field not a week's march to the south of Murshidabad, it was little wonder the Moors should give us more than customary attention. But no one of them approached us and as we neared the lake there was a general movement among them toward the mosque. Then the prayer-caller gave his lilting cry from the minaret and all the Moors emptied from the square and into the mosque. We were alone now, but for a few Hindoos, who kept at some distance from us.

'May I speak freely now, sir?' When he inclined his head, I told him what I had learned from Harry. And I told him of the state of the beaten fellow. Watts looked very grave.

'Was the man alive when you left him?'

'He was. I forbade Harry to beat him any further.'

'But he had not confessed to this allegiance to Omichand.'

'No. But Harry seemed quite certain of it.'

'It is perhaps as much evidence as may be had in such an affair. Harry knows his own people – I have let this matter run on too long.'

'What matter, sir?'

Watts made no answer. He kept his hands clasped behind his back and his eyes upon the middle distance as we walked around the lake. He was thoughtful and, by his expression, I saw that he was troubled by his thoughts.

'Is Omichand still to be treated as a friend to us?' said I.

'He shall be treated as I have ever treated him – with great care. He has a considerable power at the court here. And he is so deeply entwined with the company's affairs that we cannot now throw him off without it do us harm – perhaps a harm fatal, both to our interest and to ourselves.'

'I had thought you held him in some regard.'

'What I have learned about Omichand these past few weeks would cause the Devil to blush with shame. He has played me and all the council in Calcutta for fools. It was a good instinct made you distrust him from the first. The man is a very serpent.'

'But he was at your house just now.'

'As I have said, we cannot throw him off so easily. But I have made sure to have means other than Omichand to work the company's will at court. Jagath Seth trusts him as little as I. And there are many more in the court with a like suspicion of him.'

'Why should Omichand work upon our sepoys?'

'With that man, I fear anything is possible. But I have a worse fear that he was not the prime party in this. It is a pity Harry could not get to the truth of it.' Watts asked me then if I had noticed any disturbance in Cossimbazaar since the departure of the French, to which I answered that I had not. 'You feel yourself safe there?' he said.

'My only concern is with the many obstacles put in our way over the treaty. As to our safety, I have hardly thought on it.'

'You must think on it now. And if you request a return to Calcutta, I shall grant it.'

'I am content to stay here, sir.'

He faced me. 'It may be I shall not make this offer again. There are matters now proceeding that I cannot open to you, matters of conse-quence. How they proceed is not a question amenable to the rules of sextant and compass. Should there be a wreck, it will be chance decides the fate of the survivors – if there be any such remaining.'

'I am content, sir.'

His eye held me a moment more and then he inclined his head in acceptance of my decision. It was gentlemanly done and I saw that he now might treat me as a man, not a boy. And that is perhaps the reason why he felt at liberty to be so blunt with me as we walked back to the palanquins.

'When you return to the factory, do not ask Harry to offer up Bhaskar to you.'

'The man cannot be held for ever.'

'The fellow is most surely dead. He was condemned the minute that you left him.'

During the following few days in Cossimbazaar I did not see Harry and was glad of it, for immediately upon my return there from Murshid-abad I learned of the unfortunate drowning of Bhaskar, and there was news given to me also of one of our sepoys gone suddenly to Benares. Bhaskar's drowned body had been burned already upon a pyre and the Brahmins, who had performed the ceremony, soon came to get their payment from me at the factory. I gave them their rupees, took from them the bill Harry had written for them, asked them no questions and turned them out.

There was a girl from the black town well known to me. I sent for her and she came to me at my bungalow. She remained with me two days and gave my mind some peace, after which I returned her to her people.

After the drowning of that sepoy, Omichand kept away from the factory. But there was an increased watchfulness over us by the Moors, for now our boats, sent upriver from the squadron, were all stopped by the nawab's troops at some distance below us, and searched very thoroughly, so that no more powder or weaponry could be got through. And, though there were no violent alarms, there was an atmosphere of apprehension grew both among our soldiers in the factory and among the natives of the black town, for a number of the nawab's troops were frequently to be seen about Cossimbazaar, just as in those days before the nawab had first seized our factory and ignited the powder beneath Bengal.

It happened that I was with Hastings when the incident occurred, which flared up from nothing and might have defeated us all, but ended instead in a revelation. Hastings was not at fault in it. We were in the factory yard and I was about to accompany him down to the river to see him away (he had come up from Calcutta, and was returning now to Clive's army near Chandernagore) when there appeared at our gates some twenty of the nawab's cavalry. Their chief officer dismounted and it was at once apparent that he expected admittance.

Hastings said to me, 'Where is Scrafton?' and I told him that Scrafton had taken the hounds and gone out to hunt with Omichand on the plain. We watched the nawab's officer with some uncertainty. It was in both our minds, I believe, that neither one of us had a true authority over the factory, but Hastings was, by a few years, my senior, and my senior also in rank in the company. (And, as was proved in after years, he was not one to shirk the burdens of responsibility.) 'Whatever passes,' said he, 'we shall not surrender the factory to them.'

As we walked across to the gate, our soldiers, who had seen the Moors' arrival, made busy to arm themselves. But at our stepping out to parley with the Moor, we found no threat offered but only a letter, which Hastings broke open and read.

'It is from Mr Watts,' he told me. 'He requires that we shall open the factory to these gentlemen that they may make certain we have here only the thirty soldiers we claim. There is a report received in Murshidabad that we harbour some three or four hundred.' He raised a brow to me, for the report of such a number was manifestly absurd. He gave me the letter and instructed our guards to open the gates. He then ordered our soldiers to present themselves in the yard.

It was a rum business, to be sure, and I think the Moorish officer felt himself rather foolish as he walked down the line of our soldiers and sepoys, counting them. Once this was done, we opened the doors of our warehouses to him and I was much relieved when he made no question of the bales of cotton, for it was beneath these we had hid most of our powder. I think he understood very quickly that the report of our numbers was a lie, and yet he was as little his own master as any soldier under orders, and so we must needs open to him the smaller buildings and also the bungalows.

We had gone with him into Scrafton's bungalow and Hastings was briefly opening the doors to show the fellow each empty room, when I heard some disturbance outside. I turned and, with no good feeling, saw a hound leap onto the verandah.

'Mr Hastings,' I called over my shoulder, but it was too late. Scrafton was halfway across the yard by the time I stepped out his door.

'What the devil – what are you playing at, Douglas? Who opened the gates? I'll whip the man who opened them.' He turned to deliver a broadside at our soldiers and sepoys. He commanded them to drive the Moorish cavalrymen from the yard. Our men seemed almost as surprised as the Moors at this irruption among them and I was alarmed to see them move to obey.

'Hold!' I cried. 'Sir, it is done under Mr Watts's authority.' As I struggled to get the letter from my pocket, Hastings led the Moorish officer from the bungalow.

'The gates were opened at my order,' said Hastings.

'It is an outrage. You are in my house. Get that blackamoor down from there.'

Hastings now glanced across the yard and saw the dangerous

mischief Scrafton had made; for some of the cavalrymen had now unsheathed their swords and, though our soldiers had stopped at my cry, many of their muskets were already raised.

'Lower your weapons,' Hastings called to them and they responded at once. They well knew that Clive's army was too far off to save us should there be an over-hasty shedding of Moorish blood. The Moorish officer, who was no fool, called a command to his men and they turned and moved toward the gates.

'These people have no business here, Mr Hastings. What the devil are you about?'

Hastings took Watts's letter from me and presented it to Scrafton. While Scrafton read it, the Moors filed out of the gates.

'I did not feel that I could disobey such an order from a member of the council,' remarked Hastings. 'If I have done wrong, I am content to place myself in the hands of Mr Watts.'

'You have no business in my house.'

'You have read the order.'

'Yes, I see very well you have found a wall behind which to hide yourself, Mr Hastings. It may be you shall find that wall to be less solid than you think.'

'I am now for Calcutta, sir.'

'No one here shall detain you. Douglas, see this fellow from the factory.'

'And so they parted?' said Watts.

'Hastings left immediately. I came away as soon as I might.'

Watts touched a finger to his forehead in thought. 'I believe that I have made an error. I have sent down a note to the colonel that I must retrieve. You have ridden here, Alistair?'

'Yes.'

He snatched a paper to his blotter, wrote a quick note, affixed the company seal to it and gave it to me. 'Ride after the *cossid*. He has gone by way of Cossimbazaar. Get my letter from him and bring it back to me.'

I rode to Cossimbazaaar, but at the factory I learned that the *cossid* had already come and gone, taking the way south toward Plassey, and so I turned south to find him. By good fortune, he had been stopped by one of the nawab's *chowkays* at the edge of Cossimbazaar and I gave him Watts's note (which was in Persian) and pointed to his saddlebag and said, 'Colonel Clive.' He made no difficulty of it but offered up to me two letters bundled together with string and then I left him and returned to Murshidabad.

But upon my putting the bundle before him on his table, Watts said, 'What is this other?'

'I assumed they were both yours, sir.'

He cut the string with his letter-knife. 'This is mine – for which, Alistair, many thanks. And this—?' He turned the second letter over. 'This is also addressed to the colonel. But not by me.'

'That is Scrafton's hand,' said I, and then I understood what had happened. 'The *cossid* has given me everything he was carrying to Clive. He has picked up that letter from Scrafton at the factory.' Watts looked from me to the letter, his face darkening. I put out my hand. 'I will return it to Scrafton and explain, sir. The mistake was more mine than the *cossid*'s.'

'The mistake was Mr Scrafton's. He was to notify me of any communication he intended with the colonel or the council. I had his word upon it.' He turned the sealed letter through his hands then put it down by the knife and studied them both. I saw then what was in his mind.

'Shall I go, sir?'

'Stay.' He picked up the letter and the knife. 'This will be no better for being done alone and in secrecy.' He broke the seal and opened Scrafton's letter. 'Reach down that book of Dryden's from off the top shelf behind you.' He spoke quietly now, and glanced toward the closed door before he opened the book that I had fetched down for him. Beside the opened book he placed Scrafton's letter, and beside that an empty sheet of paper. He dipped his quill and then called me around the table to stand by him. 'You are aware that important communications of the company are enciphered.'

'I have heard of it.'

'Well now you see it,' said he, and commenced letter by letter to write upon the blank sheet. Scrafton, I saw now, had written not words but only numbers in his letter. And in the inner margin of the Dryden was a list of the letters of the alphabet, each one coupled with a number. 'You see the key?'

'Yes sir.'

'It is upon page one hundred. You will take care to remember that.'

We were silent then for twenty minutes while he decoded Scrafton's letter. When he was done, he returned the quill to the inkpot, read the transcription over, and then turned in his chair and gazed out the window, very thoughtful. I feared, almost, to look at him, for the transcription contained such remarks upon him as no man could read without feeling.

My dearest Sir,

The nawab has sent his soldiers to the factory to inspect our strength. Omichand tells me the nawab has now a suspicion of me. Mr Watts remains at the court locked in an interminable and useless parley. He is a man too timid for such an affair as this. Only let the council pass the charge of it to me and you will see then what may be done with boldness and a steady resolution.

Nothing is more certain than that this delay is a danger to the whole enterprise. A sharp attack upon the palace is all that will now answer to the regrettable situation we are placed in by the indecision of Mr Watts. If you will send to me a hundred good men, I will answer for our capture of the nawab. Omichand clears the way with the court. The Seths will be with us if only we act with more definite purpose.

Hesitation is now our greatest enemy. If Watts be withdrawn it shall be one obstacle the less.

Let me know your will in this.

My compliments to Mr Walsh and any number of the council who may be with you.

Your servant,
Scrafton.

'Put away the Dryden,' Watts said at last.

I re-shelved the book while he continued to gaze out the window.

'Shall I destroy these?' I indicated the letter and his decipherment.

'Let them be. I shall take them with me now to Cossimbazaar.' He was very calm. 'Mr Scrafton will be leaving us. I will send him down to Calcutta. If you wish, you may go with him.'

'I have no such wish. It is a disgusting and false slur he makes upon you.'

'At least we know now what lay behind the treachery of Harry's second. Scrafton would surely have used our sepoys to attack the nawab in his palace.'

'It would be madness.'

'This morning the nawab threatened to have my head cut off and set upon a spike. I had wondered at the reason for his intemperance.'

'He would not do it,' said I in startlement.

'He would do it, and in an instant, were it not for the near presence of the admiral and the colonel. But that is by the bye.' He faced me. 'If you stay now you must come to live with me here. Scrafton is right in this, that delay is now a danger to us. There is much yet to be done and I will need a second for the work, whom I may trust.'

'Of course.'

'There is no "of course" in the matter. Nor will you bind yourself without I first undeceive you.' We looked, each of us, one upon the other. I confess I felt a deep disquiet at the directness of his gaze. 'Call the syce. You shall hear this as we ride down to see Mr Scrafton.'

What took place at the meeting between Watts and Scrafton I cannot say, for, in riding from Murshidabad, Watts told me that which caused such a tumult in me that I could not be still and wait for him peaceably at the factory, but must remove myself down to the river and think on all that he had said. To be plain, he had opened himself to me on the company's absolute intent to now overthrow the nawab and raise another in his place.

'And I have been chosen as the company's prime agent in the affair,' he had said. 'And if you would prefer to leave me now and go down to Calcutta, there will be no blame in it.'

How such a momentous decision had been reached, and when, he did not tell me, but he was very clear that the authority of the council in Madras was over the whole business and that the admiral and the colonel both knew of it, as well as others of the Calcutta Council. There was even a secret committee formed to assist in carrying the affair forward. Scrafton, coming into knowledge of the general plan, had evidently made a bid to inveigle himself into it, embroiling himself first with Omichand and then attempting to subvert our sepoys from under Watts's command. Watts had given it to me as his opinion that Scrafton had seen an opportunity to emulate the rise to fame of the colonel. A dangerous emulation, Watts had said, for Clive had been lucky in his famous victory at Arcot, as well as bold, and luck was too fickle a mistress to rely upon in the making of such a revolution as the company now intended.

There was no Moorish noble yet settled upon to be the nawab's replacement, but it was a question in which the bankers Seth must have a hand.

Now I walked along the ghat, north, then south and north again, turning through my mind everything Watts had told me. To overthrow the nawab was a conception so vast and of such great consequence that it was impossible for me to at once take in its full meaning. It was as though the company should become another Cromwell and throw down a king, but the king of a people in which the company had no part. But, as Watts had also said, had not the Moors done the same when they first came into the country? And what would then be changed in Bengal? And what continue impervious to change? And should the revolution succeed, where must true power then lie – in the court of the new nawab, or in the company? To decide one question was to open another and yet another which itself must reopen the first, so that there was no end to the chain of consequences that crowded upon my mind as I walked by the river.

As to any peril I might share in, as the aide of Mr Watts, I make no boast when I say that I did not regard it. I knew that I could not leave him, in spite of the danger, for, did I leave him and he fall in this dangerous enterprise, it must be a blot of dishonour to me through my whole life.

By the time of my return to the factory, the interview between Scrafton and Watts was long ended and there was a palanquin and the bearers already waiting in the yard. As I came in at the gates, Scrafton and Watts came out from the bungalow and there was no word spoken between them. Scrafton settled his wig and put on his hat and came down into the yard with a deliberate and unhurried step. He looked as haughty as if he had been descending the stairs of his club in St James's. The soldiers watched the scene with some curiosity from the shade by their quarters.

'You have some hours till sunset, Mr Scrafton,' called Watts. 'You will be sure to make a good use of them.'

Scrafton's foot paused upon the step of the palanquin and his whole body stiffened as though he might suddenly turn and fly at Watts's throat, but he got in and pulled the shutters closed. The palanquin went first, followed by six sepoys and a number of servants, and then a cart loaded with Scrafton's trunk and the camp-goods he must need for the journey.

Last of all, and with two Hindoo cattlemen, came a line of bullocks, which I had bought at the Cossimbazaar markets in the preceding weeks at Watts's order, but without knowing their purpose. This was another thing Watts had now revealed to me – they were draft beasts to pull Clive's field guns should he need to march north to meet the nawab's army.

CHAPTER FORTY-ONE

'*I*f I am poisoned or killed, you must flee Murshidabad. Give the order at the Cossimbazaar factory for all our men to leave and you must go with them to join the colonel.' I made no answer to Watts, but only listened, for this was but the crowning instruction of the many he had given me as we rode back to Murshidabad after the departure of Scrafton. Watts was at pains to warn me against all the servants in his house, and many others besides, adding now, 'You must assume that you are watched at all times. And not only watched, but heard. There is no safety but in our own discretion. Remember it.'

I asked what my relations should be with Omichand.

'Guarded,' he replied. 'No – much more than guarded. Disclose nothing of your mind to him. He will take it ill that I have sent Scrafton away.' And upon my wondering if it were, perhaps, not better Omichand had been sent away also, Watts said, 'There is no reason I should withhold this from you now – there is one of the Moorish nobles put forward by Omichand to replace the nawab. The man is Latif Khan. Omichand is the means by which I have some communication with him. I see you do not like to hear it.'

'You know my thoughts on Omichand, sir.'

'Aye. But till now he and Latif Khan have been the only material I have had to hand. I could wish it otherwise. Indeed, I shall now renew my endeavours to make it otherwise. And I trust that you will help me in that.'

We soon came to the outskirts of Murshidabad and thereafter rode on in silence.

When he came to call upon us the next day Omichand was very quick to heap abuse and scorn upon Scrafton's name and made a ridiculous pretence that he had been unaware, till he came to us, of Scrafton's departure from Cossimbazaar. By such signs it was clear just how much it displeased him to have Scrafton gone. Watts did not trouble to question him upon any involvement he had with Scrafton's wild scheme of an assault upon the palace and they retired to the inner-courtyard garden for some while to speak together in private. After Omichand was gone, Watts withdrew to his study. When he called me to him there in the evening, he had a letter prepared. He did not tell me its nature, but put it into my hand and gave me an instruction as to the particulars of its delivery.

'You will be followed by one of those beggars who are always out there in the street. Pass the letter only if you are sure no one may see it done.'

'I will lose him first.'

'You will not lose him, Alistair, though you attempt it from now till the morning. And any such vain attempt would only serve to excite a suspicion of you. Do as I have said and behave as you are wont to behave.'

'But till now I have avoided the temple girls here.'

'You must now make an exception. Have you money?'

I showed him what I had. He put a few more coins in my purse, telling me to give those, with the letter, to the one-eyed Brahmin priest I should find in the Vijaya temple. And he gave me also the words I must say.

As Watts had foreseen, I was followed, but I took care not to look about me or give any sign that I knew it. I kept to the main streets where the lamps and torches were all lit and the stallholders crying up their wares. I came, after several minutes, to the Vijaya temple, which was a place very sacred to the Hindoos of the city. In the street outside were many stalls selling garlands of flowers, vessels filled with milk and many Hindoos colourfully dressed, the women wearing golden bangles and suchlike jewellery, bringing their own offerings. When I had climbed the steps to the broad platform by the main doorway, I turned as though to inspect the view. There were at least three fellows in the street standing apart from the others and dressed like fakirs, any one of whom might have been my shadow. I turned again and went in.

Inside was a pillared hall, with such carvings of dancing Hindoo gods and goddesses upon the stone pillars as seemed almost alive in the flickering torchlight. The burning torches were set mainly around the *lingam* (which is a smoothed and upright stone). A Brahmin priest, stripped to the waist and with a crimson thread draped like a sash over his shoulder, stood by the *lingam*. He took from the devotees who came to him those flowers they had bought, which he put onto the altar, and the vessels of milk, which he poured onto the *lingam* so that its surface shimmered like black silk in the torchlight. The smells of crushed flowers and burning incense were very thick upon the air and the babbling of excited voices very raucous, and over all played cymbals and flute and drums from a dark alcove behind, so that to stand in the midst of it was to get some rare quickening of the senses.

I was ignored by the devotees, but a Brahmin soon came to me and well knowing what I did there (for the Vijaya temple was a byword among the young men of the European factories), he took me from the pillared hall into a side chamber. There were a number of girls seated upon the floor, with a great pile of flowers near to them. The girls worked deftly with their hands, making those same garlands I had seen being sold in the street outside, and though they continued to work and talk together I saw that there was some novelty in my presence, for they must have seen very few Europeans since the French departure. I felt myself under a critical, if glancing, inspection. The Brahmin called three of them to me, I chose one, and she took a torch from the wall and led me further into the temple. And here, as Watts had told me to expect, was the one-eyed Brahmin.

He sat upon the step of a small altar and the girl directed me to him and went herself into a room close by. The fellow extended his bowl to receive my offering to the temple. When I had dropped a few coins into the bowl, he put it aside, and then I said to him, '*Golaub que foul.*' He turned his good eye upon me and repeated the words back to me. I looked along the passage to make sure that we were alone and then I took the letter from my jacket and gave it him and also those coins from Mr Watts. With a deft movement, he folded both letter and coins into the folds of the material about his waist. But when I turned to leave, he clicked his tongue in sharp warning. He shook his head severely and made me to understand that I must go into the room with the girl. I did not know if the reason of it was some superstition of the religion, or a fear in him that I might bring a suspicion upon us both by leaving her so quickly. But he was very decided in the matter. And the girl was comely.

When I came out from her room the next hour, the Brahmin neither rose from his step nor clicked his tongue, but, in peaceful indifference, let me pass.

All through the following days Watts busied himself about Murshidabad, going from the nawab's court to call upon Omichand, from Omichand to call upon the bankers Seth. And at our house there was an almost daily arrival of letters delivered by both the *cossids* and our own company people, who still came and went (though in numbers very small) between Cossimbazaar and the towns downriver. Also there came letters from Mrs Watts, which Mr Watts at first deciphered himself. But once the press of his business became too heavy, these letters too he delegated to my care. There is no question but that these from Mrs Watts gave us the best report of the situation to the south of us. In the quiet of the evening, and when I was not on some excursion about the town on his behalf, Watts would sometimes have me read to him from the deciphered letters while he worked his quill at his desk. And it was by one such letter I learned that Mrs Watts was fully apprised of – and indeed played her supporting part in – what was afoot against the nawab.

My Dearest Husband,

There is no reinforcement to be expected from either Fort St George or Bombay, but all who might be spared here are gone upriver to join Colonel Clive.

Since your departure there has been much talk of the French general, Bussy, and of the soldiers he keeps in Orissa. I have been at pains to discover what truth there is in such talk, but that is no easy matter. The nawab's soldiers have struck a mortal fear into the hearts of the villagers near to Calcutta, and I am finding our usual helpers somewhat reticent in their assistance to me. Isaacson is much recovered and offers to make a journey to Orissa. I have refused him. Such a journey would undo all the good of his convalescence whilst profiting us little by way of timely information. By my best estimation Bussy has no intent upon Calcutta. Nor have our people in Chinsurah and Chandernagore made any report that the French parolees there look to Bussy's arrival. As to what Bussy may intend to the northward, you must have better information than I.

Governor Drake is more than settled now in his authority since the departure for London of Mr Holwell. Indeed, the very sight of Holwell has been more irksome to the Governor than any of us knew. Whatever the Governor's misgivings concerning Holwell's report to the directors in London, they are as nothing against his evident relief to have the man gone from Calcutta; and our Governor now makes no scruple to refuse any invitation he does not care for, and scorns to have the good opinion of the senior traders who he now believes can do him no harm. We shall see what comes of it.

Omichand's jamindar is returned here. He lives openly in Omichand's house and carries on Omichand's business, while the Council leaves him free and unmolested. I have it from Mrs Drake that the fellow is left in peace at Admiral Watson's order, and that so long as Omichand is useful to your enterprise the wretched jamindar will keep his liberty. I have taken one of his servants into our pay as some small surety against any malicious connivance the fellow may intend.

The rebuilding of the Settlement continues, though trade is by no means restored, and European, Hindoo and Armenian now look toward Murshidabad with some trepidation. For myself, a deep trust in my husband is matched with an equally deep fear for him, and I must block my ears to the many street tales of the violence now practised by the nawab at the court. I have promised the children you will be safely returned to us soon. You will not make a liar of me, William.

Tomorrow a boat sails for Fort St George. Its captain has in his keeping that letter to Governor Pigot which you bade me relay.

I conclude with a firm hope in the successful end of the great enterprise, and with a womanly trust that we will not be parted for so very much longer. Be assured that you are ever in the heart of your loving wife,

Frances

The strain that Watts was under through all his secret dealings at the court was very apparent to me, and the personal parts of these communications from his wife he held dearly, as being a remembrance of why he laboured and a promise of the life he might again live once he had piloted the 'great enterprise' to its end. She would often ask, in these letters, that both she and her children be remembered to me, which was a kindness very touching.

The company letters, however, were our more familiar daily business. For at the arrival of every packet, I would retreat with Mr Watts to his study and there decipher the words of Colonel Clive, Admiral Watson or the council in Calcutta (and sometimes all three from a single packet), for they were in a fever at this time to be always connected with us and informed of how matters proceeded. Watts answered those letters in a manner most instructive to me – for almost none of them did he answer immediately, but only after some days, and then with a complete disregard to any question in them but the main which touched upon the revolution. This I knew, for I enciphered the letters immediately he had writ them. It was while we applied ourselves to this work, at his desk one morning, that I looked up from the Dryden and found Watts not writing, but watching me.

'Sir?'

'It is a tedious labour, is it not?'

I answered that it was necessary and therefore no labour at all.

'I meant that after all your military adventures, it must seem very dull.'

'I do not find it so.'

'You need not humour me, Alistair. There are those born for a life in the field.' He gestured to the letter from Clive which lay before him. 'And there are those, like myself, who are not.'

'The matter in the letters is not dull. I had never thought to see such things. It is more than interesting to me.'

'Indeed. But it is very far from the flash and thunder of the guns.'

'It is.'

'And you do not mind that? When you returned from Madras – when we were at Fulta – the colonel made mention of some application you had made to him.'

'It was refused. I think no more on it.'

'When a thing is wanted, a man will not baulk at a first refusal. You will make a second application.'

He continued to look at me as if expecting a more definite answer, and so I said that which surprised me. 'Perhaps.'

He nodded to himself, and with no more said between us we continued our work.

Mr Watts having no need of me one afternoon, I had taken my sketch-book to the royal burial ground near to the palace, for the Moors have a considerable skill in architecture and the mausoleums they build for their great people are often very fine and picturesque. It was a welcome refreshment to my spirits to spend an hour or two sketching details of the arches and domes of these buildings, and welcome also to be solitary awhile, as such a thing had been scarcely possible since my coming to stay in the city. We were watched always by the nawab's spies. And though I knew myself watched while in the burial ground, the thought gave me no concern, for the fellow kept himself by the gate and away from me while I busied myself at the study of the Moorish arches and quoins.

And it was because of my absorption that I did not see the young lad till I stepped fully inside one small pavilion and found him there. He seemed almost to expect me, though I know not how, unless it be that he had watched me and come deliberately in at the other side. I took him for a beggar at first, but then he held out to me a folded note. 'What is this?' said I, with an immediate suspicion and, I confess, with some annoyance at this disturbance to my recreation. He made no answer to me. And now that I looked at him more closely, I found his face somewhat familiar. 'What is it that you want?' He raised his hand and touched his ear and then his lips. It was only then that I recognized him for one of the deaf mutes that the Seths kept about them. 'Is it for Mr Watts?' His eyes implored me to take the note. When I did so, he retreated into an alcove of the pavilion and watched me.

He remained hidden there while I departed with the note and my sketchbook and drew off my shadow from the burial ground.

'It is the best day's work that you have done,' said Watts to me, putting the note to the candle-flame and telling me of the next day's appointment to which the mute lad's note had summoned us at an *aurang* outside the city.

The *aurang* (which is a weaver's manufactory) was in a village but a few miles to the east of the city, and was familiar to me from a visit I had once made there on company business with Edward. But now I found myself required by Mr Watts to make a diversionary inspection of the weavers employed there, while he took himself into the overseers' house to meet in private conference with Jagath Seth.

It was more than an hour they were together, during which time the head weaver plied me with chai and sweetmeats till I could swallow no more, and then I must ask him to conduct me about the three long narrow buildings that made up the manufactory. Since I had last been inside there, the decline in the place was shocking to see. There were not now a tenth of the weavers there had been on the looms, and those that remained had a doleful and hungry air about them. They looked up at me from their mats behind the looms in a manner altogether pitiable. Upon emerging into the sunlight from the last dismal building, I enquired of the head weaver if there had been some terrible sickness in the place.

'No sick,' he said emphatically and he raised his hands as if aiming a musket. 'Fighting.' He took me to the warehouse and waved his arm in disgust and despair at the enormous quantity of cloth he had stored there. 'No French. No British. No rupees.'

It was the war had done it. And yet the old fellow made no complaint against us, or even against the Moors. It was a calamity to his village and I am sure to every village in Bengal that relied upon an *aurang* for its sustenance, but whatever complaint the Hindoos made of it, they did so privately, whether from fear of some retribution or because bidden to it by some stricture of their religion, I know not. But certainly when the old man led me back to his house, he paused on his way, by a small shrine at the roadside, and dipped his finger into the oil of an unlit lamp there and touched his finger to his forehead and to the forehead of the many-armed idol in the shrine.

'We may have found our new nawab,' Watts told me. He had sent the palanquins ahead of us to the far side of the grove and now we walked slowly after them, enjoying the only privacy we should have before we came into the city.

'Not Latif Khan?' said I.

'A much greater one. It is Mir Jafir, the nawab's first general and paymaster to the Moorish army. He has opened himself to the Seths. I have now agreed with Jagath Seth that he should act between us and Mir Jafir.'

'What does Omichand know of it?'

'Nothing. They have not told him. There has been some trouble between the Seths and Omichand – I would suppose it is money. But even if the Seths would bring him into the intrigue, it seems that Mir Jafir will not. He makes it a condition of his allegiance with us that Omichand have no share in the spoils of the overthrow. I cannot say that I blame Mir Jafir's distrust.'

'He is the wisest Moor I have heard of till now.'

Watts put a hand on my shoulder as we walked. 'You must continue to be a support to me, Alistair. We are now embarked upon the flood-tide and for us there is no turning back.'

Letters were written that same day to the colonel, the admiral and the council, and to each Mr Watts wrote the same advice – that the company should make a private agreement with Mir Jafir, declaring that in return for the company's support in the nawab's overthrow, Mir Jafir would undertake to fulfil all the terms of the nawab's treaty with us and make certain payments to us from the royal treasury.

Further, Watts told them of the difficulties now caused by Omichand's entanglement in our affairs, for Omichand now expected some recompense for his involvement with us, which was a thing directly contrary to the wishes of Mir Jafir and the Seths. Watts proposed no solution to the dilemma, but laid it out very clearly. Above all Watts urged the urgency of immediate action, for Mir Jafir's intended treachery against the nawab could not be long hid, the court being already a hive of agitation and rumour.

I took these letters to Cossimbazaar and gave them to Harry, who in the same hour departed downriver.

And now, in Murshidabad, we must wait – with what a trial to our nerves may be imagined, for there was no open communication to be had with Mir Jafir, who kept to his mansion on the far side of the nawab's palace to us. We went sometimes to the nawab's court and sometimes to the Seths' palace, continuing as though we expected the nawab's good faith and the proper fulfilment of the treaty, though knowing that a hidden sword hung over us now by the merest thread. For if the planned treachery be now discovered, and our role in it, there is no doubt but that our severed heads must be put on spikes to decorate the nawab's palace gates.

Such was the state of affairs, then, and Watts in further anxiety, not having had any reply to his letters though we had waited a week and more, when there returned to Murshidabad two gentlemen we had least expected to see there. They were French and none other than Sinfray and Cordet. It was Watts who saw them, as he told me immediately upon his return from the palace.

'They were in the nawab's garden, strolling about there as if they had never been away. They told me Monsieur Law remains with the rest of his party near Patna. It is likely the truth. I made sure to confirm it from some others at the court. Their return here could not be worse timed.'

'They would not be here if the nawab had not called them.'

'He has called them sure enough. But he knows better than to call all of the Frenchmen back and, if he did call, Law knows better than to come. He would not give Colonel Clive any fair reason to march north.'

'Two men cannot impede us.'

'I had rather we had received some answer by now to our letters. You will take a message to the Vijaya Temple for me. Whatever it is that Sinfray and Cordet do here, we must be certain they are watched.'

In that moment there was some noise outside the door. Upon Mr Watts's cry, a servant came in to announce the arrival of Omichand. Watts told the servant to bring him.

'He has come to tell me of the returned Frenchmen,' Watts said to me as he slumped into his chair. These visits from Omichand were a more than daily occurrence and they were becoming a severe trial on Watts's patience and nerves. 'He will have some deep and nefarious scheme to divulge to me. I pray I have the strength to hear him without boxing his ears.'

'I could tell him that you are indisposed.'

'No, let him come. It is to meet such slings and arrows I am here. And it is not much longer now we shall have to endure him.'

CHAPTER FORTY-TWO

*T*he rains were approaching and none was immune from the growing humidity and heat, neither Moor nor Hindoo nor European, but everyone in the city now worked and moved only in the morning and from the late afternoon. Throughout the mid-part of the day they kept indoors or in some place well shaded. Because none ventured willingly into the street I first noticed the single palanquin while it was still at some distance from where I sat reading upon the verandah. Though I continued to read, its ever-nearing approach drew my eye till finally I set aside the book and looked more closely at it and its mounted escort. Then I rose and went quickly inside.

'Mr Watts. It is Harry come back.'

We returned to the verandah in time to see the palanquin and Harry and his *sowdars* come to a halt before the house.

'You have kept us waiting longer than you ought,' said I cheerfully. But beside me Watts made a sound as though he had been struck. For the door of the palanquin had now opened and out came first the fine shoes and breeches and then all the rest of the person we had thought ourselves rid of. With a sharp word to the chief bearer and none at all to Harry, the fellow came up the steps.

'Good day, Mr Scrafton,' said Watts, recovering himself. 'You are an unexpected visitor to us.'

'You need not fear I shall trouble you long, Mr Watts,' the other replied. 'Once you have the letters I have brought for you I must call upon the nawab and then I am gone.' Scrafton wiped a kerchief about his perspiring neck and awaiting no invitation brushed past me and into the cooler air of the house. I looked at Mr Watts, and he at me, and then we followed Scrafton inside.

Scrafton had brought a letter from the council and a letter from the colonel, and also some further pages, though these were not enciphered but written in plain English. Watts left me with all these in his study, with an instruction to decipher the letters while he retired with Scrafton to the courtyard garden to discover what was the situation downriver. I noticed he was careful not to tell Scrafton what I did.

By this time I had used the Dryden code so often that much of the key had become fixed in my memory, so I was now able to do the work at twice the speed of Mr Watts. It was not an hour later before I had deciphered the letters, and now I sat at the desk with the proposed treaties (for there were two of them) in my hands, and read them again in the light of what I had learned from the letters. I can only describe the quite singular feeling I had then as one of thrilled disgust.

For what Mr Watts had most strongly advised had now been accepted – the company was to make common cause with Mir Jafir and Clive's force was to march against the nawab's army. But to square the circle of the deep and now general distrust of Omichand and the simultaneous need to secure Omichand from divulging our plan and imperilling all, Clive had hit upon the expedient of a double treaty. The first, and false, treaty, written upon a red paper, was to be shown to Omichand. This granted Omichand a liberal reward for his part in assisting the revolution. The second and genuine treaty, upon a white paper, was identical to the first as to its terms between the company and Mir Jafir, but in this genuine treaty there was no provision made for Omichand whatever. Both treaties appeared to have been signed by

Colonel Clive, Admiral Watson and every member of the select committee of the council.

It was the most blatant and barefaced breach of honour, and as low as any foul practice I had ever heard of. Were a band of men (I might as easily say a gang) to attempt any such trick in London, they would certainly find themselves bound directly for Newgate Prison, perhaps even for Tyburn. I could scarce believe that a British colonel, admiral or governor had stooped to such repulsive audacity. And yet the signatures were all clearly legible and Clive's done with a bold and downright flourish. (I must add here, though I did not know it at the time, that Admiral Watson's signature was a forgery, made by one of the naval officers at Clive's order.)

When Watts came in he was alone, for Scrafton had gone to bathe and refresh himself before his attendance upon the nawab.

'There is another letter he brings to the nawab from the colonel,' Watts told me. 'It is a piece of foolery, instructing the nawab how his friendship with us now preserves him from the threat of an incursion by the Marathas. My own opinion would be that Mr Scrafton uses it as an instrument to keep himself embroiled in the greater affair.' He picked up the deciphered letter from Clive and commenced to read.

His expression changed as he understood the deception to be practised on Omichand. I said, 'They do not seem to understand that it is impossible for you to now meet openly with the other party.' (By which I meant Mir Jafir – it being a firm instruction from Watts that I should never refer to Mir Jafir by name.)

'It is to overcome such difficulties that we are here, Alistair, else the whole business might be conducted at one remove, and by letter.' He studied the treaties a moment more. 'This may answer. It is an abominable practice, but it is of a piece with the fellow and our situation.'

'We could wish for a more honourable solution.'

'When you have thought of one you will no doubt tell me of it. Until then we must set one duplicity against another. I have told you before that in a corrupt court the worst man has the best chance. But if it be of any consolation to your conscience, I would baulk myself at this, except that I am responsible for the consequences of any such hesitation. By which I mean to say I had rather the dreadful fellow be tricked by an odious ruse than that your head and mine should be skewered upon spikes.'

'I believe, sir, that I can in this instance quiet my conscience.'

'Burn the letters,' said he and inked his quill and signed both the treaties.

The great need was now to find some means of meeting with Mir Jafir so that we might witness his signature to the treaty. This meeting we knew would be no easy matter, but the next morning we learned from Jagath Seth that it was, for the moment, impossible. For Mir Jafir, either by his own inclination or at the nawab's order, had removed himself from Murshidabad and joined his troops in the field. The greater part of the nawab's army was now encamped at this time near the town of Plassey, two days' march downriver from Murshidabad. It was not here that Mir Jafir had gone, but to another encampment of several thousand of the nawab's soldiers nearer Murshidabad, for these troops were beneath Mir Jafir's direct command, and loyal to him. From this circumstance, and from other court rumours we heard from Jagath Seth, Watts concluded that Mir Jafir had some good reason to now look to his own safety. Though no breach between the nawab and his first general Mir Jafir had been publicly declared, yet there had been some sudden suspicion raised, and Watts was not long in deciding the cause of it.

'Omichand must go. And Scrafton with him,' said he, as we crossed to our palanquins in Jagath Seth's courtyard. His voice was quiet, but there was a real anger in it. And as he got into his palanquin he instructed me to fetch Omichand to our house.

Omichand's residence in the city being in the nearby merchant's quarter, I was soon alighting from my palanquin in his garden. As I went up to his door, I straightened my jacket and rehearsed in my mind the severe and brusque manner I should adopt with him. I own, I was pleased of the opportunity. But when the door opened Cordet and Sinfray came out from the house. I was so astonished that I stopped in my tracks. Sinfray, though much surprised to find me before him, simply nodded curtly and went by me to where a syce was now bringing two horses from the stable. Cordet, however, stopped. Looking toward the horses, he said to me, 'Your man Omichand is a rotten devil.'

'Why have you returned?'

'We were invited.'

'You know that Monsieur Law would return now at his own peril,' said I, and when Cordet faced me sharply I went on, 'It is not to threaten him. I have as high a regard for him as any. But he should know that he must not return here.'

'I can as little ask that of Monsieur Law as you can command it, Monsieur Douglas. If you would turn back an army, then you must speak with your own Colonel Clive.' I started toward Omichand's door, but then Cordet said, 'I have had a letter from my cousin Antoinette,' and I stopped. There was that in his voice I had not expected. 'I cannot believe that your colonel would think to hang Monsieur Le Baume.'

'A court-martial may do what it pleases. Treachery in an officer is not likely to be easily forgiven, as well you know.'

'But have you hanged Le Baume then?' said Cordet, with such a tone and look as if he had heard that I had killed his brother. The blood drained from his face.

'He is not hanged, though he was brought very near to it by your actions. The noose was almost around his neck. But no, he is not hanged.'

'My actions?'

'Those silver *siccas* that you were so careful to show all the naval officers – it became suspected that Le Baume retained a connection with you, which was your intention, was it not?'

'The *siccas* were an advance upon my pay, given me by Monsieur Rémy. It is no affair of yours, Le Baume's or any other man's.' I looked at him, but he was angered and not easily read. I still did not know the full truth of it, but, at the point of a sword, I would own, it seemed he did not lie. He dropped his own gaze as if to take hold of his own bewilderment. Then he looked up. 'But Le Baume is alive.'

'He is alive,' said I. The colour returned to Cordet's face now, which was certainly no pretence, and he made a small sign of the cross upon his chest. Then Sinfray called to him and Cordet nodded to me very formally.

'You will remember me to your cousin,' said I.

He made no answer but turned from me, and crossed to Sinfray and together they rode into the street.

Omichand treated me as he had ever treated me, with neither regard nor consideration, but when Watts greeted him at our house the wretch displayed a smiling unctuousness excessive even by the measure of an oriental court. Watts set me to sit with my sketchbook outside his study door, as a silent guard, while he consulted with Omichand inside, for it was the treaty with Mir Jafir they consulted on (or rather the false treaty on the red paper, with the imaginary payment to Omichand inserted). While I sketched the bowl and pitcher upon the table, the talk from inside the study was barely audible to me, so that I could distinguish the two voices but not the words.

My mind ran much over my exchange with Cordet. I cast back through all the small incidents I had so neatly stitched together to implicate Cordet in Le Baume's disgrace. And, I confess, I began to doubt of my own handiwork.

After some while Watts put his hand out the door. 'Mr Scrafton has just now arrived out in front. If you would go and fetch him to me here, Alistair, I would be obliged.'

I fetched Scrafton back to the study and then I sat and took up my sketchbook again. There were three voices now, but the words as indistinguishable as before. They were a further half-hour inside the study and all that while I sat wondering at what was passing between them and whether Omichand should be entrapped by the ruse and why Mr Watts had now brought Scrafton into the affair. Servants came several times into the room where I sat and each time I dismissed them, though without sharpness, so that their suspicions should receive no spur. Even so, I noticed the eyes of the old gardener frequently upon me now through the courtyard window.

When the three at last came out from the study it was plain from their inconsequential talk that their important business was concluded.

Omichand looked very pleased, Scrafton somewhat annoyed, and Watts, I thought, satisfied.

'If you need some further escort upon the road, I shall send Mr Douglas here to take some sepoys a short way with you,' said Watts to the both of them.

'That is unnecessary,' replied Scrafton. Watts then caught sight of a servant lurking in the next doorway and called for him to bring Madeira and glasses. 'That is also unnecessary,' said Scrafton beneath his breath and then, in a regular manner, 'If you will excuse us, we must be about our preparation.'

'But of course,' answered Watts. 'Mr Douglas will see you out.' Nodding to each of them in turn, he withdrew again to his study, where I soon after joined him. I found him lying prone upon the cushioned bench seat beneath the window, one foot planted on the floor and one arm draped loose across his forehead. He did not move when I entered.

'Sir, shall I have some water brought?'

'The only need I should have for water at this moment is to wash my soiled hands in it.'

'I take it Mr Scrafton and Omichand are to leave us.'

'Aye.' He sat up and looked out at the two palanquins now moving away. 'They are gone in two days. And when they are gone, you will go to Cossimbazaar and give the order for all our men there to go down-river to join the colonel. We are coming to the end, Alistair. There is one agreement more, and then we must look to ourselves.'

With Scrafton and Omichand gone from Murshidabad, I went to Cossimbazaar and gave them Watts's order to withdraw from the factory, take all their weapons and powder, and proceed downriver. The order, I may say, was very welcome to them, for they were not fifty men and the nawab's army of fifty thousand was in the field, and the rumours of an impending battle between us and the nawab growing every day.

At the nawab's court, Watts represented our withdrawal from Cossimbazaar as an act of our good faith in the nawab's intentions towards us and, remarkable though it may seem, this representation was accepted without contention by the Moors, for all the court's concern was of itself and the constant intriguing against one another now blinded each man to any interest but his own.

And at the centre of all this intrigue sat the nawab.

Jagath Seth reported to us that the nawab had grown unnaturally suspicious of his nobles at court and now spent the greater part of his time with the women of his harem and their eunuchs (these fellows were notorious for their scheming). The Brahmins who spied for Mr Watts within the palace made similar reports, but they went further and suggested that the nawab's mind had suffered some dangerous alteration. Watts was disinclined to give those wilder reports credence, till an alarming incident happened one night.

The hour was close to midnight and we asleep, when a great commotion from our servants called us from our beds. It was with difficulty we could calm the servants sufficient to learn that an escort of soldiers waited for us outside. We dressed and went out. The soldiers were not many, but they carried torches and their swords were drawn and, at that late hour, they made a very threatening sight. Watts spoke with their leader and discovered that we were summoned by the nawab.

'Must we go?' said I.

'It is not go or stay. It is walk or be dragged there by our very heels.'

The soldiers surrounded us and marched us to the palace gates, where a pair of eunuchs joined our escort. We then continued to the main door of the palace where the soldiers left us to the care of the eunuchs. Once inside, Watts protested vehemently to these fellows at our treatment. They ignored him, but seemed themselves in some fright at the whole strange proceedings.

We came at last to the outer room, beyond which lay the nawab's audience chamber. One of the eunuchs left us and went himself in there. After a minute he had not returned.

'If we must wait,' said Watts to the other cunuch, 'you will bring us chairs.'

But as Watts spoke there came a wild, unexpected and quite bloodcurdling cry from within the audience chamber. The hairs rose upon my neck. There came shouting then from the far side of the door and a loud ranting, unintelligible to me. The eunuch beside me looked ready to run. The shouting stopped suddenly and I felt my heart beating fiercely, in fear, and there was an uncomfortable perspiration on my neck. I glanced at Watts. His eyes were fixed upon the chamber door. In the next moment the first eunuch came out from the audience chamber and closed the door quickly behind him. Now both eunuchs were in a great hurry to get us out from there.

'You will not touch me!' said Watts and pulled his arm free of them. He beckoned me up beside him and so we walked, with the two eunuchs behind us. They came only as far as the palace gates and then Watts and I were set at liberty into the dark street, Watts directing such ripe oaths at their backs as surprised me almost as much as any other part of the whole incident. I began to laugh, but choked it down, for I knew it as a kind of hysteria. Watts put a hand upon my back.

'I am well,' said I. 'It is just that my throat is dry.' And once we had recovered ourselves a little and started for our house, I asked, 'Was it he?'

'I do not think so. It seemed to me some voice other than the nawab's.'

'I saw my own head upon a spike.'

'That was the intention of it. But even if it were not the nawab, it is no good sign that those eunuchs may do their will freely about the palace – even into the audience chamber. And a still worse sign that such an open contempt should be shown to us.'

'Will you protest to the nawab?'

'I will, but that is a formality. In truth, after tonight I know not whether to expect from him protection or the knife. We are no longer in any safety here. The thing must be done and done quickly.'

When we received word by Jagath Seth of Mir Jafir's return to the city, Watts sent me immediately to reconnoitre the streets about Mir Jafir's house, for it was openly spoken of by the Seths and many others that the nawab had now stripped Mir Jafir of the title of *Bakshi* (which is to say, of Paymaster to the Moorish army) and so it seemed very likely Mir Jafir would now be closely watched by the nawab.

I went on horseback, accompanied by Harry, for Watts had made it a rule now that I should not go out into the city alone as had, till so recently, been my habit. It had been my intention to make a circuit of the streets near Mir Jafir's house, but once Harry and I had got within sight of it we knew the futility of a closer inspection, for there were soldiers all about and, at our appearance, a few walked into the street ahead of us, as if they meant to impede our way.

'Continue to the left,' I told Harry and we trotted on, veering up a neighbouring street as if that were our intended route. But as the soldiers returned to their places in the shade, I saw a *dooley*, that closed carriage favoured by Moorish ladies, go by them unregarded and I noted it well.

'A *dooley*?' said Watts, when I told him my thoughts. 'But where might we get such a thing?'

'We returned by way of the Seths. Harry has spoken to their syce. If we need it we may have a *dooley* from there tonight.'

'This was more than the reconnoitring I sent you on.'

'Sir, I only thought that we—'

'Hold, hold. There is no harm done.' He kept his hands behind his back as we continued our perambulation about our courtyard garden. 'It may interest you what I have discovered of the two Frenchmen. They have been gathering up any European dross they find about the city – deserters, in the main. And they have been paying well for artillerymen.'

'How shall they use artillerymen?'

'There is no report of that. The nawab continues to supply Monsieur Law and his party with sufficient money to keep them near. But the more I think on it, the less concern I have at what the French shall do. They were broken at Chandernagore. They should not now distract us from our main purpose. Harry has spoken to the syce?'

'Yes.'

'We cannot wait longer. I will get word to Jagath Seth.' He faced me. 'It is the *dooley*, and tonight.'

We got from our palanquins out in the street, left them with the bearers, and walked into the Seths' courtyard, just as we had often done before.

Only this time a *dooley* waited for us and Watts and I climbed into it. The shutters and doors were all closed, and at once we were out from the courtyard and the syce driving the pony briskly through the city toward the house of Mir Jafir.

The darkness within the closed-up *dooley* was complete and I could not see Watts, though we sat squeezed tight together.

'It is like a coffin.'

'Quiet,' said Watts sharply. 'Or it may prove one for us both.'

I kept silence then and we bumped and jolted our way through the streets. I turned my ears upon every sound outside the thin wooden wall. Noises there were in plenty, but I could not map them in my mind.

After a time the *dooley* slowed, and when we rounded a corner the syce knocked upon his seat to tell us that we were approaching the Moorish soldiers. Inside we sat very still and I could hear very distinctly Watts's quiet breathing. A soldier called up to our syce. The syce answered him. But there was no check to our advance and we continued on another minute before we turned again and the *dooley* at last stopped. Our syce opened the door to let us out.

'*Asalaam alaikum*,' said a Moor as we alighted, and Mr Watts introduced me to Mir Jafir's son.

Mir Jafir's son was not a boy, but a young man, and he now led Mr Watts and me to his father inside the house. The house was a grand one, fitting for a Moor of Mir Jafir's station. But Mir Jafir awaited us in a small bare room of no ostentation. He rose from his cushion at our entrance and greeted Mr Watts like an equal.

'*Asalaam alaikum*.'

'*Amalaikum salaam*.'

He was bigger than Watts, and with a soldier's upright bearing. Beneath his richly embroidered coat (which reached almost to the floor) a broad belt and silver buckle were clearly visible. His beard was close-shaven, his face narrow, his skin dark, and he studied Watts very carefully. It struck me that there was no sign of strain on his face, which bespoke a degree of self-control far beyond the reach of the nawab, that capricious master he was about to betray.

He bade his son to bring refreshment for us, which I doubt if any but a Moor should have troubled with at such a time. There were no servants present and only one other Moorish nobleman, who was Omar Beg, Mir Jafir's lieutenant. Like me, Omar Beg was in attendance as a witness, and he uttered not a word but stayed always near to Mir Jafir's shoulder.

We sipped the chai and ate of the sweetmeats enough only for courtesy's sake, while Mir Jafir looked over the treaty, which Watts had written out for him also in Persian. Taking no consultation with either his son or the other Moor, Mir Jafir then signified to Mr Watts that the treaty was in accord with that prior understanding he had come to with Watts by way of Jagath Seth. There was some more discussion between them (Watts told me after it was of how Mir Jafir would behave if it came to battle between the nawab's army and Colonel Clive) and the chai and sweetmeats were then put aside.

'Stand,' Watts said to me, and I stood.

We all stepped into the centre of the room, away from the cushions by the walls. Upon the floor, there in the centre, was a Moorish reading-stand, very low to the ground, of a kind the Moorish priests use to read from their holy book, the *El Quoran*. Indeed, there was just such a holy book of rich and ornate binding resting on the stand before us.

Mir Jafir now sat cross-legged and put the treaty on the *El Quoran* and his son then brought him quill and ink. With the name of his god Allah upon his lips, Mir Jafir made no hesitation but signed the treaty boldly, as if it were not treachery he now put his name to, but only heaven's justice against a tyrant. Nor was he satisfied with this, but he rose and called his son to kneel down before him and, when this was done, Mir Jafir put a hand upon his son's head and with the other held the treaty, and there was no mistaking the weight or gravity of the oath he then made, for though the language of it was Persian, yet the act was universal.

The treaty passed back to Watts and we then left the house as we had come there, sealed up like the Moorish ladies in a *dooley*.

Our every thought now was to be away from Murshidabad.

Letters continued to arrive from the colonel and the council. One came of so alarming a nature that we saw our lives were all but forfeit, for the council wrote that the intended overthrow of the nawab was now a matter spoken of openly in Calcutta. But Watts, well knowing that ill-considered haste might destroy us, made application to the nawab that we might be allowed to take our hounds hunting down at Modipore, which was the country seat of the Cossimbazaar factory. After some anxious days' wait, the permission was granted us.

'Take nothing but what must be needed for the hunt,' Watts instructed me. 'Only that and also the Dryden.'

We rode first to Cossimbazaar and called upon the gentlemen of the small Dutch factory there. We did not linger, but told them we were to hunt that day in Modipore, but that we should return in the evening and would then welcome their company should they wish to dine with us in our factory. Having got their acceptance to this invitation, we then went to our own factory, where Watts gave orders to the few servants who remained there that they must make preparations to receive our Dutch guests in the late evening.

'And you,' said Watts, turning now upon the three servants – the nawab's spies – who had come with us from our house in Murshidabad. 'You will help these here. Make up two beds for us.' Thrown into confusion by the command, the boldest of these rascals enquired when they might expect our return and Watts replied, 'Sunset,' and turned his back on the fellow and went out.

We rode now with only Harry and two syces and, upon our coming now to the company's house at Modipore, we were joined by a Hindoo huntsman with our hounds. At the house itself were other servants whose loyalty we distrusted and Mr Watts went and commanded them to take some several household items – pots and lamps and linen – up to our Cossimbazaar factory.

'We shall dine there tonight with our Dutch guests. Be sure to be ready for us.'

After a poor luncheon of rice and salted fish, we then took our hounds and rode out onto the plain.

'We must keep our own horses fresh,' Watts quietly instructed Harry and me, riding to either side of him. 'But those two—' he nodded to the mounts of the syces ahead of us, 'those two must be ridden till they almost drop, and then a mile further. We cannot have them after us tonight.'

It is as well we had that sport of wearying those two horses, for the hunting itself was a quite dismal affair – the rain broke upon us in the mid-afternoon and continued an hour so that the whole plain turned to mud. We took shelter in an empty granary near to a village while our syces kept the horses sheltered beneath the nearby trees, but, when the rain ceased, we stepped straightaway from the granary and called the syces to us and rode out to find the huntsman and the hounds, which we heard baying to the south of us.

Riding now with Harry in that place, I thought of that day when I had tried my hand at the wild pig there and fallen from my horse and gotten up to ride again, and it seemed a quite different fellow had done those things, there was so much had happened since that time. We were at some distance from the ruined temple where I had found Mrs Watts and that *sadhu*, but I could see the broken line of its tumbled stones upon the hilltop. There was no wild pig now, nor much else worth the hunting. The nawab's army being so long in the field, the granaries about were now all emptied and the villagers had killed most of the game for their own sustenance. It was truly a place, as Harry now said, where even the jackals went hungry.

By the late afternoon we had made sure to each have ridden those two horses unmercifully hard, so that when Mr Watts told the syces that they might take that pair back to Cossimbazaar and that we would rest ourselves a quarter-hour before following them, the syces went north without demur.

Once they were out of sight, we mounted and rode south-east.

It was a hard ride those first few hours and we did not spare ourselves, for every hour put more miles between us and the nawab. By sunset we were upon the road south, but we never slackened our speed. Back in Cossimbazaar, we knew that the Dutch must now be awaiting our arrival. Very soon our servants must grow suspicious and when the syces arrived there without us, the alarm would quickly be raised. A report would have to go to Murshidabad. The nawab would have to be roused from his harem.

We rode and rode without resting.

'Here is the place,' said Harry at last. It was past midnight and I think Mr Watts could not have gone on for very much longer. Nor I, to be truthful, for I began to feel some ill effect from that poor luncheon we had eaten. We dismounted wearily and led our horses to the edge of the riverbank and there seemed nothing there but only a stone landing place.

'They have forgot us,' said I unhappily; for I was exceedingly tired and had begun to feel ill. But as I spoke there came a whistling from the trees at my left shoulder. I turned and raised my pistol.

'You would not shoot me, Mr Douglas,' said a voice and stepping out from the trees came Lieutenant Brereton and he whistled again and two boats moved toward us, rippling the moonlight on the water.

CHAPTER FORTY-THREE

*W*e joined Clive's army not that day but the next, by which time I had fallen ill with a fever and only my urgent appeal to Mr Watts had kept the surgeon from sending me back down to Calcutta. But, though I stayed with the army, I needs must suffer the ignominy of being carried as supercargo in the baggage train (though I own I neither felt nor understood much of my position in these few days), and when at last the fever lifted I found that we were at Cutwa, but a day's march south of Plassey, where the nawab's army was waiting, though we were on the far side of the river to the Moors.

The topass woman who informed me of all this then brought me some thin porage. The army was encamped and many campfires burned all about me where I sat in the cart eating. The woman told me also that the French captain had paid her to watch over me while we had travelled, and I knew it must be Le Baume. From atop the cart I had a vantage of the encampment, which stretched in a broad column along the road northward, and my abiding impression, I confess, was of its smallness, for I had grown accustomed in Murshidabad to the press of a great city and all my talk with Mr Watts concerning the nawab's army had been of its scores of thousands. But here with the colonel were no scores of thousands, but only those same soldiers and sepoys who had been at Chandernagore, their numbers supplemented by the sailors who had come up with Lieutenant Brereton. There must have been three thousand men at most. Putting aside the empty bowl, I pulled on my boots and got down carefully from the cart.

There was a slick of mud upon the ground, and as I walked up the road I saw that the sepoys and soldiers had broken branches from the trees to sit upon and keep their breeches dry. Yet they seemed in good spirits, as if they had no notion of the nawab's army lying so near at hand. The bullocks I had brought in Murshidabad now stood hobbled by the artillery train, chewing their cud and looking very weary and resigned.

'Mr Douglas, by Christ! Mr Brereton said you was unwell.'

I turned and found Midshipman Adams beaming at me merrily. He came down from his comrades to join me on the road.

'I am recovered,' said I, and much cheered I was to see him. 'But why are we stopped here?'

'You will have to ask the colonel, sir. Maybe it is to give Major Coote's men a breather.'

'Major Coote?'

'He took the Cutwa fort with just a handful. Your Moor isn't pigheaded like your Frenchman.'

'But how is Captain Coote a major?'

'Major Coote and Major Grant both – by the colonel's appointment. But what is Murshidabad like, sir? Rich?'

'It is a very handsome city. And between here and there lies a great army ready to defend it. I cannot believe, Mr Adams, that you are thinking already of plunder.'

'You should believe it, sir.'

I laughed at this and asked how many cannon we had.

'Eight. All of them six-pounders.'

'And the squadron?'

'The *Bridgewater* is by Hugli to keep the upper river open to us. The others lie further down. In which place does the nawab keep most of his treasure in the city?'

'Let your imagination be your guide. For it is all imagining, Mr Adams, and a great plundering of the city will not happen.'

He continued to smile as we parted. He thought me an innocent in such matters and so gave my opinion no credence.

At the north of the encampment were erected a number of large tents which I knew for those of Clive and his officers, and when I got there, the first man I met with was Major Coote, who greeted me very warmly and congratulated me on the service I had done for Mr Watts. He brushed aside my compliments on his promotion and of his taking of the Cutwa fort and asked, instead, if I had yet seen Captain Le Baume.

'He feels himself under a great obligation to you. Your letter was read aloud at the court-martial by Major Kilpatrick.'

'He owes me nothing.'

'That is between you and him. But you must excuse me. You will find Mr Watts in the second tent along there.'

The second tent along I found empty and, upon my enquiry of the two captains who sat in camp-chairs nearby, their jackets unbuttoned, their uniforms mud-bespattered and their spirits high as they laughed at their own deeds done against the Cutwa Moors, I discovered that Mr Watts was in the colonel's tent with Mr Scrafton and certain others. Deciding that I had no good reason to intrude upon such a conference, I then asked the captains if they knew the whereabouts of Captain Le Baume. They directed me to the makeshift batteries that guarded the camp, a hundred yards further on toward the river.

I saw the three cannon from some distance and I saw also the lone tent and the two score or more soldiers encamped nearby. The lone tent I knew must be Le Baume's, but this separate division of soldiers I did not understand, till I came nearer and saw their dishevelled French uniforms and heard the rough French they spoke, for these must be the Chandernagore deserters.

Le Baume came out from by his tent to meet me. He gripped my hand.

'It is good to see you,' said I.

'But you are not recovered.'

'I am a little weak. That is all.' I then felt myself in the next moment near to fainting, which Le Baume read in my face, for now he gripped my elbow. He had his camp bed brought out into the canopied shade of the tent opening and I sat down upon the bed and felt myself the veriest fool. It was not any sickness that enfeebled me now, but the long time I had lain idle in the cart. Le Baume had one of the Hindoo boys make a sweet drink for me, which I was grateful of. Once I had drunk it, I felt my head more steady, though from caution I remained seated on the bed. Le Baume drew up his camp-chair.

'I must repay you what you gave to the topass woman.' He snorted contemptuously at that and then I said, 'Why have you not rejoined the other officers?' I gestured toward the nearby soldiers. 'And why are you with these?'

'The colonel found himself in need of more soldiers. Those who had already deserted Chandernagore, he kept. Those who were captured, he offered a place in his army.'

'And you are now their commander?'

'Colonel Clive is thankful now he did not hang me.'

'It was an absurd business.'

'Many say so now. Major Coote, the other officers. But at the time – if you offer again to repay me for the topass woman, I will strike you down like a dog.'

'That is very gentlemanly of you.'

Smiling, he dipped his head to me. It was all the thanks I should have of him, though I knew that he would go to the wall for me if I but asked it. He enquired what I had seen of the nawab's army.

'It was never mustered in Murshidabad. You will have heard as much of it as we ever did while we waited there.'

'We are told one day Monsieur Law has gone to Patna. The next day, that he returns to Murshidabad with a force to assist the nawab. And Mr Watts says that Sinfray has gathered artillerymen to fight in the nawab's army.'

'Cordet is with Sinfray,' I said, and Le Baume peered at me. This was a thing he had not heard. 'I spoke with him. He had received a letter from his cousin. He was pleased – I believe very genuinely pleased – to hear from me that you had been cleared at the court-martial.'

'He would say so.'

'I believe he has some regret now with regard to his own behaviour towards yourself and his cousin.'

'It is a very late regret.'

'That may be. But it is also, I think, a sincere one.'

He considered this, with some scepticism, but at last he gave a shrug. 'Then if I meet him on the battlefield, I shall do him the honour of killing him very cleanly. But now you are tired.' Le Baume sent his Hindoo boy to bring fruit for me from the camp followers. When the lad returned, I ate the fruit and drank more of the sweet drink and rested again, while the French soldiers came and went from Le Baume's tent, talking and joking together, so that when I dozed again I dreamt myself on the Île de Paris, before Notre Dame, with the voices of pilgrims all about me, complaining of the heat.

It was late afternoon when I finally roused myself. Le Baume immediately came out from the tent. 'I am not an invalid,' said I, for I saw that he watched me very carefully. I stretched my arms and my back and now we both noticed the slight figure of Mr Watts hurrying toward us from the main camp.

'Captain,' Watts said, tipping his hat to Le Baume as he arrived. 'I was told you were resting here, Mr Douglas. I thought it better not to disturb you.'

'Now he is revived, you may take him.'

'It is not Mr Douglas I have come for, Captain. You are summoned to the colonel's tent. There is to be a Council of War held in twenty minutes.' He ran an eye over Le Baume's grubby uniform. 'I noticed the other officers taking some care with their dress.'

Le Baume called his boy sharply, ordering him to fetch a fresh shirt and breeches from the trunk. Then he asked Watts the purpose of the council, for he was as surprised as I that the colonel should make any official enquiry of the opinion of his officers.

'I believe there is some question of military rank to be first decided. One of the naval lieutenants asserts he must take precedence over the company's captains.' Watts raised a brow in amusement. 'Once that is

417

done, I expect there must be some discussion of our business with the nawab.'

Le Baume excused himself and retired to change his uniform.

'And if you are well enough, Alistair,' said Watts, 'perhaps you might walk with me a short way by the river.'

The river was but another hundred yards on and some of our soldiers had already come there to bathe and cool themselves, while others stood guard over them lest any of those Moors driven from Cutwa should return to revenge themselves. And yet Watts strolled along the riverbank as if it were a place no more dangerous than the embankment on the Thames, and I with him for company and also to be a private listener to the apprehensions which had evidently grown in him since our flight from Murshidabad. These apprehensions, to my considerable surprise, centred on the colonel, for Clive, Watts said, had not only taken some notice of the rumours stirred up by Omichand relating to the nawab's supposed discovery of the company's scheming, but he had grown increasingly distrustful of the commitment Mir Jafir had made to Mr Watts.

'It is as though we two had remained in Murshidabad at the risk of our lives but to no purpose,' he finished unhappily.

'The colonel cannot be afraid.'

'He is but flesh and blood. But it is not that. He has sent two letters each day to Mir Jafir – sometimes three – and yet he frets still for an answer. To be frank, he has a fear that Mir Jafir has not truly come over to us and that I have been made the nawab's dupe.'

'Mir Jafir swore upon it his son's head.'

'I have told the colonel repeatedly that Mir Jafir has promised me that he would not fight us. I have told him that Mir Jafir swore he would stand his own divisions idle when we came against the Moorish army. The colonel will not heed me. He must have a letter from Mir Jafir.'

'Perhaps it is that Mir Jafir fears discovery and so cannot write.'

'There are a thousand causes might prevent his communication with us, Alistair. And I have said so to the colonel. No doubt Mr Scrafton has advised him otherwise. You may be sure that if Colonel Clive had been convinced of the sincerity of Mir Jafir's allegiance to us, there had then been no Council of War summoned. He has baulked at the last fence and now we must see if his officers will urge him over it.'

'Can the officers outvote him?'

'They can outvote him. But they cannot overrule him. The final say must be his.'

We looked across the river to the bank opposite. Over there, and a day's march north of us, was encamped the nawab's army. The strongest part of it, Mir Jafir and his divisions, awaited our arrival so that the great revolution might happen – and nothing, nothing at all, now lying between us and them but Clive's unexpected hesitation.

'Let us return to camp,' said Watts, suddenly pivoting. 'There will be a decision made and I must meet it directly.'

There was no decision taken by the time of our return, so Watts had his Hindoo boy light lamps for us, that we might sit quietly in the tent (which was near to Clive's) and read while we waited. Our reading was shallow and distracted, for not a sound passed outside the tent but our heads rose sharply from our books in anticipation of the breaking of the council. And when it came at last, after almost two hours, Major Coote arrived at once to Mr Watts's tent.

'The decision is against an advance,' said he, with a look quite despondent. 'There was a belief we could not rely upon the Moorish support you had promised us, Mr Watts.' Watts took the news like a physical blow, and as to myself the shock was very great, for I could not conceive that all we had done to prepare the way had been so lightly discarded. Watts, when he had recovered himself, asked which way the colonel had voted: for the advance or against. 'Against,' the major replied. 'Most of the Bengal officers were "for", most of the Madras officers "against". There was fair opportunity given for all to speak. I was "for", but who can say what is right? It may be that time shall prove it for the best.'

'You do not believe that.'

'It is done now and cannot be helped.'

'That is yet to see,' said Watts, rising from his chair.

'The council is finished, Mr Watts.'

'An army is no democracy. There is one man will decide this and, if you will excuse me now, I must speak with him.'

Major Coote's surprise was at least the equal of my own, and Watts stepped out past him with no word more of explanation. Indeed, so surprised was the major, and perhaps hopeful, that he did not immediately rejoin the other officers who were now milling about the main campfire talking together. He said to me, 'Have you a notion what Mr Watts is about?'

'As little as you, sir.'

He turned to watch Watts go into Clive's tent. 'Whatever it be, I think we may wish him well of it.'

'Yes sir.'

'You will be sure to tell me immediately you hear what comes of it. I will not bid you good night yet, Mr Douglas.'

It was well that he did not, for when I called upon him the next hour it was with word from Mr Watts that the colonel had reconsidered the decision of the Council of War. Reconsidered the decision and overturned it utterly. Tomorrow we would cross the river and march north to meet the nawab at Plassey.

CHAPTER FORTY-FOUR

*A*ll the morning was taken up with getting our horses across the river and also the artillery train, bullocks – which should draw the guns – and the powder and shot. Boats there were in plenty, for the admiral had released them from the squadron and they had shadowed the army since Chandernagore (a good number of officers and men riding up in them) and now they worked to ferry our soldiers and sepoys to the eastern bank. This all happened, I may say, under the eyes of some few hundreds of the local Hindoos, who seemed not a wit distressed to have the Moors ejected by us from the Cutwa fort. They gathered in clusters on the western bank, most of them crouching on their haunches in the native style, and watched the spectacle of our army's movement with a lively interest, laughing merrily when any of our number stumbled in the mud or fell into the water.

This curiously festive atmosphere did not extend to the eastern bank, for here a general muster was made, the bullocks were harnessed to the train and the men's minds turned more fully now upon the enemy.

'You shall not require a horse,' said Watts, when he heard me call out to a syce. 'We have been offered places in one of the boats. I have taken the liberty of an acceptance on your behalf.'

'Major Coote is expecting me to join his officers.'

'You may join them when we reach Plassey. Our flatboat is piloted by your acquaintance, Mr Adams. I will come down to you in a moment.' So saying, Watts crossed to the place where Clive stood with his majors, Kilpatrick, Coote and Grant, all of them surveying the column forming before them, issuing orders and conferring together. They accepted Watts among them very readily, though his lack of uniform – his brown jacket instead of the red – marked him out as an interloper there, so that even from a distance, and across the general soldiery, I could see him very clearly. And I saw after a minute that a *cossid* arrived with a packet for Clive and that Clive spoke with Watts and the two of them drew aside from the others to break open the packet. From the green of the *cossid*'s turban, I suspected that the packet must come from Mir Jafir. I knew that Mr Watts would be some while now, so I went and found out Mr Adams. He had much to tell me of the lamentable slackness of the soldiers and of their appalling want of respect for his boats.

The boats carried munitions, the officers' trunks and various heavy but necessary items such as the tents and the ropes. Our company surgeon, Dr Forth (who was a volunteer in the expedition since Chandernagore), came in the Adams boat with Watts and me and several others. In this high part of the river the tide was no concern to us, neither was the current very strong, for it was only now the start of the rains, and the tributaries not yet in spate. We had six oarsmen and Adams at the tiller and we proceeded very slowly, with boats ahead of us and boats behind at some good distance.

Our straggling convoy kept generally abreast of Clive's column, which marched a few hundred yards inland from the eastern bank, so we had no fear of attack from that direction, but watched the river ahead of us and the small party of sepoys that Major Kilpatrick had sent up the western bank to scout out any ambush. In truth, we had little to fear from the Moorish army while we travelled, for the Moors' habit was to fight in set-pieces upon a battlefield, or about a fort, where their superior numbers might the more easily intimidate or overwhelm their enemies. And yet in spite of this knowledge, every man of us kept wide awake and watched the river and the banks very closely, all the way to nightfall, when we at last got the signal from the shore to put in by Plassey Grove.

'Tie up the bow-line if you please, Mr Douglas.'

'You will make an officer if you are not careful, Mr Adams.'

We soon discovered that it was but an advance party of Clive's column that had signalled us ashore and, learning from them that the local villagers reported the nawab's encampment but two miles to the north of us, Watts invited me to go with him to the far side of the grove of mangoes, where we might expect some view of the Moorish campfires. We left Adams and the oarsmen unloading and went through the grove and when we came out from the trees we met an earthen bank, about the height of a man. We climbed up on it and saw at once the many fires that marked out the vast extent of the nawab's camp away to the north of us. And I confess that in that moment my heart almost seized in me, for the campfires appeared as numberless as the stars.

'We must remember, Alistair, that they are not so many as they seem.'

'That is only if we can be sure of Mir Jafir.'

'Aye,' said he. 'If we can only be sure of him.'

It was past midnight before the whole of our army had arrived at the Plassey Grove and, after Clive's first inspection of the earthen bank that enclosed the trees, there was never any doubt but that the grove should be the army's base. Clive gave an order, too, that the large brick house just beyond the grove to the north and by the river should be secured, which was done without incident and with no shot being fired. Clive and his majors and Mr Watts then went down to this house and I with them. It seemed a leisure house of some wealthy person and was sufficiently commodious to give night-quarters to Mr Watts and the others. But before I came away to rejoin Adams at the riverside, I remarked to Mr Watts that the colonel seemed very brooding and ill at ease, for he had hardly seemed sometimes to hear what was said to him after we had come into the house.

'Tonight he has the company upon his shoulders. The strangeness would be if he should hear anything at all but the busy workings of his own mind.'

'But he must rest then.'

'Be assured, there is no resting place this night for the colonel.'

At the riverside, where Adams had a fire burning and some strips of canvas and blankets laid about as bedding, a crick of muskets stood near. I ate the ship's biscuit and salted beef that Adams had kept for me, but when I stretched out upon the canvas and drew the thin blanket over me I did not think that I would sleep. I watched the lowest stars sink below the horizon beyond the river and I listened to the boats knock gently together at their moorings. I determined that I should not think of war. And so I thought of my friends in England and of my mother and father who were gone. I thought of that girl in the Cossimbazaar black town and of Tamerlane's lament that he should die, and this world unconquered. I thought of a thousand things more and then I slept in peacefulness, like a child.

'Mr Douglas?' It was dawn and Adams by me, smiling, his hand upon my shoulder. 'We must clear the decks, sir. The nawab is up already and marching toward us.'

I rose quickly and ate the biscuit and beef that Adams had brought for me and then I went down to my hasty ablutions at the river. The whole grove was alive now with men hurrying about in obedience to the barked commands of the officers, while behind their shouts and curses beat the sudden drum-call to arms. Returning to my place by the boats, I found Mr Watts come down to find me.

'Major Coote will be with the colonel upon the bank,' cried he, departing at once in that direction, and I took my pistol, powder and shot and followed.

Within the grove the men were now forming into two distinct battalions and we passed through them and scrambled up the bank, where we found the colonel, his three majors and several others who would do duty as their messengers. But these we only glanced at, for on the plain before us, at the distance of barely a mile, was a sight to fill any man with awe and terror. The nawab's army, in full splendour, had come out from its camp, not with two battalions but battalions in scores, with tens of thousands on foot and more thousands upon horses and camels also. Of elephants there were a hundred and more, and the sound of their trumpeting, and the wild Moorish battle music, now came over that distance in a shrill rising wave and broke upon us on the bank at Plassey Grove.

I looked at Clive and he, through his spyglass, at the nawab's army. It is no blemish on his courage to say that his face was drawn and very pale. 'I see they mean to give us some sport,' said he to his officers, but they made no reply and peered through their spyglasses, their own faces set like stone.

It was a bigger army than had first driven us from Calcutta, a bigger and greater army than we had cut a swathe through out by the Maratha Ditch. And the question unspoken by Clive and his officers, there upon the bank, was whether that mere civilian who stood beside them, William Watts, had truly done what he had promised and cleaved the nawab's great army invisibly, to the heart. For there could be no doubt that such an army, united, must extinguish us from the face of the earth.

Watts affected no nonchalant appearance while he studied the nawab's army, but his look was grave and full of concern, as well it might be, for all our lives were now staked upon his work. I found that I admired him all the more that he did not hide himself behind a false bravado. It is a serious matter to hold another's life in one's hand, and it was clear by his look that Mr Watts felt it so and, at that particular moment, full as deeply as any man might.

'There is a movement on the right, sir,' announced Major Coote and the manoeuvre was soon visible now to the naked eye.

'It is mostly cavalry,' remarked Major Kilpatrick. 'They are making a wing there upon our right flank.'

'Order the men out from the grove. One battalion to the front here, the other on the right. You will be sure to hold them from any premature advance, Major Coote.'

The idea that any soldier might be eager to advance against the Moorish horde seemed madness to me, but Major Coote passed Clive's order to the ensign beside him immediately and the ensign, clutching the scabbard of his sheathed sword against his leg as he descended, hurried down the bank and into the grove behind us.

Watts had been studying the Moorish lines intently. 'I believe, Colonel, that it is Mir Jafir who flanks you on the right. I am sure it is his colours.'

'The colours cannot be trusted, Mr Watts.'

'If it is he and his fellows, they will hold off from you.'

'Bring up the guns, Major Coote.'

Another ensign descended the bank and disappeared into the grove.

These preliminaries continued for ten minutes or more, during which time I asked Mr Watts if I might join the grenadiers. He told me that I must stay by him for the present and he gave me his spyglass, that I might confirm his belief that it was Mir Jafir now positioned upon our right flank. I found that I could confirm nothing, for the banners of the Moorish troops were much mingled now all along their lines. But, through the spyglass, I could make out their different divisions, the cavalry and the infantry, the archers and the *buxerries*. They were no rabble, but an army under command. The Moors' bullocks pulled forward their guns. I returned Mr Watts his spyglass and he attempted a smile of encouragement, which I knew not how to answer at that moment.

Our soldiers and sepoys came now out from the grove with the drummer lads and officers leading them. It was men that drew the field pieces into position, the bullocks being kept behind the grove to the rear. Three guns were pulled into place in the front of us, and three more to our right. Our soldiers and sepoys being well drilled in their manoeuvres, their lines were soon forming behind the guns, some fifty yards out from the bank upon which we stood watching them. And while these manoeuvres were proceeding, the Moors, their line now halted five hundred yards to the front of us, opened upon us with their guns.

'The artillery may return their fire when they are ready, Major,' Clive said to Coote. 'But they must advance no further.'

Coote's messenger went down the face of the bank this time and hurried out to the guns.

The Moorish shelling continued light and, even to my untrained eye, it was very evident this was but their range-finding. But the increase of their accuracy seemed to happen more quickly than Clive had expected.

Our own guns now proceeded to give some answer to the Moors. This was not fighting between us yet, but only sparring, as if two bare-knuckle fighters should test their reach before moving in to thrash each other with blows. No shell came from our right, only useless and occasional musketfire.

'Sir, I cannot be certain of it, but if you look close at their artillerymen – surely they are not Moors.'

'That will be the Frenchmen I told you of,' broke in Mr Watts.

And hardly had he spoken but a Moorish shell fell almost directly upon our line. A number of our men went down and the shouting and screaming started instantly.

Major Kilpatrick turned to Clive. 'Our short-sixes will not trouble them sufficient. There will be worse to come.'

'Major Coote?'

'There is no doubt of it.'

'Withdraw the men behind the bank here,' ordered Clive, much vexed. 'But leave the guns forward and keep them firing.'

Major Coote went himself down the bank now and forward toward the havoc the Moors' shell had caused. He quickly took charge of the new manoeuvre.

The withdrawal proceeded very regular and our men neither broke nor ran to the safety of the bank behind them, but fell back under the firm command of their officers. And all the while Colonel Clive and Major Kilpatrick kept their spyglasses on the Moors to our right, for had they attacked us from that side at that moment, our position had been hopeless.

As the soldiers and sepoys came over the bank just by us and dropped behind the bank's cover on the groveward side, Watts and I descended with them. 'It seems you have your desire,' he said to me. 'You are with the grenadiers and are now like to see the battle as close as any.'

But in spite of our withdrawal, and to a general surprise and relief,

427

the Moors made no advance upon us. Instead they contented themselves with emplacing several of their heavy guns upon a rise by a pond some four hundred yards to the front of us and from there commenced to cannonade us briskly. Once the soldiers were recovered from their first apprehension of a determined Moorish attack, they relaxed somewhat and stayed close under the protection of the bank where I likewise kept myself, though Mr Watts retired with the colonel to the brick house by the river. In the next few hours there was only some of our sepoys killed who had gone onto the bank to try out their muskets, but apart from this, the Moorish shot and grape struck harmless into the bank or useless into the grove of mango trees behind.

Kilpatrick and Coote made several brief sallies to the crest whence they might inspect the disposition of the enemy. They decided then, and for no reason that I could understand, that our hobit (which is like a howitzer) should be sent forward two hundred yards toward the Moors. This being done, they again climbed with some others to observe it from the crest and, Watts and Clive now returning, I went up with them.

'If that is your Mir Jafir,' said Clive to Watts, studying the right, 'he is not overly forward in his assistance of us.'

'He holds his men off from us at least.'

'A man might do more to win a king's crown. The fellow has half the Moorish army with him there.' Our hobit then opening upon the Moors' emplacement at the pond, and on the first ranks of the enemy line, Clive's spyglass came quickly to the front again.

The hobit wreaked no little havoc and confusion among the Moors, as I clearly saw when Watts lent me his glass. But the havoc and confusion were short-lived, for within minutes a troop of Moorish cavalry was observed shifting its position in the line, as though moving to outflank and capture the gun.

'Signal the hobit back, Major Coote,' said Clive, as though it were but a pawn that he moved upon a board. 'We want no general engagement for the present.'

The signal was given and the hobit was smartly withdrawn across the field and back to the protection of the grove.

We came down into the grove ourselves then, for we had felt a sudden coolness and a light breeze, which were certain heralds in that season of rain. And, indeed, we had scarcely reached the first trees when the rain began to fall and, in a short while, as heavily as I had ever seen it in all the time that I had been in Bengal. The Moors' guns at once fell silent, but Clive gave the order that ours should continue. There was a hut just within the grove, but very small, and Colonel Clive and Major Kilpatrick hurried into it and called Mr Watts after them and shut the door against the lashing rain.

I stood with some soldiers beneath the useless umbrella of a mango tree. All about us other soldiers and sepoys found what cover they might and turned up their collars and hunched their shoulders, while the officers went among them with fierce warnings that they must be sure to keep their flint and powder dry. The rain fell through the trees in a torrent, soaking every one of us without the hut, and there never were three thousand men with muskets who looked less like a ready army. The ground turned to mud beneath our feet. We huddled beneath the useless shelter of the trees, peered through the rain to our lookouts on the bank and prayed that the silence of the Moors' guns was not the prelude to an attack upon us.

But in half an hour the rain ceased and there had been no attack, but only the great fall of rain which had drenched us.

When they came from the hut, Clive and Watts returned to the house, for the rain had caught them sufficient to wet them and they would now change into dry clothes. I returned with Kilpatrick and Coote up to the bank. We found the Moors unmoved from the positions they had held before the rain, and very soon their fire upon us recommenced and those of our men who had kept flint and powder dry now lay upon the bank, or just below its crest, and returned fire with their muskets. I discovered from the talk between the majors what Clive had decided while in the hut, which was to wait now till nightfall, when the enemy had surely returned into their camp, and then make a bold attack into the midst of them just as we had done at the Maratha Ditch. (I have since learned that most commanders have but one great manoeuvre which they use continually, till it finally break them, and this was Clive's.)

There was a brief alarm raised when an ensign reported to Coote that there was some sighting of Moors to the rear of us, down by the boats, but when a detachment was sent back there the report was found false and so the men returned to take up their places again on the bank.

It was near two o'clock when the Moorish guns made some noticeable slackening in their fire. And it was not long after when their guns fell silent entirely. Kilpatrick and Coote studied the nawab's lines with their spyglasses while our own men, in some puzzlement, left off their firing.

'It appears they are withdrawing into their camp,' reported Coote after a moment. 'With their guns. They have brought up the bullocks for them.'

Kilpatrick turned his spyglass on the Moors to our right. 'Where is your fellow Mir Jafir now, Mr Douglas?'

For several minutes this watching continued, with surprise at the Moors' actions very evident among the majors and the other officers who came up on the bank. When the first of the Moorish guns was withdrawn, some ruse was supposed, but then a second gun went back and a third. When the guns at the pond were withdrawn (which had been the nearest and most dangerous to us), Major Coote made up his mind that no ruse was intended and that the Moors, for some reason of their own, were indeed returning to their encampment.

Kilpatrick, after a time, agreed with him. After conferring briefly with Coote, he said, decidedly, 'Their position at the pond there is open to us. I will move up part of my division and two guns. We will see then what they may do. Send word of it to the colonel.'

'But he should give the order.'

'We cannot delay or the chance will be lost,' said Kilpatrick, calling commands now to his captains. Two of these captains now mounted and fifty or so men then began to advance with them over the muddy ground with the pair of field guns. The Moors continued their withdrawal quite heedless of our movements. Coote sent an ensign to the brick house by the river to take word of the advance and I went with the fellow.

'I gave no such order,' Clive bellowed at the ensign when he heard of the advance. 'Who has given the order?'

'Major Kilpatrick, sir.'

Clive, to my surprise, had been lying upon his bed when we came in. Now he jumped to his feet and moved quickly past us and up the stairs and onto the flat roof, where we followed him. Hearing the commotion, Mr Watts came up behind us. From the roof there was a fair view of the advancing men, for they were just now reaching the rise by the pond which the Moors had so inexplicably and suddenly abandoned. We could also see from this vantage that many of the Moors had already reached their camp, but their army was so vast that those nearer to us were still within range of Kilpatrick's musketmen, now at the pond. There was an exchange of musketfire between our men and their army's rear guard. And now another band of our men, perhaps two hundred, began a rapid advance from the grove and across the field toward the pond to reinforce the others.

'Who the devil is that?' cried Clive.

'I believe it is Major Kilpatrick, sir,' said the ensign.

'It is,' said Mr Watts, for he had brought a spyglass up with him and now he handed the glass to Clive.

Clive's face when he looked through the spyglass turned crimson. His voice quavered with the strain of self-control when he said to the ensign, 'Have a horse ready for me at the door.' He gave Mr Watts the spyglass and, without a word more, went down the stairs and into his room. When I came down, past there, the colonel had put on his jacket and was buckling on his sword and Mr Watts touched my sleeve and by his look called me away. I then returned with Mr Watts to the grove.

'Mir Jafir may be our friend, Mr Watts,' said Coote, now observing a body of Moorish horse moving on our right as though to cut Kilpatrick and his men off from us. 'But I must put a shot into those fellows.' He then ordered our remaining guns to fire upon the Moorish cavalrymen. A few shots falling among them, the cavalrymen immediately broke off from their manoeuvre and withdrew themselves to safety. Coote, then turning his spyglass forward, observed the colonel and some other soldiers, who had been guarding the house, now going up to the pond. Coote glanced at Watts.

'I believe there is a recall of Major Kilpatrick and his men intended,' said Watts.

We watched now for several minutes, expecting at any moment the withdrawal to begin, but the guns at the pond continued to fire upon the Moors. And, if anything, the musketfire of our soldiers there steadily increased.

Finally, after fifteen minutes, that same ensign rode back to us from the pond with the colonel's command that Major Coote should advance at once to the pond with two more of our guns. Mr Watts and I were both amazed after what we had seen of Clive's behaviour at the house, but Coote made no hesitation and started at once down the bank, saying to Watts as he went, 'I will take Mr Douglas. He will bring you any private message from the colonel.' Watts agreed and I had no time for amazement, then, my heart suddenly racing, I hurried down after Major Coote.

There was no horse for me, so I advanced on foot with the grenadiers. We took no fire till we had crossed the four hundred yards and come to the pond and then we lost but three men only to the Moorish muskets, before our guns were set and firing upon the enemy. From the rise where we were now established we had a clearer view of the nawab's camp and the first line of their entrenchment. There was only a part of their army in the field now, for many of the Moors were already behind their lines.

'Turn all your fire upon those guns there,' ordered Clive, and he seemed now hardly the same man I had seen at the brick house. He was upright and vigorous and moved about behind our own guns encouraging the artillerymen, with an eye always forward to the Moors. He sent the sepoys forward to a bank nearer the Moors now, that the sepoys might gall them with musketshot while our artillery plied them with our heavy metal. (It was only later I understood that Clive had arrived at the pond intending to command a withdrawal, but on seeing the situation, had changed his mind. This was, I believe, the greatest act of generalship in the whole campaign.)

The Moorish rear, though clearly unsettled by our small force having advanced so rapidly and unexpectedly, now set themselves upon a rise halfway between us and their camp and turned on us those few guns that had not yet been so rashly withdrawn behind the entrenchments.

But, as to any comparison between our artillery and theirs in the brief exchange that followed, there was none, for our gunners almost at once found the range and Coote, after several minutes, handed me his spyglass that I might see the havoc they had made upon the Moors' position, which was considerable. Indeed, some Moors were now in flight and there were two elephants lying dead and such a disorder now, at the sole mounted gun remaining to them, that it almost seemed there was no proper commander there (this was truer than I knew, for Mir Madan, the nawab's senior general, was killed in this exchange).

The confusion and disorder among the Moors seemed to increase and Clive, after fifteen minutes more, gave the order to advance upon the enemy position. With only some pause made to re-prime muskets, our soldiers and sepoys went forward, I with them, and Coote in command. Clive and Kilpatrick remained on the high ground behind us at the pond and the talk between them, as I went down, was of calling the rest of our army forward from the Plassey Grove.

The Moors fired upon us as we advanced, but with musketshot only, and all the while our own guns behind us kept up a deadly cannonade into the Moors, who fell back as fast as we came toward them. When we came to within two hundred yards of the entrance to their encampment (which was an opening through their entrenchment), we saw that the great press of Moors fleeing us had obstructed their own guns, which had in consequence been unable to come out to meet us, and the scene there now was of utter confusion, a terrified whirlpool of Moorish cavalry and infantry breaking over their own entrenchment and over each other, and striking terror into the whole army, as they fled from us back through their camp.

It was like no other battle that I had fought in. In truth, it was but a skirmish that had now turned into a rout.

'At them!' cried Coote. 'Forward the grenadiers!' The soldiers about me started up some wild shouting, urging each other forward. Soon they were rushing forward, stopping to fire and reload and them forward again, with bayonets now held at the ready.

'Mr Douglas, you will take these men along the entrenchment there and down to the river. Secure any boats that you find there.'

In obedience to Coote's command, I moved quickly riverward and two grenadiers and a handful of sepoys went with me in a single file along the hollow of the entrenchment, safe there from any stray musket-shot. The entrenchment petered out twenty yards short of the river, and when we came into the open we saw three boats being rowed away from us toward the far bank. By their clothes, we knew them for the nawab's French artillerymen. They had muskets and they fired upon us and we upon them. Then I saw another boat launching a hundred yards further on and I left the grenadiers and sepoys and hurried on alone with my pistol.

The boat was not so very far out when I stopped on the bank, certainly not so far out that I could fail to recognize the uniformed figure of Sébastien Cordet seated between the two native oarsmen. I saw him, and he me, and whether it was that he had no weapon about him in the boat or that it was there but he chose not to raise it, I could not tell, but he sat still between the oarsmen and watched me. The boat moved steadily away from me, over the river. And, whether it was that I was reminded in that moment of myself as I fled the Calcutta siege, or from some other reason, my own pistol stayed at my side. Had I known then what I know now, might I have fired upon him? Perhaps. Perhaps it is better not to know. It is no matter, for I did not fire, and by the time the grenadiers came up to me, Cordet had turned his back on us and was beyond the range of our muskets.

The nawab had fled. And, by the reports of the Moorish prisoners we took, upon a camel and in fear of his life, and this it was had caused the final rout. Clive now summoned forward the rest of our force from the Plassey Grove and Coote and Kilpatrick he sent in harrying pursuit of the pell-mell retreat of the collapsed Moorish army toward Murs-hidabad. I stayed with Watts and Clive in the nawab's abandoned encampment. A few hundred of our men remained with us and they looked now to gather the Moors' scattered bullocks, so that the captured guns might be pulled forward (of these guns we discovered almost fifty lying useless in the camp). Also there was much shot and powder to be had and some amount of easy spoils to be gathered from the hastily abandoned tents of the nawab's senior officers.

'I do not know how it is, Alistair, that the Moors have failed in killing you.'

'They must try harder, sir.'

Watts smiled. 'I expect they must.'

A guard had been placed upon the nawab's tent by Major Coote on our first entering the camp, so the nawab's papers had been secured (though little else in the tent, for the Moors themselves had plundered it), and Watts now went through these papers and selected from them any that might be useful to us. He looked an almost absurd figure, sat there cross-legged in the Moorish fashion upon a carpet, his wig upon his knee and peering closely at each paper, holding it up to his eyes to study the tight Persian script. And I, scarcely less absurd, I suppose, lying sprawled across the nawab's silken cushions and using the nawab's own quill and ink to sketch Mr Watts at his work. When he now exclaimed in surprise, I lifted my head.

'Oh, this is something to the purpose. Was ever a fellow such a fool?'

'What is it?'

'It is a death warrant – and not for one man only, but for a dozen. The nawab has written it out this very morning.' At my remark that the colonel and officers might want it for a souvenir, Watts smiled. 'It is not a warrant for them. It is written against the lives of his own people – Mir Jafir, Royab Dhul. It is almost every man of any note within his court. It is no wonder that his army should break beneath him.' Watts shook his head at the nawab's folly and put the warrant with the papers he would keep.

'Sir, I have not yet congratulated you upon the victory.'

'That is a generous thought, Alistair, but a wrong one. Victories are for soldiers and the soldiers must have their due. You will be sure to remember that when you have your commission.' He looked at me, smiling at the surprise he had caused me. 'I had meant to wait till

435

Murshidabad, but there is no reason you should not hear of it now. I have spoken with Colonel Clive and Major Coote, while we were in Cutwa. At the raising of Mir Jafir, there will be a dispersal made from the nawab's treasury. Your part in all this will be remembered. It will be no great sum, but sufficient for you to purchase a commission in the grenadiers.'

I knew not what to say and so said nothing.

Harry then came into the tent.

'He will stay there at the lake,' Harry reported and gave Watts a note from Mir Jafir. Harry had just come from the lake, nearby Plassey, where Mir Jafir had retired with his men after the battle. 'He fears to have his men near to ours.'

'That is no doubt very wise of him,' said Watts, opening the note and reading it. And then he turned to me. 'The rising nawab invites us to meet with him. It would be very churlish, I think, to refuse so kindly an invitation.'

Mr Watts sat in parley with Mir Jafir for an hour and more, arranging a further meeting the next day between Mir Jafir and Clive (for it was thought that the escaped nawab might, by then, be captured, Mir Jafir being about to send a party in pursuit of him). There was an agreement made that Mir Jafir should go on to Murshidabad and secure it peacefully, before the colonel should enter the city and see Mir Jafir installed in the palace.

But, though those arrangements were both necessary and important, it was something that I saw as I readied to leave Mir Jafir's lakeside camp that I think, now, was the real reason for our being called there.

I had withdrawn from Mir Jafir's tent to tell our syce that he might now bring our horses, and the syce finding some small difficulty with the tethering ropes, I had gone to assist. It was as I was about this – and in a place I should not have been otherwise – that I saw to the rear of Mir Jafir's tent, Mir Jafir's son, that same young man upon whose head the secret treaty had been sworn. He was deep in whispered conference with Harry Khan. I was so struck by the strangeness of the sight and in wonder at what possible business they might have together, that I did not immediately call out to tell Harry that we were soon leaving. Instead I continued working at the ropes and watching the pair; and not a minute later my wonder increased tenfold when out from the tent came Mr Watts and went himself to the rear of the tent and joined them as though expected there. The three of them now conferred a short while, with much emphatic gesturing from Mir Jafir's son (which the Moors are much prone to). Then Mr Watts parted from them and went to the front of the tent, where he received the betel from Mir Jafir's hand, while Harry and Mir Jafir's son disappeared into the encampment behind.

I brought up our horses with the syce.

Mr Watts said, 'We will leave Harry's horse. He will go on to Murshidabad ahead of us.' At my asking if the sepoys were also to go with Harry, he replied, 'They will stay with us. He is upon some personal business for me.' Then Watts mounted, and doffed his hat to Mir Jafir, who salaamed in return. So we came away from the place without Harry Khan, and Harry's business for Mr Watts still unknown to me.

CHAPTER FORTY-FIVE

*B*etween Plassey and Murshidabad were no more defences to hold us back for, at the nawab's fleeing the field, his army had either gone over to Mir Jafir or scattered upon the wind. Clive wished to advance at no great hurry, for he would first let Mir Jafir and his people go on ahead to secure the city peacefully. But, to make some assurance of the nawab's treasury (for it was a common fear it should be plundered or much depleted before our arrival), Mr Watts and I were sent on ahead with Scrafton (who had joined us at Plassey after the fight) and Clive's relation, the paymaster to the army, Mr Walsh.

We passed through Cossimbazaar on our way and found our factory there a burned ruin. The townspeople told us that the French artillerymen had put fire to it as they went down to join the nawab's army at Plassey and, though I did not like to see such a wanton destruction, yet I felt very much as Mr Watts did, who remarked to me when he saw it that he had rather lose a factory than all of Bengal. We did not linger, but rode on to Murshidabad.

'Where shall we stay, sir?'

'We will take back the house we left,' Watts replied and then asked

Mr Walsh if they would stay with us. But Walsh declined, which I was not sorry for. We found later that Walsh and Scrafton had insisted upon taking quarters within the nawab's palace, where was Mir Jafir, and also the nawab's treasury.

For three days there was an almost continual round of consultations with Jagath Seth, Mir Jafir's senior courtiers and the treasury officials who had not already filled their pockets and fled (and this was but the beginning of the negotiations and wrangling over those payments which were to be made to us under our treaty with Mir Jafir). At last, on the 29th day of June, Clive entered the city.

'I have this account still to finish,' said Watts when I came to fetch him. Indeed, he had been very busy with the report he was writing in every spare minute when he was not about the business of the treaty. 'You go on if you will. But be sure to be back here at midday. We will go straight to the palace.'

Clive had left most of his army with Major Kilpatrick back near Cossimbazaar, and now he rode into the city with only a few officers and a guard of some three hundred soldiers and sepoys. They were not marching as at a triumph, but quiet and orderly and with no drummer, just as Mr Watts had advised. But all the Moors and Hindoos had heard of Clive's coming and some thousands had come to the Cossimbazaar road to witness his arrival. I had come down to the corner near to the palace gate to witness it and to see the reaction of the native people (for, as Clive rightly said after, they were so many and we so few, that had they wished it they might have driven us from their city with only sticks and stones). But there was neither joy nor hatred in the press of people, only an excited curiosity, and the sole accostment or impediment the column suffered was from Hindoo boys, who ran beside them, laughing and stumbling sometimes, near their feet.

Clive – very upright in his saddle, his gold buttons all shining – made no show of emotion, but looked about him very calmly and spoke to his officers and they to him, as though it was but a small town in the Carnatic he was entering and not Bengal's royal city. Near to the palace gates, he commanded the column right (again, it was by Mr Watts's advice he kept from there at his first arrival), and then he led the men up to the house which Mr Watts had got for him near to ours, and by the time I had made my way back through the people, he had dismounted and gone in to prepare himself for the midday ceremony we should all attend at the palace.

As I came back to our house, someone came out from it, and down into the crowd and I called, 'Harry!' but he was gone and nor was I even sure that it was Harry I had seen.

'Is that fellow done with my boots?'

'They are here,' called I, and Mr Watts came from his room in his stockings, still fixing the pin at his collar. He sat down by me in the passage and we pulled on our boots, with the servant standing near. When we stood, the fellow knelt again and wiped at our boots again with his cloth. 'It is a very different way we went before, sir.'

'What is that?'

'To the nawab's audience chamber.'

'Dear God, mention it no more.'

'Sir, is Harry come back now?'

'Why do you ask?'

'I thought I saw him outside just now.'

'I do not know where he is.' He called for his jacket and another servant came out from his room with it, and as Mr Watts put on the jacket he said to me, 'Today I will give you no warnings, Alistair. When we are there, you must speak as you please and to whom you please. For today we are the masters of ourselves.'

In the road, two new-painted palanquins waited and we got into them in our full finery, for today there would be no walking to the palace or even riding, but everything must go on in that manner suited to the high occasion and as decreed by the colonel. I confess, the swaying motion of the palanquin, for once, gave me no discomfort, and as we passed through the palace gates and the Moorish guards there rose briskly to salute our entrance, I felt myself quite lordly, if also a little ridiculous.

There were many other palanquins gone in before us, but standing empty now in the courtyard, and so we did not wait but went directly in after our Moorish escort and found the door to the audience chamber opening almost as we arrived. Clive, Walsh and Scrafton were there, and the officers, and also Jagath Seth and Omichand and several others. They had all been waiting together and there was a cheerful and expectant liveliness in their talk, as if it were the talk of a supper party in Mayfair and the host's footman now opening the door to let his guests spill into the master's dining room.

In the audience chamber was that same dais, but no one upon it, only the *musnud*, the carpeted cushion which is like a throne to the Moors, sitting there solitary. All about the dais, except to the front of it, stood the Moorish nobles in their silk robes, very fine, and turbans of every colour and sashes tied about their waists. Foremost among these was Mir Jafir. He gave Clive his salaam, at which Clive bowed in return, and then some official of the Moorish court – the fussing fellow reminded me of Drake's man, Cooke – went onto the first step of the dais. All now falling silent, he commenced to read out in Persian the proclamation of Mir Jafir's rise to the Nawabship of Bengal.

Watts left me then and went forward to Clive and the others, and in a low murmur gave them the substance of the thing, so that all might be certain there had been nothing inserted beyond our agreement. This tedious proclamation after several long minutes being at last completed, the officious fellow made some intimation that the moment was now come for Mir Jafir to go up on the dais and take his seat upon the *musnud*.

But Mir Jafir turned aside, as if the intimation from such a lowly fellow displeased him, and spoke now privately with his son.

The Moorish official appeared in some perplexity what to do. He spoke again to Mir Jafir and still Mir Jafir very pointedly ignored him. Now the Moorish nobles themselves began to seem uncomfortable at this unscripted delay. But then, whether prompted by a look from Mir Jafir's son (for I noticed that he turned toward Clive now) or by some other previously made secret arrangement, the colonel unbidden stepped forward.

Clive put his foot on the first step of the dais and held out his hand to Mir Jafir. Now there was no further hesitation from Mir Jafir, but he took Clive's hand and allowed himself to be led up onto the dais and, still holding Clive's hand, he lowered himself to his seat on the *musnud*. Clive released Mir Jafir's hand and came down from the dais. He turned and bowed to Mir Jafir very solemnly, hailed him as nawab, and then made a gentlemanly Moorish salaam.

At our departure from the audience chamber we were ushered to another part of the palace which had been always closed to us till now. Here was a great room, like to a ballroom, and all one side of it pillared and opening onto a terrace which overlooked the palace walls onto the river. There were Moorish musicians here waiting, with drums and flutes, and there were tables laden with sweetmeats and syrups and the finest delicacies to be had from all the city's bazaars. The musicians commenced to play at our arrival and a number of small girls came from a sideroom and made a whirling dance in front of them. After a few minutes, Mir Jafir and his nobles not yet come to join us, we most of us went out onto the terrace.

I looked up behind us to the many windows of the palace and wondered where in that vast building the defeated nawab's wives were held and whether they could hear this small celebration and, if they heard it, did they weep.

'I will go with the colonel to the treasury tomorrow,' said Mr Watts, coming to join me at the balustrade. 'If you wish, we may then settle the business of your commission.'

'I have not yet spoken with Major Coote, sir.'

'Have you not?'

'I did not like to trouble him with so small a matter.'

'It is no small matter to you.' When I said nothing in reply to this, but only looked out over the river at the great houses of the merchants opposite and the boats by the ghats, he said, 'There is nothing done yet, Alistair. It is not put in stone and you may yet remain with the company if you would.'

'I cannot be a writer again.'

'In a year you would be a factor.'

'I mean no disrespect to you, sir. But I have seen enough now of what life I might expect as a factor, or even a trader, with the company.'

'There are many would be only too happy of such a position. But if you are so decided—'

'I am. My only regret of it, sir, is that I should disappoint your expectation of me.'

'It is no disappointment to me. Your life must be your own. But now is perhaps not the time for this. We will talk again later.' At this point we saw the colonel and Scrafton approaching us. Watts said to me before they came, 'But I would ask, in the meantime, that you should hold off from making a formal offer of your services to Major Coote.' Clive and Scrafton then arriving by us, I had no opportunity to ask Watts the reason of his request and the talk now moved to some small arrangements Clive must make with Mr Watts concerning our soldiers in the city.

Scrafton broke in upon them, saying quietly, 'He is here,' and when we followed his gaze, we saw coming between the pillars and out onto the terrace the stout figure of the wretch Omichand. I felt at once that the three of them had been waiting for him all the while (for he had stayed behind with the Moors after the ceremony) and that there was some matter of importance afoot.

'The time is now come, I think, to let Omichand in upon the secret,' said Clive. At Watts's nod of agreement, Clive turned to Scrafton, saying, 'You have the treaty there?'

Scrafton drew it from his coat.

Omichand, having seen Clive now, came toward us in some hurry and with a look of considerable agitation on his face. The colonel greeted him very civilly, which Omichand ignored, saying at once, 'The nawab will not pay me.'

'Pay you?' said Clive. 'And why might the new nawab wish to pay you? At this time he must have some more important demands upon his treasury than to think of making gifts.'

Omichand looked much astonished at Clive's words. He began to speak of the treaty.

'Ah, the treaty,' said Clive.

443

'He must pay what he has put his name to. It was agreed.'

'Mr Scrafton?' said Clive.

And Scrafton, with no sign at all that he had ever been friendly with Omichand, or indeed intrigued in league with him, then made some show of opening up the treaty that the company had made with Mir Jafir. He stepped up by Omichand and showed him the words written there, which made no mention of any payment to Omichand.

'But this is not the treaty. The treaty was written on a red paper.'

'And this treaty,' said Scrafton, 'is upon a white.'

It took a few moments yet before the full weight of the deceit descended on Omichand. But, when it finally struck him, he made a moan and looked at Clive and Watts with disbelief.

'You are undeceived,' said Scrafton. 'There is nothing owing to you under our treaty with Mir Jafir. Had you not first practised to deceive us at every turn, it might have ended otherwise.'

Scrafton refolded the treaty and Omichand was silent, as though the shock had robbed him of speech, and a rage like madness burned in his eyes. He was undone, and undone from a quarter he had never thought to doubt, and by a practice he might use against others, but never thought to have turned upon himself. I thought of Edward in that moment, and I confess I was now not sorry for the baseness of that false treaty, but almost glad of it, as a fitting poison for Omichand. He was an evil presence and his fall too long in the coming, and I felt no pity for the wretch at all. But when Clive, Watts and Scrafton then turned away from Omichand as though their business with him was done, and they rid of him once and for all, I saw that he fixed his gaze on their backs as though he might bury a knife into each one of them. It was a look of the purest malice, and I started at the look, but then he saw me and turned away, and immediately after withdrew himself from the celebration. I did not tell the others what I had seen (for what was it but to report Omichand's fury, which was a thing they already knew?) but after that sight I was not so sanguine that Omichand was broken, or that we had witnessed the last of his evil meddling in our affairs.

CHAPTER FORTY-SIX

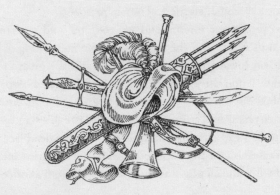

*T*he deposed nawab, Siraj ud-Daulah, was captured within days and brought back to Murshidabad and made a prisoner in the palace.

'What shall happen to him?'

'That will be for the nawab to decide,' said Mr Watts, who had brought me the news. 'But that is not our affair. There is that which you must do for me in Cossimbazaar.' He told me then of the problem that had arisen since the discovery that there was not as much in the palace treasury as he and the colonel had expected to find there (I have since learned this to be a familiar disappointment after most revolutions) and so, to recompense Jagath Seth for his aid of us, there had been an agreement now made that he should have the goods remaining at the French factories in Bengal and any coin in them up to a certain value. For this reason Mr Watts now asked me to go down to Cossimbazaar, in the company of one of Jagath Seth's agents, to discover what might be got from the French factory there, for the place had been sealed by Mr Watts at our passing and our soldiers kept out of it, from the certainty of their plundering.

We stayed at the French factory but one night, and it was as we returned into Murshidabad the next morning that we came upon a great commotion and hubbub in the streets. We stopped a Hindoo merchant who was going toward that crowd, now emerging from a street to the front of us.

'It is the nawab, Siraj ud-Daulah,' said he to our question. 'He is dead.'

'How dead?' said I, startled. 'He is a prisoner.'

He had no answer for me and we rode on, and we saw now the elephant at its centre and the Moorish cavalrymen riding in escort. As they came on toward us we moved aside and the great crowd came surging past. Upon the elephant lay Siraj ud-Daulah's corpse. He had been stabbed not once but many times over, and the Moorish soldiers upon the elephant had a grip on Siraj ud-Daulah's hair, and by this means kept his head raised so that all might see the dead face and know it without question for the deposed nawab. It was a grim and very ugly sight, and when the elephant was gone by us, I went at once to tell Mr Watts.

'I have heard already,' said he and kept his eyes down and his quill moving over the report he had been writing when I burst in upon him.

'He was killed while a prisoner.'

'There were some of the Moors not altogether accepting of Mir Jafir's rise. I am not surprised it should have ended so.'

'Then it was done by Mir Jafir's order.'

'I should say, rather, with his blessing. How seemed the crowd?'

'Some were displeased, but there were many more threw dirt at the body.'

'Nor am I surprised by that. They are well rid of him.'

'What will happen now?'

'Now?' He raised his eyes. 'Now they will bury him. It is over with.'

'And that is all, sir?'

'We will now have our reparations from the new nawab that we are owed under the treaty. What else might there be?'

When I made no answer, he dipped his quill in the inkpot and bent his head and calmly continued with the writing of his report.

*

The treasure which was the company's reparations was put into crates before it left the vaults and carpenters fixed down the lids and nailed them tight before the soldiers brought the treasure down. At the ghat we weighed the numbered crates before loading them into those boats brought up from Plassey for the purpose. I kept a tallybook, as did another fellow put there by the paymaster, Mr Walsh.

When we came to near the end of the loading, I looked up frequently to the palace gardens where I must soon go to meet with Mr Watts. He had told me that morning that he must speak with me privately, and I knew it was on the matter of my prospective commission, which must now be settled. And what must I say to him? That I had seen the soldier's life, just as I had seen the writer's, and that it was not all that I had expected it to be?

The loading done, a guard of soldiers and sepoys was now set on the ghat, and the sailors who had come up from Plassey now armed themselves and went aboard the boats, where they must stay the night before launching for Calcutta in the morning

'Will we see you in Calcutta, sir?' called Adams from the stern of the last boat.

'Perhaps. I am not my own master. You will give my compliments to the admiral.'

'I will, sir. I think you are not so sceptical now, sir, of what the King's Navy may do.'

'I am not so sceptical now, Mr Adams.'

Pleased to have got the concession from me, he went to join his fellows, and I, with heavy steps, went up to the nawab's garden.

Mr Watts was standing already at the arches and looking down at the ghat and the river. There was no other person in the garden and I went to him and gave him the tallybook. He only glanced at the figures, but then put the book in his pocket, saying that there would be time enough for that. 'Let us walk a little,' said he. So we walked, he with his hands held together behind his back and his head somewhat bowed, as he talked to me. And I talked with him, as I could with no other, of the many things that we had been through and of all the battles and strange turnings that had brought us to this day. As we talked of them and recollected them to each other, it seemed almost a miracle to me that we should have done those things and yet come safe to the end.

'It is a hard road you have travelled, Alistair, since first you came to us in Cossimbazaar.'

'It is a hard road that we have all travelled, sir.'

'That is true. But it is right that you should know your part in this has not passed unregarded. I am very conscious of your aid to me and much obliged to you for it.' I inclined my head in acknowledgement of his generous remark. 'And throughout I have ever striven to be as open with you as I might, which was not always so open as you may have wished. Yet you never complained of it and I am much obliged to you for that also.'

'I did not regard it, sir—'

'Allow me to finish, Alistair. There is that now which I would say to you. To begin – when you asked me the other day of Harry Khan's whereabouts, I replied that I did not know of them. I must tell you now that was a lie. For Harry has gone to Benares.' I looked at him, but Mr Watts's eyes stayed down and he continued to walk. 'I think you will understand the meaning of it.'

'He must wash his soul clean there.'

'That is enough to say. We shall not speak of this again, but I may tell you that there could be no other end to it. Mir Jafir could have no security as nawab while the other lived. There was no help for it. What must be done was done and Harry is gone to Benares.'

We walked in silence awhile and I thought of Siraj ud-Daulah's muti-lated body carried on the elephant and of all our dead in the Black Hole in Calcutta, and the change there had been in Harry after his return to us from the Murshidabad prison. I found (to my own surprise) that there was some small pity in me for the murdered nawab now that he had paid for his crimes with his life. I remembered him in his *durbar* tent when I had first seen him, how he had looked scarcely more than a boy. And I remembered the time when he had hunted with his hawk, momentarily free from the courtiers whispering poison in his ear. He had come to manhood and power on a rising wave of intrigue and violence, and for a short time he had been carried forward on the wave,

448

but now it had broken over him indifferently, and I saw clearly now that the young man and the nawabship were things distinct, and that Siraj ud-Daulah had lived always in the shadow of his own violent death. But neither could I forget Edward Fairborough.

'I am not sorry that ud-Daulah is gone.'

'Nor I,' said Mr Watts. 'I thank God this is all in the past now. But it is not of the past that I wished to speak with you, Alistair. For there is something else I must tell you, which I would not have done had I seen in you any proper anticipation of the commission which is yours, you know, but for the asking.'

'I know it, sir.'

'But you do not reach for it. By which reluctance I must conclude that it is no longer to you the prize it once seemed. Very well. There is this then to say. That report which I have been writing almost since we left Plassey is now done. And it is not, as I led you to believe, for the council in Calcutta. It will go to London. To the Board of Trade.'

'You mean the company's court of directors, sir?'

'I know very well what I mean. It will go to Mr Fitzherbert, who sits on the Board of Trade and Plantations and also on the king's Privy Council. And from Mr Fitzherbert's hand it will pass to the king – I see that I have at last surprised you. But let us not stop. It is too little chance we have had to enjoy the nawab's garden.' So saying he walked again, and I with him, in some wonder now at his words. 'It is not the first report I have sent, nor will it be the last, but I will venture that I shall never send another of greater import, which is why I now feel the loss of that good man Reverend Bellamy all the more, for it is he would have carried it to Mr Fitzherbert and no worry to me in its honest passage there.' He glanced across at me. 'You see, Alistair, where I am tending.'

'Was the Reverend Bellamy then in your employ, sir?'

'He was a friend to his country – as am I and as you have proved yourself to be, in your aid of me. It is my further belief you may do some greater service yet for your country and your king. You have gathered such experience here as would be profligate for us now to waste.'

'If you mean, sir, that I should carry your report—'

'I mean more than that. This war with France, I fear, will be a war in very earnest. Our interests and theirs must clash now, and with bloodshed, in many more places than Bengal. Mr Fitzherbert must certainly feel the heat of it, and the strain, for the king's friends are but thinly scattered through the colonies and the great companies. I cannot answer for him, Alistair, but I think I know Mr Fitzherbert well enough to say that my recommendation of you to him would carry such weight as to get you the security of his patronage. At least it shall serve you till my own return home.'

'And will you return?'

'I do not mean to bury my wife and children here. And you may know that once the nawab has finally settled with us, I shall be a wealthy man. I must then return to England to make a proper establishment of my family, and you would ever find a familial welcome among us.'

'That is very kind.'

'If you do not now purchase a commission, I shall make certain that an amount equivalent is put aside for you, that you do not return to England with an empty purse. But that is a small matter. The greater is whether you should throw over all your prospects here, that you might put yourself in your country's service.'

'What would I do for Mr Fitzherbert?'

'That he must tell you, but it is unlikely that you should stay long in England.'

We reached a wall, stopped and came slowly back, neither one of us speaking for a time. The prospect he had opened before me was too vast to be taken in completely, and what he had told me threw such a light over his own actions these past months as I only began dimly to understand the meaning of. But I own that his proposal had struck to my very heart, and I could not keep my thoughts steady, for I recognized the gate that was opened to me and it was not the gate of riches, which was the company's, nor yet of military glory, which the army might offer me, but it was the gate I had been brought to by my own turnings, and beyond that gate I now glimpsed the path into my own proper life.

I asked more questions of him then and he gave me what answers he could. But, in truth, there was little more he could tell me, for how could he answer for a man half the world away in London? In his own mind he was very certain that I should be wanted by this Mr Fitzherbert of the Board of Trade and that such use should be made of me as would give me no reason to complain of the dullness of my days. Nor would there be any want of honour in it, but all should be done, though veiled, beneath the service of the king.

We ended seated in the alcove of the great arches overlooking the river, below us our boats, loaded with plate and coin. There was a calling from the mosque near to the palace and on the far bank the Hindoos bathed and made their prayers.

'You would have to go down with the treasure to Calcutta,' said he.

I did not answer him at once, but only looked at the fading sunlight falling on the water, and at the city's shadows and the flower garlands drifting down. It was very beautiful, and I, in that moment, very glad to have no sketchbook near, but content to see and to wonder at all the things that I should leave behind me.

CHAPTER FORTY-SEVEN

Our passage down the river was almost a moving festival. We stopped by Cossimbazaar, where I bid Le Baume farewell, and also at Plassey, before passing into the greater river where the boats of the squadron had come up to meet us. Flags and banners were raised and there was no town we went by but heard the beat of our drums and our cheering. And, though I could hardly bear to look at Hugli from the remembrance of the things we had done there, yet by Chinsurah and Chandernagore I smiled to hear the great cheering of our men, for I was not sorry that all the people in those towns should know the pride and joy there was in our victory and that we should not now be remembered only for our first cowardly abandonment of Calcutta.

At Calcutta we were greeted as heroes, with a salute of guns from the bastions of the fort, and all of those who had weathered those hard months at Fulta now came to the Great Ghat to welcome us and to see the treasure crates we had brought down from Murshidabad.

It was only ten days that I stayed there in Calcutta, settling Edward's affairs, buying diamonds from the Hindoo merchants and making ready to leave. I kept from the many dinners that were held about the town in honour of our victory, saving only that small one held by Mrs Watts with Admiral Watson and Lieutenant Brereton and several men and women of the settlement, though no one of the council was invited. Governor Drake I did see, but only at a distance and fleetingly, for he and the other members of the council were continually met in conference in the fort at that time, debating what their proper shares of the nawab's treasure might be.

On the morning of my leaving, I went to the burial ground and there was an old Hindoo scything the grass there which had sprung up with the return of the rains. I gave him something, that he might be sure to tend well Edward's grave and also the Reverend Bellamy's and some others that I knew, and after I had said in my heart a prayer for them all, I came away and put off my melancholy, for I was young and the strength of life very full in me.

'Mr Fitzherbert will be very glad of your assistance, though you must not expect him to say so. And I fear he will not allow you to rest long in London.' So said Mrs Watts as we neared the waiting boat. Her children ran on ahead of us, and as we watched them I remarked that where I was most useful, there I would be most content. 'There you shall be most in danger,' said she, 'but I do not seek to dissuade you. You have seen sufficient these past months to know what manner of thing it is you enter into. And there is the whole voyage home to ponder your decision.'

'It will not change.'

'This path once set cannot easily be altered. And though you know it, one day you shall feel it and, when you do, I would that you may look back upon this time without bitterness. I would not have you deceived.'

'I cannot think that of you or Mr Watts.'

'It was not me or my husband I meant, but your own self.' We stopped and she gazed out at the ship mid-river, and I at her. She was thoughtful and her face very still. While my trunk was passed into the boat, she turned to me. 'We have a fond hope of you, Alistair.' She produced a small silver medallion from her purse and put it into my hand. 'I have kept this about me these past months as a charm. You will think I am become as superstitious as a Bengali.' At my demur, she said, 'It is no matter. We are through the fire and you must keep it as a token and a remembrance. I will not say that you must write to us, for we shall follow soon and be with you next year in England.' She bent toward me and put her cheek to mine. Next I shook young George's hand and then I crouched while Amelia hugged my arm.

I got down into the boat and, as the boat pushed off from the ghat, I turned and called to Mrs Watts with feeling, 'I shall not look back on this time with any bitterness.' But she only inclined her head to me and smiled and I glimpsed then in her face something deeper than just the sadness of farewell. I have often thought of it since and, as often, wondered what she saw at that moment – a foolish youth? A hopeful but misguided young man? I raised my hand in farewell to her and the oarsmen pulled for the ship.

On the fort's southern bastion the British flag now flew proudly and the two soldiers there rested at their ease against the parapet and watched my boat draw out to where the *Protector* lay waiting for the tide. Soon my trunk was aboard and then I, with nothing to do then but see everything stowed safe in the cabin that would be mine till we were in England again.

Lieutenant Brereton then came across from the *Kent* to bid me farewell and he brought with him the admiral's good wishes for the journey. How could we, either of us, know then that within a month the admiral would be stricken with a fever, waste away quickly and die, and be buried with Edward and all those others? Much else, too, lay hidden from me of the future. For the Watts family would not follow me as soon as they expected, only after Mr Watts had first been made governor in Calcutta, before himself passing the office to Colonel Clive. And Mr Watts's own saying that in a corrupt court the worst men have the best chance would be confirmed to me in later years by Scrafton's rise to the company's court of directors. Nor, as I had surmised, was Omichand's fall as final as so many had fondly supposed, for he returned in later years to insinuate himself into the new nawab's court and repay our deceit tenfold. The fate of Colonel Clive, all the world knows. But of soldiering still to do, it was Captain Coote who would fight the most battles, before taking that great victory at Wandiwash, which finally sealed what Clive had begun. Drake must return to England to die in a comfortable obscurity, and Le Baume too would come to England, in an attempt to lift from his name the blemish put on it by Clive's breaking of him.

And Cordet I would meet again, though in circumstances very different, and each of us much changed since our time in Bengal.

But all of this was yet to be.

For the present, I came to the rail of the *Protector* and watched Lieutenant Brereton's return to the *Kent*. Then I looked across to the fort and the settlement and the black town, and though there was the sadness of departure in me, when the cry at last came to weigh anchor and the ship began to move on the tide, I went not to the stern to see Calcutta falling behind us, but to the bow, where I stayed till we were past Tanner's Fort. Our sails were filling and the tide running strong and soon we must pass out from the great river and into the open sea.

The author would like to thank:

Eli Dryden, Editorial Services
Neil Lang, Design
Jeremy Trevathan, Editor
Ellen Wood, Marketing